THE CODICIL

A NOVEL BY

TOM TOPOR

HYPERION

NEW YORK

Library of Congress Cataloging-In-Publication Data

Topor, Tom, 1938–
      The codicil / by Tom Topor. — 1st ed.
         p.   cm.
      ISBN 0-7868-6153-3
      I. Title.
   PS3570.065C63   1994
   813'.54—dc20   94-36986
                                         CIP

Design by Holly McNeely
FIRST EDITION
10 9 8 7 6 5 4 3 2 1

THE CODICIL

CHAPTER I

HERSCHEL DIDN'T TELL ME in advance he was stopping by with her, so I missed them when they came in—I was on the stand, testifying. But they must have slid in as discreetly as burglars, because Neuberger was the kind of judge who commonly halted everything if anyone entered his courtroom once he'd taken the bench.

"We'll just wait till our guest is seated," he'd say in his sandpapery voice. "We wouldn't want our guest to miss any of the proceedings, would we, counsel?" And the assistant U.S. attorney, the lawyer for the defense, the court clerk, the recorder, the bailiff, the officers, the witness, and the twelve jurors and four alternates would all turn to stare at the hapless interloper as he or she stumbled to a seat. I knew; he'd done it to me.

The defense lawyer, a crafty veteran named Jeff Abramson, was spreading a set of Polaroids on the clerk's desk. "Your honor, can we label these Exhibits twenty-four through twenty-nine for identification?" Neuberger nodded, and Abramson brought the photos over. "Mr. Bruno, do you recognize these photographs?"

"Yes, I do," I said. "I took them at the defendant's building last week."

We went through the ritual of my confirming that it was my handwriting on the back of each picture and that I had dated and signed them.

"Who asked that you take these photos, Mr. Bruno?"

"You did. You wanted to show the jury the defendant's hallway and door."

"To the best of your recollection, Mr. Bruno, do these pictures show the entire hallway?"

"Yes—this is from the south stairway, this is from the north stairway, this is from the elevator, this is from the incinerator unit."

"Your Honor, may I enter these in evidence?" Neuberger nodded grudgingly—all his movements were grudging—and the clerk marked the photos. "Mr. Bruno, so far as you know, have there been any renovations or modifications to this hallway?"

"Objection. Calls for speculation." Neuberger turned a withering eye on the objecting assistant U.S. attorney, Cecile Boulanger, and slowly shook his head. Boulanger, who resembled Naomi Campbell, but with smarter eyes, lowered her chin and sighed. Anyone else would have responded to that sigh—I'd seen other judges offer her a glass of water and mean it—but Neuberger simply pointed to me. Abramson shifted a step, giving me a clear pass at the jury.

"According to the super, and the landlord, and the buildings department, there have been no changes in that hallway since 1988." I glanced at Boulanger, who was starting to get up, then at Neuberger. "I'd be pleased to offer the court my transcripts—or original tapes—of those interviews." Boulanger sank back down.

We went picture by picture, each time hammering home to the jury that no matter where he was standing, sitting, crouching, or squatting, no FBI agent or Immigration or Treasury agent could have seen from the hallway into the apartment.

"Mr. Bruno, if I tell you that an agent of the federal government testified that—"

Boulanger was up and waving. "Your Honor!"

Neuberger wiggled the tip of his forefinger at Abramson. "Mr. Abramson, this isn't a state court. We obey the rules of evidence here."

Abramson suppressed a grin. He'd done what he needed to do. The jury got the point: The feds had sworn that they'd seen into the defendant's apartment. My pictures showed they couldn't have. "Nothing further." Abramson bowed slightly to Boulanger, who stood, smoothed her skirt, and came over.

As she did, I glanced around, and that's when I saw my former partner Herschel O'Hara in the back row. With him was the kind of woman Herschel usually married—and then divorced: blond, blue-eyed, and WASP to her tiny, tasteful earrings and her double strand of pearls. Herschel pointed to his watch and raised his brows in a question. I shrugged. Boulanger came close enough for me to smell her Chanel.

"Mr. Bruno," Boulanger said, "before you became a detective, you were a lawyer, were you not?"

"Relevance?" Abramson called out.

"Goes to credibility, Your Honor." Neuberger hesitated—the relevance was questionable and he knew it—but then he nodded. He must have been bored. Boulanger came a bit closer. Her eyes were hazel. "Were you not a lawyer, Mr. Bruno?" she said.

"Yes. For fourteen years."

"But you're no longer a lawyer?"

"No."

"Were you disbarred, Mr. Bruno?"

"No, I was not."

"You were not disbarred?"

"Asked and answered," Abramson called out.

"Were you disciplined in any way?" Boulanger said.

"No."

"You were not called before a disciplinary body . . . ?"

"Yes. But I was not disciplined."

Boulanger turned away from the jury to hide her chagrin, then turned back. "Mr. Bruno, what kind of law did you practice?"

"Criminal."

"Did you ever represent defendants accused in federal criminal cases?"

"Yes. Many times."

"What would you say is your attitude toward enforcement agents of the federal government—the FBI, or the Drug Enforcement Administration, or Immigration, or Alcohol, Tobacco and Firearms?"

"Relevance?" Abramson said.

"Goes to bias, Your Honor." Again, Neuberger gave her some slack. "How do you feel about federal agents, Mr. Bruno—do you consider them your enemy?"

"No."

"No?"

"Only in the professional sense, Ms. Boulanger—they wanted to put my clients away."

"Like today . . . ?"

I gambled. "Your Honor, I'm confused—it's no secret that the cops and the crooks—the alleged crooks—are adversaries. By definition. I don't get what Ms. Boulanger's going after."

Neuberger twisted and stared at me. He reminded me of a vulture eyeing his lunch from the top of a tree. "You're supposed to let Mr. Abramson make the objection, Mr. Bruno." He swiveled to Boulanger. "Counselor, are we heading somewhere, or is this merely your way of tantalizing poor, puzzled Mr. Bruno?—I mean tantalizing solely in the professional sense, naturally."

"What I'm going after, Your Honor, is, given Mr. Bruno's history as a lawyer and given his notoriety vis-à—"

"Object!" Abramson shouted, but Boulanger rode right over him:

"—vis law-enforcement agents, I wanted to know how far he would go to put them in the wrong."

"Objection!" Abramson shouted even louder.

Neuberger put his handkerchief in front of his mouth and coughed, but I got the feeling that he was swallowing a laugh. He lowered the handkerchief and turned to Boulanger. "Counselor, I'm an admirer of yours, so, if you insist, I'm going to allow the witness to answer. But if I don't find the answer relevant, playtime's over, and I'm going to strike everything beginning with 'What would you say is your attitude . . .' " He smiled his vulture's smile. "Do you insist?"

Boulanger looked as though she'd had a tooth drilled without Novocain. She nodded deferentially and soldiered on:

"Mr. Bruno, given your history of antagonism toward law-enforcement personnel, how far would you go to put them in the wrong? You're under oath."

I shifted to my left so I could see around her to the jury. "As far as I could." I lowered my head, raised it, and grinned. "Legally." Three jurors grinned back at me. "Just as I assume the cops would go as far as they could. Legally. I would not tamper with evidence, if that's what you want the jury to infer. Just as I'm sure they would not tamper with evidence. Would they?"

"They would not, but—"

"Stop right there, Ms. Boulanger," Neuberger said. She glanced at him, and the evil old bastard made her sweat before chopping her off at the knees.

"Jurors, please disregard everything from . . . 'What would you say is your attitude toward agents of the federal government' . . ."

Boulanger was the color of cappuccino, so she couldn't turn scarlet, but her shoulders and her mouth made it clear that Neuberger was lucky—and so was I—that she wasn't strapped. She took a breath for composure. "No more questions."

I stood up, nodded to Abramson, and walked toward the back of the courtroom, where Herschel and his WASP companion were waiting in the aisle. I followed them into the hallway, and changed my life.

The WASP's name was Mollie Wharton, and she spoke quietly, but not gently, as though there were reserves of strength that she couldn't quite keep hidden. Radcliffe. Michigan Law. *Law Review*. She'd been at Dunlop, Tyler & Laird for six years; trusts and estates. She and Herschel had met when her younger brother had been busted on a misdemeanor possession charge, and her loyal colleagues at Dunlop, Tyler & Laird made it clear they didn't do misdemeanor possession cases, not even for relatives. Herschel got it knocked down to next to nothing, and he and Wharton became . . . what? Neither would say, but I'd known Herschel for twenty years, and been partners with him for ten, and so far as I could remember he never made friends with a woman unless he slept with her at least once. It was one of his most dependable principles.

We were sitting in a corner booth of a restaurant near the courthouse; it was too late for the lunch crowd and too early for cocktails, so we had the place to ourselves.

"Thus you see," she was saying to me, "we believe that with your legal background, you'd be the ideal person to help us find this beneficiary. Mr. Bruno—your glass is empty!" Wharton signaled the waitress and turned back to me. She didn't smile a lot, which I liked her for. But I could see nothing behind her eyes.

"My legal background is criminal law—is your beneficiary a criminal?" I said.

"No, no, not at all."

"Is there a crime connected with the estate somehow?"

"Absolutely not." She glanced at Herschel for help.

He leaned forward and poked me. "Adam, why are you being such a prick? Mollie wants to give you work."

"Right." I turned to her. "Ms. Wharton, I know Dunlop, Tyler & Laird, and I know the kinds of estates you represent, and I know this isn't the first time you've had to hunt down a beneficiary—and I know which detectives you usually hire to do your hunting. Why me?"

She glanced at her watch. "Mr. Bruno, I need to get over to surrogate's court. My senior partners will be back at the office at five-thirty, and if you stop by then we'll explain this to you properly. Can you do that?"

"What's the estate worth, Ms. Wharton?"

"Why do you ask that?"

"You're not telling me anything else, Ms. Wharton, so I at least need to know whether it pays even to talk to you—the way I work, the larger the estate, the larger the bonus." She avoided looking at Herschel, which meant she hadn't told him. "If you don't tell me, Ms. Wharton, there's not a chance I'll be there at five-thirty, or any other time."

She smiled, but this time like a model on a runway. "The estate is worth one hundred and five million dollars, perhaps more, depending on the value of Tel-Mat stock." She stood up, dropped twenty dollars on the table and picked up her purse. "Can I expect you?"

"Yes, you can."

CHAPTER 2

MY GUESS IS THAT Dunlop, Tyler & Laird had a score of conference rooms—the firm had 140 lawyers—but the one we were in was surely the sanctum of the most senior partners. The chairs were leather, the books were collectibles, and the table was teak, which is common; but the paintings were real French pre-Impressionists, which is not. There was no bar, or coffee machine, or anything that suggested self-service. The view was about 240 degrees: in one direction, the harbor, with the Statue of Liberty; in another, the Hudson and the World Trade Center towers; in another, the Empire State Building. And in every direction, sky and clouds and setting sun. The room, which was soundproofed, was meant to exude safety, comfort, taste, and effortless control, and it did.

I sat in the middle on one side of the oval table—there was room for twelve—and Wharton sat opposite me. To my left was Thomas Schuyler, Wharton's boss in trusts and estates. Across from Schuyler was a pair I couldn't help tagging Frick & Frack, though their names actually were Dieter Gunther and Paul VanHoven; they did tax shelters and other money stuff.

And at the head of the table, filling the Wedgwood cups from a sterling silver coffee carafe, sat Wilson Laird. Or, depending on how well you knew him and the circumstances of your meeting him, Judge Laird, he'd served on the Virginia bench; or Senator Laird, two terms, Republican of Virginia; or Vice President Laird, one term.

"You said black, one sugar, Mr. Bruno . . ?" I nodded, and he passed my cup to Schuyler, who slid it to me. Laird waited till I took a sip and gave him a slight bow before he poured for the others. When everyone had a cup, and had stopped stirring, Laird carelessly opened a file in front of him, which was a cue for everyone else to do the same.

"Mr. Bruno, let me give you a little background before we go to the file." A sip of coffee for drama. "Eleven days ago, my friend and client Matthew Marshall died of a stroke at his cabin upstate—I'm sure you saw the obituary in the *Times*. Matt was only fifty-one—five years younger than me. He left a wife—my friend Beth—and three children, my god-children, Matt junior, Fred, and Wendy. He also left a good-sized estate."

"One hundred and five million, I was told."

Laird glanced at Wharton and smiled. "Were you, Mr. Bruno? That's about right, perhaps more, once the paintings on loan to museums are taken into account. According to the terms of Matt's will, that estate was divided, via trusts, among his wife and named children, his brother and sister, plus some generous bequests to various charities. I am the executor of the estate." He took another theatrical pause.

"Just before the Fourth of July weekend, Matt called us, to make an adjustment to his will. I was in Capri, Tom here was on the Cape, so Mollie was watching the store. Mollie is a brilliant lawyer and Tom trusts her with everything in his bailiwick—as he should—and she was never told that everything connected with Matt's legal work should—strictly as a courtesy, not for monitoring—be run through me."

Wharton's eyes were lowered, so at first I couldn't tell how she was reacting. But then I saw the two tiny red spots appear on her pale cheeks. I felt for her—she was being put down so deftly she couldn't protest and so viciously she couldn't help but implode.

"So Matt came in and dictated a codicil to his will. Normally, we don't do codicils—we rewrite the entire will—-but since Matt was leaving town for the summer, Mollie went over the terms with him, checked the codicil for legal language, called in two secretaries as witnesses, and added the codicil to the file, with a marker to Tom to incorporate the provisions after a final consultation with Matt. Mollie did not question what Matt told her—we don't encourage associates to question a client's instructions—but she did tell him Tom would be going over the codicil with him to make sure of its effects on the main will. Mollie then simply sent Tom a memo giving a summary of what she'd done." Another sip. "Because Mollie had no instructions to speak to me—I owe Tom a brisk spanking for that," he chuckled paternally. "I first found out about all this when Matt died and Tom retrieved the will so we could file it with the surrogate for probate."

Laird picked up two stapled pages from the open file before him. Reluctantly, he passed the pages to me. "In house, we refer to that as the

Saigon codicil. May I have your cup?" Schuyler passed my cup to Laird, and he filled it while I skimmed the codicil.

It was simple, to the point, and devastating:

In August 1971, while I was serving in Vietnam, though I was married at the time to the former Beth Moore, and had my oldest child with her, I fell in love with a Vietnamese native whom I called Cricket. Some months later, Cricket became pregnant. Before the birth of this child—who I have no doubt was mine—we were separated by the fortunes of war, and I never saw Cricket again.

Some time after I had returned to the United States and to my wife and some time after she had borne me two more children, I learned that Cricket had emigrated to the United States and was living here with our child.

Because of these events, I am changing the terms of my original will, dated 23 April 1993, in accordance with the following:

In addition to the personal and material items listed below, one-half of my residual estate, after taxes and executor's fees, is to go, via trust, to my child by Cricket. My child by Cricket shall also have the absolute right to use the name Marshall if he or she wishes.

In the event that my child by Cricket is dead, or has returned of his or her own free will to Vietnam—and either of these facts can be demonstrated to the satisfaction of my executor and the court—then one-half of my residual estate shall be used to establish the Foundation for Vietnamese-American Bastards (yes, that is explicitly the name I wish to give the foundation), to be administered by my executor according to the terms attached.

In the event that neither of these facts can be established to the satisfaction of my executor and the court, then this codicil shall be considered null and void.

In the event that any person or entity designated as a beneficiary of this will challenges any or all of its provisions, including this codicil, for any and several reasons, that person or entity shall be stricken as a beneficiary of this will.

The provisions in my original will therefore shall be adjusted as follows . . .

It went on to list the terms and the adjustments, which I figured I'd read later. It didn't take a genius to deduce why everyone in the room looked as if they'd been told Kübler-Ross was coming over for coffee and cake. Good old Matt Marshall had just taken at least $50-odd million from all the rest of his family and left it to his Vietnamese-American bastard. I raised my eyes, looked at Laird, and said, "I did criminal law, Senator, not trusts and estates. What do you think of this?"

His answer was obviously rehearsed: "At the time of his meeting with Mollie, Matt appeared his normal, competent self—shrewd, charming, flirtatious—so there seems to be no question of any mental defect. Nor, given the wording of the codicil, does there seem to be any question of coercion by a third party."

"You're saying the codicil is legal."

"The *document* is legal, yes, Mr. Bruno. I doubt very much that the *document* could be successfully challenged." He smiled cheerily. "Technically, Mollie is one of our best."

"What about . . . 'the Foundation for Vietnamese-American Bastards'?"

"Matt was notorious for his earthy humor. His dogs are named Bitch One and Bitch Two, and his schooner is named *Velvet Triangle*." Laird manufactured a rueful laugh. "I'd hate to tell you his nickname for me."

I turned to Wharton, who had somehow pulled herself together. "Ms. Wharton," I began and then changed tack. "I have a few questions—are you free later?"

She nodded yes quickly, and I faced Laird: "Do you believe this, Mr. Laird—do you believe he fathered a child over there?"

I thought the "Mister" would catch him off guard and make it easier to see if he lied to me; I was wrong. He furrowed his brow intensely and tapped a manicured nail with his Mont Blanc fountain pen. "I don't know; it's possible." He tapped some more. "Matt Marshall was a decent, honorable man, but he'd been away from Beth a long time, and that sort of thing was very common in 'Nam. I can't tell you it's out of the question. I wish I could, but I can't." He smiled complacently, as though he'd just recited a magnificent anecdote, and said easily to Wharton:

"Mollie, it's way after six—why don't you call it a day? Dieter, Paul, you, too. Tom and I can handle this."

Laird and Schuyler watched patiently while Gunther and VanHoven gathered their stuff and headed for the door. As they left, I realized that they hadn't said a word in all the time I'd been there. Wharton scribbled her number on a piece of paper, handed it to me, murmured, "I'll speak to you later," and followed them out.

Laird waited till he heard the door click shut and then turned to me. "As executor of Matt Marshall's estate, I am legally obligated to enact the terms of his will. In the codicil, Matt has directed me to give one-half of his estate to a nameless—and perhaps imaginary—child." He held up his left hand, spread his fingers, and counted off his points:

"One, did Matt impregnate a Vietnamese native? Two, did she bear his child? Three, did she emigrate here with the child? Four, is the child alive? Five, if it is, did it return to Vietnam or is it still here? Six, if the child is still here, can it demonstrate—to the satisfaction of the Manhattan surrogate—that it was fathered by Matt Marshall?"

"What do you want me to do?" I said.

Schyuler opened his mouth, but Laird touched his sleeve to quiet him. "We want you to look for this nameless—and perhaps imaginary—child."

"Yes, but do you want me to find him? Or her?"

For the first time, a tremor touched Laird's smooth facade, and he coughed raspingly to cover it. "I don't understand the question, Mr. Bruno . . ."

"You haven't told me the terms of Mr. Marshall's original will," I said, tapping the codicil, "but I have to assume that this plays havoc with the family's shares, and you mentioned that you're friends with Mrs. Marshall and godfather to their children." I smiled a bit. "So I'm wondering about the . . . dynamic here."

"What is it you're implying?" Schuyler snapped.

"I'm not implying anything, Mr. Schuyler," I said. "According to this paragraph—the null and void paragraph—if I don't find the child, or prove its existence, the codicil is null and void, and the original will applies. I'm trying to figure out in whose interest it is to find the child—other than the child's, I mean."

"No. You're questioning the senator's integrity," Schuyler said. "You're demeaning him and, by extension, demeaning this firm, and demeaning me."

"No. I'm trying to calculate the actual parameters of the job."

For a trusts and estates lawyer, Schuyler had a raw temper. "Assuming you get it," he snapped.

"Assuming I get it. By the way," I said to Laird, "why am I being considered for it?"

Carefully, Laird said: "You have a reputation, Mr. Bruno, for tenacity and discretion and—if I may say so without implying any offense—a gift for reading the criminal mind." He tapped the codicil. "You can surely understand our concern: Amounts like this frequently attract dishonest persons, not so?"

"I see. You're offering me the job because I'm discreet and tenacious and understand crooks?"

"At this moment," Schuyler said, "we are merely *considering* offering you the job."

I'd had enough. "Senator, if you're going to offer me this job, do it now, please."

"Wilson," Schuyler began, "let me say that—"

As I stood, I cut him off: "Otherwise, Senator, I'll be forced to assume you're not serious about finding this child. I'll be forced to assume you called me not because you thought I was discreet and tenacious, but because you thought I was just shady enough not to look very hard but just respectable enough so the surrogate would believe me when I reported that the child couldn't be found, and its existence couldn't be proved.

"Senator, I don't want to assume that. I want to assume that as well as being the executor of this estate, you're a man of probity, and that you would never consider deceiving the surrogate." I paused. "I'm a member of the bar, Senator; I'm an officer of the court."

After a freighted silence, Laird solemnly said, "Mr. Bruno, you're perfectly correct. My first duty is as the executor: I want you to find the child and serve a notice of probate." He rested a hand on Schuyler's arm to keep him silent. "Can you begin immediately?"

"I'll send a contract over by messenger in the morning," I said. "My regular fees are one hundred dollars an hour or six hundred dollars a day, plus expenses—you get itemized receipts for all of those. I file summary reports weekly, and I get paid by return messenger; for this case, I'd want a six-thousand-dollar retainer. If I find your beneficiary, you pay a bonus of fifty thousand dollars before I serve a notice of probate. If I prove he or she is dead, you pay a bonus of one hundred thousand dollars—it'll all be in the contract."

"That's extortion!" Schuyler snapped. "We won't agree to such an arrangement."

Laird pretended Schuyler wasn't there and spent a while studying my face; finally he nodded and rose, with his hand out: "A pleasure, Mr. Bruno."

I took his hand, and before releasing it said, "May I have a copy of the original will?" As Schuyler began to shake his head from side to side, I leaned closer to Laird's ear. "Or if you pre—"

"Out of the question!" Schuyler yelped.

"—If you prefer, I can go down to surrogate's court and apply there for a copy. Whatever's easiest for you . . ."

Before they could say anything, I nodded to Laird and walked out.

Mollie Wharton had changed into tailored pants—not jeans—and a chambray shirt; she looked like what Herschel used to call the ultimate shiksa, by which he meant he would have fucked her in Barney's main window on sale day. Her living room resembled a page from an antiques show catalogue. I had no idea how much of the stuff was genuine and how much reproductions—for all I knew, Wharton came from a long line of potato farmers—but it certainly gave the impression of wealth and breeding. On the oiled coffee table next to my steno notebook and pen stood a bottle of impressive Bordeaux, and she made sure her glass was constantly filled. I stayed with club soda. Until a few years ago, I could drink and ask smart questions at the same time; not anymore.

I'd spent the first hour letting her roam free, gossiping decorously about Laird, Schuyler, and the firm, and how she'd expected to practice a different kind of law, mergers and acquisitions, say, or product liability or international financing, but had wound up in trusts and estates because her father had said that's where the real leverage was. "You'll protect the great fortunes," he'd told her. "You'll make certain the dynasties remain intact." She didn't talk about her father much, but whenever she mentioned him, whenever she said "Dad," she faltered, as though he might disapprove of her familiarity.

The way she talked about Herschel made me suspect that she still hadn't made sense of him; Herschel belonged to the world of felony arraignments and high bail and maximum-security prisons. He hung out with the kinds of people who ran down the courthouse steps with their raincoats over their heads and their jackets hiding the handcuffs. If she and Herschel had ever slept together it had to have been in his bed—I couldn't conceive of her letting Herschel O'Hara loll around on her antiques, genuine or fake.

She had moved on to the day Marshall came by, so I took a microcassette recorder from my case, put it on the coffee table between us, and turned it on. The tiny red *record* light glowed vividly, and she stopped in midsentence to look at it. She smiled. "Are the notes to back up the recording, or is the recording to back up the notes?"

I smiled back. "Yes," I said.

It only took her an instant to laugh, and it was a real laugh, not loud or full-throated, but not tinny, either. "Ask your last question again . . ." she said.

"Did he dictate from something—notes?"

"He had the points typed out—one sheet of paper, single-spaced."

"Did you have a stenographer with you?"

"No, I did it myself."

"Did he leave his notes with you? Is his sheet of paper in the file?" She nodded. "Does what's in the codicil match what he'd typed out?"

"Yes. Exactly, except for legal stuff and transitions."

"While you were putting the codicil together, did he go into any detail—did he embellish?" She shut her eyes to help her remember, opened them after an instant, and shook her head no. "What about when he told you the name of the foundation—did you say anything, make a joke?"

"I said, 'I'm not sure the AG—the attorney general—will let that one pass,' and he said, 'that asshole will do anything I tell him to, I helped elect him.' "

I picked up my copy of the codicil and read: " 'Some time after I had returned to the United States and to my wife and after she had borne me two more children, I learned that Cricket had emigrated to the United States and was living here with our child.' Did he say when he learned this?" Wharton shook her head no. "Did he say how—phone call, letter, card, fax?" Again, she shook her head. "And you didn't ask him about it?"

"It wasn't necessary," Wharton said. "The answers wouldn't have affected the wording of the document."

"Did you ask him why he decided to change the will now, this year, and not last—or next?"

"There was no reason to, not unless he wasn't mentally competent. He was of sound mind," she said, pointing to the codicil. "He swore to it, and so did the witnesses."

"Did you ask him anything about Cricket or the child? I mean, weren't you curious about *anything*?"

Wharton's lips tightened; she glanced at the recorder. Though she chose her words cautiously, she couldn't hide the distaste in her tone. "I'd only had a couple of dealings with Mr. Marshall, but my experience was that curiosity led to small talk and small talk took Mr. Marshall's mind off the business at hand."

"Just what is it you're saying?" I asked.

After a pause, she said, "He seemed to believe small talk from a woman meant . . . an invitation."

"What kind of invitation?"

Again, she glanced at the recorder. "Maybe I misread him. Maybe I'm hypersensitive to that sort of thing." She looked hard at me. "Can we stay focused on the codicil?"

I went over it with her, and then again, and, though it was evident she was getting irritated as hell, one last time. But she didn't give me anything more. I leaned forward and shut off the recorder, and behind me I heard her sigh softly in relief. I turned to her and said, "Can I have something to drink now? If you have any vodka . . . ." She nodded, jumped up, and went to the kitchen. After a minute, she returned with a fresh bottle of wine, a Baccarat glass, and an iced bottle of Russian vodka. She poured me a reasonable shot, filled her wineglass, and raised it to me. As we drank, each of us watched the other's eyes over the rims of our glasses.

I asked her the same question I'd asked Laird: "Do you believe he fathered a child over there?"

She laughed, without mirth. "Just one?"

I trod carefully. "Do you know of others?"

"No, no, I just meant . . . what I'm saying is . . . I mean, from what I heard . . . rumors, you know, gossip . . . he didn't concern himself too much—" She looked at the recorder.

"It's off," I said.

"He didn't concern himself too much about where he dropped his seed." She got off it in a hurry. "Is your father a lawyer?" she said.

"No."

"Why did you go into law?"

"Every fourth Thursday afternoon, my father was busted. He used to be a bookmaker, the kind who accepted bets. Taking the fall every fourth Thursday was part of his arrangement with the people he worked for. Misdemeanor possession of gambling instruments. He was photographed, printed, and taken to night court. There, Mr. Carillo the lawyer would show up, pay my father's fine, take him out to dinner, and drive him home. I wanted to be like Mr. Carillo."

"Is that really why you went into law?"

"Isn't it a good enough reason?"

"It sounds like the sort of thing somebody would say to make himself seem more interesting."

I grinned, nodded in agreement, drained my glass, put it carefully on a napkin, then deliberately turned my back on her and started packing my things.

"Are you offended, Mr. Bruno?" she said flatly. I glanced over my shoulder at her, grinned again, and continued packing. "Are you?" she asked, more belligerently.

"Thank you for your help, Ms. Wharton," I said. "I'll probably have some more questions once I've done a little work on the case."

I started for the door, and she grabbed my arm. "I asked you a question, Mr. Bruno."

Very slowly, I turned to her. "Yes, you did, Ms. Wharton." I made her wait. "And such a dumb one." Quickly, I put my forefinger on my lips. "Let's make a deal, Ms. Wharton: I won't underestimate you if you don't underestimate me. Okay?"

She inhaled sharply and said quietly, "Deal." We shook hands formally, and she walked me to the door and opened it. "Did I help at all?"

"A bit," I said. "Not much."

"You really know how to charm a girl, Mr. Bruno."

"Not part of our deal, Ms. Wharton."

"Are you divorced?" she said.

"Is it that obvious?"

"Yes." She smiled. "Sleep well, Mr. Bruno."

CHAPTER 3

BUT I DIDN'T SLEEP well. I stayed up most of the night typing into a notebook computer a summary of the conversation with Laird and Schuyler, a transcript of the talk with Wharton, a condensed version of the Saigon codicil, and lists and lists of questions. Most of the questions were about Matthew Marshall, and I knew that until I got a handle on who he was, anything else I learned was strictly filler.

When I dig into a person's life, I begin with the obvious: newspaper and magazine articles, biographical dictionaries, professional directories, like that. If the person's dead, there's always an obituary someplace, and at the very least that gives me a framework. After the surface layer, I go down a step: work history, medical history, criminal records, credit reports, overt bank balances, secret bank balances, stock holdings, partnerships, open corporations, dummy corporations, real estate, permits, licenses, judgments—the list is as long as I feel like making it. Years ago, doing this sort of research took days of legwork, but nowadays most of it can be done from a chair: All you need is a computer and a modem. There are about 1,000 on-line services through which you can hook into more than 5,000 data bases, private and government, and in those data bases is enough information to blackmail anyone you do a real search on. Getting into a data base either costs a few dollars or takes a little ingenuity—about as much as a shrewd high school sophomore uses to cheat on a term paper. Maybe less.

When I got to the office in the morning, I punched up a publications data base, and I knew I was in for a long, long day. Though Matthew Marshall wasn't a business celebrity—he didn't belong to the Lee Iacocca or Ted Turner or Bill Gates class—he'd made lots of money for himself and other people, and done it in a fashionable trade, electronics and communications. So there were hundreds of listings for him, and those referred only to articles in mainstream newspapers and magazines. They didn't include trade publications. I flagged what I thought I might use, got a list of the rest, and started with his obituary in the *New York Times*.

If you'd bought the paper the Wednesday after Labor Day, this is what you'd have found out:

> Matthew Marshall, founder and chairman of Tel-Mat Industries and a longtime patron of the Whitney Museum, the Film Society of Lincoln Center, New Amsterdam Hospital, and his alma mater, the University of North Carolina, died over the holiday weekend at his cabin in upstate Knickerbocker County.
>
> Although the cause of death had not been determined at press time, the Knickerbocker County sheriff, A. J. Holloway, said it appeared that Mr. Marshall, who was alone in the cabin, had suffered a stroke. He was 51 years old.
>
> Tel-Mat Industries, which Mr. Marshall founded in a garage in Chapel Hill in 1975, after his return from Vietnam, designed and manufactured computerized switches and software for telephone and cable TV transmission equipment.
>
> For the first few years of its existence, Tel-Mat, which in those days was privately held, depended on Pentagon contracts for its survival. Mr. Marshall, whose degree was in electrical engineering, had invented—along with his late partner, Arthur Macintosh—a device that cleaned up "noise" on communications lines. The device is still used by military forces throughout the world.
>
> In 1984, when the Reagan buildup of the Pentagon was at its apex, Mr. Marshall foresaw that the days of getting rich on defense contracts were numbered, and he maneuvered Tel-Mat into position to exploit the revolution in communications that was on the horizon.
>
> In 1988, Mr. Marshall and Mr. Macintosh took the company public, becoming wealthy in the process and giving Tel-Mat a huge financial base from which to expand.
>
> Last year, Tel-Mat, which has its operations headquarters in Raleigh and its financial headquarters in New York, had revenues of nearly $2 billion and earnings of more than $330 million. It had plants in three states, Hong Kong, Jakarta, the Yucatan, and Manila. Rumors have been circulating in the telecommunications industry since

January that Mr. Marshall was about to close a deal for a major installation in China.

Mr. Marshall jokingly referred to himself as a "country boy from North Carolina," but in fact he was very much part of the New York charity circuit. He and his wife, Beth, could be found at most of the more visible benefit events of the season.

Though their legal residence was in Tuckahoe, the Marshalls maintained a co-op at the Olympic Towers, and as likely as not they would spend the night in the city as in Westchester. They also maintained homes in Corfu, Antigua, Telluride, and Chapel Hill.

When Tel-Mat went public, Mr. Marshall endowed two chairs at the University of North Carolina Engineering School and became a patron of both the Whitney and the Film Society.

Because of his service in Vietnam, he also built and endowed the burn unit at the New Amsterdam Hospital and a blood bank to go with it, along with blood banks at existing burn units at hospitals around the country.

Matthew Luke Marshall (he legally dropped the Luke on his 21st birthday) was born outside Durham, N.C., on June 7, 1944, to Luke and Antoinette Marshall. He was the youngest of three and was delivered while his father was storming the beaches of Normandy. In civilian life, Luke Marshall operated a Shell station and Mr. Marshall worked there for two years before enrolling at the University of North Carolina.

During Mr. Marshall's undergraduate days, he joined the ROTC, and at a dance given by a sorority for the cadet corps he met Beth Moore, a fine arts major. They were married the day of his graduation in June 1968.

In 1969, soon after the birth of his first child, Mr. Marshall began his first tour of duty in South Vietnam, during which he won a Bronze Star and a Purple Heart. He served another two tours, winning several more decorations, and left active duty in 1972 as a captain.

In addition to his widow, Mr. Marshall leaves three children, Matthew Jr., of Manhattan; Frederick and Wendy, of Tuckahoe; a brother, Paul, of Charlotte, N.C.; and a sister, Rachel Marshall Pollock, of San Francisco.

Former Vice President Wilson Laird, Mr. Marshall's lawyer and a longtime friend of the family, said that funeral arrangements were incomplete.

I reread the obit and made myself a pot of coffee. Even allowing for the *Times*'s gift for making anyone dull, Matthew Marshall seemed too bland to be true: ROTC, college sweetheart, 'Nam, electronics entrepreneur, three children, cozy home in Tuckahoe, safe charities, no hint of booze or drugs or corruption or scandal. Nothing. The most arresting thing about Matthew Marshall's life was that he could hardly wait to shed his father's name. Was this the kind of man who'd call his schooner the *Velvet Triangle* and rewrite his will to leave half his fortune to a child he'd never seen? On the face of it, no. Which meant Matthew Marshall was much more interesting than the *Times* suspected; and which also meant that I was about to enjoy myself a whole lot.

CHAPTER 4

THE MARSHALL ESTATE IN Tuckahoe had a long, twisty driveway, and at first I didn't realize just how big the property was. Then, I came around the last curve: The meadow and woods behind the main building, which looked to be fifty rooms big, went on for miles. To the left of the house was a formal garden, complete with stream, waterfall, and beds of flowers and a maze; to the right was a paddock in which three horses nibbled grass. Behind the paddock, grouped in a gentle arc, were four guest houses. I assumed the pool and tennis courts were around someplace, but I couldn't see them.

I'd expected a servant, perhaps even a butler in morning clothes, to answer the door, but I got a surprise: Before me stood a striking woman of about fifty. She was five-seven or so, slender, with long but curly hair—auburn touched with silver—and large blue eyes. She wore a dress that shaded from pewter to black, and the coloring and cut were so subtle that instead of being severe it was serene. She paused an instant, enough for courtesy—or effect—and held out her hand; her fingers were graceful and her touch silken.

"Mr. Bruno, I'm Beth Marshall," she said, and even in the few words I could hear North Carolina. "Thank you for driving up here. Please come in."

I followed her through the foyer—that's when a maid appeared, to shut the door behind me—and into a library. We were moving too fast for me to notice much, but I could see that Marshall's generosity to the Whitney wasn't just for show: The paintings on the walls were by artists whose work was reproduced in *People* magazine because of the prices they got.

The library was the kind of room that you usually see only as a stage set: spacious, high-ceilinged, bookcases filled with real books, books you could reach and books you would read; an antique globe; and the sort of furniture that Mollie Wharton only dreamed of.

Before I could enter the room, I was greeted by two large, black, standard poodles—Bitch One and Bitch Two, I assumed—who both tried to nuzzle my empty left hand; my briefcase was in my right. I patted each of them on their flanks, and they preceded me into the library.

As I stepped into the room, I saw what had to be two of the three Marshall children rising simultaneously from a crinkled leather sofa. Beth Marshall confirmed it: "Mr. Bruno, my daughter Wendy and my younger son Fred."

They had their mother's manners. Each stepped forward, hand out, confident but not aggressive, smiled in welcome when we shook, and murmured, "How do you do, Mr. Bruno?" as though they meant it. Like their mother, they were slender and attractive, and wore similarly subdued outfits. Tasteful grief was the motif. They had her hair and hands, but their eyes, from what I recalled of Marshall's photos, came from their father. They looked to be about twenty or twenty-one.

As we all sat down—the children on the couch, their mother in a Victorian rocker, me opposite them and the poodles between us—the maid came in, rolling a bar before her. She looked at Beth Marshall, who said, "I'll serve. Thank you, Celia." The maid nodded and left the room, and I took a notebook and tape recorder from my case. Everyone watched while I stood the recorder on a coffee table, flipped open the notebook, and carefully made a test scribble with my pen.

"You don't mind, do you?" I said, as ingenuously as I dared. "I have a terrible memory and a worse handwriting. If I don't record and take notes, I mess up."

Beth Marshall laughed softly. She had a caressing kind of laugh; it made you believe for an instant that everything in the world was going to be okay. "Really, Mr. Bruno? You don't look like somebody who has a terrible memory. In fact, you don't look like somebody who messes up. But perhaps I'm overestimating you. Whatever. We don't mind, do we . . . ?" Both children shook their heads. "Can I offer you something?"

"A bit later," I said. I smiled what I hoped was a disarming smile. "Let me plunge right in, Mrs. Marshall. Did your husband ever mention to you—or to any of your children—that he planned to change his will?"

"No," she said. The kids shook their heads.

"So the first you heard about it was when?"

"When Wilson—Senator Laird—told me."

"Did your husband ever mention fathering a child while he was in Vietnam?"

She inhaled sharply. "You don't believe in an excess of tact, do you, Mr. Bruno?"

"I do. But I'm not good at it. Sorry."

"No, Matt never mentioned it."

"Did he mention a romance over there? An affair? A one-night stand? Did he ever mention falling into bed with somebody when he was, say, depressed, or drunk?"

"My husband didn't fall into bed with people, even when he got drunk," she said lethally. "Which was seldom."

"What about during a fight?"

"I don't follow you, Mr. Bruno."

"Did he ever mention anything during a fight? People sometimes say very ugly things during a fight—wounding things, and sometimes those things are true—'I *say* I love you, but I *really* love so and so, and she and I had something you and I will never have'—like that?"

She lowered her eyes for an instant. "No. No."

"Did you ever hear the name Cricket?"

"No, never."

"Was your husband the kind of man who'd have suffered a guilty conscience over a one-night stand?"

"He was an honorable man, if that's what you mean."

"Who might he have told about something like this?"

Wendy Marshall conspicuously cleared her throat. "Mr. Bruno, your questions assume that what Daddy said in the codicil is true. We don't think it is."

"You don't?" I said, feigning astonishment.

"No," Fred Marshall said.

"Hmmmm." I flipped a notebook page as though I were reading something. "If it isn't true, then why did he compose the codicil?" Nobody said anything; I moved my pen down the blank page. "Do you believe he'd lost his mind? The lawyer who wrote it up for him seems to think he was fine."

"She didn't know him very well," Wendy Marshall said.

"She certainly didn't!" Fred Marshall added.

"But you knew him," I said, and the three of them nodded spiritedly. "Was he acting strangely around the July fourth holiday?"

"We were all away," Beth Marshall said.

"Was he acting strangely at any time in the past few months, say, back to the first of the year? Any behavior enough out of the ordinary that he'd do something like this? Think about it—don't rush." They didn't. They reflected, they glanced at each other, they reflected some more, before finally shaking their heads no.

Again, I moved my pen down the blank page. "If he wasn't crazy, did he write the codicil because he wanted to hurt you? Any of you? All of you?"

In unison, and forcefully, they said, "No."

I let it hang. "You see why I need to assume it's true?" They looked at each other in discomfort, which was fine with me. "So," I continued, "who might he have told about something like this—who was his best friend? Who did he trust with his deepest secrets?"

"Me," Beth Marshall said with perfect confidence.

"Of course," I said reassuringly. "But who else—who did he confide in, or hang out with who wasn't a friend of yours, or, at least, who was more a friend of his?" I coughed a couple of times to forewarn her. "Man or woman."

Tightly, she said, "He had many, many friends." She inhaled deeply, then exhaled. "I'd have to go through all his address books."

"I don't mind doing it," I said. "Do you have them?"

"I have one small personal book, the one he carried with him. His assistant at Tel-Mat has the others."

"And she is . . . ?"

"Trish Twomey." She spelled it for me, and I printed it. "I'll send you mine as soon as I've had a chance to make a copy."

I put on my kindest at-your-service smile. "I have state-of-the-art copying equipment. If you give me the book now, I'll messenger it back to you tomorrow morning."

She started to protest, then changed her mind. "Fred, in your father's night table . . ." He nodded and left the room. "Are you ready for a drink yet, Mr. Bruno?"

"Not quite," I answered. "But I'd be happy to pour you one."

"We'll wait for you," she said, with an amused smile, and patiently folded her beautiful hands in her lap.

"The names of his doctors are in the address books, aren't they?" She nodded. "What about the names of people he served with in Vietnam?"

"I don't think so," she said. "So far as I know, he didn't stay in touch with anyone."

"Did he keep a journal or a diary?"

"Only a business diary. Trish would have that."

"Did he ever keep one—say, while he was in Vietnam?"

"Not as far as I know."

"What about letters?"

"You mean, from Vietnam?" I nodded. "He wrote to me, he wrote to his mother—she's dead. He might have written to Rachel and Paul, his brother and sister. I don't know." Her lips curled very slightly. "In his letters to me, I can't recall his mentioning a lover or a child."

Fred came back into the room and handed me a small leather address book before taking his seat.

"Did he talk about the war at all?"

"No," she said neutrally.

I turned to Fred. "What about to you?"

After a cautious look at his mother and sister, he said, "Not really, but once . . ."

"Once *what*?" Beth Marshall said.

"Once," Fred Marshall said quickly, "he took us to the wall—in Washington, I mean—and made us touch some names."

"Twenty-three names," Wendy Marshall said, with a brief shudder. "I counted."

"Did your brother go with you?" I asked.

"Uhuh," Fred Marshall said, a bit awkwardly.

"Where can I reach him—is he listed?"

"I'm sure my husband never talked to Matthew about the war," Beth Marshall said.

"I'm sure not, Mrs. Marshall," I said agreeably, "but he is the oldest. . . . Is he listed?"

Beth Marshall smiled placidly before saying, "Either at his gallery—it's called Reflex, in Soho someplace—or in the address book I lent you, Mr. Bruno." She twisted slowly to face her children, and after staring at them just long enough to make them fidget said, "When was this?"

"June of eighty-six," Wendy said. "You were in Wyoming, at the spa."

"He made us promise not to tell you," Fred Marshall added hastily.

"Did he say why?" his mother asked.

"No. Only . . . only . . . that it was our secret," Wendy Marshall answered.

While we were all digesting the word "secret" the doors swung open and the maid ushered in Wilson Laird. He strode straight to Beth Marshall, kissed her, did the same to Wendy Marshall, shook Fred Marshall's hand, and stopped in front of me. "Mr. Bruno." Instead of offering me his hand, he held out a fat 10-by 14-envelope. "The nineteen ninety-three document," he said. I took it, and Laird glanced around, saying in mock surprise, "It's after five on Friday, and I don't see a single glass!"

"We're totally dependent on Mr. Bruno," Beth Marshall said lightly, inflating her accent. She leaned my way and touched the back of my hand with her forefinger. "Mr. Bruno, please, may we have a cocktail now? It is nearly sunset, and we have been so very, very cooperative . . ."

Obviously, there was no way to refuse, and I didn't. Once we had drinks in hand, Laird sat on the ottoman in front of Beth Marshall, touched his glass to hers, and smiled at the children. They didn't smile back. "Blessings," Laird said, in his practiced pol's way, and sipped. "How's it going?"

"Mr. Bruno is diligence itself," Beth Marshall said. "He's already seduced Matt's personal address book out of me and unearthed a secret Matt had with the children."

"What secret?" Laird said.

"Matt took the children to the Vietnam Memorial—the wall," she said lightly, "while I was busy making myself beautiful for him."

Laird nodded sagely. "I can understand that, giving his children a sense of the hardest part of his life. It's painful, but I'd do the same."

Wendy Marshall sniffed and said, "Would you?"

"Wendy . . ." her mother said, with a gossamer touch of reproach, "Dear, please . . ."

"Wouldn't you be embarrassed?" Wendy Marshall said to Laird.

"Don't be rude, Wendy. Please," Beth Marshall said, but it was in no way a request.

"Right," Fred Marshall apparently agreed. "Wilson is a dear friend of the family—Mr. Bruno," he said, as though the thought had just popped into his head, "you should ask Wilson if my father told *him* anything. I'll do it. Did he, Wilson? Did my dad tell you about what happened in Vietnam?"

"No, he did not," Laird said shortly, and something in his tone made Bitch One and Bitch Two growl very softly.

"Maybe he's not such a dear friend, after all," Wendy Marshall said. "Who can tell?"

"That's enough," Beth Marshall said, and by then I was on my feet.

While I gathered my things, I said to Laird, "Do you know anyone Mr. Marshall might have talked to about Vietnam?" He shook his head no. "Was he the kind of man who kept souvenirs?"

"Souvenirs?" Beth Marshall said, puzzled.

"The kind of man who took his children to the memorial might be the kind of man who kept souvenirs . . . ?"

"No," she said. "Not here." She thought about it. "Not anywhere we lived."

"Does he have a storage locker anyplace?"

"You'd have to ask Trish."

"What about the cabin, the one upstate?"

"I wouldn't know," she said. "That was his retreat." She turned to the children. "Did he ever take you there? Is that another secret?" They both shook their heads vigorously.

I made a farewell circuit and stopped in front of Beth Marshall. "Thank you," I said, "you've been very helpful, and forgive me if I warn you that I'm sure to pester you again." She smiled understandingly, shook my hand, and bent toward Laird as I headed out. At the door, I stopped. "Mrs. Marshall . . ." She raised her head to look straight at me.

"Yes, Mr. Bruno?"

"Did you save his letters from Vietnam?"

Calmly, she said, "Only as long as I needed to."

CHAPTER 5

I DIDN'T HEAR HIM come up behind me—I was busy trying to unlock the front door of Marshall's cabin. What I did hear was the inimitable double-clack of a shotgun round being chambered, and I stopped moving and started sweating. I thought for an instant of raising my hands high or spreading them wide, so he'd see I had no weapon, but I didn't dare. My experience with people holding guns on me is that it's urgent—mortally urgent—to do nothing until they give you instructions. There's no way of knowing in advance what somebody with a gun might find threatening. So I waited, frozen, my left hand curled around the doorknob, my right thumb and forefinger pinching the key.

The lock, I noticed again, as I had when I put the key in it, was a Yale, which was hardly a surprise; Yale locks are very popular. The doorknob, I noticed, was slightly damp, and I couldn't tell whether it was the remains of the morning dew—it was only a bit past eight-thirty—or my sweat. Whoever was behind me said nothing, nor did he move. All I heard was breathing. It was labored, like a smoker's, but didn't sound close. By then, sweat had started dribbling down my back and from my scrotum to the insides of my thighs. By then, knots were forming all over—my shoulders, my stomach, my forearms. The temptation to move, to shake, to wriggle, to jump—anything to get rid of the tension—was overwhelming, but I stayed immobile, bent over the key in the Yale lock in the front door of Matt Marshall's cabin in Knickerbocker County.

Without moving my head, I glanced at the ground, just to exercise my eye and face muscles. A chameleon scampered from behind a rock to the left of the door—the same rock under which I'd found the key. People are strange about keys to country houses: Nobody who lives in the city would leave his key under a hallway rug or on a doorway ledge, but they do that all the time in the country. Not that I'd completely counted on that. I'd brought a set of tools and been prepared to pick the lock if I needed to. I almost laughed. Was this my punishment for being ready to break into the cabin? Someone with a pumper behind me.

In my left jacket pocket I had a letter giving me permission to enter the cabin. The letter was fraudulent—I'd forged it the previous night—but there was no way the person behind me would know that. Of course, people with shotguns tend not to be impressed with letters of permission, even genuine ones. I wondered if it was safe to clear my throat; if I swallowed, would he—I assumed it was a he—see the back of my neck move, and would that startle him? I badly needed to swallow; my throat was as dry as old bread.

Before I could make up my mind, the breathing seemed to stop. Then I felt something hard and cool touch the base of my skull. I couldn't feel the shape—that's a myth that you can feel whether something is round, or oval, or oblong, or square—but I could feel the density and the temperature, and if it wasn't the barrel of a shotgun, it was something enough like it for me to reflexively close my eyes and start counting backward to myself. When I was a kid, whenever I got really scared, I would count backward, just to focus on something, anything, other than the fear.

The barrel tip moved slightly and a hand patted down my upper body, not professionally but expertly enough for me to guess that he'd done it before. I held my breath as the hand moved to my thighs. I'd known lots of cops—DEA thugs especially—who when they did the lower body grabbed your balls and twisted till tears came to your eyes. He didn't. The barrel tip disappeared. "You wanna turn around, man . . . ?"

The voice was gravelly—cigarettes and booze, I guessed—but not nervous, which was a break. Slowly, opening both palms and spreading my hands, I turned around.

If it hadn't been for his eyes, he could have worked as a model for Eddie Bauer or L.L. Bean: tall, slender, sandy hair going on gray, strong jaw, straight nose, forgiving mouth. He wore hunter's clothes, up to and including the reflective vest so other hunters wouldn't mistake him for game. He looked the way lawmen in movies used to look—Gary Cooper or Alan Ladd—open and honest and decent and kindly. Except for his eyes. His eyes belonged to the kinds of people who never blink during their sentencing hearings, not even when relatives of their victims describe the torn and mutilated bodies.

He gestured with his shotgun to the driveway, moved aside to let me pass, and then fell in step behind me. I paused as I reached my car, but he prodded me lightly and I continued, up the 800 or so yards to the county road. The going wasn't easy because autumn had truly arrived, and golden leaves, wet and treacherous, lay in odd-shaped patches all along the gravel. At the head of the driveway, parked obscurely behind a hedge, was a pickup truck. With his hand he pointed to the passenger side, and I opened the door and climbed in. With the shotgun, he gestured to me to slide over, to the driver's seat. After I had, he climbed in and, without taking his eyes or the gun off me, pulled the door closed. From his shirt pocket he took a key and handed it to me; I put it in the ignition and waited for his signal. Above the windshield was bolted a double gun rack; one set of clamps was empty. The other held an AK-47 rifle.

He nodded. I started the truck and pulled onto the roadway. "About eleven miles," he said. "Then a right."

I checked the odometer for the mileage and sped up to around fifty. Out of the corner of my right eye, I could see the barrel of the shotgun pointed at my ribs. With his free hand, he pushed a button on the cassette deck and the Rolling Stones' "Mother's Little Helper" came out of the speakers.

He muttered something, but I didn't hear it over the music. "What'd you say?" I asked.

"Rock and roll," he said gaily. "Rock and roll."

"Right."

"The thing was the booby traps," he said.

"I beg your pardon?"

"Gooks like to booby trap everything. 'Specially babies. We're suckers for babies—they know that. We buy all those Hallmark fuckin' cards; so you go in a hootch and there's this baby, lying in a basket, crying, so you figure it's hungry, it's shit itself, it wants to puke. Baby stuff. So you pick it up and bam! Bam bam bam!" He laughed uproariously. "Rock and roll! They're not all stupid, gooks. They figured out about the fuckin' babies."

"I see what you mean."

"You got to watch the grass and the plants. Which is a pain, 'cause then you always got your eyes down. You walk around like a fuckin' drunk lookin' for a dime. See, a branch is too straight, it's not a branch. Bam! No more leg. Up to the knee, bam! Bam! Goat shit. Pig shit. They're real good with shit. We hadda learn that from them. Bam!"

The music changed to Janis Joplin's "Another Little Piece of My Heart," and he sang along for a few bars. "Fuckin' Yahoo. I was picking pieces of Yahoo outta my fuckin' hair for days. Bam! Him and Talcott and that mongrel E-5 from Georgia, they were really suckers for kids. I mean, that fuckin' Yahoo would *kiss* a gook kid. Bam! No more Talcott, off with his head, said the Queen, pudding all over the walls and ceiling. Blood pudding." Once more, he laughed in sheer enjoyment.

"The secret is not to try to waste 'em in their hootches unless you use a grenade. You use a grenade, it's cool 'cause the firepower goes up; you roll a couple on the ground and it's gorgeous. Like Radio City! But that doesn't work too good 'cause they figure out pretty quick what you're about. Even a gook can do that. You gotta get 'em outside somehow, but if you shout VC! VC! VC!, they just cower like frightened fuckin' dogs. The best way is to talk real soft, like you were talkin' up some bitch in a bar at four in the morning, throw in a few French words—gooks think if you talk French you're actually saying something to 'em—and get 'em to line up. Hold out some chocolate for the kids; maybe some rice or some thread for the *mama-san*; then they follow you, tippie toe tippie toe.

"Once you get 'em outside, you make sure there's some ground behind 'em, needn't be much, a few inches is good, and if you don't have a sixty, or a quad, you put your sixteen on auto, and you aim for the legs; you gotta aim for the legs, 'cause a sixteen, I don't give a shit how strong you are, that mother jerks up on rock and roll, you aim for their legs, you get 'em in the gut or the chest." Another healthy laugh. "You got a spare piece, you got enough magazines, you do it right, you can cut a VC right the fuck in half. 'Specially a baby."

I wanted to wipe my face—the sweat was dripping on to the steering wheel—but it didn't seem like a great idea to move my hands. I glanced at the odometer; we still had six miles to drive before the turn, and I had no idea where we going from there.

"I love Joplin," he said appreciatively, as though we'd been having a friendly discussion about music. He hummed a couple of bars. "Gives me a hard-on."

"I can understand that," I said, just to move my jaw.

We had reached the turn and I swung right. Carefully, I said, "How far?"

"Not far," he said. "Maybe three miles from the perimeter. Maybe three and a half. Watch out for goat shit." The music changed to Otis Redding's "Dock of the Bay," and he sang along to himself. I glanced his way: The shotgun barrel remained steady, pointed at my midsection.

A little more than three miles along the road, I saw a sign that read, KNICKERBOCKER COUNTY SHERIFF, which, as it turned out, was where he was taking me.

As I pulled into a parking slot, a middle-aged deputy emerged from the squat building and strolled over to us. "Morning," he said to me. "Hi, Tim." He looked briefly into the truck. "Tim, you want to do me a favor and put the shotgun in the rack . . . ? Sheriff catches you with it like that, he's gotta fine you." As Tim thought that over, the deputy opened my door and signaled me to climb out.

Tim carefully put the gun in the overhead rack, removed the keys from the ignition, and got out on the passenger side. The deputy offered his hand and Tim shook it. Tim waved toward me: "Caught him trying to break into Matt's place. My guess, he was about ready to frag it."

"Ummmmm," the deputy said, as though he were genuinely thinking it over. "You find a grenade on him, Tim? Any kind of explosive?"

"Fuck you, Sklar," Tim said flatly.

"Hmmmmm," the deputy repeated. He looked at me, and by then I had my fake letter in my hand.

"I'm doing an investigation for the Marshall estate," I said. "I have permission to enter the cabin. I wasn't breaking in, I was using the key. It's still in the lock."

The deputy took the letter, unfolded it, and skimmed it. "You got any ID, Mr. Bruno?" I passed him my wallet, and he flipped through various cards, checking my face against anything with a photo on it. He held my driver's license in front of Tim's face. "His papers are okay, Tim."

Tim stared at the license, then at me. "Fuck your papers. You're a fragger," he said. With a nod to the deputy, he jumped into his pickup and drove off.

The deputy gave me the wallet and the letter. "I'll run you back to Marshall's place." He glanced at my face, which must have been shiny with sweat. "You want a coffee?"

They gave me coffee, and doughnuts. What is it about cops and doughnuts? The deputy's name was Ephraim Sklar, and he'd worked at the 74th precinct in Brooklyn before moving upstate. His boss, the sheriff, was A. J. Holloway, and he'd been Sklar's sergeant at the 74th. For the first pot of coffee, they went out of their way to be pleasant—after all, it wasn't every day a harmless stranger got taken to their offices at the point of a 12-gauge pump-action. We chatted about the weather, and the hunting season, and the merits of Mossberg and Savage rifles, and how pleasant life was upstate.

But by the second pot, they stopped chatting—they'd adjusted to the country some, but at heart they were still city cops, and city cops like to ask questions, and get answers to their questions; they believed getting answers to their questions was their natural right, like tax exemptions for church real estate. Since I didn't believe it was their natural right, we'd stopped being buddies. I tried a legalistic approach: "Sheriff," I said, "of course you know that unless what I'm doing is connected to something you're doing, I don't have to answer your questions. This is a private matter."

"I decide what's private," Holloway said.

I tried diplomacy: "Sheriff, help me out. Give me a reason to answer your questions."

"Gimme a fuckin' break," Sklar interjected.

"I don't have to give you reasons, Bruno."

"No; and I don't have to answer your questions."

"Fine," Holloway said savagely. "Eff, take him back there, put him in his car, and point him to the city."

"Sheriff, I have permission to go into that cabin. You send me home today, I'm back tomorrow. You do it again tomorrow, I'm back the day after; you do it too often, I'm back with a court order. You know that."

"I don't know shit! Eff, take him back there, put him in his car, escort him to the thruway, and make sure he gets on it. Fuck you and your court order, Bruno."

I'm not sure why I didn't believe the explosion—maybe because I'd been around too many city cops and seen too many of their numbers—but I didn't. I nodded deferentially, stood up, and started out. Holloway's voice stopped me before I got three steps. "Bruno . . ." I looked over my shoulder. "You got a first name?"

"Adam."

"Adam," Holloway continued, dredging up an awful smile, "sit down, sit down. You need more coffee? Here." He poured. "Eff, give him some sugar." Holloway stirred his own coffee far, far too long before talking, and when he spoke, he had trouble getting the words out.

"Matt Marshall was a friend of ours—not a close friend, not a drinking friend, but he liked us and we liked him. Donation every Christmas and every election, too. He had high blood pressure—no secret. Okay. You have high blood pressure, you're vulnerable to strokes—my old man went that way. I hear Marshall had a couple of minor ones—cerebral incidents, they call 'em; no secret. Okay.

"Labor Day weekend, Tim comes by, says the light is on in Marshall's place, says he knocked, Marshall doesn't answer, says he looked in the window, Marshall's sitting in his chair, says he knocked again, loud, Marshall still doesn't answer. So he goes in—Marshall never locks the door—and checks on him. Marshall's not showing any signs; he does CPR; zip. Tim can't call anyplace. The only phone's in Marshall's car, and Tim doesn't have the code, so—"

"Where's the car?"

"We got it here. Laird asked us to put it in storage," Holloway said, irritated that I'd interrupted his narrative. "Okay, so Tim comes by to get me. I go over to Marshall's place—"

"You and Deputy Sklar?"

"No, just me. I drew the holiday, tough shit on me. Marshall's dead. Dead. From my car, I call Dr. Hewitt—this is midnight, mind you—and Hewitt says he'll come by in the morning. I seal the house. Next morning, eight o'clock, Eff and me meet Hewitt—he knows Marshall's history, he's even prescribed whatever that shit is they take for blood pressure—and he writes up a death certificate. Right date, right time, right cause. No bullshit, but . . ."

"Eight hours later, and no autopsy," I said.

"Oh, get off it," Sklar said. "The fuck does he need an autopsy for? He got a stroke."

"He needs an autopsy because no doctor was in attendance when he died," I said. "Right, Sheriff?"

"Technically," Holloway begrudged.

"You got a number and address for Hewitt?" I said.

Holloway didn't hesitate. He scribbled on a pad, tore off the top sheet, and slid it to me. "We got nothing to hide, Bruno. Adam. You talk to Hewitt, anyone you want."

"What's Tim's last name?"

"Cleary," Sklar said. "He lives three miles west of Marshall." He smiled venemously. "You want to be careful approaching his place."

"Thanks for the tip," I said.

"Listen, Adam," Holloway said, with some urgency, "nobody fucked up here, okay? This is the country—we don't have nine-one-one, we don't have EMS, we're kinda catch-as-catch-can up here—but Hewitt wrote up a legit death certificate for a legit death. This is not a big fuckin' deal, okay?"

"Fine," I said. "Can I go back to the cabin now?"

They looked at each other. "You're okay on this?" Holloway said.

"It's none of my business," I said.

They both exhaled slowly, and the tension left their faces. "Well, what *is* your business?" Sklar said.

"Not yours," I said. "How about that ride?"

CHAPTER 6

It took me a good thirty seconds of staring at the photo to find Tim Cleary. He was squatting on the dirt, bare-chested, a rocket launcher cradled in his arms. He had a lovely smile in those days—the picture was dated 1970 and marked Pleiku—and his eyes were clear as a child's. Why not? He wasn't much more than a child back then. Neither were any of the others in the shot.

The room, which was the largest in the cabin—maybe 20 by 25—was a shrine to Marshall's tours in Vietnam. One wall was devoted to photos of soldiers and nurses—that's where I started and that's where I found Tim Cleary; a second to weapons, both American and captured; a third to souvenirs: patches, decorations, articles of Vietnamese clothing, menus from bars, towels from hotels, items from aid kits, food packs, junk.

The fourth wall was less revealing. The photos there, unlike the combat stuff, weren't dated or place-marked, and the people in them—except for one Vietnamese in uniform—were civilians. Some wore hard hats, some sipped drinks at an open-air restaurant, one sat at the controls of a cargo plane, one talked into the microphone of a portable recorder, one held a machete over a sack marked LONG GRAIN RICE PRODUCT OF TEXAS.

In a corner were two metal file cabinets, which I badly wanted to ransack, but I decided that would be my reward for the scut work. I fetched a camera and tripod from my car, took off my jacket, loosened my tie, and began to shoot everything in the room. Shooting pictures of dozens of other pictures and of dozens of objects mounted on walls is as dull as walking back and forth in a blank hallway, but harder, because in a hallway you can at least think about anything you like—the women who've loved you, or the friends you've protected, or the deeds you did that made things better, or the deeds you did that made things worse. It doesn't take much concentration to walk back and forth. But shooting pictures does take concentration, and if you start to think about women or friends or good or bad deeds, you lose concentration and make mistakes. Which I did. Often.

By the time I'd finished shooting, it was after one and I was ravenous. Much of the stuff in the refrigerator was spoiled, but I found a pantry, which contained several 100-pound sacks of kibble and enough canned and packaged goods for humans. I could put together a tolerable meal. There was a fancy coffeemaker—it ground the beans and offered either regular or espresso—and I made myself a full pot of regular. The coffeemaker wasn't the only elegant appliance. There were a dishwasher, built-in oven, built-in microwave, built-in stovetop, and every kind of laborsaving cooking tool I'd ever seen. Despite all that, the kitchen had a homey, pleasant feel, with oak floors, exposed beams, and an old-fashioned ceiling fan.

After I cleaned up, I took a quick impressionistic tour of the rest of the house—cabin was a misnomer, the place was at least 4,000 square feet—just to get a sense of the building, and in the hope (vain, as it turned out) that anything unusual would make itself instantly visible. Every room in the place gave off the same care, warmth, and appeal as the kitchen. Marshall had spent a lot of time and money to create his safe harbor—his retreat, Beth Marshall had called it—and create a safe harbor he had.

After the quick tour, I got my notebook and went room by room, starting with the master bathroom. For a man his age, Marshall had been in pretty good shape. All he had for himself in the medicine cabinet were a half-empty bottle of Capoten for high blood pressure; aspirin, ibuprofen, and acetaminophen—all for headaches; and a decongestant. In another section of the cabinet—it was one of those large, mirrored, three-doored jobs—were supplies for guests: three brands of tampons; two brands of sanitary napkins; two brands of panty-liners, douche, spermicidal jelly, applicators, condoms, and several packages of Today, a contraceptive sponge. I began to see why Beth Marshall didn't feel welcome at the cabin.

In the master bedroom, mounted in the wall opposite the king-sized bed, was a 27-inch TV set; under it were a VCR, a stereo set, and a shelf filled with videotapes. Marshall's taste ran to musicals—Fred Astaire and Ginger Rogers, Gene Kelly—and Italian neorealism and French New Wave, the result, no doubt, of hanging around with the aficionados at the Film Society. I made a note of the titles and, leaving the night table till last, moved on to the closets, the bureaus, and the oak trunk at the foot of the bed. Nothing special in any of them. The guest's night table—I assumed it was the guest's because there was a box of pink Kleenex on it—was empty but for a small bowl of Godiva chocolates.

In Marshall's night table was a travel alarm clock, a pad, two pens, a scientific calculator, a sealed pack of 3.5 diskettes, three loose condoms, and a 9-mm Smith & Wesson, loaded. I felt around at the back of the shelf and found a backup magazine, full, for the piece. I also found another pad; on the top page was written #651594.

I made a note of the entire inventory, copied the number, put everything back, and did the three guest bathrooms and the three guest bedrooms. Nothing. It seemed to me they hadn't been used in years.

Downstairs, in the living room, the den, and kitchen, I came up just as empty. There was another 9-mm Smith & Wesson in his desk in the den, but all that told me was that Marshall had a thing for 9-mm Smith & Wessons. I was frustrated and exhausted—it was dark by then, and Holloway had made it clear that he wasn't about to let me stay in the cabin overnight—so by the time I got back to the Vietnam room, I was burning to find something.

Which I did. What I found first were Beth Marshall's letters to her husband. They were in the top drawer of the left file cabinet, three bundles, organized by dates and carefully bound with clean, straw-colored twine. There was no sign of his letters to her.

Tempted as I was to start reading, I put the letters aside. I was too eager to search the file cabinets completely. Beth Marshall's letters were here; the room was his homage to his Vietnam past. I *knew* I would find some evidence of Marshall's lover and child—a note perhaps or a birth certificate, a scribbled address, a canceled check, a brokerage account, a deed on a house, a receipt for a stroller, a report card, or a document in Vietnamese. Something. Anything. I didn't.

Instead, I found military stuff—copies of letters to soldiers' wives and mothers; copies of recommendations for medals; maps, logs, battle plans, injury reports, grave registration reports, leave requests, reprimands, formal charges, courts-martial transcripts, but no complete rosters and no key to the photos on the wall. Moreover, everything dated from the war; there was nothing to indicate that Marshall stayed in touch with any of the people he'd served with; no way of knowing which of those people he was closest to.

Sometimes fatigue makes for stupidity. The people he'd been closest to, whether he'd stayed in touch with them or not, were the people whose pictures were on his walls. I sat down and stared at the combat pictures; they still told me nothing except a date and a place.

Suddenly I had an image of my mother, sitting at the kitchen table on Amsterdam Avenue, hair wrapped in a kerchief, the crimson cardboard album in front of her, the stack of photos to her right, the tiny white triangular mounting tabs to her left. I remember her picking up a photo as if it were a butterfly, gazing at it, polishing it tenderly with a tissue, turning it over and murmuring, "Adam and Mama in Vermont," and writing that on the back of the picture.

I jumped up and turned over the photo with Tim Cleary in it. On the mounting cardboard were printed several names—all first names or nicknames. Next to some of the names were tiny asterisks. I copied what was there and moved on to the next picture. The same: first names and nicknames, some with asterisks. All the photos on the combat wall were like that, as were the photos on the civilian wall, the mystery wall. The only difference was there were no tiny asterisks next to any civilian names.

Returning to Beth Marshall's letters, I pulled a half-dozen from each bundle—there were too many to read all the way through, and I didn't have enough film to photograph them—to try to get a sense of how Beth Marshall felt about her husband, and whether those feelings had ever changed.

You can never be sure, of course—people can be brilliant liars, especially from 8,000 miles away, and especially on paper—but between the letters I read and the letters I skimmed, I doubted very much that Matt Marshall had ever told his wife anything about his Vietnamese lover. This was in one of the last of his wife's letters:

> . . . When you wrote me you were wounded, I was so scared I would never see you again—actually, *sure* I would never see you again—that I searched the closet for the beachball you gave me the weekend we went to Cape May—do you remember?—and when I found it, I sat down on the closet floor, put the valve to my mouth and very slowly, as slowly as I physically could, sucked the air from it—because you had blown it up and I needed to taste your breath. I needed to be filled with your breath. I cannot tell you what losing you would mean, I don't know how to express that loss, the terror of that loss, but I *do* know that the very thought of it, the very thought of forever without you is darker than the darkest night. I love you.

As I started to reread the passage—it was impossible to resist the emotion in it, impossible not to envy the person who aroused that emotion—I heard the faint sound of a car engine and caught a glimpse of distant headlights through the window. Quickly, but carefully, I put the letters back in the file cabinet, and—the memory of Tim Cleary vivid in my mind—fetched the 9-mm Smith & Wesson from the den and went quietly to the hallway. While hiding the pistol under an old newspaper on a table near the front door, I heard the sound of footsteps on gravel. Then, a harsh knock.

Without thinking—thinking would have paralyzed me—I pulled open the door and crouched at the same time. Standing in the doorway, looking down at me in surprise, was Sklar. Clumsily, I got myself upright. "I thought you were Tim," I said too loudly.

Sklar chuckled. "Nah. He'd never knock on the front door, anybody'd figure that out." He tapped his watch. "Time for you to get outta here."

I gave it a halfhearted try: "If I leave now, I'll only have to come back—it's a big house."

"Then you'll have to come back," he said.

I nodded and turned to go to the Vietnam room; he shut the front door and followed me. Just before we reached the room, I stepped aside to let him pass—if he'd never been in there, I wanted to see his reaction. He walked in, stopped, inhaled sharply, and began slowly turning 360 degrees, halting occasionally to absorb what he saw. He looked at me accusingly. "Did you take anything?"

I pointed to my camera. "Just pictures."

He leaned over and stared at my briefcase and camera bag. "I got a good mind to search these."

I gestured in invitation. "If it makes you happy . . ."

"Forget it. Let's move out." While I packed my camera, lights, and film, Sklar moved from wall to wall, examining the photos and the souvenirs and muttering.

"What'd you say?" I asked.

"Least, he hasn't got any goddamn ears on the wall," he grunted. "Are you ready yet?"

I finished packing and went through the cabin, turning out the lights; as I shut the door to the master bedroom, something nagged at me, but I was too tired to pursue it. Sklar and I stepped outside. A light, fine rain pattered on the trees, and the air smelled sharply of fallen leaves. He watched me as I locked the front door, walked me to my car, and stood beside me as I started it. Just as I was about to drive off, I figured out what was nagging me: the sealed pack of computer diskettes.

"Sklar," I said politely, "when you put Marshall's car in storage, did you search it?"

"Uh uh—no reason to."

"Did you happen to spot a portable computer? They're usually in a canvas—"

"I know what they look like," he said. He thought for a few seconds, then shook his head.

"Do you mind if I check out the car? His son thinks maybe he left his computer in it." I gave him no time to reflect. "There's a term paper in it . . ."

He snorted, nodded yes, climbed in his car, and headed up the driveway, with me behind him. As he approached the road, he flicked his headlights to bright, and when I followed him onto the highway, I saw why: Cleary's pickup was parked on the shoulder, under the trees.

The notebook computer, in its black canvas case, lay under the passenger seat of Marshall's Range Rover. "Got it," I said over my shoulder to Sklar, and hoisted it out. He moved forward to shut the door, but I held up a palm. "Hang on," I said, "let me just see if there are any diskettes."

Blocking Sklar's view with my back as best I could, I pointed my penlight into the glove compartment: owner's manual, maintenance record, insurance receipt, accident report form, printed list of emergency numbers, bridge tokens, flashlight, pen, beer can opener.

"Hey, come on, Bruno," Sklar said irritably, "it's wet out here."

I matched his tone. "Give me a break, pal, it's a goddamn mess."

Swiftly, I checked every piece of paper for any scribbling; at the bottom of the printed list of emergency phone numbers was written #651594, just as it had been written on Marshall's bedside pad.

One more sweep of my light turned up nothing—the car was bare and immaculate. I eased my way out and faced Sklar. "Thanks," I said. "By the way, where's the phone?"

"What do you care?" he said nastily, slamming the Rover door and deliberately locking it.

I cared because I thought I'd find a list of speed-dial numbers taped to it, but I couldn't say that. Instead, I said, "Can I mail you a receipt?"

"FedEx," he snapped, and trotted to his car.

CHAPTER 7

"SHIT, SHIT, SHIT, SHIT, shit, shit!" I yelled at my walls. "Shit!"

Sunday dawn was breaking, and I ached with fatigue; every muscle was sore, every bone was heavy, and my eyes stung as though pepper coated the lids.

On the ride back to the city, I'd felt almost giddy with accomplishment. To come across that much tangible information on one trip was rare in my business—the pictures, the nicknames, the letters, the military stuff, and, as a miraculous bonus, Marshall's own computer.

The trouble was I couldn't get into his computer.

When I turned it on, it hummed and a message appeared saying: TO INVOKE PROGRAM, ENTER PASSWORD.

I tried all the obvious choices—variations and anagrams of his name; his birthday; his phone numbers, home and office; his address; his zip code; his hometown; his state; his wife's name; his kids' names; his parents' names; and, of course, the number I'd found written on the pad in his night table and glove compartment. All I got every time was a message saying: INVALID PASSWORD.

Finally, at 5:20, I had a brainstorm and entered CRICKET; hum hum, buzz buzz, click, click: INVALID PASSWORD. That's when I stood up yelled at my walls.

Yelling is good for tension, but it doesn't solve encryption problems; and even in my place—I lived in a converted loft with thick walls—if I kept shouting "Shit!" at dawn on Sunday, one of my neighbors was sure to complain, and I wasn't in the mood for a fight with a neighbor. I shut off Marshall's computer and opened the swollen envelope Laird had given me. I was too irritated to sleep, and I needed to do something to feel useful. Reading Marshall's will and codicil seemed like a good idea.

It wasn't. Even with the help of several standard texts on trusts and estates, my eyes began to throb every five pages, and the main body of the original will was a couple of hundred pages long. Then, there were all the trusts—one for each child and two for Beth; then the cash or stock bequests to nonrelated individuals; then the cash or stock bequests to charities; then the particular and singular material items—the software patents, the houses, the cars, the boats, the planes, the first editions, and, of course, and endlessly, the paintings and sculptures. What I wanted to find out was exactly what each of the original beneficiaries stood to get, but every bequest was so hemmed in by conditions—if this, then that; if that, then this, interminably—that for a few hours I felt like a blindfolded man trying to build a model railroad.

Finally, after a pot of coffee and another bout of shouting at the walls, I broke through.

In the original, Marshall had divided his pile this way: 5 percent each directly to his brother and sister; 13.333 percent each, directly and in trusts, to the three children; and 26.666 percent, directly and in trusts, to Beth Marshall; 1 percent to Patricia Twomey; and the rest, around 19 percent to various charities, including two burn wards.

At first I thought the codicil simply halved everything for everyone—half for the unknown child (or the foundation), half of his or her original take for everyone else; but it was a shade more complicated—and painful—than that: brother and sister kept their 5 percent each, and Patricia Twomey kept her 1 percent. But the charities dropped to 9 percent.

And Beth Marshall dropped to 12 percent—$12 million and change instead of $28 million. Each child dropped to 6 percent—$6 million and change instead of $14 million.

I was so pleased with myself for sorting out what was in the will and codicil that I switched my computer back on and went to work entering my notes and making lists of questions—MM's office password? E-mail? office strongbox? address books? diaries? speed-dial list? buddy list? home strongbox? mail drop? and so on, and so on.

By the time I broke to make an omelette and another pot of coffee, I no longer felt stupid and stymied, only exhausted. I copied my notes to a diskette to take to the office and looked up the address of Tel-Mat. Monday morning, bright and early, was a good time to go see the person who kept Marshall's diaries and phone books: Trish Twomey.

CHAPTER 8

SHE WASN'T COMPLETELY VISIBLE at first. When I approached her desk, she was finishing a phone call, facing three-quarters away from me. Then she hung up and turned my way, and I felt a slight tremor: Her hair, combed up, was darker—not far from black—and she was younger, maybe thirty-five; but everything else about Trish Twomey—her nose, her jaw, her cheeks, her lips, her huge blue eyes, the touch of her long slender fingers—so echoed Beth Marshall that she easily might have been her sister.

In fact, when she opened her mouth to greet me, I half-expected to hear North Carolina; instead I heard second-generation New York Irish. If you've ever listened to the college-educated children of cops and firemen, you know the sound. "Mr. Bruno," she said, "thank you for coming in."

"Thank you for giving me the time," I said.

She rose and led me toward a set of double doors, which she unlocked, to usher me into Marshall's office.

Had I not seen the estate, or even the cabin, the office might have impressed me: It was big—maybe as big as my loft, and my loft was 1,900 square feet; light, with windows facing north to the Empire State Building and west to the river; and decorated in what I was beginning to discover was Marshall's taste: elegant but austere. A Lichtenstein and a Bacon hung on one wall and a Rauschenberg and a Johns hung on another. In a windowed corner was a conversation area, leather chairs and couch, and a granite coffee table; in a walled corner was a round teak conference table, with five upright chairs—obviously the spot where real talk took place.

The one oddity was the desk, an old and scarred monstrosity that looked as if it had been conjured straight from the pages of Dickens. It was so out of keeping with the rest of the room—especially because of the two computer terminals resting in the middle of it—that I couldn't help but draw close to stare at it and then run my palm along its nubby surface. "Did he actually work at this?" I said.

"Oh, yes," she said brightly. "When Mr. Marshall and Mr. Macintosh first formed the business, they could only afford to buy one desk. They tossed for it, and Mr. Marshall lost; so he went to the dump and found this. The business prospered so well that he kept it for luck."

I thought it over. "How much of that is true?"

She shrugged wittily. "Most of it," she said, "the only thing that's . . ." she paused to search for a word, ". . . intensified is that he kept it for luck. He kept it because of the way you reacted—nobody comes into this room for the first time without being seduced by the desk. Mr. Marshall said it gave him a definite edge. He liked that."

"Don't we all?" I said mildly, and gestured to the round teak table. "What did Mrs. Marshall tell you?" I asked as we sat down and I got out my notebook.

"She said you wanted to see Mr. Marshall's address books, and that you'd probably ask for any private diaries."

"Did she say why?"

Twomey paused, then said, "More or less."

"Which means?"

"She told me *what* you were doing—that you were looking for people Mr. Marshall confided in about Vietnam—but she didn't tell me *why* you were looking for those people." She leaned back, smiled winningly, and said, "But then, perhaps I'm not supposed to know why . . ."

I wasn't certain what was going on. "Does your help depend on your knowing?"

She took a long time to weigh that. "I wouldn't put it like that. Let's just say that Mr. Marshall was good to me, very good to me, for twelve years, and if what you're looking for can hurt him, I don't want to help you."

"Why would you think I want to hurt him?"

But before she could reply, there was a soft knock, and the door opened to disclose two senior executives—they must have been that, because though they were young, maybe late thirties, their suits were too well cut and expensive for them to be climbers. They looked expectantly at Twomey, who, to my surprise, didn't bother to get to her feet or give them any greeting. "Mr. Macintosh, Mr. Shaeffer, this is Mr. Bruno."

They came toward me with their hands outstretched, as though they were playing touch football. I rose and shook their hands and they smiled together.

"Welcome to Tel-Mat," Macintosh said. He had an effortless, open smile and the kind of hard, complacent mouth people develop when things always go their way.

"Thank you."

"Is Trish helping you all right?" Shaeffer said. His face, on the other hand, showed years of striving; it was the face of someone who would always be unsure whether he belonged in the first-class section of the plane.

"Better than all right," I said.

Both instantly looked her way, then back at me. Macintosh cleared his throat. "Trish is always very helpful."

It was Shaeffer's turn. "Extremely helpful."

"Yes," I said. I smiled at them, sat down, opened my notebook, wrote something, and closed the notebook.

"We wondered if there was something either of us could help you with . . ." Shaeffer said.

"Anything that might be beyond Trish's purview," Macintosh added.

"I can't tell," I said. "We've only just begun."

"What is it exactly you wanted to find out, Mr. Bruno?" Shaeffer said.

I glanced at Twomey; her face was composed and unreadable. "Do you know why I'm here?" I asked.

"We understand you're prying into Matthew Marshall's private life," Macintosh said.

"What a way to put it, Mr. Macintosh," I said blandly. "Actually, I'm looking for people Mr. Marshall confided in about Vietnam. I'll also be looking for people he served with in Vietnam." I put on my best boyish face. "Did he confide in either of you about Vietnam?"

"No," Macintosh said.

"Did either of you serve with him in Vietnam?"

Shaeffer's turn: "No."

"Do either of you know anybody he might have confided in, or served with?"

In unison: "No."

"Did he leave any personal records with either of you"—I ticked them off on my fingers,—"address books, diaries, journals, computer disks, or anything at all that might lead me to somebody he confided in about Vietnam or somebody he served with in Vietnam?"

This time, they simply shook their heads.

"Well, gentlemen, there is nothing you can help me with." I stood up and offered my hand. "But it was a great pleasure to meet you. Mr. Macintosh, are you related to—"

"My father was Mr. Marshall's partner."

"Are you related to anyone, Mr. Shaeffer?"

"No. I mean, nobody connected with Tel-Mat. I'm the chief financial officer. Jay—Mr. Macintosh—is the acting CEO." He swallowed. "Why are you looking for these people?"

"Because I'm being paid to."

"That answer is unacceptable," Macintosh said curtly. "Why are you looking for these people?"

I pushed my chair back and rose. Speaking very softly, I repeated, "Because I'm being paid to, Mr. Macintosh." I moved close enough so he had to back away a step. "And since you are not the person paying me, you are not entitled to any answers at all."

It only took a few seconds. He knew he couldn't back away another step, not without losing whatever face he had left, so he turned abruptly on his heel, gestured sharply to Shaeffer, and strode toward the door. Shaeffer hopped ahead of him and opened it. Macintosh stopped to stare at Twomey.

"I expect an inventory of whatever you show this man, Ms. Twomey."

"Of all Tel-Mat material. Of course, Mr. Macintosh."

They left, pulling the door shut behind them. I rejoined her at the table. "Will they come back in?" I asked.

"Not Mr. Macintosh. Mr. Shaeffer."

"More than once."

She smiled. "Oh, yes."

"Well, why don't we get together away from here. Can you make copies of what I need?"

"Of course. Could we go over it once more?"

"Address books, diaries, journals, call logs, scraps of paper with anything that's not about business. Would there be anything in the North Carolina headquarters?" She shook her head no. "Does he have a personal assistant there, or anywhere else in Tel-Mat's universe?"

"I traveled with him," she said.

I looked around. "Does he have a safe in here at all?" She shook her head no. "What about in Raleigh?"

"No," she said. "He's got a safe-deposit box, I believe at Chemical—Mr. Laird would have that information."

"Did he have a storage locker or a mail drop—post office box, that kind of thing?"

"Not that he told me about."

"Did he keep private files on his computer here?"

"I don't know. I don't think so."

"Can you get into his files?"

"Three levels down; after that—assuming something's there—I'd need either Mr. Marshall's private password or we'd have to hire a hacker. And I doubt that would do much good. We are a high-tech company, after all."

"He didn't give you his private password?"

"Only the first three."

"What were they?"

"They changed every time you logged on."

"Did the private password change that way as well?"

"No; since it was user-only, everyone invented his own and kept it to himself."

"Did Marshall have a nickname?"

She caught on immediately. "Of course: for a password." She reflected before shaking her head. "No."

"Did he leave any floppies here?"

"He took them with him every night."

I read from my notebook. "A list of the speed-dial numbers on all his phones—would he have kept a separate file of confidential numbers in his computer?"

She smiled. "You've never been an executive, have you, Mr. Bruno?"

"Is it that transparent?"

"Executives of Mr. Marshall's rank don't have lists of confidential numbers because they never dial the phone themselves. That's what their assistants do."

"What about if he were going to call, say, perhaps, somebody like, maybe, oh, for instance, a—"

"A lover?" she said dispassionately.

"Now why couldn't I think of that word?"

"They called him."

"They . . . ?"

"It's a clumsy use of the pronoun," she said. "She."

"And if he needed to call them—her—back, maybe to cancel, or rearrange, or pick a fight?"

"He sent me to make coffee."

"What if there was a fresh pot?"

"He sent me to make *tea*." She looked away for an instant. "He believed in discretion."

"Are their numbers—sorry—is her number on any of the speed dials?"

She flushed. "Not any longer."

I let her recover before asking, "Did you purge any other numbers from the speed dials?"

"No."

"Did you erase anything from the other material I asked for?"

"No. Just her number."

I cleared my throat. "You will include it in the stuff you bring me, though—right?"

"Of course."

"Do you think you could have it all ready by this evening?"

Before she could answer, Shaeffer opened the door and stuck his head in.

"It's Mr. Shaeffer," I said to Twomey. "Hello, Mr. Shaeffer. What can we do for you?"

He tried to grin, but the result was more like a grimace. "Just checking to see if you need any help. Do you need any help?"

"Actually, I'm just leaving," I said, and stood.

"So you learned what you wanted to know . . . ?"

"Does one ever?" I found a business card and scribbled the name of a restaurant on it and a numeral 8. I handed the card to Twomey and waited till she'd read it and nodded. "Great," I said. "Thanks for everything." I picked up my case, joined Shaeffer at the door, and before he could step into the room to harass her, I gently guided him into the hallway, saying, "Mr. Shaeffer, Ms. Twomey tells me you were very close to Mr. Marshall . . ."

CHAPTER 9

". . . Of *course* everybody knew. You don't smuggle a five-year-old girl on a fire truck without the other firemen knowing—what's the matter with you? I didn't find out till years later that he could get suspended for it. I think, once, he actually *did* get suspended for it. I was so proud of him. Everybody else's father worked for Con Ed, or was a motorman, or a cop; but Trish Twomey's dad was the only dad who put out fires. And rescued people. He *rescued* people; he gave people the kiss of life! People he didn't know! People he couldn't stand! Where I grew up, you didn't touch black people or Spanish people, never mind give them the kiss of life. He was on the front page of the *Daily News* and the *Post*—HERO FIREMAN SAVES TWO TOTS. He's bent over this tiny, tiny black baby, giving it breath; life. The next day, before school—I'm not sure it was even light—I took the subway down to the News building and bought a hundred copies of the paper. I brought them to school and work—I had a part-time job—to confession, I brought them everywhere. I was so proud. I didn't know the expression "bursting with pride" meant anything till that day—my buttons were popping! How about a cognac?"

I signaled the waiter, while Twomey sipped her coffee. I'd arrived at the restaurant at one minute after eight, and she was already there, sitting at the tiny bar. On the stool beside her was a shopping bag filled, it turned out, with all the things I'd asked for—including an inventory. She'd also worked up a list of useful contacts at every one of Tel-Mat's facilities, direct-dial numbers, the works. And she'd changed her clothes and let her hair down. She seemed to be a woman who worshipped control, so I anticipated an evening of uphill work.

But after three shots of twelve-year-old Jameson's, with the nuts; half a bottle of red, with the stuffed mushrooms; and half a bottle of white, with the swordfish, Twomey's tension had melted and her face glowed golden in the candlelight. She obviously was overflowing with talk, but so far she hadn't said a word about Marshall. That might have been inadvertent, or it might have been because I hadn't prodded her, but somehow neither explanation rang true.

". . . I suppose I married him because he reminded me of my dad, but now I can't figure out in what way he reminded me of my dad. I mean, my dad only had a GED, but he was smart. My husband graduated from Fordham, but if he got any dumber, you'd have to water him twice a week. Was your wife smart?"

"I beg your pardon?" I said; I didn't recall mentioning my wife.

"Your wife," Twomey said. "Was she smart?"

"Did I say I'd been married?"

She drained her glass, signaled for another cognac, and patted my hand. "Was she?"

I thought about it. "In some ways. Yes, very. In some ways."

"What ways?"

"She always knew what I was thinking—no, I take that back—she always knew what I was feeling."

"Did you know what she was feeling?"

"Uh . . ." I couldn't help lowering my eyes. "No. I wasn't paying enough attention." A thought surfaced through the haze of wine. "Did he always know what you were feeling?"

"My husband?"

"Matt Marshall."

Without warning, a tear formed in her left eye and slipped down her cheek. She blinked, which brought a tear to her right eye. "That wasn't fair," she said, and raised her napkin from her lap to blot her face.

"Did he?"

"Yes."

"Did you always know what he was feeling?"

"I thought I did." She dabbed at her face again. "I was wrong."

I waited till she returned to looking at me. "What did the Queen say to Alice?—start at the beginning, go—"

"Go on to the end, and then stop. Sure." She drained her cognac and signaled for another. "I was working for a temp agency, and they sent me to his office because his personal assistant was pregnant—no, he wasn't the father. It was October twelfth nineteen eighty-three—a Wednesday. A beautiful day. You know how New York can be in October: clear, cool, bright but not hurtful, everyone moving as though they really wanted to get somewhere. I don't know why people think spring is the time of renewal. Maybe in the country, not in New York."

She took a deep breath: "When I walked into his office, he stood up and came from behind his desk to say hello—you have to remember that I was twenty-three years old and a good Irish Catholic girl from Sheepshead Bay—I hadn't moved to Manhattan yet. In my family, in my neighborhood, the men didn't stand up to greet the women. They didn't take their hands and say, 'I'm Matt Marshall, I can't tell you how glad I am that you're here.' " She laughed fondly. "Later on, I found out he greeted everyone like that, and he made everyone believe it was true.

"He led me to the couch and he interviewed me—no, we interviewed each other. After, oh, maybe fifteen minutes, he showed me to his regular assistant's desk, where you met me this morning, and I went to work. The temp. I thought. Just before six, he called me into the office and asked me whether I'd be interested in working for Tel-Mat on a permanent basis. I must have hesitated, because he said, 'Actually, not for Tel-Mat, for me.' I didn't say anything right away, but he saw what I was thinking—I was very transparent in those days—and said, 'Anne's going to be home for at least three months, and I know she wants something with fewer hours and more flexibility, so you wouldn't be stealing her job.' " Once more, the loving chuckle. "It's hard to resist a man who offers you a job and promises to do right by the person you're replacing, all in the same sentence."

"How long did you resist him?"

"Forty-eight hours. Not because of any principle—he was busy Wednesday night and Thursday night."

"Where'd you go—your place?"

"I was still living at home in Sheepshead Bay—nice Irish Catholic virgins didn't live by themselves."

"You were a virgin?"

"Once removed. We went to an apartment—"

"The one in Olympic Tower?"

"*No*. That was *their* place. He had a small place on East Forty-eighth, Three five five East forty-eighth. That was *his* place. We had dinner at a Japanese restaurant—I'd never eaten Japanese food—and we drank a lot of sake. I was very nervous, shaking actually. I mean, sleeping with a married man, sleeping with my boss. I didn't know how many sins I was about to commit. What was I supposed to tell Father Julius? What if I couldn't tell Father Julius—did that mean I'd have to find another priest? Did it mean I'd have to leave the church? How would I tell my mother? Or my cousin, the Franciscan? Or my sister, Bernadette, who believed—believes—if you touch a man *down there* your fingers will wither and fall off. I mean, I was so scared I was pissing in my pants!" She burst into exultant laughter, then dipped her head shyly to say, almost inaudibly, as though revealing a miracle: "There was nothing to be scared of."

Once more, a few silent tears crept from her eyes to her cheeks, and once more she blotted them with her napkin. She cleared her throat harshly and raised her face to mine. "That's when it began, Friday, October the fourteenth, nineteen eighty-three, and it went on—our . . ."

"Romance?"

"What a sweet word. Yes, romance, for three years."

"Was it a problem—continuing to work for him."

"Of course it was a problem!" she snapped. "Don't you think you'd find it a problem?" She stopped, shut her eyes to regain control, and said. "I'm sorry. Yes, some days were torture. Some days, I would come into work so saturated with love I could barely see."

"So you were very close?"

"As close as two human beings can get and still be two human beings."

"Did he ever talk to you about Vietnam?"

"No."

"Did you ever ask him about it?"

"No."

"Why did it end?"

As though she'd been rehearsing the line for years, she said: "It wasn't going anywhere." I was about to ask where she'd expected it to go, but I sensed that I didn't need to, and I didn't. "I loved him, and I think he loved me—I *know* he loved me. But he said he didn't believe in love anymore. He said he'd lost a piece of his heart, maybe all of his heart.

"Right, I thought, sure, I thought, typical married-man bullshit, anything not to have to admit that you're not ready to leave your wife and kids and probably won't ever be ready to leave your wife and kids. Right! But, I think maybe he was telling the truth."

"Why?"

She laughed ruefully. "Maybe because I need to think that. Maybe because I can't stand the idea that maybe he didn't love me. I don't know." A sudden shift from self-pity. "Yes, I do know! We broke up nine years ago, and I'm pretty certain I know everybody he's fucked since then. And unless I missed something, nobody ever lasted more than three months. Nobody. There was Beth, and there was me. And there's no need to point out how much I look like her."

"So it's unlikely he would have talked to any of the others about Vietnam."

"It's not unlikely; it's out of the goddamn question. He didn't talk to *me* about Vietnam. He didn't talk to Beth about Vietnam. He certainly didn't talk to Ms. Bimbette."

She reached into her purse, found a compact, and redid her eyes, nose, and mouth. I waited till she'd returned the compact to her purse.

"Can you think of anybody he was particularly close to—brother, sister, friend, partner, lawyer, accountant?"

She thought. "Maybe Mac—Mr. Macintosh's father. When Mac was alive, he and Matt were close."

"Anyone else in the company like that—an old-timer, somebody who was around in the early days?" She reflected, then slowly shook her head. "What about his children?"

She was quicker this time. "I can't imagine anyone telling anything important to those kids. Wendy and Fred would use it against you somehow, and Matt junior would repeat it to everyone he knows. Especially if you made him promise to keep it secret." She shook her head in mock regret. "They are some flock. Do you think being raised rich does that, or do you think there's a wayward gene someplace?"

"Both."

"Aren't you diplomatic," she said, with just enough edge for me to guess she wanted to pick a fight.

"Some people call it agreeable."

"Some people call it hypocritical."

"Can I ask you something?"

"Can I stop you?" she said.

"Do you think it's fair—when you're feeling cranky—to pick a fight with anyone who's handy?"

She leaned across the table till her face was six inches from mine. "No. But I don't play fair; I'm Irish."

"Was your husband Irish?"

She shook her head and laughed. "You really are not going to get sucked into this, are you? How come? Don't you like to fight?"

"I do," I said, "but only when it concerns me and the person I'm fighting with."

"Christ, how safe. Yes, my husband was Irish—I mean, he still is Irish, he's not my husband."

"What does he do?"

"He works for the city, in the Corporation Counsel's office. The joke goes, if you ever sue the city after you break your leg in a pothole, pray my husband handles the case, because that way you'll make a fortune."

"Why'd you marry him?"

Breezily, she said, "He hates sports, he sends cards with beautiful poems, he's not territorial in bed, he has real charm, especially when he's drinking, and I thought he reminded me of my father." Looking past me, she said, "There was a vacuum in me and I had to fill it."

"Are you going to leave Tel-Mat?"

"Oh, sure. But not on my own; I'm going to make them buy me out. I have a contract with nearly five years to run, and I'm not leaving till I get the money."

"How much money?"

"With bonuses and stock options . . ." she grinned mischievously, ". . . a lot."

She didn't sound like somebody who knew she was due to inherit more than a million dollars. I tested the water. "Will it be enough to retire on?"

She laughed. "Very cute—no, not unless I die in five years."

"Still, sounds like you're a good catch."

"Better believe it!"

Twomey asked me to wait in the cab till she opened her front door, but since my place was only a few blocks from hers—she lived on Ninth Street, in a renovated walkup a couple of doors west of University—I got out with her. She had trouble with her key—I could see she was holding it upside down—but I let her fumble. She was too proud to lightly accept a man's helping her open her own front door.

"Ahhh," she said, when she finally got it. "One cognac too many to open my own lock." She looked over her shoulder. "Do you want to come up?" Instantly, she corrected herself: "Let me rephrase that. Do we need to talk some more?"

"Uhuh, but why don't we do it another time—I'm not thinking very clearly right now."

She tilted her head and stared at me. I felt like a specimen on a slide. "Hard to believe, Mr. Bruno," she said. "My guess is you're thinking clearly all the time."

"Don't I wish," I said. "If anything else occurs to you—the name of a friend, a document, a cache—" I stopped to pursue the obvious: "While you were involved with him, did he keep any documents at East Forty-eighth Street?"

"No."

"Any floppy disks?"

"No."

"No journal, no diary, no scribbled notes?"

" 'We need Vienna roast coffee and rice cakes.' Like that. He dipped rice cakes in his coffee."

I waited till she came back to the present. "After you broke up, did Marshall keep the apartment?"

"Of course. He had it before I arrived, and he had it after I left."

"Have you been there since you broke up?"

"When my marriage collapsed, Matt let me hide out there. And no, he didn't visit to comfort me."

"So it still belonged to him when he died?"

"Yes." She shivered. "I'm getting cold—either come upstairs, or let's do this next time."

"I'm done for now," I said, and slowly extended my palm. "If you could just lend me your key . . ."

She looked at my palm, then into my eyes. She opened her mouth to say something, but instead shrugged and passed me her key ring. "My hands are chilled—you do it." Each key bore a little colored plastic sleeve at its base. "The purple is East Forty-eighth Street," she said. "Eleven-B."

I removed the key and passed the ring back to her. "Thank you, Ms. Twomey."

"Trish. I think a man who has that key can use my first name." She stepped into the vestibule. "The coffeemaker, the one that makes regular and espresso, *I* bought it for the apartment. Do you think I could get it back?"

Before I could tell her of course, no problem, she turned her head away, brought her splayed fingers to her eyes, and bolted for the inner door.

CHAPTER 10

WHEN I GOT HOME that night I found five messages on my machine from Herschel O'Hara. The last, and most poignant—and when he wanted a favor Herschel became the prince of poignant—was delivered in a husky, trembling whisper: "Adam, it's after one, and this is it for the night. Renny Duclos's decided to withdraw his plea and stand trial—remember Renny? You interviewed all his witnesses for me in April. I *need* you in court, Judge Sheinberg's part at nine forty-five tomorrow. Unless you've got another case—another *big* case—you have to be there, pal. Sheinberg's part, one eleven Centre. We're talking ten to twenty-five here."

It was too late to call him back, and I knew he wouldn't answer his phone in the morning—it was his tried and true technique for making sure people showed up.

I called his office machine: "Herschel, I have to search an apartment on Forty-eighth Street tomorrow, so forget it. In any case, you manipulative shit, you haven't paid me for the Renny Duclos job yet."

While I was waiting in the hallway outside Sheinberg's courtroom—witnesses aren't allowed in till they take the stand—I reviewed my notes on Herschel's client.

Renny Duclos worked at a day-care center and had been charged with fondling five of his pupils, boys and girls both. What I'd found out persuaded me pretty well that Duclos hadn't done anything—you can never be 100 percent sure in abuse cases—but I had a feeling my testimony wasn't going to help the sorry sonofabitch. Duclos was skinny and on the small side, maybe five-seven, and he would have been harmless-looking except for a tiny cast in his left eye, which made him appear a little bit demented. On top of that, he was an illegal—from Haiti—with a forged green card. Even if Duclos hadn't been an illegal who looked deranged, and even if he hadn't done anything, it was easy to understand why he'd originally copped a plea. That was the season of high indignation. If you were a scoutmaster, or a priest, or a Little League coach, or a day-care teacher, if you wiped a kid's ass after he shit in his pants, any paranoid parent could put you away.

Just before noon, Duclos changed his mind again, and copped to sexual abuse one, which is a Class-D felony. I didn't see any of this, of course. Herschel told me at lunch: "Pathetic, ignorant, fucking Port-au-Prince street cleaner! I mean, this shithead is dumb. This shithead is dumber than a Republican vice president. This shithead is so dumb you could lobotomize a rodeo cowboy and the rodeo cowboy would outthink this shithead. You want a beer? I'm going to have a beer; I don't give a shit what it does to my liver. Lee, two Chinese beers." He tapped my arm with his chopsticks. *"Today* he first gets it that if he wins, if those twelve middle-class executioners let him go, he's on the boat back to Port-au-Prince; he's on his way back to the guys with the machine guns and machetes. *Today.* Two weeks ago, I make a deal for him for sexual abuse two, Class-A misdemeanor, a year max. Okay, he says, you very smart, Mr. Herschel. Okay.

"He speaks to his mother, and his mother says, in whatever fucking language she communicates with him, but you didn't do it, Renny, you did nothing. Lee, where are our beers—if I'm going to ruin my liver, I don't want to have to do it on your goddamn Peoples' Republic schedule."

"What will he do?"

"We got a mayor and a governor and two senators going on TV every hour on the hour to tell us that the only thing wrong with this fucking country is illegals. He'll do the whole thing." He rapped the table hard with his knuckle. "Seven fucking years is what he'll do!"

Everyone in the place heard that one, and for a loaded moment the chatter stopped. I didn't even bother looking around to indicate, as I once might have, relax, it's only my lunatic partner Herschel coming down after losing a case he cares about. Don't duck, don't call 911. He's like this. It's why we all love him, those of us that do. Lee arrived with the beer and poured it. Herschel gulped his in one go, as though draining the glass would quench his rage.

"How you coming with the Marshall thing?"

"I'm just starting," I said nonchalantly.

"Just starting as in just starting, or just starting as in, mind your own business?" I hesitated a tick too long. "Mind your own business, huh?" he said sardonically.

I bobbed and weaved: "Herschel, it's awkward for me, okay? I mean, I don't know what your . . . understanding is with Mollie Wharton, and she's an associate of the executor, and the executor is my client."

He played with his food for a second. "I don't know what my understanding is, either." He chuckled. "She likes me to go down on her; her WASP guys can't stand the smell." He daintily sniffed the wedge of bass trapped in his chopsticks. "I don't get why—she smells fabulous."

"Do you talk?"

"What kind of question is that?"

"Because if I tell you anything about the case, and you talk to her—when your mouth isn't filled with her pussy—then she—my client—knows I've betrayed her confidence. So: Do you talk?"

He tilted his palm from side to side. "Okay, I see your point."

"Thanks."

He gestured for the check, and Lee was over in a flash. Herschel was a regular customer, but Lee was always just as happy to see him exit as enter. "You should pay for this," he said, "because you never did testify."

"No, you should pay because you wasted my day."

"Fuck you and the horse you rode in on."

"You've got cowboys on the brain."

He paid the check, left a gargantuan tip—Herschel believed all immigrants lived on the verge of starvation—and we went out to Pell Street. There we ceremoniously shook hands; he didn't release me. "Are you a hundred percent okay on this case?" he said.

"Why do you ask that?"

"Because you have the look."

"What look?"

We'd been partners for a long time, and Herschel, beneath all his mania, was as sharp as anyone I knew. "The look that tells me you don't one hundred percent completely totally absolutely definitively trust your client."

"Who does?"

Instead of responding with a crack, he surprised me by saying, "Maybe you left the firm, pal, but in my head, we're still partners. See ya." He let go of my hand, waved, and vanished into the Chinatown throng.

After I'd picked up my prints from the lab, I took the subway uptown and walked to 355 East 48th Street. It was a well-maintained prewar building, unassuming, but moneyed enough to have a doorman. He looked lost in his comic-opera uniform, and when I nodded to him in greeting, he smiled broadly, showing a lot of foreign dental work, brought his feet together, and flung his hand to his cap in a salute that he must have learned by studying movies about the British Empire. "Si, sir . . . ?" he began. "How is it to help you?"

I found a business card from the old days, which identified me as Adam Bruno, Esquire, of Bruno & O'Hara, Counselors at Law, and showed it to him. "I'm here on behalf of the family of eleven-B," I said in a man-to-man murmur.

"Si, eleven-B," he said, nodding enthusiastically. "Very good, very good."

I took Twomey's key from my pocket and showed it to him. "I have to go upstairs."

"Upstairs. Si, eleven-B. Empty. No home." He smiled eagerly. "Very good." When I said nothing, he signaled me to move closer, glanced around furtively, cupped his left hand in front of his right, and rubbed his right thumb along the tips of his right fingers. "Mr. Eleven-B very good, always."

I fished a five-dollar bill from my pocket and let him see it. He stretched out a tentative hand, and I pointed a forefinger upward. "Eleven-B." I showed him the key again.

Very slowly, his smile retreated from his face. He nodded philosophically and led me into the lobby, unlocked the inner door, steered me to the self-service elevator, pushed the button to open it, and stepped aside to let me pass. I thought he was going to accompany me, but he simply stood there, waiting. I held out the five dollars, and he bowed slightly while taking it. "Very good," he said, his smile restored. "Very good."

Eleven-B, which Twomey had described as a small place, was a two-bedroom apartment of around 1,500 square feet. It wasn't high enough to have a view of the East River, but the light wasn't blocked either, and it had fireplaces in the living room and the master bedroom, a whirlpool bath, and a sauna. The furniture wasn't anything like what he had in Tuckahoe, or even as nicely designed as the things upstate, but it wasn't outlet stuff, either. Marshall obviously liked his comforts wherever he slept.

The second bedroom doubled as an office, so I began there, not truly expecting much—rich men usually try to keep important documents away from their girlfriends—but committed to the search, anyway. On top of the desk were a mug holding pens and pencils; a blotter—nothing written on it; an answering machine with a built-in phone—no speed dial; and an invitation to an opening at the Whitney. The middle drawer held writing paper, envelopes, plain postcards, those stick-em pads that secretaries rely on, and four full books of American Express checks, $50,000 worth. The signature was Marshall's.

In the right-hand drawer was a file folder, which contained a single sheet of names and phone numbers; at the bottom left corner of the sheet, in faint pencil, were the lower-cased initials, tt. The left-hand drawer contained two thick stacks of invitations—to the Whitney, to the Modern, to the Castelli Gallery, to the Pace Gallery, and so on. I flipped through the first stack, looking to see if he'd marked them at all. I was sure he hadn't saved them for any reason. My guess was that he'd gotten an invitation in the morning, stuck it in his briefcase, and then left it in the apartment so he wouldn't have to take it home to Tuckahoe. I went even more rapidly through the second stack, but stopped when I came to an invitation from Reflex. Reflex, my notebook confirmed, was the gallery owned by Matt Marshall, Jr. I scrutinized the invitation, but I couldn't spot anything out of the ordinary—no names or numbers scribbled on it, no words underlined. It was as unremarkable as the others.

There was nothing else helpful in the office, so I copied the names and phone numbers from the sheet of paper—though I was certain Twomey had typed them and they'd match numbers in Marshall's address books—and went through the rest of the apartment. The guest bathroom was bare, not even a toothbrush or a bottle of aspirin in the cabinet, and only a face towel hanging from the rack. The living room seemed comfortable—a good stereo system and a 27-inch TV, some magazines, a coffee table book of Georgia O'Keeffe—but it had the feel of a cunningly decorated waiting room, a space to hang out in before moving on.

Twomey's coffeemaker was safely in the kitchen, along with an elaborate microwave, a hand blender, a toaster oven, a dishwasher, and, uncommonly, a yogurtmaker. In the refrigerator were six pint jars of homemade yogurt, a dozen bottles of imported beer, some spoiled bean sprouts, lemons, limes, and mineral water. I checked the freezer carefully—my mother used to hide hundred-dollar bills under the ice trays because my father never used the freezer—but the only thing in it was a half-gallon of raspberry sherbet. In one drawer of the kitchen cabinet were perhaps twenty-five takeout menus—Chinese, Italian, deli, Japanese—but nothing was written on any of them, either.

Next to the wall phone hung a scratchpad; on it were scrawled five numbers. I had a pretty good idea what they were, but rather than go through all the menus again, I simply dialed the numbers: They belonged to restaurants.

I did a last circuit, ending in the office so I could copy the American Express numbers. I went through the desk drawers again, feeling deep inside for slips of paper, finding none. I finished with the museum and gallery invitations, scouring each page for handwritten names, addresses, numbers, anything at all. The last invitation I examined was the one from Reflex. It, like the others, showed only a printed message on one side, a mailing-label address on the other.

I opened the drawer to put the invitations away when my eye was stopped.

Beth Marshall had said that her husband would never have confided in Matt junior; and Trish Twomey had said that if you told anything important to Matt junior he would repeat it to everyone he knew, especially if it were a secret.

But on the invitation from Reflex, the invitation to his father from the unreliable, tattletelling Matt Marshall, Jr., the mailing label read:

Matthew Marshall
355 East 48th Street
New York NY 10022

CHAPTER II

REFLEX OCCUPIED HALF OF the mezzanine level of a gussied-up, century-old factory building in Soho, in lower Manhattan. One of six galleries in the building, it was a bright, airy space, with a parquet floor and ivory-colored walls hung with framed photographs. Until the late 1960s, Soho had been home to small garment manufacturers and job printers. Then, as the printers and manufacturers fled to nonunion states, the artists moved in. The floors were huge and in those days, since nobody wanted the space—it was illegal to live there—the rents were cheap. (The neighborhood was so unfashionable it had no name; Soho stood for SOuth of HOuston in real estate agents' shorthand.) Then the seventies became the eighties, the law changed, and the rents weren't cheap anymore; the artists moved to Red Hook and Williamsburg and Hoboken; and the brokers and the bankers moved in, followed, hungrily, by the boutiques, the gourmet shops, and the galleries.

A young receptionist eagerly offered me a brochure and a price list. She looked truly disheartened when I waved them away, handed her my card, and said, "I'm here to see Mr. Marshall." While I waited I roamed around the gallery.

I was drawn to a picture of a small, emaciated Palestinian boy in traditional Arab clothes holding a blowup of Yasir Arafat to his chest.

"It's wrenching, isn't it?" a voice behind me said.

Matthew Marshall, Jr., had a handsome face, the face of an actor, even a young leading man—except that his eyes were too intense. Intense eyes usually hinder leading men; they work better for character actors. He spoke nicely, too, modulating effortlessly so that his voice conveyed multiple meanings with every word. It was the voice of a seducer.

"Don McCullin," he said, pointing languidly at the picture. "Mr. Heart of Darkness himself. People in my racket find him too journalistic, but then they said that about Walker Evans, too." He extended his hand. "Matt Marshall. I used to announce, Matt Marshall, junior, but that's no longer necessary." We shook hands while he scanned my card. "Adam Bruno—you're the detective that Wilson Laird hired . . ."

"Oh, your family told you?" I said.

"Mollie Wharton was kind enough to let me know what's going on. Please . . ."

He led me through another room hung with pictures and into a hallway, where he stopped at a little alcove to murmur to a young Latino assistant seated at a computer: "Elena, no calls please—oh, excuse me, Elena Jimenez, Adam Bruno." She smiled briefly, and we continued down the hallway to a small, plain, private office.

After closing the door, Matt junior moved his chair out from behind his desk so he could sit next to me, poured us both bubbly water from a stoppered glass decanter, and smiled helpfully. "Well, Mr. Bruno. What can I do for you?"

"I'm looking for people your father confided in about Vietnam. I'll also be looking for people he served with in Vietnam."

"Because of the codicil?"

"Yes." I opened my case and took out my recorder and an envelope of blowups. "These are copies of pictures your father had in his cabin upstate. Unfortunately, the people in them are identified only by nicknames."

One by one, I placed on his desk a half-dozen photos and invited him to look at them. As he put his glass on a coaster and leaned over the desk, I turned on the recorder; he paid it no attention. Taking his time, stopping occasionally to square a print so it was even with the one beside it, he moved from shot to shot. He picked up the fourth picture, of a pretty nurse with a pageboy hairdo, squinting and grinning foolishly into the camera. "This is the best one—I think it captures her quite nicely."

"You know her?"

"No, not at all—but I get an acute sense of her from this—she's crazy about somebody on this side of the camera."

"Could it have been your father?"

"Who took this?"

"Or who's she's crazy about? Or both?"

His smile was oddly peaceful. "Oh, for sure."

I drew another six photos, and we went through the same exercise, and then again, and again, until we'd exhausted all the pictures. In each batch, he would hunt for any shot he liked—as a photograph—and he would show genuine pleasure if he found one. When we were done, he said, "I'm sorry, Mr. Bruno, I don't know any of these people."

"Do any of the names or nicknames mean anything to you?" I asked, and read from a list.

"No."

"Did he ever talk to you about Vietnam?"

He surprised me by turning to the window and taking shelter in stillness—a stillness that didn't permit invasion; after more than a minute, he emerged and pleasantly said, "He took me to the wall."

"Did he talk to you there?"

"He looked up where the names were, and we found the names and he read the names aloud to us. Twenty-three names."

"That's all?"

"Uhuh. After the first time, we just strolled in silence; occasionally, he'd cry. Nothing gaudy, nothing demonstrative, but tears just the same."

"When you say 'we,' do you mean, all of you?"

"Oh, no. Fred and Wendy had had enough the first time. Just Dad and me."

"Did he ever take you up to the cabin?"

"No. I asked once, and he said the cabin was for him and strangers. No friends, no enemies, no loved ones." Matt junior laughed mordantly. "I spend my life trying to figure out which of those categories I belong to."

"Did you take any other trips—apart from the wall, I mean, any other father/son trips?"

"No."

"Were you close to him?"

Matt junior made a mocking, clucking noise. "Mr. Bruno, I'm the disappointment. Right this minute, I'm supposed to be telling young Macintosh what to do; I'm supposed to be running the empire, wearing the golden garb, and carrying the silver scepter. I'm the firstborn, Mr. Bruno. I'm the apple of Matthew Marshall's eye. Unfortunately, the apple has a worm in it—forgive the triteness of the image." He brushed his fingertips across his lips. "Were we close? No. Yes. Sometimes. Rarely. I don't know. Do you love your father, Mr. Bruno?"

"When I'm not mad at him."

"Ahhh. You see, you have the luxury of getting mad at him. You feel strong enough, *you* enough to get mad at him. I envy you, Mr. Bruno. My father—" He stopped. "Dad—" Again, he stopped. "No. We weren't close."

"What about to your brother or sister?"

"Not unless they've changed a great deal."

"And your mother?"

Matt junior thought about that. "Once."

"When?"

"Long time ago."

"What about to his brother and sister?"

"Paul and Rachel?" He deliberated. "I don't think so. I got the impression that his success made them uncomfortable." He shrugged and smoothly added, "Or perhaps their modest success made Dad uncomfortable. Either way."

"Can you think of anyone else—a friend, lover, anyone he might have talked to?"

Again, he withdrew to a stillness. "You have to keep in mind, Mr. Bruno, that my father kept his life in very separate compartments. Even if there were somebody like that, I wouldn't know about it."

"And he didn't talk to you—you weren't close?"

"I said no."

I reached into my case, found the Reflex invitation, and passed it to him, address side up. He read the address, and tendered me an ironic bow. "Nice. Shrewd."

"Did he give you the address?"

"No."

"How did you get it?"

"Does it matter? I got it."

"Did he ever say anything about your having it?"

"No."

"He never said anything to let you know he knew?"

He started to shake his head, stopped, and grinned. "Well, in a way." The grin exploded into laughter. "He came to an opening once and handed the invitation to Elena when he walked in. The sly, malevolent sonofabitch."

I stayed quiet, hoping he would do my work for me, and he did: "Ahhh." He snapped the invitation. "You suspect that Dad and I were closer than I'm conceding?" I nodded. "No, Mr. Bruno. Sorry. It was a game. I wanted him to understand that I knew about his little—what's the expression, love nest?—and I didn't care. I loved him anyway—I loved him in spite of his philandering, in spite of his callousness, in spite of his greed, in spite of his tyranny, in spite of his indifference. I loved him in spite of all the things I hated about him.

"Which is what I wanted from him and which he would never give. How can I put this, Mr. Bruno? My father, Dad, believed only in conditional love. If you didn't speak the speech, if you didn't do the deed, if you didn't toe the line, if you didn't live up to the *junior,* he loved you less.

"He didn't stop loving you, he just loved you less. And less. And less. And less. And less." He held out his thumb and forefinger and slowly brought them closer till barely any light showed through them. "Among his innumerable gifts, did I mention cruelty?"

He exhaled sharply, like a smoker clearing phlegm, then smiled buoyantly. "Well, that's better. Almost as good as an hour at the gym."

Without preamble, I asked, "Do you believe it?"

"The story in the codicil?"

"Yes."

"There is no question in my mind that Dad could have fathered a child in Vietnam. But . . ." he stopped to grapple with a thought. "But what's strange—bizarre—is that he would care. That I find hard to believe. Near impossible."

"Because he was—" I looked at my notebook, "philandering, callous, greedy, and indifferent?"

"And cruel. Did you ever hear the expression He'd fuck the crack of dawn if it held still long enough?"

"In junior high school."

"That was Matthew Marshall. He didn't care whom he fucked, he didn't care about us, why would he care about some Vietnamese—what did he call her? Cockroach?"

"Cricket."

"Cricket. It doesn't compute, not even a little."

"When was the last time you saw him?"

"Memorial Day—we went to the wall."

"This Memorial Day?"

"Yes. Usually, he preferred Veteran's Day, but this year, for some reason, he wanted Memorial Day."

"How did he seem?"

"The same. Matthew Marshall. Father. Dad."

"Nothing unusual, nothing to indicate that—"

Harshly, he cut me off: "Mr. Bruno, Matthew Marshall wasn't some petit bourgeois who had to maintain a respectable persona. Matthew Marshall was a hugely wealthy self-made man. He could behave any way he wanted. He could behave, if you will, like an artist, like a star. Artists and stars and hugely wealthy self-made men are allowed to behave any goddamn way they like. It's impossible to determine if they're behaving strangely. On Memorial Day of this year, I saw nothing strange about Matthew Marshall's behavior."

"Was that the last time you saw him?"

"As a matter of fact, it was."

"Can you describe it for me."

"I told you, we went to the wall."

"Did you go to Washington together? Did you meet him there? Did you stay overnight? Did you have breakfast, lunch, dinner? Did you come back together? Did you—?"

"We met at the wall—he came in from Raleigh. I took the Metroliner, we didn't have breakfast, lunch, or dinner. He flew back to New York, I stayed over a couple of days—I have friends in Washington. Good enough?"

"How long were you at the wall?"

"I don't know—forty-five minutes, an hour. I didn't know it was the last time I'd see him, so I didn't watch the clock."

"Did you talk at all?"

"Chitchat."

"Can you remember any of it?"

"Not really—it was social noise."

"Anything might help . . ."

In a chipper singsong, he replied: "We said hello, how are you, fine, great; your mother sends her regards; thank her for me; I saw a review of the Robert Frank show; did you read it; no, I just saw the name Reflex and knew you were still in business; nice of you to keep tabs; hey, what's a father for; don't ask me; are you okay; yes; you're being careful; I'm being careful—I wear two condoms; maybe I should buy Trojans stock— here we are . . . And then we stopped and he touched a name, and we moved on and he touched a name, and so on, and so on, and so on and then he wept." Once more, Marshall unconsciously touched his fingertips to his lips. "It was like any of the other times."

"But he didn't say anything to you?"

"He didn't *look* at me. It was his private grief. I was allowed to watch it, not share it. Not that I had any right to share it." He shrugged. "But I wanted to—I wanted to cup my hands and catch his tears. I wanted very badly to do that." He glanced at his watch. "Will you need me much longer, Mr. Bruno?"

"Just a couple questions more—if I think of anything else, I can always come back."

"And you will be more than welcome. Go ahead."

"About the philandering . . ."

"Yes . . . ?"

"Did he ever talk to you about it?"

"Moi?" he said, breaking up in laughter. "No. He never talked to me about it."

"How did you know?"

"He never bothered to hide it. He didn't rub Beth's nose in it—didn't sleep with her friends, or with the wives of anyone they knew—but otherwise . . ." He gestured to take in the rest of the universe, ". . . fair game."

"Can you think of anyone he might have talked to about his romances—anyone he might have bragged to, anyone he might have asked advice from?"

"Doesn't sound like his style."

I was reaching for the recorder to turn it off, when I remembered: "By the way, did your father have a nickname?"

"What an interesting question." He thought. "If he did, I never knew it. Have you asked Beth?"

"She said he didn't."

"She should know."

As I turned off the recorder and packed up, he stood, stretched, picked up a pen, and smiled teasingly. "May we put you on our mailing list, Mr. Bruno?"

I don't know if he was heckling me or not, but I gave him my work address, zip code and all. He noted it on a pad, opened the door, let me precede him, and followed me to the exit, stopping en route to give Elena my address and take a sheaf of messages from her. As we shook hands, he said, "Are you making progress, Mr. Bruno?"

"From whose point of view?" I said.

"I see what you mean," he said. "If you make progress, it's going to cost us all a fortune."

"You don't seem very disturbed," I said, meaning it.

"Don't be fooled, Mr. Bruno—I am. I don't intend to let my father do to me in death what he did to me in life."

CHAPTER 12

I SPENT THE REST of the day and evening, and half the night, driving myself quietly crazy. First, I made the rounds with the blowups from Marshall's cabin.

I went to Dunlop, Tyler & Laird and showed the pictures to Wharton, Schuyler, and Laird: Nothing. I went to Tel-Mat and showed them to Twomey: Nothing. (To avoid making Twomey's life more difficult, I also showed them to Macintosh and Shaeffer: Nothing.) I went to Tuckahoe and showed them to Beth, Wendy, and Fred Marshall: Nothing.

Nothing is not unusual in the detective business—it had been a long shot that anyone would recognize the people in the pictures—but by the time I got back to the office I was in no mood to work and too furious to stop. Instead of going to dinner, I made a pot of coffee, sat down at the computer, and invested my rage in the hunt.

I began by scanning dozens of articles about Marshall, looking for anecdotes about fishing companions, hunting companions, climbing companions, tennis partners, squash partners, golf partners, scuba partners, softball teams, football teams, bowling teams. I looked for the names of surgeons who'd sliced him, masseurs who'd stroked him, chefs who'd fed him, pilots who'd flown him; chauffeurs who'd driven him; I looked for bankers who'd lent him millions and brokers who'd played with those millions; for gardeners who'd watered his plants and veterinarians who'd wormed his poodles. I looked for anybody, friend or enemy, lover or acquaintance, Matt Marshall might have trusted enough to confide in.

Then I cross-matched likely names I'd found in the articles with names in his phone books; there were lots of matches, but they all were in the business books. Not a soul mentioned in an article about Matt Marshall, other than his wife and children and his brother and sister, appeared in his personal phone book. But from what I could tell, most of his personal phone book wasn't that personal.

It listed two ambulance services, an internist, a proctologist, an immunologist, a cardiovascular man—that would be for his strokes, a dental surgeon, a periodontist; three car services, two helicopter services, two flower shops, three 24-hour drugstores, two 24-hour health clubs; five different lawyers, three bankers, two accountants; Sheriff Holloway, an assistant district attorney in Westchester, two assistant district attorneys in Manhattan, half a dozen judges, the governor, the former governor, the mayor, the former mayor, four councilmen; the manager at the Tel-Mat building, and the super at 355 East 48th.

He did include all the numbers of all his homes—I guess that was personal; numbers for Matt junior, his brother, Paul, his sister, Rachel, and Trish Twomey; and numbers for about two dozen other women. All the women's entries but one were marked "86," which is saloon code for banished, exiled, forbidden, nevermore. The number of the current entry, an Eileen Dillon, matched a number on two of Marshall's three office speed dials.

If Marshall had kept any friends who weren't involved with him professionally—any guys he grew up with, or went to school with, or, most important to me, served with—it wasn't detectable from his personal phone book. Of course, Matt junior had said his father kept his life in compartments, and maybe this personal phone book wasn't truly personal. Maybe there was another personal phone book someplace, one with the names of his real friends. And yet, his lovers were in this book; his firstborn was in it; so were his brother and sister. So was Trish Twomey.

I went through the book again, checking under C for Cricket, V for Vietnam, N for 'Nam, S for Saigon, W for war, A for army, R for ROTC and for reunion, and through every initial letter I could think of connected to his time in service, even, as a last resort, D for dink, G for gook, and S for slope. Then, I looked for scratchings out, erasures, codes, superscripts, subscripts. Nothing.

In the morning, I hooked my recorder up to the phone and began the truly maddening part, making the calls. My basic spiel was simple: "Hello, my name is Adam Bruno. I've been asked to edit a memorial volume of reminiscences about Matthew Marshall, particularly his time in Vietnam. I understand you were close to him. Did he ever talk to you about his experiences during the war—or any other personal experience that would help our readers understand who Matt *really* was? Any little thing at all would be most helpful . . ."

Since I was pretty sure the business books, the diaries, the phone logs, and the speed dials would yield even less than his personal book, I left that till last and started with A in Marshall's first business phone book. Name by name, I worked my way forward, calling until the end of the business day in California, which is nine at night in New York.

I did that the following day and the following day and the following day and the following day.

By five o'clock of the fifth day, I had gotten to M of his first business book, and I could hardly punch the buttons of my phone.

Worse, every one of the people I managed to reach—and I reached only two-thirds of the people I tried—told me, yes, he (or in eighty-nine cases, she) was indeed close to Matt Marshall, very close, as close as brothers (or sisters, or lovers), and, yes, Matt did indeed talk to him (or her) about all kinds of things close, personal, intimate things, oh, yes, but, unfortunately, unhappily, unhelpfully, Matt, dear old Matt, brotherly old Matt (loverly old Matt), Matt their closest connection in the world, bar none, Matt, who was open and candid and honest in all things, especially with me, his dearest friend (lover) in the whole world, Matt, for reasons I cannot divine, did keep his Vietnam experiences to himself.

For the sake of neatness, I finished the M's, then got up to pace, hoping—vainly—to purge the frustration.

Matt Marshall lived more than half a century, helped build a giant business, enjoyed a crowded—and public—social life, had a wife and three children, a brother and a sister, a slew of lovers, and enough professional and commercial acquaintances to populate a small town. Yet, so far as I could see, he had constructed his privacy so artfully that he was like a perfect hologram—visible to all, touchable by none.

As I paced back and forth, trying to decide whether I had stamina enough to start on N through Z, there was a recognizable double tap on the outer door. Before I could get to it, Sandy, the UPS route man, strolled in. "Hey, Mr. B, here you go."

He passed me an overnight envelope and held his tiny computer steady so I could sign the miniature screen. While he let himself out, I examined the SHIPPED FROM section of the airbill. I was expecting a check from Jeff Abramson, and hoping for one from Herschel; but the envelope wasn't from Abramson or Herschel.

It was from somebody named A. Nonni Muss, who lived, according to the airbill, at 777 West 42nd Street, New York, NY 10036. Seven seventy-seven West 42nd Street would be just about in the middle of the Hudson

River—a perfect address for A. Nonni Muss. I slit open the envelope, expecting to find a practical joke as juvenile as the name.

Instead, I found four unfolded sheets of Xerox paper, covered on both sides with elegant cursive handwriting. Nothing else—no note, no business card, nothing.

At first, I didn't recognize the language—the letters were Roman, but all kinds of dots and lines and squiggles hovered above each word. But as I turned the pages over, searching for a combination of letters that might be familiar, I remembered a little handbook I'd been given in the Coast Guard; just in case, they said.

The language was Vietnamese.

The first thing I did was call UPS to try to trace the sender. All UPS could tell me was that the package had been dropped off during lunch hour at the World Trade Center office—one of their busiest—and paid for in cash. Neither the receiving clerk nor the day manager could recall anything about A. Nonni Muss—male or female, young or old, black or white or brown or yellow; nothing.

The second thing I did was call Herschel, who barely let me say hello before growling, "I've got a client. Later."

"Thirty seconds," I said. "I need a translator, for a document in Vietnamese, someone good, and trustworthy. You ever use anyone in a trial?"

"My Orientals are Chinese," he said. "Try Phil Rabinowitz—he did that gang thing in Jersey last year."

"Phil the fuckup?" I said. "Would you trust anyone he suggested?"

"Now that I remember," Herschel said, "his guy did get three life terms. Let me think about it, okay?"

"Soon as you can."

"No shit, Sherlock."

Three days later, the call came, but not from Herschel or a translator: "Mr. Bruno, this is Cecile Boulanger. I understand you're looking for a Vietnamese interpreter."

"Er, er, yes, I am," I stammered.

"That's what Mr. O'Hara told me," she said, and by then, I could hear the gentle relish in her voice. "Could you tell me a little more, so I can recommend the best person?"

"Well, to begin with I need a handwritten document translated. And down the road I anticipate I'll be doing some interviews, and my guess is there'll be more documents."

"So you can't really describe the full extent of the job?" she said.

"If I did, I'd be lying."

"What's the pay?"

"Excuse me, Ms. Boulanger, but are you acting as representative for a translator?"

"Not exactly, Mr. Bruno, but the person I have in mind is very much in demand. If she's going to work for you, I'd like to assure her that it's worth her while."

"Whatever her going rate is—and of course I can find that out—she can bill me at, say, a hundred fifty percent of that rate."

"Sight unseen?"

"Ms. Boulanger, you're the sponsor—I know you're going to recommend somebody wonderful."

"Are you stroking me, Mr. Bruno, or mocking me?"

"Ms. Boulanger, I don't know you well enough to stroke you, and I admire you too much to mock you."

"Mr. Bruno," she said, with a velvety laugh, "if this is your way of making up to me for your court appearance—"

"No, not at all," I interjected.

"It's a shade too slick," she continued, then paused. "But not entirely ineffective."

"Thank you. I think."

For a second, she was silent, then, airily: "Mr. Bruno, even though I don't formally represent the interpreter, I do require a very modest finder's fee—payable in advance."

"A finder's fee—can an assistant United States Attorney do that?"

"I said very modest, Mr. Bruno. I'd like you to take me to dinner. I have some questions I want to ask you." Her tone was straightforward, nothing ominous in it at all; nothing flirtatious, either.

"I can't tell you about this case, Ms. Boulanger."

"I don't expect you to," she said.

"Or any other active case."

"I understand, Mr. Bruno. Well . . . ?"

CHAPTER 13

BOULANGER LET US EAT two appetizer courses and most of a main dish before she sprung her trap, and I was so busy cooling my overheated mouth I nearly fell right into it. She liked her food spicy, she'd told me—her hometown was New Orleans—and sweetly asked if I'd mind Indonesian. Not at all, I said gallantly. She took me to a place that served a national dish called Ristoffel, which was so incendiary that no matter how many beers I drank, I could hardly stop huffing. Boulanger washed her Ristoffel down with coconut milk, and never took a deep breath; that should have alerted me.

She lowered my guard even further by animatedly describing her life as a black Louisiana woman in a white male citadel like the New York U.S. Attorney's Office.

"You have no conception of what it takes to deal with these guys, not to mention some of the troglodytes in the defense bar. Either they walk around on eggshells because they think I'll shriek if they use the word nigger—I grew up in the Confederacy, for chrissake!—or they assume that the only thing that would make all my dreams come true is to sleep with a pot-bellied, middle-aged, married, strutting white lawyer whose ass I'm about to whip in a federal courtroom." She drank some coconut milk. "I must say, your partner—I mean, your ex-partner—isn't like that."

"Yes, he is," I said. "But you're not his type."

"Meaning?" she said, and—hearing the steel in her tone—I got a glimpse of just what it did take to be a black Louisiana woman in a white male citadel.

"Meaning Herschel's father is Irish Catholic and his mother is Austrian

Jewish, so he only goes for blond Protestants. He's not bigoted, he's just bent."

"What are they called? They have a funny name."

"Shiksas."

"Right: Shiksas. May I?" she asked, and took a sip of my beer. "How long were you partners?"

"Years and years."

"What broke it up?" she asked innocently, and at last I saw where she was heading and perceived that her finder's fee wasn't so modest at all.

"You want to know why I don't practice law anymore—that's what these questions are leading up to?"

"Uhuh."

"Why?"

After a pause, she said, "You embarrassed me in court, and I *hate* being embarrassed."

"Didn't you ask around?"

"Of course. I asked before you took the stand for Abramson, and I found out you were summoned before a disciplinary committee."

"And you assumed they'd punished me?"

"Yes. Dumb of me, wasn't it?" She shook her head in chagrin. "Then, I asked before I called you."

"What did you find out?"

"I confirmed that the committee didn't punish you."

"That's all?"

She grunted in irritation. "Everyone's very reticent about it—you must have a lot of friends."

"Just enough."

"Why didn't the committee punish you?"

"The committee didn't punish me because I didn't give them any actual grounds."

"If they didn't punish you, you're still licensed to practice law. Why don't you?"

"The committee made it clear, excruciatingly clear, that if I practiced law in New York, my clients would suffer. Every client. So I stopped."

Without asking this time, she took another sip of my beer. "What did you do?"

I leaned back and looked at her, but the scrutiny didn't enlighten me. She had an open, trustworthy face, but so did a lot of lawyers I knew. It meant nothing. Good lawyers are good actors, and the faces they give you are designed to serve a purpose or achieve an end. On top of that, southern women as attractive as Boulanger—especially black southern women as attractive as Boulanger—were as hard to read as invisible writing. And on top of *that,* she was a federal prosecutor.

I took a dollar from my pocket and spread it flat on the table. "That's a retainer. If you accept it, anything I say to you about this is said under lawyer-client privilege. If you don't accept it, we talk about something else. And if that costs me your translator, so be it."

It was her turn to stare at me. Finally, she reached into her purse and drew out a pen and a black leather notebook; she flipped it open, scribbled on a blank page, ripped the page out, and passed it to me. It read: "Received one dollar ($1) as retainer for professional services from Adam Bruno. Cecile Boulanger, Esq."

I folded her receipt and slipped it in my pocket, and she folded my dollar and slipped it in her notebook. I signaled the waiter for more beer. My mouth was hot and dry, and I knew I'd need the beer simply to talk. After he vanished, I drank half a glass, and began: "I had a case in state supreme court, a narcotics case. Here's the gist: A dealer is caught delivering three quarter pieces of coke to an address on Avenue A; or maybe he's picking it up; not clear. The dealer's girlfriend is sitting behind the wheel of his car. My client is the dealer's girlfriend's sister. Nineteen years old. Mother of two infant children. You with me so far?" Boulanger nodded.

"The ADA turns the girlfriend; she gives up the dealer. The dealer's brothers go to visit the girlfriend; she changes her mind. The ADA goes to my client—mind you, at this point, my client hasn't been busted. The ADA tells my client that if she testifies against the dealer, her sister's boyfriend, nothing will happen to her. If she doesn't, she'll go to prison and lose her two babies.

"She hasn't done anything, my client says. Yes, she has, the ADA tells her. Her sister swears that my client watched the dealer wrap the coke in his apartment and load it in his car, while she, on the other hand—the dealer's girlfriend—saw nothing and simply got in the car while it was parked at the Avenue A address."

"Was your client in the car?"

"No." I swallowed some beer; sweat was gluing my shirt to my armpits and back. "My client maintains she hasn't done anything, that she wasn't even in the apartment; she was in Tompkins Square Park with her two babies. The ADA is young, he's ambitious, he believes what helps him. The ADA puts the dealer's girlfriend in front of a grand jury, and she testifies that her sister helped her boyfriend wrap the coke. The grand jury indicts on criminal possession one, which is an A-one felony; fifteen to twenty-five, no parole.

"This is where I come in. I owe a favor to the Legal Aid guy who caught the case at the arraignment, and he asks me to take it over. My client—she is that now—tells me her story. I have no idea whether to believe her or not. As far as I know, the girlfriend might be telling the truth. The ADA thinks she is. In fact, by now he thinks it so faithfully, so devoutly, he's only got one offer—my client turns on the dealer, or he takes her to trial on the A-one felony.

"The ADA asks a hundred thousand dollars bail, I scream. It's imposed. The judge orders my client to Rikers. She goes berserk—who's going to take care of her kids? The judge is not interested in her kids. The corrections people hustle her away to Rikers and put her under a suicide watch.

"I get a baby-sitter for the kids, and I go to work. I find out that the girlfriend turned and then recanted. I find out that my client is not a user and is not a whore; I find out she has no sheet. I also find out that there are two independent witnesses, not wonderful witnesses—a lady super who likes her wine and a kid playing hooky—but two independent witnesses who put my client in Tompkins Square Park with her babies— it's the babies the witnesses fix on—while my client is allegedly wrapping the coke in the apartment.

"I talk to the ADA. He doesn't want to hear it; he wants this dealer. If I'm that confident, he says, take it to trial. I go back to the lady super and and the kid, and after two hours with each of them, I *am* that confident. I go to Rikers to tell my client not to worry, I'm going to kick the ADA's ass. But I don't get to tell my client I'm going to kick the ADA's ass because it turns out that the suicide watch at Rikers is a shade less than a hundred percent effective.

"My client has hanged herself. Dead."

Boulanger was leaning forward, listening very hard, her eyes locked on my face.

"I might add," I said, fighting the pain in my throat, "that my client not only was a nineteen-year-old mother of two, she was a nineteen-year-old mother of two who'd never been in trouble, no arrests, no complaints, no desk appearances, nothing. Not even JD. Did I say that already? I'm sorry. I repeat myself sometimes. Do you drink cognac?"

"Yes," she said. Before I could do it, she signaled the waiter, ordered two Remys, and turned back to me.

"Here's the good part," I said. "I go to work again. This time on the ADA.

"I find out he's cheating on his wife. Even better, I find out he's cheating on his wife with three different girls, not women, girls—one sixteen, one fifteen, one thirteen. Multiple drug offenders. There's a little hotel on Twelfth and Second where they go. I make a deal with the desk clerk and the security guard at the little hotel, and I make a deal with each girl. Whoever lands the ADA first calls me. I get lucky: the thirteen-year-old calls me. I go to the hotel, I'm shown to my room. I take my pictures."

The waiter put the cognacs on the table, and we each picked up a glass. "Cheers," she said, and we sipped.

"Luck," I said in reply. "I develop my pictures, my sharp, ravishing color pictures, longshots and closeups; profiles and full faces. And bodies. The best. Keep in mind, the girl is thirteen, but she's a druggie—she looks maybe eleven. I select the best of the best, I make blowups and—one week apart—I send a set of the best of the best blowups to the ADA's wife; to his mother; to the Manhattan district attorney; to the chief administrative judge of New York; and to the Bar Association committee on codes and conduct.

"I overdid it. He killed himself right after the district attorney got his set." I wiped my face and neck with my napkin. "Sorry about this," I said. "The combination of the food and beer makes for a lot of sweat."

She thought for a while. "All you did was send the pictures?" I nodded. "You made no demands, you made no threats?" I shook my head. "You didn't send the pictures to the media, you didn't mount them on a public bulletin board?" Again, I shook my head.

Flatly, she continued: "You merely distributed them to a restricted group of people—all adults, which would undermine any prosecution for pornography, especially since you weren't offering the pictures for sale." She raised her glass in mock admiration. "Smart. I see what you mean when you say you gave them no actual grounds. They must have been furious."

"They were."

For a few seconds, she avoided looking at me. Then: "Did you anticipate that he'd do what he did?"

"If you're asking did I expect him to kill himself, that answer is no. If you're asking did I want him to kill himself, the answer is yes. I didn't send the pictures around just so he'd blush in public, or resign, or move to Honolulu. I wanted what happened to her to happen to him."

"Well," she said, and exhaled noisily. "I certainly understand why you retained me."

"If it makes you uncomfortable," I said, "we can abrogate it."

"Aren't you afraid if I have you on the stand I'll use this material to impeach you?"

"No."

"Why not?"

"That's not who you are."

"I'm a prosecutor."

"Yes. But that's a job title, not a character disorder. I don't hate prosecutors, I hate hateful prosecutors, and I can make the distinction. We both know who the Torquemadas are in your trade, and you're not one of them."

"I might be."

"Yes, you might—I could be wrong about you, and if I am, you'll carry out your threat."

"You seem blissfully indifferent, Mr. Bruno."

"Well, Ms. Boulanger," I said, leaning close and pitching my voice at its most menacing, "You already know what I do to prosecutors who burn me . . ."

She jerked back, and for a second she stared at me as though I were a mugger who'd trapped her in an elevator. Then she relaxed and said, "I'm sorry you're not practicing anymore, Mr. Bruno—it would be real fun to appear opposite you."

"For me, too."

We sat in a pleasant silence for a moment, letting whatever tension was left between us dissipate. When I gauged the moment was right, I said, "Before we move on to anything else, the translator . . . ?"

She nodded, took her pen and notebook from her purse, and wrote as she spoke: "Her name is Nicole Maldonado. She's finishing a trial in Brooklyn, and she'll call you when it's done."

CHAPTER 14

FORTY-EIGHT HOURS AFTER MY dinner with Boulanger, Nicole Maldonado called for an appointment. Her voice was lightly accented, moderately young, and immoderately quiet—I'd have been willing to bet that more than one judge had instructed her to speak up. She was mannerly but a bit timid. When I tried to ask her some questions, she said she was uncomfortable on the telephone and preferred to submit a CV—her phrase—either in writing or in person. Did I want her to send it before I interviewed her, or could she simply visit? She could simply visit, I said. We fixed a time—5:30 the next afternoon, she confirmed the address, and asked if there were any particular reference books I thought might be useful for the job; if so, she would bring them with her. I told her I had no idea. She again confirmed the time and address, thanked me, and hung up.

At 5:25 the next day she knocked on the door. I'm not sure what I'd been expecting—maybe somebody like most of the translators, male or female, in the court system; somebody gray and bookish, somebody bordering on invisible.

I wasn't expecting somebody with a face that was the greatest argument for miscegenation I've ever seen. Somehow, the two major strains within her, the Asian and the Latin-American, had fused to form something unique. Not because she was beautiful—to this day, I'm not sure of that—but because the combination—skin, bones, lips, teeth, cheeks, eyes—was so *right*. "Mr. Bruno?" she said tentatively, and even more tentatively offered a hand. "I am Nicole Maldonado."

I showed her to a chair, put her canvas briefcase on my desk, sat next to her, and spent five minutes interviewing her. I should have taken longer, but she had a way of lowering her head slightly and turning it sideways so that whenever she looked at me, there was something mysterious and promising in her oval brown eyes. Since she looked at me every time she answered one of my questions, I found it hard—though it made no sense—to avoid feeling beguiled. Later, I discovered how habitual the movement was, and later still I discovered how innocent it was; Vietnamese are raised not to look directly in other people's eyes. It's considered rude.

After learning that she was fluent in French and Vietnamese (via her mother), Spanish (via her father), and English (via the public schools), and that she was more than happy with the money, I found a confidentiality agreement.

"Ms. Maldonado, I'm going to need you to sign this before we can go to work. If you like, you can take it home and study it, but I would like an answer by tomorrow."

She took the agreement from me, skimmed it, and stopped to reread a passage. "What does this mean?" she said, pointing to a paragraph.

"That means the agreement is strictly between us, unless I legally assign it to somebody else. It means that you report solely to me, orally or in writing, and not to anyone who's hired me—at least, not without my say-so."

Gravely, she nodded. "I understand," she said. She finished reading the agreement and gestured toward a pen on my desk. "May I?"

"You're sure you don't want to think about it overnight, Ms. Maldonado?"

Deliberately, she shook her head, and I handed her the pen. She signed the agreement; I did, too, and gave her a copy. She folded it in thirds and put it in her briefcase.

I drew the Vietnamese letter from a folder and placed it in front of her. "Ms. Maldonado, I'd like you to translate that for me. Can you do that?"

She leaned over the letter and read the first couple of sentences. "Yes." She glanced up and saw me waiting expectantly. "Oh, you mean now?"

"If you could . . ."

She frowned slightly. "If you wish, Mr. Bruno. But I have to request that you permit me also to submit a proper written translation." To my surprise, she blushed. "It is important that my work maintain its standard."

"Of course," I said. "Take a minute to look it over." While she did, I made a fresh pot of coffee and put my recorder on the desk in front of her. "Tell me when you're ready," I said.

"Do you have the original?" she said.

"No, that's what I was sent."

"I am ready," she said. I started the tape and signaled. She sat up very straight, as though she were in court, and translated:

Dear Captain Matthew:

I hope this reaches you. I have given it to somebody I cannot really trust, but I know he has the means to escape and it is the only way I am able to send a message. I have been very much on the lookout for your friend—

Maldonado stopped and looked up. "This word can also mean special friend, or even relation." I nodded, and she went on:

I have been very much on the lookout for your friend, but it is extremely difficult to know if she is here. There are one thousand or even one thousand five hundred prisoners at Bien Hoa, and unless you tell me more, I do not know where to look for her.

Most of the prisoners here are common criminals, and I must ask you in all pity whether your friend could be considered a common criminal? I beg your forgiveness for asking this—it is the extremity of rudeness between comrades-in-arms—but our captors make their own definitions. If a woman has given herself for money to a member of the invading forces, she is a prostitute, and thus a common criminal. Please forgive me, my dear companion, but has your friend ever done this? If, to her shame, this is the case, you must give me much more information—not merely a physical description and the name you called her. I cannot look for somebody with only the nickname you affectionately imposed on her. I must have her own name, at the least the name of her village. Do you know if she has the child with her? This is of paramount importance, and not only to help me with my search.

If a woman has given herself freely to a member of the invading forces and borne his child, she can, if the Communists are so inclined, be considered a political prisoner. There are political prisoners here who have spent years in solitary confinement. This is not normally done to women—unless they are caught with incriminating documents. Those with such documents are treated as spies. I myself am now a political prisoner—in my tenth month among the criminals, an informer exposed my rank for a bowl of rice—but I am not considered a spy. We are treated very harshly, but there are many fewer political prisoners than criminals, and if your friend is political, it would make it easier for me to conduct a search. (If I have a name and a village.)

I understand how urgent this is to you, but I must borrow a few lines to beg you again to use all your influence on behalf of my family. I realize with all my soul that your government has no influence in Vietnam anymore, but the government of our captors I believe still pays heed to the importunations of your humanitarian cadres. Do you have any acquaintance with the American Friends, or with the Quakers? If you do, I beg you to appeal to them to help my family escape. I will stay here and follow them when I may.

I pray that this missive reaches you, and that you are thriving in your homeland. I salute you and wish you all my admiration and affection.

She paused, read the salutation to herself a couple of times, and said, "It is signed 'Ghost.'"

"Ghost?" I said.

"Yes," she said, pointing to the signature at the bottom of the last page. "Here—*ma,* written like this, means 'ghost.' With a little mark here, it means 'mother.' It can also mean 'horse,' or 'hemp,' or 'cheek,' or 'but,' or 'grave,' or 'effigy,' depending on one of these little marks—you see them, all throughout his letter. Each little mark indicates a tone. Vietnamese is a language of tones, not words." She studied the letter again. "Yes, ghost. This is an educated writer; he would not make a mistake in his farewell to his comrade-in-arms." Carefully, she put the letter on my desk, folded her hands, and lowered her eyes.

I pulled the nickname key up on the computer screen. There was no Ghost.

But, seven lines down, there was a Ma.

The name belonged to the Vietnamese in uniform whose photo hung on the mystery wall. I found the photo and studied it. All it showed was a Vietnamese in uniform. He wore no insignia or patches, so I couldn't tell his rank or unit.

Gesturing to the letter, I asked, "Is there a date?"

"No, but . . ." she started but stopped.

"But what?"

"I believe it must be 1976, at the earliest."

"Why do you say that?"

"Bien Hoa is in the south. The Communists did not take control of the south until April 1975, and Mr. Ghost has been a prisoner in the Bien Hoa jail at least ten months." Anyone else might have gloated a bit; she did the opposite, lowering her eyes and saying apologetically, "Mr. Bruno, if you tell me a little more, perhaps I would not have to guess so much."

"The letter is all I have," I said, and the way she nodded in reply— respectfully but woodenly—made it plain she knew I was lying.

Whether she realized it or not, she had put me in a bind, or, rather, she had exposed the bind so clearly that I had to deal with it. My professional instinct was to tell her as little as possible for as long as possible. The trouble with that was the second I came across something else valuable— another Vietnamese document, a Vietnamese person, whichever—I would need Nicole Maldonado, or someone like her, to translate. And the odds were that sooner or later a document or a person would reveal all or part of what I was up to. So the question really wasn't whether to tell her more, but when. I glanced at her. She sat quietly, her gaze directed considerately through the window.

"Ms. Maldonado," I began, and she tilted her head very delicately in my direction. "What I mean is, that's all I have in Vietnamese."

"Ahh," she murmured, and I could have sworn the corners of her mouth curled up minutely.

"I am looking for the illegitimate child of an American soldier and a Vietnamese woman. The soldier deserted the mother in Vietnam, but the soldier believes she and the child found their way to the United States."

She inhaled deeply before saying, "I see, the father is still looking for the child, and you are working for him, this . . . Captain Matthew?"

"Not precisely. He's dead."

"Then who is looking for the child?"

I hesitated. "The father left the child something in his will. A bequest. The executor of the estate has asked me to find the child so he or she can receive this bequest."

"And you don't know the child's name?" I shook my head. "Or the mother's name?" I shook my head again. She referred to the letter. "What about the name Captain Matthew called her—the name he 'affectionately imposed upon her'?"

"Cricket."

"Cricket?" she said. I nodded. "Cricket the sport, or cricket the insect?"

"The insect, I imagine," I said.

She shook her head in puzzlement, then went on: "Do you know when they are supposed to have come to this country?"

"No," I said. "Nor where they went when they came here. I know almost nothing." I paused, then continued: "Until you translated that, I didn't know for sure whether there was a child."

She brushed the letter with her fingers. "Do you know anything about Mr. Ghost?"

I touched the photo. "Only what you see here—that he was a soldier."

She spread the pages of the letter in a fan, skimmed them, and stopped at a passage. "He says—" she tapped the line with her nail, "—he and Matthew are comrades-in-arms, and that an informer exposed his rank and he is now a political prisoner. This means, as I'm sure you see, that Mr. Ghost was an officer, a high officer, in the Army of the Republic of Vietnam. A simple soldier would not be in danger if his rank were exposed."

Obviously, I hadn't seen it, just as I hadn't known enough about Bien Hoa and the conquest of South Vietnam to deduce the earliest date of the letter.

For a wild moment I was tempted to offer her a partnership; Bruno & Maldonado had a nice exotic ring to it. Clients preferred their detectives to sound foreign and disreputable. It allowed them to feel superior. But I let the moment pass. Instead, I nodded strenuously, as though she were merely expressing my own thought, and walked across the room to the coffee machine. I had the feeling she was laughing at me behind my back, but when I turned around to offer her a cup, her expression was as serious and composed as usual. "Do you have tea?" she asked.

Luckily, I did. When I brought the cups back to the desk, she was examining the letter and jotting notes on a pad. Her handwriting was microscopic, neat but far too small for me to make out any words. "Find something else?" I asked, indicating the notes.

"Sometimes," she began, "prisoners use words that perhaps mean more than one thing and—" She stopped, unsure how to continue. Then, a shade less tentatively: "Mr. Bruno, may I have your permission to confirm my translation with my mother and my aunts?"

"Your mother and your aunts—are they all interpreters?" I said sarcastically, which only goes to show how slow I can be when I really put my mind to it.

Again, she blushed and lowered her eyes. When she finally raised them, they were shadowed with pain. "No. They were all prisoners."

This time, I was less stupid. "Were you?"

"No. I was rescued during the fall of Saigon," she said, pausing. "April twenty-fourth nineteen seventy-five."

"Who rescued you?"

"My father."

"But he didn't rescue your mother?"

The pain in her eyes deepened, and when she finally spoke, I easily sensed she was telling me something she desperately wished she could forget:

"That day, there were only two places, and my mother believed that it was safer to send me with my father while she and my aunts would follow later. If I stayed with her, she believed, both of us would be punished much more severely; perhaps even my aunts would be punished. My father and I left. Some weeks later, my mother and my aunts tried to escape by boat and were caught."

"When did she get here?"

"August fifteenth, nineteen eighty-one."

"Six years after you escaped?" I said, trying—but failing—to imagine what that would be like for a child.

"Six years, ten weeks." She smiled slowly and joyously. "A hot, sunny, spectacular Saturday!"

With some effort, she composed herself. "Mr. Bruno, may I have your permission?"

"You may, Ms. Maldonado."

CHAPTER 15

HERSCHEL USED TO SAY that my interim reports were the last surviving form of short fiction in American letters, but Herschel never did understand that it's hazardous to burden a client with too much information. Unless the facts you offer a client are conclusive, he has questions. If you can't answer those questions, he gets upset. So, the goal is to offer the client just enough conclusive facts—phrased in an encouraging manner—so that he asks no questions but lets you keep working (and billing) anyway.

Dear Mr. Laird:

This is to bring you up to date on my assignment (Contract #L572). As per your instructions, there will be no case caption on any of these interim reports.

I am happy to inform you that I am making slow but excellent progress in this matter.

Most crucially, I have learned through a top-secret source (an employee of a clandestine agency of a Southeast Asian government) that some months after the fall of Saigon (April 30, 1975), Mr. Marshall used back channels to inquire about the fate of a female Vietnamese national (name so far unknown) and her child (sex and name so far unknown). This piece of information (which I find reliable) appears to confirm that Mr. Marshall did in fact tell the truth in his codicil.

More mundanely, as of today, I have reached (by phone) nearly 92 percent of Matthew Marshall's business acquaintances, and, as I previously alerted you to expect, he did not confide his Vietnam experiences to any of them.

I have also reached (by phone) more than 85 percent of Mr. Marshall's personal friends and acquaintances (as determined by the telephone numbers in his private address book), and Mr. Marshall was similarly close-mouthed with this group. For this reason, I am reluctant to visit all these people to show them the photographs that I showed you.

(On the other hand, among those in the private address book are his brother, Paul, and his sister, Rachel, and although they both deny that Mr. Marshall discussed his war experiences with them, I believe it would be worthwhile for me to visit them, both to show them the photographs and to prod them further. Since Paul lives in North Carolina and Rachel lives in San Francisco, please be forewarned of travel expenses—flights, hotels, rental cars.)

As you anticipated, the inventory of Mr. Marshall's safe-deposit box at Chemical Bank yielded nothing useful to my investigation. Nor did the inventory of the contents of Mr. Marshall's wallet. Thank you for sending them to me. At your convenience, can you supply me with a list of all of Mr. Marshall's bank accounts and copies of all of his keys? As you may surmise, I am looking for either another safe-deposit box, or any sort of lockaway where Mr. Marshall might have secreted private papers.

Starting next week, I will devote most of my time to tracing those people Mr. Marshall served with in Vietnam. I have already sent requests to the Pentagon and various veterans' organizations, and I am conducting daily searches of all relevant data bases. As you doubtless know, the Pentagon is singularly reluctant to give out any information, so tracing these people—excluding any personal interviews—will be time-consuming and expensive. However, I am confident this will prove to be our most fruitful field of attack.

Attached please find an itemized account of expenses. If you have any questions, please feel free to call.

I printed two copies, one for Laird, one for Wharton, and called for a messenger. When he arrived, he was soaked—what had been a shower, he said, had turned into a violent squall, with rain, hail, and cutting winds. I gave him a big tip—Laird, I felt sure, would stiff him—packed my floppies to take home for the weekend, and slumped back wearily in my chair.

The elation I'd felt when Maldonado translated Ghost's letter was long gone. Since then, though she'd related more anecdotes about conditions in the Bien Hoa jail and more history of the fall of Saigon; she and her mother and her aunts had found nothing in the letter that helped me: no double meanings, no codes, no secret writing.

The words of Ghost, Maldonado explained disappointedly, appeared—at least so far—to mean only what they said.

Once again, I was shaken with the sense that Marshall was eluding me, that I would perpetually be taking three steps back for every two steps forward. And what most unsettled me was the suspicion, conviction, really, that tracing Marshall's Vietnam colleagues the way I'd promised Laird in my report was not only ludicrous—it would take months, if it could be done at all—but, at bottom, was nothing more than a feeble excuse to avoid calling on Tim Cleary.

CHAPTER 16

IT WAS SMART OF me not to have taken a gun, and smart of me to have pumped my horn when I turned into his unweeded driveway, and smart of me to have shut off the engine and sat waiting with my hands visible on the steering wheel.

I tried not to let slight rustlings alarm me—the day was windy and the shrubbery in his yard maintained a nervous ripple—because I wanted badly not to fidget. Tim Cleary struck me as the kind of hunter who would empty a magazine into any living thing that fidgeted. The minutes went by slowly—if you've ever sat immobile and unbearably coiled in tension, you know how slowly—but I stayed in place. It was his territory, and he would dictate all the moves.

He must have been lethal in the field. He appeared noiselessly at the passenger door—the faultless choice. Had he appeared in front of the car or behind it, I might—if the engine were on and in gear—have run him down. Had he appeared at the driver's door, I might—if I were agile enough—have deflected the M-16 aimed at my head.

He opened the passenger door, leaned in, pulled the key from the ignition, and stepped back all in one flowing movement. For a few seconds, he simply watched me, as a snake might watch a mouse, then signaled for me to leave the car. I pointed to my case on the passenger seat and started to reach for it. He fluttered the M-16 barrel gently—astonishing how much the motion resembled a man saying no—and I froze my hand in midgrasp. He again signaled me to leave the car, and I did, one cramped limb at a time. When was I out, he signaled me to go to the front of the car and spread-eagle my trunk on the hood. I did.

There, he joined me, to toss me as efficiently and painlessly as he had the first time. Once he was done, he trod backward to the passenger door and balanced the rifle on the rearview mirror so the barrel pointed at the top of my head. For an instant, he vanished, and I realized he had gone into a crouch so he could remove my case from the seat. When he reappeared, he was holding the case rigidly at the horizontal; carefully, he placed it on the hood, bent his head, and inspected the clasps and the hinges. When he was satisfied, he retrieved the rifle and signaled me to pick up the case and precede him to the door of the house.

The living room fit him: functional unpainted shelves and chairs—I wouldn't have been surprised if he'd built them himself; a huge round coffee table that had once been a spool for electric company cable; a cast-iron pot-bellied stove; bare painted walls, no pictures; polished oak floors, no rugs; three locked gun cases—pistols, rifles, shotguns; and thick dark curtains on the windows. There was only one incongruous note: the expensive stereo set and hundreds of shelved cassettes occupying a full wall.

As soon as he'd put the M-16 in the rifle case, he loaded a Rolling Stones cassette into the stereo and turned it on. Ignoring me—or so I thought—he disappeared, to return a minute later with two bottles of local beer. He opened the bottles, handed me one, put the other to his mouth, swallowed, wiped his lips with a bandanna, and, without preamble, said:

"They're these mines—they're Russian maybe, or Chinese, or Yugoslav, some Commie country with scientists—and they're much better than anything Charlie does himself—all Charlie does is modify a Claymore or put a spring in an old C-ration can—and they're maybe the size of your hand—no, no, littler, the size of a gook's hand—and they're plastic with a rubber pressure pad on top. They take about ten pounds' pressure to blow it." He shook his head ruefully. "Gooks weigh much less than we do, so they always set the pressure too light. Stupid. They lose a lot of food that way, 'cause any animal, a dog, a big rat—they eat rats, gooks—can set it off. They lose a lot of kids, too, 'cause a kid, even a little kid, can set it off, not that anyone would miss a gook kid, least of all a gook. Now what's cute about these mines, and why for sure they're from someplace with scientists, is that some of 'em've got a little gizmo in them, no more than this big, and the gizmo is like a detonator hooked up to a carpenter's level, and if you tip the little fucker more than like so—say, maybe five degrees—" He picked up my briefcase and excruciatingly slowly tilted it, "—it blows. Bam!"

"Ahhh," I said, "I see," and drank some beer.

Cleary nodded, disappeared again, and this time returned with bread, cheese, and two Granny Smith apples, which he arranged neatly on the coffee table. He drew a combat knife from his boot and cut the cheese in cubes and the apples in wedges. He handled his knife—it was a K-bar, I'd been issued one in the Coast Guard—as well as he handled his guns, which was altogether too expertly for the civilized world.

For a few moments we sat and ate and sipped our upstate beer.

The scene reminded me of the time Herschel had talked me into taking the case of a gruesomely overweight Ukrainian mother in the East Village who'd drowned five of her eight children in the bathtub. This was after the guy in San Francisco won with the Twinkie defense.

We pled her not guilty by reason of insanity, and actually put her on the stand. She explained to the jury that she killed the five children because if she hadn't she wouldn't have had enough to eat. During his cross, the ADA, a wiseguy, asked her if she planned to eat the children, too (this was also after Jeffrey Dahmer, the Milwaukee cannibal). She crossed herself, broke down in tears, begged the good Lord to forgive the ADA for his terrible blasphemy and to pray that he had no children, and asked the judge if she could have a bite to eat. The jury acquitted her in three hours.

While we were prepping the case, I spent hours with her, and I never knew what to expect. Sometimes she would scribble notes for her remaining kids, or demand to see their homework, or decipher reports from their pediatrician. Other times she would explain that it was exceptionally hard to drown the children, especially the last two, because by then she was losing her strength—she hadn't eaten in nearly three hours—and the last two were the oldest and strongest and put up a savage struggle.

She would explain that it was easier to drown a child not by trying to force its head under water but by tying its hands, holding the child by the feet, and slowly dipping it into the tub. That way, she explained, the only muscle the child could rely on to prevent its drowning was its neck, and neck muscles weren't well developed in a child. It helped marginally, she explained, to put detergent in the water—it provoked coughing and coughing made a child drown quicker.

As with her, so with Cleary: I didn't know what to expect. For the moment, he seemed as docile as an old hound. He ate, he drank, he hummed to the Rolling Stones. His guns all seemed safe in their locked cabinets, and the handle of his K-bar was closer to me than to him. Offhandedly, I said: "Say, did you guys have a nickname for Marshall?"

He ignored me, picked up the K-bar, and carved the seeds from two apple wedges.

"I don't mean to his face—I know you wouldn't use a nickname to an officer's face—I mean, when he wasn't around to hear it . . . ?"

Continuing to ignore me, he speared each apple seed with the tip of his knife and brought it to his mouth.

"You ever come across the nickname Ghost?"

Cleary peeked at me, smiled winningly, and made a throat-slashing gesture with the K-bar. "Ghost," he said.

"Did Ghost do that a lot?" I asked.

He made the gesture in the other direction. "Ghost."

"Maybe an ARVN officer?"

But Cleary had had enough of Ghost, and he resumed concentrating on his snack.

"Did Marshall have a girlfriend—a local?"

Cleary's head jerked up, and he looked directly into my eyes. A leer slithered across his face.

"You ever fuck a VC?" he asked conversationally. "It's great, 'cause you don't have to worry about VD." Another chuckle. "Yes VC, no VD. Bam! VC don't sell their pussy on Tu Do, 'cause VC are killers. You gotta be another VC to fuck 'em. Or you gotta be U.S." He sang a burst of "America the Beautiful." "They're tight, 'cause they're not used to it. They're used to leaving booby traps under their babies, they're not used to cock. So you really gotta work at it, get a good rhythm goin', bam! bam! bam! bam! bam! bam! thank you, ma'am, bam bam! 'Course, after a few guys—'specially a few U.S. guys, *big* U.S. guys, guys with peckers like no VC ever saw, they get looser. Like, you know, your average Alabama homecoming queen." A huge cackle. "The last guy in sloshes around like some poor schmuck stumbling around in a fuckin' swamp." A sigh. "Still, there's compensations: The last guy in gets to stick a K-bar in her snatch and slice her all the way up to her Adam's apple. You're lucky, she's still alive while you're pulling her guts out. Rock and roll!"

"Did Marshall have a VC girlfriend named Cricket?"

He spread the fingers of his left hand and touched them one by one with the tip of his knife:

"Hit her, stomp her, fuck her, blind her, gut her."

"Who?"

"Rule One."

"Whose rule was Rule One?"

"Hit her, stomp her, fuck her, blind her, gut her."

"Was it Marshall's rule?"

"Rule One."

"Did he follow that rule with his girlfriends?"

"Hit her, stomp her, fuck her, blind her, gut her."

"Did he break the rule with any of his girlfriends?"

"Rule One."

"Did he talk to you about any of his girlfriends?"

Cleary half-rose, leaned over the coffee table, and spat his words in my face, "Don't give me fuckin' orders about gooks, Captain."

He sat back down, then jumped up, grabbed the two empties, took them to the kitchen, and returned with two fresh beers. For a few minutes, we simply sat, nibbling, sipping, and listening to the Rolling Stones.

After Cleary had finished half his beer, I decided to take another gamble. Pointing to my case, I said, "Can I show you something?" He neither looked my way nor said anything. I took that as a yes and reached for the case.

When I unsnapped the clasps, he blinked once, but didn't glance at me. I turned the case sideways—the last thing I wanted was to raise the lid so it blocked his view of me—opened it, and drew out a set of blowups. Though he didn't appear to be watching me, my hands started to sweat and I had trouble separating the photos. After blowing on my fingertips, I spread the photos on the coffee table so that they formed a half-ring around his food. He glanced at them, gave no reaction, and went back to his food.

The first sign that they made an impression came when some crumbs fell from the bread he was bringing to his mouth onto one of the pictures. Taking his bandanna from his pocket, he began to brush the crumbs away. But when the crumbs were all gone, he continued to brush; and with each pass of his bandanna his stroke became more and more tender.

The picture was of two soldiers—a small, slender, impish, dark corporal was being hoisted into the air by a bare-chested blond giant. Painted on the giant's helmet was a skull and crossbones above a peace symbol. The smile on the impish corporal's face was undercut by the deep, spectral circles under his eyes.

Surreptitiously, I checked my nickname key: The corporal was Doc; the giant was somebody called Yahoo.

Cleary was still stroking the photos. "Is Doc a corpsman?" I asked casually.

"Officers say corpsman," Cleary snapped. "He's a medic. Doc."

"What about Yahoo?" I said.

"Bouncer. 'Stead of getting his feet and legs, it bounced up—bam!" Cleary dropped to his knees, and his hands reflexively came forward and formed a cup, "Balls and belly." Gently, he pushed his cupped hands up a few inches, then let them drop, then pushed them up again. As he did, he kept staring to his left, his head jerking and his eyes shifting as though he were watching something or somebody.

For the next eight minutes, while I sat opposite him, he stayed kneeling, his hands cupped. After a while, I realized that he was trying to catch the flow of Yahoo's innards as they drained out of his body. While he knelt and caught, he murmured tenderly to Yahoo, not words, but sounds, the same sounds a mother makes when she cradles her weeping infant and rocks him to sleep. Finally, he went mute.

And then, his face as drained of expression as an embalmed corpse, he nodded to the figure to his left and watched as that figure injected invisible ampule after ampule of morphine into the figure before him, the beloved friend whose palpable life was slopping into his cupped hands.

Cleary raised his face and murmured, "I didn't have the balls—I made Doc kill him."

"Where is Doc?" I said.

"He should have said, 'You love him, you shoot him.' "

"Do you remember his name?"

"He should have made me do it."

"What did you call him?"

"If he tells me to, I would have done it."

"What did you call him?"

"I told you, Doc."

"Doc what?"

"Doc Dopey."

"Doc Dopey?"

Cleary mimed a hypodermic.

"Did he answer to Doc Dopey?"

"He did with me."

"What about with the others?"

"Doc Mickey."

"Mickey what?"

Cleary lowered his head to stare at the photograph.

"Is Mickey his first name or last name?"

"All you had to do is tell me, I would have shot him."

"What did Captain Marshall call him?"

Cleary raised his eyes. "Who?"

"Doc. What did Captain Marshall call him?"

"Doc Wolf."

CHAPTER 17

HE SPELLED IT WOOLFF, but the sign-carrying pickets blockading his ranch house in central Florida spelled it any way that popped into their heads:

Wolf, Wolfe, Woolf, Woolfe, Wulf, Wulfe, Wulff. On several of the signs, the name was ornamented with a crude drawing of a wolf devouring a newborn; blood dripped from the wolf's fangs onto the newborn's mutilated face and then dribbled down beneath its body to form the words BABY KILLER.

I heard the pickets before I saw them, but that's because Woolff lived in the bend of an S on his pretty suburban street, and they were hidden until I reached the midpoint of the curve. They were divided into two groups: a dozen on one side of the street, marching and shouting; four on the other side, pacing silently in a line in front of Woolff's house. My guess was they were operating under some kind of court restraint, otherwise they'd all have been in front of his house, if not actually in it.

It hadn't taken long to locate Woolff. On a hunch, I'd begun with medical directories and found a listing for him in less than two days—Michael B. Woolff, M.D., ob-gyn, practicing in Lakeland, Florida, which is between Orlando and Tampa. When I'd called him and told him I wanted to talk about Matt Marshall, he'd sounded puzzled. The war, he reminded me, had ended more than twenty years ago. But after a minimum of pushing on my part—I told him that Marshall, before he died, had tearfully praised Woolff's noble work in the field—he agreed to see me, and suggested I come for dinner rather than go to his clinic. "I'm always terribly busy there," he said, ingenuously enough, "and it's a hectic atmosphere."

As I left my car to walk the twenty feet to Woolff's pathway, I could imagine what he meant. If this is what they did to him at home, they must have made life around the clinic a nightmare. When I came even with the silent picketers—the noisy ones across the street had stopped shouting to watch my progress—a middle-aged man with a large cross around his neck shifted his weight and spread his arms to block my path.

"If you're going to visit the murderer—" he began in a weird mixture of growl and falsetto, but by then I was around him, and moving fast. He spun on his heel to chase me, but slipped to the ground. Immediately, the other pickets formed a clumsy barrier.

Stick first, carrot later seemed the best tactic, so I brought my elbows high and accelerated, slamming with all my weight into a scrawny teenager and knocking the wind out of him. A woman, his mother by her looks, lunged at me; I sidestepped her and did a sudden about-face just in time to greet the middle-aged man with the cross. I raised my palm.

"Please, Reverend," I said, loud enough for the others to hear, "I am present in an official capacity, and it's in your interest to let me do my job." I lowered my voice: "If you interfere with me, I will have you arrested . . ." I waited till he started to sneer—pickets of all sorts love to be arrested; they get to be martyrs on the six o'clock news—then continued, ". . . on charges of feloniously assaulting a federal agent." I raised my voice again: "That's not five days in the county jail, Reverend, that's ten years in Leavenworth, with no parole."

Across the street, the other picketers were bunched in a clumsy phalanx, watching for a signal from the man with the cross. I didn't want to give him a chance to think. I shook my head brusquely, reached into my pocket, and drew out a slip of paper. "You have the right to remain silent, you have the right to an att—" Startled, the man with the cross waved in my face as I continued my supposed reading of Miranda. Finally, his wave turned into a gesture to his followers to back away, and I stopped reading, pocketed the slip of paper, nodded to the man with the cross, and strode up the bluestone path to Woolff's front door.

". . . Did you ever look at the face of a pro-lifer? I used to see faces like that in country—Special Forces guys, or ARVN mercenaries, or doorway gunners—people who really *love* to kill; people who love to make *mama-sans* beg for mercy before they gut-shoot them; people who love to pack their seventy-nines with phosphorous loads and empty them into hootch hospitals; people who love to ram finger charges up the vaginas of six-year-olds. People who *come* when they watch their enemies die.

"They know everything, too; they've got the same direct line to God.

God tells them what's right and what's wrong, and they're going to kill anyone that God tells them is wrong. Kill the abortionists! Kill the patients of the abortionists! Kill the counselors of the abortionists! Kill the nurses of the abortionists! Kill the receptionists of the abortionists! Kill the cleaning women of the abortionists! Kill the wives of the abortionists. Kill the children of the abortionists. Kill the enemy! Pro-life!"

It was nearly ten, and Woolff was working on the bottom third of a liter of vodka and showing no signs of drunkenness at all. He was still dark, still small, still slender, and still had spectral circles under his eyes; he wasn't impish, though, not a bit. He had plenty of energy and he could make jokes, but his jokes were all about pain. He ran on pain. And rage. He reminded me of those burned-out lawyers who handled appeals for prisoners on death row.

We'd been in the living room for about seventy minutes, and all he'd talked about was what it was like to do abortions in central Florida. At dinner, he'd talked about going to college on the GI bill and going to medical school and getting married and having children and relocating to Lakeland because he adored his wife and that's where her family lived. He'd avoided any talk about Vietnam, and I hadn't forced the point: It wasn't, after all, a great subject for mealtime chatter.

Woolff sat on a crimson leather knockoff of an Eames chair, I was opposite him on the couch. His wife was in the kitchen, doing the dishes; their children, an eleven-year-old boy and a ten-year-old girl, were helping her. I opened my case, took out some papers and a set of blowups, and turned on my recorder—but left it in the case. I had a feeling that setting it in front of him would scare him into silence. "Dr. Woolff," I said, "your nickname in Vietnam was Doc, right?"

"All the medics were called Doc."

"Did most of the people in your outfit have a nickname?"

"I dunno. I guess." He frowned. "The trouble with nicknames is people lay them on you, and unless you're big enough, you can't order them to use your own name."

"Did you have another nickname?"

He glanced at the door. "Not really."

"Tim Cleary says—"

"Tim Cleary is a psychopathic murderer, and anything he says comes from a murderer's head!" He exhaled. "My only nickname was Doc."

"Did Cleary have a nickname?"

"Polio."

"Polio?" I said.

"Cleary left you crippled or dead."

"Did Matt Marshall have a nickname?"

Woolff thought for a second. "Not that I recall."

"You never heard anybody call him anything but his name or rank?"

"Uh uh—of course, I didn't hang around with most of them. You hang around with them, the next thing is they get wounded and you gotta deal with them. You can't fix them up if you know them too well."

"Did you ever come across the nickname Ghost?"

"Ghost?"

"He might have been an ARVN officer . . . ?"

"I stayed as far away from them as I could, unless I had to take care of them on the field—and I did that as little as I could get away with. I never met an ARVN officer who wasn't a thieving, homicidal piece of shit."

"Dr. Woolff, does the nickname Cricket mean anything to you at all?"

"Cricket? No."

"Did Marshall have a girlfriend?"

"Sure. They all did."

"A local?"

Again, Woolff glanced at the door. "I don't know who the officers were mixed up with."

"Were there any women around?"

"Around? Not around, actually. But there was access. You got field hospitals, you got Red Cross girls, you got USO girls, you got a lady reporter once in awhile. Officers got lots of access."

"I mean natives, Vietnamese . . ."

This time, he paused for a full thirty seconds. "Vietnamese are for grunts. Officers stay clear of Vietnamese."

"If he'd had a native girlfriend, would you have noticed?"

"I told you, I don't care who the officers are mixed up with."

"And you never heard the name Cricket?"

"I told you. No."

"If he'd had a native girlfriend, would you have heard about it—would it have been the subject of gossip?"

"How many times do I have to tell you, I didn't hang out with them; I didn't hear gossip."

"Who would have heard it?"

"I don't know."

"Who was Marshall closest to?"

"I don't know—I kept my distance, I told you."

"You weren't close to him?"

"Not me. Shit! This is empty. Hon! Hon! Hon!"

His wife, whose name was Miriam and who seemed very sturdy beneath her docility, appeared in the doorway. "Yes?"

He waved the empty vodka bottle. "We got another one of these anywhere?"

She glanced my way disapprovingly, nodded to him, and went to fetch it.

I spread the blowups on the coffee table. "These were Marshall's private, personal photos from the war, the only ones he saved. Here you are, Dr. Woolff. If you weren't close to him, why do you think he saved your picture?"

"I'm not by myself, am I?" he said pugnaciously. "See? Look."

"Yahoo," I said.

"Right, Yahoo."

"You think that's why he saved the picture?"

"He didn't save it for me."

I pointed to another picture. "Isn't this Yahoo here?" I said.

"He's in back in that one, you can hardly see him."

"So you think Marshall and Yahoo were close?"

"He saved his picture, they must have been."

"You were with him when he died, weren't you?"

Without warning, he leaped from the chair. "Okay, okay, okay, I had another nickname. Dopey. Are you satisfied now? My other nickname was Dopey. Dopey." He collapsed back in the chair, passed his hand across his eyes, and sucked in breath after breath before continuing:

"Whenever somebody yelled, Doc, and I got there, there'd be pieces missing, legs usually—that was the mines; sometimes arms; sometimes arms and legs—that was the mortars. Insides on the outsides, there was a lot of that—let me tell you, in country people *really* wore their hearts on their sleeves. The casualties weren't clean. Never. Or they were so clean, you could spend an hour looking for the goddamn entry wound and never find it. I prayed I'd just find somebody who'd been hit with an ordinary bullet, and just stick a tampon in the hole. The only time that happened was if there was a sniper around, and most of them couldn't shoot straight.

"So I get there, and I do what I do, and somebody tries to clear a landing zone, and somebody calls in the Medevac, but it's hard to clear an LZ if you're under fire, and the Medevac won't come in if he can't land, and in the meantime, I got five guys in bits and pieces and no surgeon, not there, not Tokyo, not stateside, is going to put him back together—Humpty Dumpty is in Olympic-medal shape compared to this guy—and the guy is begging me to take him out." The tears were spilling through his fingers. "Dopey."

His wife, who was in the doorway with a bottle of vodka, sped to him and crouched at his side. Turning away from me, he put his arms around her and let his wet face fall desolately on her shoulder.

Miriam stared at me, making it clear she wanted me to leave, but I ignored her bitter signals. I didn't know if Woolff had anything for me, but I wasn't about to walk away from someone as primed to erupt as he was.

I opened the fresh bottle, poured us each a drink, and put his glass in his free hand. He glanced up, nodded gratefully, and gulped. I returned to the couch and waited till he pulled away from the safety of his wife's body. Then I found the photo with Yahoo in the background and slid it closer to him. "What was Yahoo's real name, do you remember?"

He thought for a moment. "Bailey, I think."

I pointed to another soldier in the picture. "What about him?" I looked at my key. "His nickname's Angel."

Woolff bent over the blowup and studied the face. "Right, the Medevac pilot—Angel, what's his name, Angel . . . Angel—he came from the sky, so they called him Angel—Angel . . . it was like that old movie—Amberson! Don Amberson."

I pointed to another soldier. "Him—Philly?"

Woolff peered at the image and shrugged. "Dead."

"What was his name?"

"Frederickson."

I pointed to the last image in that picture. "What about him—Red Dog?"

"Like the designer, Halston, but with a Y. Mark Hoylston sounds right," he said, and spelled it for me.

I turned the picture face down and showed him another. "What about him?—nickname Spearmint."

"Er, er . . . Poloski . . . Growloski . . . Sodoski . . . something from Eastern Europe. Lewis, I think."

"Him—Wanda?"

"Wanda? Oh, yeah, Wander! He was always walking off and getting lost. Stefani. He's dead, too."

"And this one?" I indicated a black soldier, standing almost hidden in the background. "N.P.?"

Woolff bent to look, stopped, touched the black face with his forefinger, and raised his suspicious eyes to mine. "Why are you asking about these guys?"

"I need to talk to everyone who was close to Matt Marshall."

After staring at the photo for a few seconds, he looked me hard in the eye and defiantly said, "He's dead."

"Who's dead?"

"N.P."

"N.P. is dead?"

"I just said so, didn't I? He's dead. Just like the others. Angel, Philly, Red Dog—who else did we look at?"

"Spearmint and Wanda."

"Right. They're dead, too. Dead." He snapped his fingers. "That's why Marshall kept the pictures—they're what do you say?—in memoriam. Why didn't I think of that?"

"You're not dead."

"I told you," he snarled, "he didn't save that picture for me!"

"What was N.P.'s name?"

"I don't remember!"

"Do you remember what the N.P. stands for?"

"No."

"You're sure all those guys are dead?"

"I'm sure—I was there, they're dead."

"Okay," I said, finding another picture. "What about . . . Shylock?"

"He's dead, too." He glanced at Miriam for help. "Don't make me resurrect all this shit."

"It'll only take another few minutes," I said, and tapped the photo. "What about—"

"Mr. Bruno," Miriam said, "he's had enough."

"It's only a few more pictures; let's do—"

"Don't make me resurrect all this shit!" he shouted. "Are you deaf?"

"Why don't we do three more photos, and I'll—"

But by then he was moving, spilling his vodka as he sprang from the chair and stumbled brokenly from the room, almost knocking down his frightened children, who had sneaked into the hallway to eavesdrop on their father's anguish.

CHAPTER 18

INSTEAD OF FLYING STRAIGHT to New York, I stopped in Washington, to visit the wall. It was the easiest way to find out whether Woolff had lied to me. He had.

Of the names Woolff and I had gone through, only those of Bailey, Frederickson, and Stefani were chiseled into the polished black granite. They'd died a few days apart, in the summer of 1971.

The others—Don (Angel) Amberson, Mark (Red Dog) Hoylston, and Lewis (Spearmint) Sodowski—had not been killed in Vietnam. Nor, I suspected, had the mysterious N.P.—the soldier whose ebony image silenced Woolff and whose true name he stubbornly refused to summon.

This was great news—lies in my business are always great news because they mean somebody is hiding something—and on the shuttle to New York I felt the lovely rush of the hunt as I plotted how I would track down Angel, Red Dog, Spearmint, and—most intriguingly—N.P.

But the hunt was going to have to wait. The shit, it turned out, had hit the fan.

Awaiting me were several messages from Wilson Laird, the first group requesting, the second group requiring my presence at a meeting at Dunlop, Tyler & Laird.

The morning after the night I landed, I was back in the conference room, and Schuyler was in full cry, his face scarlet, his voice screechy, his tubby little frame vibrating with righteous indignation: "I repeat, Mr. Bruno, a 'top-secret source' is not adequate. 'An employee of a clandestine agency of a Southeast Asian government' is not adequate. Who is this source? What is this agency? How did you find this source? How did you

105

communicate with this source? By letter? By telephone? In person? In what language? Did you use an interpreter to communicate with this Southeast Asian source? How did you verify this source's bona fides? Your unsubstantiated assertion that *you* find the information from this source reliable is not adequate. I repeat, not adequate. We're waiting for your responses, Mr. Bruno."

The configuration was a bit different from the last time. I was on one side of the huge table; Laird, Schuyler, and Wharton were on the other—the classic intimidators' lineup. My recorder was in the middle of the table. I shifted my gaze from Schuyler to Laird.

"Mr. Laird, there's nothing in our contract that obligates me to give you the kind of information Mr. Schuyler is demanding. How I find my sources and how I verify my sources is my business. In the event—"

"We have the absolute right—" Schuyler began.

"In the event that you need essential details for a litigation—for a litigation, not because some pompous asshole wants his curiosity satisfied—I supply those details in my final report."

"We have the absolute right to make our own judgment about your source's bona fides," Schuyler finished.

"Is that your position, Mr. Laird?" I asked.

Before he could answer, there was an insistent knock at the conference room door. As Wharton hopped up, the door swung open and a covey of Marshalls—Beth, Wendy, and Fred—marched into the room. Behind them, looking sheepish, was a flustered secretary, who hastily said, "I'm sorry, Mr. Laird, but Mrs. Marshall insisted."

For a second, nobody moved and nobody spoke. Finally, Laird smiled his glossy smile, rose to his feet, pulled a chair out for Beth, and said, "Don't worry about it, Gretchen. Thank you."

Gretchen left, Beth Marshall sat, and the children followed suit. Now, I had six opposite me. "Good morning, Mrs. Marshall," I said. "Ms. Marshall, Mr. Marshall . . ."

"Mr. Bruno," Beth Marshall said civilly. Wendy and Fred barely acknowledged me.

Laird had resumed his seat, and I looked at him: "Is there something I'm missing, Mr. Laird?"

"Do you mind the family being here, Mr. Bruno?" he said, with enough of a spin to let me know I'd better not mind.

"Not at all," I said, "but—"

"But?" Beth Marshall said, civility diminished.

"But maybe you could explain why they're here."

"It's obvious, isn't it?" Schuyler said.

"Not to me," I said. "Mrs. Marshall . . ."

"Yes, Mr. Bruno?"

"Can you tell me why you're here?"

"I understand that you are convinced that my husband told the truth in the codicil," she said, doing her best to retrieve all her southern politeness.

"Yes."

"In other words, that he had a Vietnamese lover and she bore him a child?"

"Yes."

"Can you tell me whether—"

I cut her off: "How do you understand that, Mrs. Marshall?"

"How?" she said.

"Yes. How?"

"The point, is not how," Laird interjected, "the point is that—"

"The point is, what we have here is—at the very least—an appearance of a conflict of interest," I said. "I'm not a trusts and estates lawyer, but even I can see that."

"Oh, I don't think so," Laird said affably.

"Mr. Laird," I said, "does that mean you unequivocally think that there is no conflict between the interests of each and all of the Marshalls and the interests of Matthew Marshall's estate?" Laird furrowed his brow to avoid responding. "Ms. Wharton," I said, "what do you think?"

"I'm the senior trust and estates attorney here!" Schuyler snapped petulantly.

"Fine. What do you think?"

Before Schuyler could tell us what he thought, Laird waved a nonchalant hand: "Under ordinary circumstances, you'd have a point, Mr. Bruno, but we're all friends here. There's no conflict, I assure you."

"Mr. Laird," I said, giving him my most trusting smile, "you've made me feel a lot better."

Ostentatiously, I pushed my recorder closer to him. "Mr. Laird, will you please confirm that you passed the contents of my interim report on to the Marshalls?"

"Why is this necessary?" Laird said.

"Will you confirm it, please?"

"Why is it necessary?" Schuyler echoed loudly.

Wharton angrily explained: "It's necessary because in the event of any litigation, Mr. Bruno wants the surrogate to know that *he* did not pass this information on to parties who were not his clients. As I mentioned to you, Mr. Schuyler."

Schuyler almost spit at her in rage: "Thank you, Ms. Wharton. That is enough. That is quite enough. You have duties elsewhere. Now!"

"I'd like Ms. Wharton to stay," I said.

Before Schuyler could display his choler again, Laird restrained him. "Tom, Ms. Wharton is Mr. Bruno's liaison to the firm; she belongs here." He turned to me and nodded contritely, like an alcoholic addressing an AA meeting.

"Mr. Bruno, I acknowledge that I passed the contents of your interim report on to Beth—Mrs. Marshall. I do acknowledge it. Now perhaps a literal-minded lawyer might see a conflict of interest in that; I don't. Nor do my partners. Nonetheless, if you sincerely believe that I overstepped my bounds by informing Beth of your report, I apologize. It was done purely in the spirit of openness and cooperation. And since all the Marshalls know we represent the estate, there's no question of nondisclosure. It's unthinkable that the surrogate would hold me—or the firm—blameworthy."

This was so patently said for the benefit of the recorder that Wharton—much to Schuyler's unabated fury—could hardly stifle her laughter.

"I accept that in the spirit in which it was offered," I said, almost matching Laird in hypocrisy. "I think, though, just to avoid any misunderstandings, I'll forgo interim reports and submit only a final report."

Laird pretended to think about it. "I accept that you might prefer that course, Mr. Bruno, but we've found your interim reports so valuable and timely that we'd sorely miss them. Why don't we give you our pledge that none of your reports will be shown to anyone other than Ms. Wharton, Mr. Schuyler, and myself? That should reassure you . . ."

"It should," I said, "but it doesn't." I shrugged apologetically. "Mark me down as a paranoid and humor me."

Schuyler couldn't contain himself any longer. "Wilson, I insist on making my views known." Laird took in Schuyler's contorted face and nodded eagerly, like a scoutmaster encouraging his favorite klutz to climb a jagged rockface.

Schuyler wasted no time: "It seems to me that Bruno is living up to his original promise of extortion. He declines to submit further interim reports, thus leaving us completely in the dark as to his methods and sources. Additionally, he has not mentioned the matter of billing. If he continues to bill us weekly, we will pay for time and expenses that we cannot monitor. If he bills us in one lump, with his final report, we are vulnerable even further to his inventions.

"May I suggest that our policy be this: We expect Bruno to submit detailed interim reports. We further expect him to identify any anonymous source whose credentials we wish to verify. We further expect him to properly document his expenses. An item such as—" He flipped pages, "—I quote, 'Special Research, N. Maldonado, eight hundred dollars,' is unacceptable." He glared at me. *"That* should be our policy."

Schuyler slapped my report down on the table and leaned back in his chair.

For a moment, nobody said anything. Then, Laird chuckled: "Oh, Tom, that's a bit stern. Mr. Bruno's not only very industrious—we all agree to that, even you—but there's not a hint of any fiddling with expenses. No, no, I think we just need to find a comfortable middle ground where we can all come out winners. Don't you agree, Mr. Bruno?"

"No."

"I beg your pardon?" Beth Marshall said, as though I'd just told her her underwear was dirty.

"No. There's no comfortable middle ground. If you want me to stay on the case, I won't submit any interim reports, and I'll continue to submit weekly bills."

"Then," Schuyler said, "I suggest we do not want you to stay on the case. Correct, Wilson . . . ?"

Laird glanced to Beth Marshall, but she was still staring at me.

"Beth . . . ?" Laird said.

I raised my palm to him and said: "Mr. Laird, I don't know what you're asking Mrs. Marshall, but I'm confident you're not asking her whether the estate should continue to employ me? Are you, Mr. Laird?"

Laird's eyes shot to the recorder. "Absolutely not. It never entered my mind. I was about to ask Mrs. Marshall if she wouldn't mind stepping outside—along with Wendy and Fred—while the executors discuss this. Beth . . ."

I had to hand it to her; she inhaled, nodded, smiled at everyone— including me—rose, and led her children toward the door. "Mrs. Marshall," I said, stopping her. She turned gracefully, as though somebody had called to her across a ballroom floor. "Before we got sidetracked, you were going to ask me another question about my report. Do you recall it?"

She thought for a second and nodded, but said nothing. I shut off the tape, "Off the record, Mrs. Marshall."

"You said that sometime after the fall of Saigon, my husband used back channels to inquire about the woman and her child—what back channels?"

"I don't know."

"How long after?"

"I don't know."

"If you know so little, why do you think the information is reliable?"

"Because of the source."

Caustically, Schuyler said, "The mythical employee of a clandestine agency of a Southeast Asian government."

She ignored him. "And you find the source reliable enough to believe that my husband was telling the truth?" As much as she tried to hide it, there was a plea in her voice, and the plea was for me to say, no, I don't.

"Yes, I do."

"Ahhhh," she said, and shut her eyes for longer than a blink would need. "Did the source tell you whether the woman and the child are still alive?"

"No. Otherwise it would have been in my report."

"Do you have an opinion on that, Mr. Bruno?"

"Mrs. Marshall," Schuyler interrupted, "we really—"

"I asked for Mr. Bruno's opinion, not yours," she said, so acidly that Schuyler actually shrank. "Do you?"

"No," I said.

"Thank you, Mr. Bruno." She nodded to the others and led her children out.

After Fred Marshall shut the door behind them, Laird said, "Do you have an opinion, Mr. Bruno?"

"No."

"Well, now," he said expansively, "how are we going to solve our little problem?"

"What problem?" I said.

"The problem of your conditions of employment," Laird replied easily. "We really need to come to terms."

"Of course," I said. "Before we do, may I ask you something?" Laird waved benevolently. "Did you pass the contents of this interim report on to any other of the beneficiaries in Marshall's original will?"

"What a question!" Laird said.

"Could you answer it, please?"

"Absolutely not," he said.

"You're certain?"

Laird's amiability slipped a bit. "I understand why you're pursuing the point, Mr. Bruno, but absolutely not."

"Thank you. Now, as to terms: I won't submit interim reports, and I'll continue to submit weekly bills."

"Mr. Bruno," Laird said, silencing the ever-ready-to-pop Schuyler, "I don't believe that's acceptable." He sighed deeply. "If you insist on those terms, Mr. Bruno, I fear we would have to consider making a change."

"Unquestionably!" Schuyler said.

"Mr. Laird, I want to stay on the case. I want to find this child," I said, and I meant it, badly.

"Yes, Mr. Bruno, but we have our requirements, too, and unless you meet them, we must make a change."

"Mr. Laird," I said, after giving him a chance to preen a little, "if you make a change, if you replace me, that gives me the freedom to work for another party."

"Which party?" Laird said sharply.

"Oh, there are so many possibilities," I said. "Which beneficiary wouldn't want to find this child and make a deal with it—Matthew junior? Ms. Twomey? Paul Marshall? Rachel? Not to mention Mrs. Marshall and Fred and Wendy . . ."

"Mr. Bruno, I can't bring myself to believe you would actually consider such a step."

Smiling ever so sweetly, I said, "Mr. Laird, I can't bring myself to believe you would consider replacing me . . ."

After the most distressing of silences, Laird allowed himself a crooked, rueful smile, and said, "Mr. Bruno, if it wouldn't be betraying any confidences, what do you expect to do next?"

"Interview soldiers who served with Marshall."

CHAPTER 19

". . . THEY'RE CLEARING THE SEMI from the overpass now, Lilly, but Edgemere to the tunnel is a better bet than Sixty-four. Across the river, the upper deck on-ramp of the bridge is backed up maybe twenty minutes. Use the lower. Local east-west avenues look pretty good, but if you're heading north, take Maple. This is Don Amberson in the KRLL traffic chopper. Here's Chris Kennedy with the latest weather."

Amberson banked the helicopter left and flew toward a knot of interchanges about ten miles distant. Before I could resume my questions, he waggled a finger at me and began fiddling with switches and dials.

We'd been in the air for nearly forty minutes, and for the last twenty, Amberson had managed to deflect my questions either by turning them on me or finding work to do. Since he'd greeted me at the landing pad on the pier and handed me a container of coffee and a muffin, his attitude had changed markedly, and I was retracing all the steps in our conversation to pinpoint the moment when it did.

At the start of the trip, we chatted about Woolff—Woolff was a great medic, he said, and it was a pity about the pickets, and he wished he'd stayed in touch; and about flying. The Angel had aged well: no puffiness in his face, all his hair—though the temples were gray—and the same taut, stocky frame as showed in the twenty-year-old photo. I mentioned that he seemed like a contented man. True enough, he said, but on some days, he confessed very man-to-man, on some days, in the midst of telling commuters which route to take home, he missed the Medevac missions. He missed descending into the action, the guns below and the guns on the ship; he missed the adrenaline pumping as he lifted his overloaded Huey up from a hot LZ and took it just above the trees; he even missed the sticky blood on the floor of the chopper as he carried his damaged men to safety. He missed *flying,* he said.

Which, of course, is what led me to him. Eventually.

The Pentagon won't give out any information about anybody—last known address, phone number, hometown, you name it—unless the person is on active duty, and neither Don Amberson nor Mark Hoylston nor Lewis Sodowski were on active duty. Nor were they members of the American Legion or the Veterans of Foreign Wars or the Vietnam Veterans of America.

So I turned to two data bases that between them have put me on the scent of people faster and more often than any other method of tracking. The most useful was an outfit called Information America. For a monthly fee, plus search charges, you could look for anyone you wanted. You typed in the name, and if Information America had the data—and they had it around a third of the time—they would tell you the prey's last known address, length of residence, phone number, property ownership, liens and court appearances, and God knows what else.

One by one, I typed in the names, last name, first name, and did a search. Nothing, nothing, and nothing.

Next, I tried National Demographics and Lifestyles, which is a service that keeps records of appliance warranty cards. If you buy a TV or a VCR or a CD player and send in the card, National will make a copy of it—and sell me your last-known address.

Here, I did better: Sodowski and Hoylston came up: Sodowski in Hagerstown, Pennsylvania, and Hoylston in Missoula, Montana. Pennsylvania information told me they had no phone listing for Sodowski at the address I gave them; Hoylston was listed in Missoula.

Following my usual pattern of saving the most likely for last, I started with Sodowski. The lack of a phone might have meant he'd moved, or, with luck, he didn't have a phone or hadn't paid his bill. I persuaded myself I felt lucky and began a paper chase to find him.

If Information America doesn't have what you want, the best way to do a paper chase is to start with the smallest unit—a town or village—and work outward, to county, then state. Because small towns don't keep many useful records—they lack the money for it—county is normally the first worthwhile stop. You call all the possible county sources and follow up with fax requests in case they're reluctant—usually they are—to give you information on the phone.

At the county level, you check:

Court records—civil, criminal, and probate; the register of deeds for home sales; the tax assessor for property tax payments; voter registration lists; commercial licenses for the owners of businesses; the Better Business Bureau for complaints against those owners; union locals for membership lists; utility companies for forwarding addresses, likewise the local post office; public libraries, private libraries, videotape stores; moving companies, car renters, truck renters; newspaper morgues for obituaries—or births; United Fund and other charities for contributors.

If you expand to the state level, there are even more sources, the most valuable of which are the motor vehicle department and the state licensing board. Whatever you want to do in this society—hunt, or fish, or massage, or marry, or sell hot dogs or dirty videos, you need a license to do it.

While I was waiting for all the agencies to respond about Sodowski, I tried Hoylston. I called at 6:30 in the evening, Montana time, which is the time to call if you're friendly; if you're not, you call at 6:30 in the morning. A woman answered cheerfully, "Hi, there."

"Hi," I said, "is Mr. Hoylston in?" I could hear her tense up—the "mister" probably had been a mistake.

"Are you collection people?" she said.

"No, no," I said. "This is Adam Bruno, I'm doing a book about a man Red Dog served with in Vietnam."

"Red Dog?" she said, wonderingly.

I tried for lightness. "That was his nickname over there. Do you call him Mark?"

"I call him sweetie," she said, then shouted, "Sweetie! Sweetie—he's just coming out of the shower. Shit, did they really call him Red Dog?"

"Yes, they did."

"Sweetie, there's a guy on the phone, he wants to talk to you about somebody in Vietnam."

In the background I heard a deep voice say, "Fuck him, the war's over," and she covered the phone. After a good minute, she came back on. "He doesn't really want to talk right now," she said uncomfortably.

"Could you tell him it's about Matt Marshall?" I said in my humblest tone. "Captain Marshall."

Again, she covered the phone, then: "He says, the war's over. Period. The war's over."

"Mrs. Hoylston—it is Mrs. Hoylston, isn't it?"

"Yeah, but everyone calls me Cindy."

"Cindy, I need him for thirty seconds, just to confirm a date; if he doesn't want to be thanked by name in the book, we can use his initials. Help me out, Cindy . . ."

She left the phone uncovered while she said, "Sweetie, he just wants to talk for thirty seconds."

I heard a small, sharp cry. Then, the deep voice:

"Listen, buddy, I don't give a shit about your book; I don't give a shit about Marshall; I don't give a shit about what happened; I don't give a shit about Vietnam—you got it? The war's over and I don't give a shit."

"Mr. Hoylston, if you'll just—"

But he loudly hung up on me. I waited ten minutes and called back. "Hi, there," Cindy said.

"Cindy," I said quickly, "it's Adam Bruno again. If your problem with the collection agency isn't too high, maybe I could ask my publisher to—"

Once more, I heard her small, sharp cry. Once more, the phone crashed down.

Lewis Sodowski came up in several different records, county and state, and they all pointed to the same conclusion: He had abandoned Hagerstown, Pennsylvania, in April 1993, leaving no forwarding address.

I was left with Amberson, which was to be left with nothing. To find somebody whose home address you don't have, whose county and state you don't have, whose social security number you don't have, whose occupation you don't have is the work of months. You always begin by trying to eliminate a negative, the person's death, so if Information America can't locate a death certificate, you do an obituary search.

There are around 1,600 daily newspapers in the United States and Lord knows how many weeklies and biweeklies, each of which prints obituaries; not of everyone, of course—the homeless don't get obituaries, unless they're hideously murdered; neither do convicts; neither do people too poor to afford undertakers, because undertakers are the ones who call in the obits to the newspapers. Moreover, to do an effective obituary search, you need a date of death—or a week, or a month, or a year. I had none of those, so even the most basic task was strewn with obstacles.

If I found an obituary for Amberson, he became, in the most literal way, a dead end. If I didn't, that proved only that he wasn't memorialized, not that he wasn't dead.

My head ached, badly. I turned off the desk light, swiveled away from my computer, leaned back, and closed my eyes, believing I'd merely take a break from thinking for awhile. Instead, I drifted off.

An hour later, I was trapped in a nightmare, fighting huge white-flecked green waves as a merchant seaman clung to my knees and dragged us into the depths of the Gulf of Mexico. The Coast Guard cutter I worked on shrank to the size of a child's toy boat; the guard rescue helicopter floating lazily above us sprouted fangs at the ends of its rotor blades, and its winking belly lights turned into eyes swollen with blood.

Sweating and scared, I jerked myself awake and forced myself to remember the actual rescue, not my dream of it.

We had saved all but three of the crewmen on the oil tanker; we had never found two of the three we'd lost—nobody had clutched my knees or anybody else's—and the third died on the helicopter, exposure or oil in his lungs, no one was sure. We had lost nobody from the cutter and nobody from the helicopter. It was a *good* rescue—we actually celebrated that night, except for the chopper pilot who blamed himself for the death of the third tanker crewmen, because the seaman had bought it on his ship.

The pilot—his name was Rick Liebling and he was an older guy who'd recently come over from flying fixed-wing in the Navy—got very drunk that night; it was his first fatal, and he was terrified the Coast Guard would ground him and he'd have to take a desk job; I mean, petrified.

"Thank you, Rick!" I shouted, and turned back to my desk and the present.

Flyers love flying and will do anything to keep at it. Some things you guess, and some things you know; I knew Angel Amberson was still flying a chopper somewhere, and there were only so many civilian chopper pilots in the United States: at charter flight services, large law-enforcement agencies, the Red Cross, and at radio stations that cover traffic.

I remembered the moment: Amberson and I had been in the air for about fifteen minutes, and I'd been asking questions similar to those I'd asked Woolff: "If Marshall had had a native girlfriend, would people have gossiped about it?"

"Maybe," Amberson said, "field officers didn't have gook regulars, so there could've been talk."

"Did you hear anything at all?"

"Not me—but, I wasn't in his unit."

"Did you ever hear the nickname Cricket?"

"Cricket? Uh uh."

"What about Ghost—an ARVN officer, maybe?"

"Ghost? Uh uh." After a thoughtful pause, he added, "Who was it said Captain Marshall had this gook girlfriend?"

"He did."

"Who—this Ghost?"

"No. Captain Marshall."

Sarcastically, he said, "From the grave?"

"He told us in his will."

"In his will?" Amberson said disbelievingly.

"Yes. In his will, Marshall says he fell in love with a Vietnamese woman he called Cricket."

"Weird," Amberson said, meaning, bullshit.

I let him brood on it, then asked, "Did Captain Marshall have a nickname?"

"I don't know," Amberson said. "If he did, I wouldn't have heard it."

"Your nickname was Angel, right?"

"Angel of the skies—nothing special, half the guys who flew Medevacs were Angel."

"And Hoylston was Red Dog?"

"Uhuh."

"And Woolff's was Doc?"

"All the medics were Doc."

"Stefani was Wanda?" I said.

"Yeah, but he's KIA—what's with the nicknames?"

"Marshall left some mementos, and I have to match the real names with the nicknames. Spearmint was Sodowski?"

"Uhuh."

I gambled that I'd blown enough smoke: "N.P. was Frederickson, right?"

"Uh uh, Philly was Frederickson—N.P. was Lincoln."

Chuckling, I said, "Abe?"

"Jake," he said.

"Now I'm mixed up. Is Lincoln from Philadelphia, or is Frederickson from Philadelphia?"

"Frederickson, but he's KIA. Lincoln's from Texas."

"Let me make sure I've got this right: Jake Lincoln's from Texas, and he was N.P.?"

"Right."

"What does it stand for?"

"No Prisoners," he said.

To round things out—and to avoid showing my hand—I said, "And Tim Cleary was Polio—is that right?"

A fractional pause. "You talked to Tim Cleary?"

"Couple of times."

"What'd he have to say?"

"Not much," I said, "you know Cleary."

"No," he said flatly, "I don't."

That was the moment.

.   .   .

We had reached the complicated interchange and were circling over it; Amberson scribbled notes on his pad.

"Is there something about Tim Cleary that got you so quiet?" I said.

He gestured for me to keep still, patched into the station, cleared his throat, received his cue, and said: "Hi, everyone, this is Don Amberson; I'm over the Mead Lake interchange, and if you're coming in from Route eleven, take the next exit—there's a school bus with a flat tire in the right lane. North on Four is backed up about two miles, but it's moving. Watch for the construction guys at the west exit on Flower—they show up early on sunny days. This is Don Amberson in Chopper KRLL; over to Chris for the weather."

He disconnected, smiled uneasily at me, reached under his seat, and drew out a two-inch .38, which he pointed at my mouth. "I want to see some ID." As I put my hand in my jacket, he said, "Slow."

Slow is what he asked for, slow is what he got. I took my driver's license from my wallet and passed it to him. He read it, then gestured with the .38 for more. One by one, I passed him every document in my wallet—auto registration, charge cards, insurance certificate, library cards, the works.

When he'd checked them all, he let them slide to the floor and said, "The feds are real good at doing fake ID—you got anything that tells me you're not a fed?"

"A fed?" I asked, completely confused.

"I think you're CID," he said.

"Why do you think that?"

"Nevermind why I think that!" he shouted. "You better show me you're not or you're going right outta here."

For a moment, no idea occurred to me; then, I meekly said, "Would you believe the captain's will?"

He hesitated, nodded, and watched vigilantly while I pulled my case near, opened it, drew out the codicil, and held it out to him. "Read it," he muttered impatiently.

I read him the opening paragraph: "In August 1971, while I was serving in Vietnam, though I was married at the time to Beth Moore, and had my oldest child with her, I fell in love with a Vietnamese native whom I called Cricket. Some months later, Cricket became pregnant. Before the birth of this child—which I have no doubt was mine—we were separated by the fortunes of war, and I never saw Cricket again."

He asked me to read it again; I did, and he said, "This isn't about anything else?"

"No."

"You got nothing to do with CID?"

"No."

After a few seconds, he permitted me to gather my documents from the floor and put them in my wallet while he put his .38 back under his seat.

"What was it about Cleary?" I finally said.

"He's a fucking scumbag."

"Why'd you get so quiet?"

"What did he tell you?"

"Not much," I said, "his mind's not in great shape."

"It never was," Amberson said.

For a few minutes, I let him fly in peace. "What would the CID want from you?"

"What did Cleary tell you?"

"Nothing useful—his brain's fried."

"You said you saw him a couple of times—he must have told you something."

"He told me Rule One."

"Rule One—what the hell is Rule One?"

"Hit her, stomp her, fuck her, blind her, gut her—Cleary's policy for Vietnamese women."

"I wasn't there!" he shouted. "I didn't shoot anybody. I didn't torch anything. I landed when it was all over. I can't testify to anything. I wasn't there."

CHAPTER 20

"YEAH, I WAS THERE," Jake Lincoln said very calmly, "and if you want to know about it, keep your mouth shut and let me tell it my own way at my own pace."

The Vietnam photo hadn't shown how big he was—six-three, 220 pounds—nor did it capture his force, or his anger. Jake Lincoln was a cop, a detective with fifteen years on the job, and I'd met cops like him before. They were the kind of cops who neither lost evidence nor faked it; who neither beat prisoners nor believed them. He was the kind of cop who made my life as a defense lawyer sheer torment, because on the stand his testimony stood up, and so did he. It was easy to understand why his fellow soldiers had named him No Prisoners.

We were in a roadside bar not far from my motel near the airport in Austin, Texas. My tape recorder was clipped onto my belt, and I had a tiny mike in the buttonhole of my jacket. Both of us were drinking club soda: I was working; he'd given up booze. Finding him had taken only a few hours of phone calls—Jake Lincoln was something of legend in Texas because he'd been one of the first black men hired as a cop in Dallas, one of the first to make sergeant, and the first to throw a white lieutenant down a flight of stairs for ordering Lincoln not to let a diabetic suspect take his insulin shot. Soon after that, Lincoln left Dallas and moved to Austin, which, by Texas standards, is a liberal city.

"Now the time we're talkin' about, nineteen seventy-one, anyone who's been in the field knows what's goin' on. This ain't sixty-six or sixty-seven, nineteen sixty-seven, when we believe the command. By now, we know they're full of shit; we know what the VC can do, and we know how the NVA can fight. And we know how ARVN can't fight.

"See, when we go into Vietnam, we just put on our white fuckin' hats and get in our white fuckin' planes and load our white fuckin' bombs and go in stompin'. 'Cause that's how white men fight wars. They don't bother learnin' anythin'—this country's like this, and that country's like that. Shit, no. All those yellow and brown and black countries are alike. They don't do like we tell 'em, us white men'll bomb the fuckers back to the Stone Age.

"Trouble is, man, it don't work if a country's in the middle of a civil war 'cause you never know *which* fuckers to bomb into the Stone Age. You bomb North Vietnam, you got the VC to deal with. You waste everybody you think is VC, there's nothin' left in the country but snakes and trees. You don't waste everybody, you gotta keep an army there till Jesse Helms sucks Jesse Jackson's black dick.

"See, you white men are so sure you all know God, you never learn nothin'. Maybe you ain't naturally dumb, maybe you got dumb 'cause till now it be so easy for you. Till now, you got all the money and all the guns, you don't got to be smart. You just wave a piece, or a piece of money, and you take what you want. No more, man. Now, you gotta be smart as well as white. You gotta know where you are.

"The Vietcong—and the NVA—they are smart, and they know where they are. Shit, man, it's their country—but nobody tell us that. They tell us the VC is the enemy, they ain't *real* Vietnamese. They might look like Vietnamese, they might talk like Vietnamese, they might eat like Vietnamese and shit like Vietnamese, but they ain't Vietnamese, they're the enemy. And we believe it. Which make us even dumber than white folk."

Lincoln drained his glass and signaled the bartender for two more. The place had begun to fill up, and the noise level had risen by a couple of decibels. We no longer had our end of the bar to ourselves—three good ol' boys, in plaid shirts and cowboy hats and boots, were knocking back shots and beers. Lincoln went on: "Matt Marshall is ROTC, not regular army, not West Point. RA lieutenants, most of 'em, do one tour, six months, because that's enough to get their tickets punched.

"Matt Marshall do three tours. Now most guys do three tours, they be one of four things: guys who love the action; guys who love Vietnam; guys who love America; and guys who love rank. Marshall ain't any of those.

"By the time I meet him, on his third tour, he's a real good officer. Now, a real good officer is a complicated thing. 'Cause, the better he is, the more his men hate him—not hate him the way they hate a dangerous shithead, or hate him the way they hate an RA motherfucker, who just want to prove he can take your stripe, but hate him 'cause to keep 'em alive he gotta keep 'em sharp. And if you in the field for awhile, you don't want some cracker lieutenant makin' you work, harassin' the shit outta you to keep you sharp so you stay alive. You *know* how to stay alive. You think.

"Now the same time they hate him, they depend on him; the firin' starts, they say, 'What we do, sir?' It's not like the fuckin' movies, where the grunts take over. Grunts don't take over less the commander—*and* the NCOs—be out of it. Now the commander's gotta stay very cool; he's gotta be here . . . ," Lincoln held his left palm three inches from his left temple, ". . . and there." He held his right palm the same distance from his right temple. "Here, but there, you follow me? He get too close, he can't make no decision without somebody gettin' killed. He get too far, he stop watchin' out for his people. Matt Marshall, he keep just the right perfect distance. Here, and there." He moved his palms back and forth to indicate Marshall's sense of balance.

"See, man, Matt Marshall is very, very sharp. I mean, that motherfucker can hear *thinkin'*. He take care of his people, 'cause he pay attention. He knows who's worth a shit and who isn't. For a long, long time, our casualty numbers are down here—and not because we are not in it. But because we got a CO who pay attention."

From the jukebox came Marvin Gaye's "What's Goin' On?" and Lincoln stopped talking to hum a few bars. One of the good ol' boys next to us glanced at Lincoln and smiled slyly at his companions. Lincoln returned from the music.

"When I first meet Matt Marshall, it ain't easy for me. He's officer, I'm NCO; he's college, I scuffle through high school. I don't wanna be in recon, I wanna be in intelligence, but when I go in, which is sixty-eight, intelligence isn't for us. Top of everythin', Matt Marshall is one hundred percent white North Carolina, and I got as much use for that as I got for AIDS. So, him and me—"

"Did you say you got AIDS?" One of the good ol' boys asked in a loud, cutting tone. From behind their long-neck beers, his two buddies watched in spiteful anticipation.

Lincoln turned his whole trunk very slowly. "Sorry, my man, I missed that. One more time . . ."

"I said, did you say you got AIDS?" the good ol' boy repeated, winking at his buddies.

"You sure you're talkin' to me, man?" Lincoln said, his voice filled with incredulity.

"Yeah, I'm sure," the good ol' boy said. "I'm talkin' to you, the nigger—beg pardon, the African-American—with AIDS. Are you deaf?"

"No, I hear you," Lincoln said.

He smiled sorrowfully and started to turn back toward me. But before he completed the movement, he spun hard the other way and hit the good ol' boy just under the heart with a pointed-knuckle blow so hard it made me wince. And as the good ol' boy clutched his chest, Lincoln rose and smashed the edge of his other hand into his throat. Instantly, Lincoln slipped behind him, twisted his arm into a cruel hammerlock, and put the good ol' boy's head down on the bar. He did all this so swiftly and so discreetly that only the good ol' boy's buddies and I caught it. Not even the bartender noticed.

The buddies started to move, but Lincoln pulled his shield from his pocket and slapped it on the bar where they could see it. "You," he said to the closest one, "reach into his pocket and put his wallet up here. Now." Nervously, the buddy pulled a wallet from the good ol' boy's hip pocket and placed it on the bar.

By then, the bartender had seen the head on the bar and the badge, and drifted over. "I need a pad and a pen," Lincoln said to him, "and a teaspoon."

"A teaspoon?" the bartender asked.

"A teaspoon," Lincoln repeated. When the bartender brought everything, Lincoln slid the wallet, the pad, and the pen toward me. "Detective Bruno, copy this man's name, address, and license number for us, will you?" I opened the wallet, found a driver's license, and began copying.

"See," Lincoln said to the bartender, "I don't want to take this man in if I don't got to, but he sure look like the murderer in that wanted poster, don't he, Detective Bruno?"

"On the money," I said.

"Now, it's dark in here and I might be makin' a mistake, so we're gonna check out his ID," Lincoln said.

"He's a regular," the bartender said warily.

Lincoln smiled. "So are lots of murderers." He looked at me questioningly, and I passed him the pad. "Give his wallet to his pal." I did. "Put it back in his pocket." The pal did. Lincoln squinted at the pad and read: "Leach, Theodore—" He looked at the bartender. "You know this man as Leach, Theodore?"

"Ted Leach, right," the bartender said. "Ted."

Lincoln leaned close to Leach's head. "Ted, can you hear me? Grunt, if can hear me . . ." Leach, who was still gasping for breath, managed a feeble grunt. "Great. Ted, I got your address here: I know where you live, I know where you drink. You hear me, Ted? You hear what it is I'm tellin' you?"

He leaned even closer, so his lips almost brushed Leach's ear: "Now, Ted, you used a bad, bad word before. You know what word I'm talkin' about? Grunt if you do." No grunt. "You don't? Shit, man. Detective Bruno, hand me that spoon." I passed him the teaspoon, and he brought it close to Leach's left eye.

"Ted, when I was in country, intelligence used to let me watch 'em work, just in case one day I got good enough to join 'em. Now, they take a teaspoon like this, they stick it in hot water—you want it sterile—and they bring it right up here to the corner of one of Charlie's eyes. Right here.

"And then they pop that motherfucker right out of its socket—but not out of Charlie's head. The idea, Ted, is to let that eye hang there by a membrane. 'Cause it hurt, I mean, *pain,* Ted, and on top of that, Charlie can see it with his good eye. I swear to you, Ted, those intelligence guys don't get that handle for nothin'."

Leach's visible eye was doing a mad dance, and a forlorn whimper came from deep in his body. His sweat reeked of fear, and any minute I expected him to wet himself; I took a step back.

"Ted," Lincoln said almost tenderly, "do you know what bad word I'm talkin' about? Grunt if you do." He touched the corner of Leach's eye with the edge of the teaspoon, and Leach grunted. "Great. Now you tell me—in a sentence with the bad word in it—you tell me you'll never say that bad word aloud again. Come on, come on . . ."

Leach muttered something unintelligible. "I didn't get that, did you, Detective Bruno?" Lincoln said.

"Not me."

"Give it another shot, Ted. Suck in some air, and give it another shot."

Faintly, and quakingly, Leach said, "I'll never say nigger aloud again."

"All right!" Lincoln said, and, grinning happily, slapped his palm on the bar. "All right!" He pulled Leach upright and slid a stool under him. "You want a fresh drink, Ted?" Leach shook his head vehemently. "You're sure, Ted—I mean, we're all cool here now." Again, Leach shook his head. "Maybe you're right, it's gettin' late." Lincoln glanced at the pad. "You got a pretty fair drive, Ted, maybe you better call it a night—you don't wanna get nailed for DWI . . ."

Leach shook his head, grabbed his money from the bar, and, followed by his pals, hastened out. "Ted!" Lincoln called, stopping them in their tracks. He tapped the pad with his forefinger. "Safe home."

After they'd gone, he ordered fresh sodas and, without any fumbling, resumed.

"Like I said, when I first meet Matt Marshall, it ain't easy for me. But it gets easier, 'cause he's not a fuckin' menace. Normally, it don't pay to be anyplace near an officer in a fight, 'cause he'll get you killed. For sure. Marshall don't. Not for a long fuckin' time. Then, our luck run out. It happens, man. You're in the field; if there's VC or NVA around—and those fuckers are always around—your luck is gonna run out. We walk into a bad ambush—that was a Friday, I think—and we lose five. Saturday, some shithead calls wrong coordinates, and we lose two to friendly mortars. Sunday, a gook kid around seven rolls a grenade into a latrine hootch—that's two more. Monday, we get a break, we go into a hamlet that's been cleaned, no VC."

He sucked in air between his teeth. "Mines, booby traps, finger charges, then, VC and NVA regulars come pourin' outta the trees like goddamn rats.

"The Cobras can't do shit 'cause the fightin' is too tight, most of the Medevacs won't come in 'cause the LZ is so hot, and the ones that will come in can't get off the ground 'cause they can't hover—it's humid in Vietnam, you can't hover with a normal load, and these guys are shit scared to overload. But we make 'em overload 'cause otherwise they're leavin' people to die. Man, we are in the fuckin' toilet, and Charlie is pullin' the chain."

"Did Angel come in?"

Lincoln laughed. "You tell Angel, your landing zone is in Hell its own self, he come in. He come in, and take off eight hundred pounds over, and everybody go home. Fuckin' Angel."

"Was that when Yahoo got it?"

"Right: black Monday, man. We lose nine dead; Christ knows how many wounded. We got body parts all over the place, and the poor corpsmen are goin' crazy tryin' to match this foot with that leg, and this arm with that shoulder. We got chest wounds, we got gut wounds—that was Yahoo—we got head wounds—those are the guys so fucked up they get to spend the rest of their lives bein' doorstops—we got about a dozen of those. Man, it be as bad as bad can get." He paused to press hard on his eyelids with his thick fingers.

"So, Thursday maybe—I think it was Thursday—we go into another village. We see a couple of dogs, we see a buffalo; we see a little kid takin' a shit over a log; Cleary is on point and Cleary is good, he's a real Apache in the field, and Cleary signal sniper! Sniper in hootch three."

He sat up straight, as though he were giving evidence in a trial.

"I can't remember how many hootches were in that village—Marshall put down some number in his report—but we start with hootch three and we do every one of 'em. We light 'em, or we fire phosphorous into 'em, or we toss regular grenades into 'em or we sixty 'em. When the gooks come out, we report contact, we fault our radios—you gotta fault your radio if you're gonna really hammer—and we shoot. Some we line up, but that's a pain in the ass, so we just shoot. Rock 'n' roll.

"Contest: Who can cut somebody in half fastest with a sixteen? With a sixty? With a quad? Contest: Who can slice two gook ears quickest? Who can scalp a *mama-san* with his wrong hand? Who can chop off a gook's dick and stick it in the gook's mouth while he's still alive—without him makin' any noise? Contest: Who needs the lowest number of whacks with a machete to take off a baby's head?"

He stopped to gulp some soda; he wouldn't look at me. "Was Marshall there?" I said.

"Sure, he's there."

"Did he join in?" I said.

"Uh uh. But he don't stop it, neither. Not right away." He saw my expression. "He lose a lot of people, and the ones he don't lose need payback. If he stop it, they don't never take orders from him again."

"You said . . . not right away?"

"You ever kill anybody?"

"No."

"Killin' is . . ." He paused to choose the precise words. "A certain kinda killin', in the field, with a enemy you hate, that kinda killin', on the right day, gets very hot—you know what I'm tellin' you—sex hot? You're mad enough, you hate enough, you shoot somebody, you cut somebody, you beat somebody, you do it over and over, blood is hot: You get a hard-on. A lotta guys get hard-ons, and the girls who aren't dead—maybe even some girls who are dead—they fuck. They kick 'em down and fuck 'em right there. Fuck 'em right on top of a buncha corpses. Then, after they're done—"

"Stomp her, fuck her, blind her, gut her," I said.

"You talked to Cleary, huh?" he said. "Right: stomp her, fuck her, blind her, gut her." He drummed his knuckle harshly on the bar. "You got kids?"

"No."

"I got a boy in high school and a girl at the University of Texas. Nineteen. Smart. One day, she's gonna be the first black woman governor." He looked at me directly. "She wasn't born till after the war, so I was too dumb to understand. Marshall, he understand. He see Cleary and this E-four, Starger, kickin' these two gook girls—they look maybe thirteen, but gooks always look young—kickin' them in the cunt, and the Captain, he say, 'Fun's done, Sergeant, put a stop to it.' And we did."

"Just like that?"

"Cleary kick his girl a couple times for luck, Starger say to me, 'Fuck you, nigger,' slash his girl's tit, and reach for his prick. I shoot him in both knees.

"Doc fix him up, he fix the girls up, we call in a Medevac, and Angel take 'em all to the field hospital. We report one unit casualty—that's Starger; two allied civilians wounded—that's the girls; and seventy-one VC adults killed—we don't count the kids. All in a day's work."

"And that was the end of it?"

"See no evil, hear no evil."

I waited a moment. "Were you close to Marshall?"

For a few seconds he worried his upper lip with the tips of his teeth. "Close enough," he said, looking away too casually. "For an NCO."

"Did he talk to you about personal stuff?"

"Here and there."

"Did he have a girlfriend?"

He laughed. "Does a dog have fleas?"

"A local, I mean?"

In amazement, he said, "A gook?"

"Yes."

"Not a chance."

From my pocket, I drew the first page of the codicil and began reading: "In August 1971, while I was serving in Vietnam—"

He stretched out his hand, and I passed the page to him and offered him my penlight. He refused it, tilted the page toward the neon beer sign above the cash register, and read, tracing the words with his finger. When he was done, he passed it back to me. "I never heard of Cricket."

"And you think you would have heard—I mean, about her or any other Vietnamese woman?"

"I would've heard."

"Even if he worked to keep it quiet?"

He started to answer, stopped, and considered. "If she's in Dalat, or Nha Trang, or Saigon, he can keep it quiet. Not if she's anyplace near the base."

"Would anyone else have heard?"

"If I don't, nobody do."

"Can I show you some pictures?" I said. He wasn't pleased, so for form's sake, I added, "If you like, we can do it tomorrow."

Curtly, he shook his head; I drew a batch of blowups from my case, and we went through them, starting with the civilian photos. He recognized nobody, he said. Briskly, he identified everyone in the combat photos, giving me real names to go with the nicknames.

"Is there anyone here who was close to him?"

"Me."

"Who else?"

He riffled through the combat shots and paused at a picture of a nurse—the pretty nurse with the pageboy hairdo, the woman who Matt junior had believed was crazy about somebody on the shooting side of the camera. "Her, maybe," Lincoln said dismissively. "Lieutenant McGowan."

"And she was close to Marshall?" I said.

"They fucked. Sometimes that's close."

"Do you know where she's from?"

"Uh uh."

"Where'd they meet?"

"Field hospital."

Sometimes what's too good to be true is true.

With my fingers crossed and my hope rising, I asked, "Didn't you say Angel took Starger and the two girls to a field hospital?"

"Uhuh."

"The same field hospital where McGowan worked?"

He was about to toss off an answer, but he caught himself. "Got it," he said. "You think one of those gook girls is Cricket."

"It's possible, isn't it?"

"It's a stretch, man."

"Did he go over there regularly?"

"Sure," he said, "if one of our people is hurt, he go there. Or he go to see McGowan."

"So he could have met the girl there?"

"He don't go in gook wards."

Debating him, I said, "His men have torched their village, slaughtered their families; he feels guilty; he stops in to see if the girls are okay. Next time he's there, he stops in again. And again. One of the girls—let's call her Cricket—turns him on, and when she gets better and leaves the hospital, they start something. Is it possible?"

Lincoln laughed. "Till this moment right here, I thought you had brains: Man, this is a white cracker captain who can do any fuckin' woman in Vietnam—why does he want to start something with a gook?"

"I don't know. But can he? Can he get something going with her and keep it secret? Is it possible?"

"Not if it's around the base."

"Can he keep it secret if it isn't around the base?"

"What does he want with her?" he demanded angrily.

"I don't know," I said. "Love. Can he?"

"Love? In 'Nam?! The only love in 'Nam is in a fire zone between the *men!*"

"Can he—is it possible?"

"Oh, sure!" he said scornfully. "The gook is lyin' in her bed, and Captain Marshall is whisperin' Cricket, Cricket and ticklin' her little twat—and Lieutenant Eve McGowan is pluggin' in the IV and changin' the dressin'. Now, man, that sounds real cool."

CHAPTER 21

"HE CALLED HER CHAU Chau," Eve McGowan said, with as much expression as an information operator. "It's as close as their language gets to cricket—I think *chau chau* actually means grasshopper. But who knows? Every word in Vietnamese has about a hundred meanings—it's a slippery language." She smiled, but only with her mouth. "A slippery language for a slippery people." Her intercom chimed softly. "Yes?"

"Pediatrics wants to talk about your revisions of their budget," said a disembodied woman's voice. "Is tomorrow at eight okay?"

McGowan scanned a calendar on her desk. "Seven forty-five. And Marge, remind him that this isn't a souk, it's a hospital; I'm not interested in haggling with him." She clicked off and looked at me, waiting for my next question.

Eve McGowan was perhaps fifteen pounds heavier than she'd been in Vietnam, and she was still pretty, but whatever had shone in her eyes in her photograph—youth, or daring, or infatuation, or love—didn't shine in them that day. She was all business, from her tailored gray wool suit to her filled-in Month-at-a-Glance calendar to the long trestle table piled neatly with budget estimates of her many departments. The only homey touch was a mason jar filled with M&M chocolate candies that rested on the visitor's side of her desk.

Her official title was deputy administrator of operations, but it wasn't hard to figure out that she ran the hospital. The nominal head man was a world-famous retired heart surgeon who'd been hired for his celebrity value: His main job was to appear on the evening news to explain to concerned TV reporters that doctors were saints, not businessmen.

Eve McGowan had been at the hospital—Liberty Memorial, outside Atlanta—for six years. Before that she'd been an administrator in Denver, and before that a nurses' supervisor in Phoenix, and before that a trauma chief in Portland, where she'd been born and gone to school and—after the war—gotten married. That's how I'd traced her, via a marriage-license data base: Eve Rebecca McGowan, to Jonathan Marcus Hartman, September 9, 1977, Portland. Framed color pictures of Hartman and their two teenaged boys stood on a bookshelf behind her desk, facing visitors rather than her.

"Did you ever hear her real name?" I asked.

She laughed. "Real name? Probably it was Nguyen—over there, Nguyen's as common as Smith; or maybe Binh, or Minh, or Canh, or Nhat, or Ghon. That's assuming she gave a real name, which is unlikely—she was VC, and they never gave us real names. But I wouldn't have known, anyway—I didn't draw duty on the native ward very often—everybody knew I was a menace in there."

"A menace?" I said.

She glanced at my tape recorder, then shrugged indifferently. "I hated them. All of them. As far as I was concerned, they were all shits. ARVN were shits because they could be counted on to run away from a fight, and the others were shits because they were VC and were killing and crippling my guys. The supervisors and the doctors knew that if they put me in there, I'd do nothing for them unless somebody forced me to. I'd let their dressings putrefy, I'd let their wounds suppurate, I'd let their IVs run dry, I'd give them sugar water instead of morphine. I'd do everything short of killing them, and if I'd had the courage I'd have done that."

Her intercom chimed. "Yes?"

"Dr. Weissman wants to stop by to discuss reinstating Dr. Ruskin's privileges."

"Tell Weissman that if we reinstate Ruskin we'll lose our insurance. Diplomatically." She clicked off. "Ruskin's a butcher. Slash and hack." She grimaced: "We had a lot of Ruskins in country. 'They're only enlisted men, for chrissake,' they'd say. 'You expect invisible mending for enlisted men? Captain or above for invisible mending.' " She laughed conspiratorially. "I learned: 'He's a major, Doctor, maybe a colonel.' We got away with it because officers in the field always hid their rank—otherwise the snipers would get them. And the enlisted men hated wearing their dog tags. Either they thought it was bad luck—if you're okay, you can *tell* people who you are, you don't need dog tags—or they made too much noise, jangle, jangle, jangle, so they put them in their boots. 'Course, since a lot of the injuries were lower-body amps, they didn't *have* any boots—or feet. It wasn't hard to promote them to major on the spot: invisible mending.

"We had one surgeon, Neuberger, I think his name was, Abraham Neuberger, Jewish liberal from Great Neck, Long Island; he was the only one we didn't have to lie to about rank. He did everybody right. He even did Commie POWs if the orderlies didn't waste 'em first. He did not care: You were hurt, he fixed you. I think he was some kind of Commie himself—he went back after his tour—after the Americans were out of there; late seventy-three maybe. Him, and two nurses. They joined the Mennonites, or the Quakers, one of those. Stupid bleeding-heart bullshit! We lost fifty-eight thousand for them, we didn't need to go back and fix them up!" She stopped, retreating behind her administrator's facade. "I'm ranting. Sorry. I haven't talked about it in a long time."

I gave her a moment, then cautiously asked, "Since you didn't go in the native ward very often, how do you know he called her Chau Chau?"

"He told me. Matt was very unusual—he knew when not to lie. He was the only guy over there who always told women he was married. Always. 'I'm married to a girl I met in college, and we have a son, and I expect to go back to her. If that's a problem for you, let's stop right now.' That's what he told everyone. It was like a politician's stump speech." She laughed with genuine gaiety. "And, naturally, we all believed we were the exception; we would take him away from Beth." She glanced at the photos of her husband and sons. "We were all wrong." She was silent for a few seconds.

"One night, we were having a drink, and he asked me if I'd heard what went down. Well, of course I'd heard, everyone had heard—it's hard to keep a massacre secret. Especially when Tim Cleary is going around telling whoever'll listen that Captain Marshall stopped him from gutting his little gook." Again, she glanced at the photos of her family.

"He said, 'I feel responsible for them,' but he meant her, Cricket, Chau Chau. 'And right now, they're using up all my emotions.' That's what he said—'they're using up all my emotions.' How do you compete with that? Here's an officer whose troops have just wiped out a hamlet, and his heart is going out to the survivors—what can you say to him? Anything you say makes you a monster. *Anything*." She chuckled.

"As a manipulator, Matt Marshall was in a class by himself. I mean, I believed him—I actually believed he was telling the truth. He wasn't interested in *her,* he was taking care of the poor little orphan survivors. They were using up all his emotions. Dumb. Chau Chau!" She looked away from me. "We never made love after that night."

"Did he ever tell you anything more?"

"No."

"How do you know he took up with her?"

"Tim Cleary."

"Cleary told you?" I said, unprepared.

"He came in one day to con a doctor into giving him a circumcision—a lot of them did it; it was good for two weeks off, and the doctors went along. I knew he and Matt were close so I stopped in to see him once in a while, and he told me. 'Captain's learning gook,' he said. 'Gets the kids to help him so if he makes a mistake they won't laugh. Got a gook gash.' I knew right away. 'Chau Chau? Cricket?' I asked him. 'You got it,' he said. 'Some kinda bug.' "

"And you believed him?"

"Cleary was crazy, not stupid."

"Did you talk to Marshall about it?"

She answered passionately: "I was twenty-two years old. He was a married man, with a child. What was I supposed to say—I know you're going back to your wife, but how dare you stop sleeping with me, a first lieutenant in the United States Army, and start sleeping with a Vietnamese orphan named Cricket?!!"

She slammed her fist into her palm so sharply it sounded like a gunshot, and the echo hung in the charged air between us. Rancor flooded her eyes, and the blood drained from her lips. She touched the intercom button.

"Yes, Ms. Hartman," Marge's voice said.

"No calls," she said, leaned back, and inhaled deeply half a dozen times. Then: "I'm sorry. I didn't realize I remembered so much."

"Did anyone else say anything about it to you—apart from Cleary, I mean?"

"No."

"No gossip at all?"

"Not a word—and I would have heard it. I *did* have an interest."

"Who else would have known?" I asked.

She thought. "Maybe Doc Woolff—she wasn't completely okay when she left here—I mean, when she left the hospital, and she would have needed some attention."

"Did Cleary tell you she got pregnant?"

"No," she said, so softly I barely heard her.

"Did you ever hear from anyone she got pregnant?"

"No," she said more emphatically, pointing at a copy of the codicil in my lap. "You brought me that piece of news." She dipped her head mockingly. "Thanks."

"Do you believe it?"

After a silence, she said, "I don't want to." More deliberately: "Everything in me doesn't want to. Everything." She smiled very gently, and for a moment she became Lieutenant Eve McGowan, twenty-two years old, and crazy about the man on the other side of the camera. "But I do."

As I opened my case to take out both sets of blowups, I recalled my standard question: "Did he have a nickname?"

She swallowed, then said, "Not that I ever heard—not a regular one."

"Did you have a nickname for him?"

She blushed. "Why does it matter?"

Gesturing to the computer console to the side of her desk, I said, "I'm trying to find the private password that'll get me into his files."

Shyly, she waved at the Mason jar. "M and M."

I put the blowups in two piles in front of her. She glanced down at the top combat-era picture, but couldn't give it her attention. After a pause, she said:

"Did you ever meet somebody who you believed understood you? I mean, *really* understood you. Understood you so you never had to explain anything—you just had to say it, to *tell* it, whatever it was, makes no nevermind how awkward, or ugly, or painful, or stupid, or even evil, if you just told it, the person would immediately get why you were thinking what you were thinking and feeling what you were feeling? Would *get* it. Did you ever meet somebody like that?"

I didn't need to think. "No."

"Did you ever meet anybody who touched you so intimately you believed your bodies weren't separate? Did you ever meet somebody like that?"

"I'm not sure. Maybe."

"Did you ever spend a night with somebody and just before you fell asleep say to yourself, There's nothing more than this, I don't care if I die now? Did you?"

"No."

"Well, I have, all of it. I *have*." She glanced at the family photos. "I love Jonathan, and I really love my boys, I swear I do, but I don't believe a day's passed in twenty-four years when I haven't daydreamed about Matt Marshall."

"Did you ever get in touch with him?" I asked.

She gave me a pitying look, the kind you bestow on someone you believe is beyond help. "No."

She lowered her eyes and briskly went through the combat-era blowups. She knew nobody whose name I didn't already have. She switched to the other stack, the mystery pictures, and stopped at a shot of several tropically suited men having drinks in a rooftop restaurant.

"I can't tell whether I know anybody here, or I just recognize the place—it's that bar in Saigon where all the big shots went. A two-star took me for drinks there once. He thought he'd get lucky." She rested her forefinger on the image of a man with a rakishly tilted straw hat. "This guy looks familiar, but maybe it's the hat."

I referred to my nickname key. "B.H.," I said.

"B.H.? Doesn't ring a bell," she said, and continued with the rest of the photos. She stopped at a picture of a jolly-looking plump man in a White Sox cap, seated at the controls of a cargo plane. "Isn't this Terry Quinn?"

I checked the key. "Terry; right. Who is he?"

"He ran that charter airline—what was it? World, or Universal, or Global, or Trans-National—I don't remember. He flew anything or anybody anywhere." As I was listing the possible names of Quinn's airlines, she added, "Didn't he get killed taking kids out of Sarajevo, in ninety-three? I thought I heard that." She went through the rest of the photos and then skimmed both batches one last time. "Terry's the only one I recognize in these," she said.

"Can you think of anybody else Marshall might have been close to over there?"

She smiled wryly. "Me." She looked up at the ceiling in mock prayer. "Cricket." She turned up her palms in a theatrical shrug. "That's it."

"What about at home? Did he talk about anybody—a special friend, a confidant?"

"Uh uh," she said.

"Beth . . . ?"

"I wouldn't know—we didn't discuss her."

"You can't think of anyone?"

She shut her eyes to reflect. "He wrote a lot to his brother and sister—especially the sister. I don't remember her name."

"Rachel."

"Rachel? That doesn't sound right."

"Rachel Marshall, now Rachel Marshall Pollock."

"Rachel . . . Rachel . . ." She frowned. "It was something else. A middle name maybe. No, no, it was something else, something strange. Rachel . . . Rocket . . . Rooster . . . Wrench . . . Roach! Roach—that was it." Suddenly, she laughed. "You think Matt had a thing about bugs? Cricket . . . Roach . . . ?"

CHAPTER 22

WHY MATT MARSHALL CALLED his sister Roach I had no idea, but I'm sure if I'd asked her she'd have told me—she was that kind of person. Whatever you asked Rachel Marshall Pollock, either she would answer truthfully or she would laughingly apologize and explain that if she answered that particular question, it would hurt somebody she didn't feel like hurting, and so she couldn't. With anyone else, I'd have dismissed the excuse for the bullshit it normally was, but I found it just about impossible to disbelieve Rachel Marshall Pollock, and I'm sure I wasn't alone.

She was in her early fifties, and had lived a busy life: When she was eighteen, she'd fled North Carolina for San Francisco, where she worked as a cashier for a music promoter named Bill Graham, who was most famous for operating a place called the Fillmore. Then, she'd taken a degree in anthropology and run what used to be called a home for wayward girls, basically a hostel where unmarried mothers lived with their babies. Some of the wayward girls formed a band, called the Neo Natals, and Rachel managed that for a couple of years. Next, she got involved with a food program for old people, persuading restaurants to deliver their leftovers to shut-ins and persuading the Bank of America to pay for it. Along the way, she married a man named Aaron Pollock, who'd performed in the sixties with a radical outfit called the San Francisco Mime Troupe and then had become, like his father, a pediatrician.

Rachel had lines on her face, but they were benign—true laugh lines. I got the feeling that she found the world a fascinating, complicated place, a territory to explore and enjoy, rather than confront or fear. That evening, as she and her brother Paul and I sat in the living room of her comfortable hillside house, she was enjoying the world even more than usual: Her youngest daughter, Abigail (there were two others, and a son) had not only gotten married that morning, but was about three weeks away from giving birth.

Rachel and I had met on the phone the day before. After leaving McGowan, I'd picked up my things at the motel and gone to the airport. While I waited for my flight home—it was delayed ninety minutes—I called San Francisco, and a breathless Rachel Marshall Pollock got on the phone:

"That idiot Wilson Laird said you might call," were her opening words. "Doesn't he remind you of Jesse Helms? Or that other one—what's he called?—he's named for an English building parcel—Trent Lott. Imagine growing up with that, his mama yelling, Trent, oh Trent! Or, in school—Lott, oh, Lott! And his poor spouse. Think of it: Lott's wife. We all know what happened to her. Dum dah dum dum." She was laughing by then, and so was I.

When I recovered, I asked her whether Laird had told her what I wanted.

"Oh, sure," she said, "in his smarmy, indirect way. He said Matt had himself a byblow over in Vietnam and decided to leave it half his money." She laughed wholeheartedly. "Beth must be passing blood instead of urine."

"When would be a good time to talk you?"

"After the wedding," she said.

"Wedding?" I said, sounding a bit backward.

"Abigail, my youngest. She's *so* gorgeous. You won't believe it. How did I do it? I don't know. I did, though. Gorgeous!"

"Congratulations," I said. "So, when . . . ?"

"Don't come 'round before two-thirty or so—the ceremony is just for family. Do you have the address?"

I explained that I was in Atlanta.

"Ah," she said understandingly, "so you'll need directions from San Francisco Airport. Got a pencil?"

"A pencil?" I repeated stupidly.

"Mr. Bruno—wait, what's your first name?" she said with sisterly patience.

"Adam."

"I love that name—I lost my virginity to an Adam! You want to talk to me, get on a plane and come talk to me. Atlanta is some kind of hub—you'll get a flight real easy. Paul is here, too. You can talk to Paul. See? A doubleheader. You can dance with my Abigail. What more do you want, Adam? What's your problem? Don't you like weddings?"

"It's been a while," I said with a shade more of an edge than I intended.

"I hear gloom and doom. Leave the gloom and doom in Atlanta, Adam. This is my daughter's wedding, not yours." She paused, then said straight-forwardly: "It breaks my heart my baby brother won't be here."

At the reception, she didn't act heartbroken—just the opposite. So, naturally, the party went spectacularly well. The food was good, and plentiful; the champagne flowed unstoppably; the band honored all re-quests and knew to the measure when to change tempos; the cake stuck to the roof of everyone's mouth; the toasts were traditionally ribald and corny; and Rachel and her husband, Aaron, made sure I didn't feel left out. Like everyone else, I had a great time, so great a time that when the bride and groom took their leave, and Abigail offered her flushed, moist face to be kissed, I didn't hesitate for a second, and I kissed her as though I were a legitimate guest, a true friend of her mother's. It was a wedding out of a romantic comedy, including the indulgent parents, the gleeful relatives, and the bride with the mountainous belly and the prepartum glow.

"I'll tell you, Adam," Rachel said, her eyes dancing, "when Matt called to say he was going to marry this girl he'd met at school, this Beth Moore, Paul and I were *sure* she had a bun in the oven. Weren't we, honey?"

"You were sure," said her brother indulgently.

"All right, I was sure. Adam, top us up, honey."

By then, all the guests had gone, and the three of us—Rachel, Paul, and myself—were sprawled around the living room. Paul had removed his jacket and tie, Rachel had removed her shoes. We'd graduated from champagne to coffee laced with Irish, and I was relieved my recorder was doing my work for me. I added coffee and Irish to each of our cups and waited for Rachel to continue.

"Of course I was sure—it's not as if we didn't know what Matt was like: That boy was wicked, truly wicked." She made wickedness sound like the last, best virtue. "He didn't want to get married, he wanted to deflower every coed at Chapel Hill, and from what we heard, he was well on his way to doing just that. So, when he called to say he was going to get *married,* I naturally assumed—Paul, tell poor Adam the truth—didn't you assume it, too?—that the wedding would be incomplete without Father Moore standing behind the happy couple with a double-barreled twelve-gauge in his respectable bourgeois paw." She shook her head in recol-lected puzzlement. "We were wrong."

"You were wrong," Paul said without animosity.

"Oh, you are getting to be such a hypocrite, Paul Marshall. Are you seriously saying to me you weren't surprised that Matt married that girl?" He hesitated, and she pounced. "Ahah! You see, Adam, you see?"

"Not because I thought she was pregnant. I was surprised because I didn't think she was his type."

"His type! What type?! Every type is his type. You are reprehensible, Paul. You are such a snake. Now that I think of it, you always were a snake. Adam, let me apologize for my brother, the snake." She glared at Paul accusingly. "I remember you at the wedding, I remember you very well, and I remember that whenever you were anywhere in Beth Moore's vicinity, you found some excuse to touch her belly. Didn't you? Tell the truth, snake!"

"Only because you asked me to," he said innocently.

"Ohohoh!" Rachel cried operatically. "Ohohoh! Adam, quickly—a measure!" She pointed to the Irish, and I refilled her cup. "Paul, I have nothing more to say to you."

"Promise?" he said.

"No, I do not promise," she said, and abruptly left her chair, went to a cabinet filled with videotapes, searched, found what she was looking for, loaded it in the VCR, and switched on the TV monitor. As she returned to her seat, she leaned over me and murmured, "I need him here."

After a few seconds of pebbly leader, an image appeared of Abigail, looking a bit younger, and without her belly. She stood between two director's chairs under a sign that read DEPT. OF COMMUNICATIONS. Into the frame strode a tall, attractive, middle-aged man—the kind of man who had he been an actor would have been a star. He bowed slightly, smiled slightly, and sat in one of the chairs. Abigail nervously attached a microphone to his lapel. Then, she attached a mike to her sweater, sat in the other chair, cleared her throat, and said, "Welcome to another edition of 'On Campus.' I'm your host Abigail Marshall Pollock. My guest today is Matthew Marshall, founder and chief executive officer of Tel-Mat, and we're going to talk about interactive media." She hesitated and smiled awkwardly but endearingly.

"In the cause of full disclosure, I have to warn our audience that this interview may be a bit tougher on the guest than usual. That's because I have a conflict of interest: Mr. Marshall also happens to be my uncle Matt."

During the next fifteen minutes or so, as niece interviewed uncle, I studied the screen. I had no idea what other footage of Matt Marshall was available—quite a bit, probably, because these days big-time electronics executives appear on the tube regularly—but I was certain this was the only footage in which Matt Marshall talked to somebody who loved him. And Abigail loved him—that was obvious from every gesture and every look.

After a while, I got a sense of why.

Matt Marshall had the gift, or discipline, of truly paying attention. Twomey had mentioned it, and so had Lincoln, and there it was, on the screen in front of me. Though he must have heard Abigail's questions dozens of times before, and though she was merely a student—and his niece—he listened to her and answered her as carefully and as intelligently as he might have listened to and answered the Grand Inquisitor himself. Effortlessly—or, at least invisibly—he created an atmosphere in which she felt grown up, smart, and unique. It was the kind of performance that made you want to write him a letter—not to congratulate him but to invite him to dinner or a weekend.

At the close of the interview, after Abigail said, "Thank you for coming, Mr. Marshall," he replied, "Thank you for having me, Ms. Pollock." Then he topped himself: Once she'd undone her microphone and stood in front of him to undo his, he rose, smiled dazzlingly enough to melt ice, enfolded her in his arms, looked in her eyes, and said:

"Sweetheart, I knew you would turn out okay, but this is ridiculous!" Ceremoniously but tenderly, he kissed each cheek and led her from the set.

An instant later, the screen went gray; a click signaled the end of the tape. Rachel rose and shut off the TV. When she turned back to us, I half-expected her to have tears in her eyes, but she was merry as ever. She sat down, drained her cup, refilled it, and, as though there'd been no interruption to watch the tape, said, "To tell you the truth, I don't know why he married Beth."

Without missing a beat, Paul said, "She's beautiful, she's smart, she's gracious, she's sexy, she's—"

"Sexy?" Rachel interjected. "Beth isn't sexy."

"In a refined sort of way, she is," Paul said. "Like Grace Kelly."

She snorted in derision. "Kitty is like Grace Kelly, not Beth."

"Kitty?" I said.

"You danced with her twice, Adam," Rachel said. "The strawberry blond with the green eyes. Paul's wife." She made the traditional school-room sign at me for a faux pas—stroking one forefinger with the other—and said, "Adam, do you find Beth sexy?"

"It's hard to say," I answered, truthfully. "I might, if we'd met under different circumstances."

"All right: Try and imagine her twenty-five years ago. You have the

choice of any woman on campus, would you pick her? And not just to
screw her, but to marry her?"

"That's meaningless," I said. "I'm not Matt Marshall."

"Thank you," Paul said.

"Oh, don't rub it in," Rachel said. "I don't like her, it's true. I think
she lives for display—tasteful display, elegant display, but still display. Her
clothes, her furniture, her children, her husband, they're all part of her
interior decoration. She has no soul."

"You're not being fair," Paul said.

"I know I'm not being fair," Rachel said, "but she did everything in
her power to keep him from us, and he's dead and she isn't, and that drives
me completely, utterly crazy!"

"Is that true?" I said to Paul. "Did she do everything in her power to
keep him from you?"

"He asked me!" Paul said to Rachel before she could leap in. "The
Moores were in real estate. Not in a terribly big way, but they were
prosperous. Close to rich. The Marshalls, on the other hand, were—"

"Nothing," Rachel said with perverted pride.

"Near enough," Paul agreed. "Papa had a gas station that made no
money, and he drank what he made; Rachel went to work during high
school; I went into the Air Force. When Matt met Beth, he was just a
poor, bright kid getting through college via ROTC."

Rachel cackled. "All he had were looks, brains, and charm. Otherwise,
he was a total loser."

Paul continued: "Yes, but from the Moores' perspective, he was no
kind of catch. None at all."

"How come they accepted him?" I asked.

"Beth gave them no choice," Paul said. "From what I gather, she told
her family they could learn to live with Matt or learn to live without her."

"I thought she had no soul," I said.

"That's Rachel's notion, not mine," Paul said, with a touch of asperity.
He stopped to sort out his thoughts. "I think she wanted to keep him away
from us—"

"You see!" Rachel cried.

"But I think—to what degree and for how long I can't be sure—Matt
collaborated in that . . ."

I expected Rachel to explode, but instead she simply watched her
brother closely and waited for him to elaborate.

"I think there was a part of him—a minuscule part, if you like—but a
part of him that enjoyed the display as much as she did. He *liked* getting
all dressed up and going to a fancy benefit. He *liked* receiving awards from

hospitals and museums, and watching investment bankers grovel outside his office. He *liked* having the beautiful belle of a wife and the three photographable children. We grew up very poor, and it's hard to resist that stuff when it comes along." He gestured widely to take in the house. "For any of us."

"Okay," Rachel said flatly. "Let's say that's true. Let's say he didn't want to hang out with poor white trash. But I haven't been that for years, and neither have you. There's more, and she's the more."

She addressed me: "I won't pretend that I'm not half the problem. I'm not easy; I've got a real big mouth. But she knows how we feel about Matt—I'm his big sister, Paul's his big brother. This is Paul and me."

She hooked her thumbs together. "And here's Matt." She curled her palms around her hooked thumbs. "I think she hated that—not because she was jealous of us exactly—but because she never had that with him."

"You don't know that," Paul said.

"Okay, I don't know that," Rachel said witheringly. "Matt's connection with Beth was so wondrous, so meaningful, so deep, that Adam is searching for a child Matt had with a Vietnamese woman he only knew for a few months. Get a life!"

Since the opening was there, I took it: "Do you believe it—that he fathered a child over there with a Vietnamese girl?"

"For sure!" Rachel said.

"I don't know," Paul said.

"Did he ever mention it to you, either of you?" I said, finding a notebook.

They shook their heads simultaneously.

"Did he ever mention a person he called Cricket?"

"Cricket? No," Rachel said.

"What about Chau Chau?"

"Chau Chau?" Paul said, wonderingly.

"It's Vietnamese for Cricket," I said.

Once more, they shook their heads.

"Did he ever mention any women over there?"

"He wouldn't have done that," Paul said.

"No," Rachel assented. "Not unless he was going to leave Beth."

"He never mentioned Eve McGowan?"

They looked at one another, and again shook their heads simultaneously.

"What about Ghost, or Ma?—that's Vietnamese for Ghost."

"No," Rachel said.

"Can you think of anyone else your brother was really close to in those days—anyone he might have confided in? Take a minute to think about it."

Finally, and tentatively, Paul said, "Beth."

"Yes, Beth," Rachel said. She smiled. "Not that I think he would have confided in her about—what's her name?"

"Cricket. Chau Chau," Paul said.

"No," Rachel said. "Or about—who's the other one, Eve some-thing . . . ?"

"McGowan," Paul completed.

"What about later on?" I said. "What about recently? Did he ever mention anybody he talked to? Did he ever toss out a name so you got a sense that whoever it was was a regular in his life? Somebody he really trusted?"

A shimmer of regret passed slowly across Rachel's face before she said, "Matt was an open, gregarious man who liked to keep parts of himself secret from everyone—from Mama and Papa, from Paul and me, from Beth, from everyone. I mean *really* secret. So secret it would take torture to make him expose it." She smiled wanly. "Torture or trust."

She recovered her spirits. "My guess is he talked to Bitch One and Bitch Two. Matt always trusted dogs a whole lot more than he trusted people."

"Did he keep a journal or a diary?"

Once more they looked at each other. "You mean during the war?" Paul said.

"Anytime," I said.

"I don't think so," Paul said.

"If he did," Rachel said, with a needling snicker, "he'd have kept it secret."

Hiding my disappointment, I said, "If I could just run this by you once more. In his letters to you, he never mentioned: Cricket, Chau Chau, Eve McGowan, Ma, or Ghost?" To each name, they shook their heads no. "Did he ever write about a . . . skirmish—a bloody skirmish—in which his men rescued two Vietnamese girls and took them to a hospital?"

Uncertainly, Paul said, "I don't remember his describing battles, really. Not to me." He smiled in memory. "Even then, Matt was very clever about writing to his reader's interest. I was in college, studying literature and anthropology, so he wrote about the country—how beautiful it was, and its culture, and the effects of air raids on rice paddies." He glanced at Rachel, waiting.

"His boys, and what it was like to command them," Rachel said. "How people died. How they were wounded. He asked me once how I'd like to be informed if he got killed. He wanted a model letter."

"You never told me that," Paul said sharply.

It was her turn to smile in memory. "He didn't want me to tell you. He figured you'd be upset that he asked me instead of you."

"He's right, I'm upset. Bastard."

"He didn't describe a skirmish in which two native girls were rescued?" I said.

"It doesn't sound familiar," she said. "It's not the kind of thing I'd disremember. Do you want me to look?"

Involuntarily, I sat up ramrod straight. "You mean, you still have his letters?" I said.

"For sure," Rachel said, and Paul nodded yes.

After a breath, I said, "Could you send me copies?"

They glanced at each other. "Why not?" Paul said, and Rachel nodded in accord. Then, she added, "Do you need copies of all of them?—some are just, you know, hello-how-are-you-I'm-okay-bye . . ."

"It's as easy to copy all of them as to try and pick out what's useful," I said. "About how many are there?"

Paul counted mentally. "Maybe fifty, sixty, then just a handful."

Rachel said, "Figure one every ten days or so, for three years, and then, oh, a dozen."

Their phrasing mystified me. "I don't follow you—when is 'then' as compared to some other time?"

"Then is later," Rachel said, as though she assumed I knew what she was talking about. "When he went back."

"Went back?" I said, the liquor miraculously vanishing from my system.

"In nineteen seventy-four," Rachel said.

"May," Paul said.

"April," Rachel said.

Forcing my voice to stay even, I asked, "April nineteen seventy-four, and why did he go back?"

"To work for a contractor," Paul said offhandedly. "Who was it?—AT and T, or ITT, or General Telecom, or Federal Electric, somebody wiring up the country."

"How long did he stay?"

Paul looked at Rachel. "Ten months . . . ?"

"More like a year," she said.

To cover my excitement, I licked my thumb, turned to a clean page in my notebook, printed DATE and said, "When exactly did he come home?"

"Right near the end—when was that, Roach?" Paul said. "I'm rotten with dates," he said to me.

"The fall of Saigon was April thirtieth, nineteen seventy-five," I said, mentally thanking Nicole Maldonado.

"That sounds about right," Paul said. Rachel nodded in agreement.

I looked from one to the other and said, "Is there anything in his letters from April nineteen seventy-four to April nineteen seventy-five about a girl he called Cricket?"

"No," they said in unison.

"Chau Chau?"

They shook their heads.

"About a child—an infant?"

"No," they said.

"Ma or Ghost?"

"No," they repeated.

An idea darted into my head, and I hurriedly skimmed my McGowan notes. "Did he ever mention a Terry Quinn?"

"Terry Quinn . . . ?" Paul said in ignorance. "No."

"Doesn't ring a bell," Rachel said.

"Quinn operated a charter airline," I said.

Once more, they shook their heads.

When I was done scribbling like a lunatic—"contractor," "airline," "TQ," "year," "Fall Saigon," "Beth"—and looked up, I found Rachel staring at me. Her face was pink with expectation.

"You think he went back to look for them, don't you, Adam? I take that back. You know!"

"Not yet," I said.

"Really," she said, glancing at my notebook. "How come your handwriting went all squiggly? Does it go squiggly when you get excited?"

"Jet lag," I said. "Can you copy his letters and send them to me as soon as possible?"

"That's where I'd look, too," she said, pleased.

CHAPTER 23

THREE DAYS LATER, OVERNIGHT packages arrived from Rachel in San Francisco and Paul in Charlotte. After turning on the answering machine and making a pot of coffee, I sat down and immersed myself in Matt Marshall's letters to his brother and sister.

After a short time in Vietnam, he wrote to Paul about the land:

> . . . It is a much more complicated country than I had any idea. It has lowlands, and mountains and valleys, and a huge delta, and endless forests, and the most beautiful beaches. It also has the weirdest combination of architectures you could imagine. There are buildings that go back centuries, and then there are these sort of wedding-cake French Empire mansions and government edifices . . .
>
> . . . To confirm your guess, the reason Vietnamese is written in the Roman alphabet rather than ideographs is because of the French. Do you think once we're here a while, they will learn to become illiterate?

At first, he saw the people from a typically Western perspective:

> . . . All I can say is that they're very Oriental: They bow and scrape and eat very strange shit, and never tell white people (they call us "round eyes") the truth. Somebody told me their families are very large, but it turns out they count everybody as part of the family. Every grandfather and grandmother, every aunt, every uncle, every goddamn cousin to the 50th goddamn degree. If a Vietnamese comes

up to you and says, Is it okay if my cousin stays with me in the tent? be prepared—if you're soft enough to say yes—to bid welcome to a huge, smelly crowd.

Later, he got more observant:

> . . . I couldn't figure out for the longest time how the enemy could ever mount a campaign—they're Vietnamese, too, and the Vietnamese I know are about as interested in fighting and rebelling as is the average lizard in the sun—but your point about home is on the money. It's true: We always believed our local Negroes were too dumb and lazy and shiftless to ever fight. The trouble is—if you're a round eye—you don't pay much attention to what the natives are up to.

To Rachel, he wrote less about the Vietnamese and more about his own men:

> . . . I'm not sure it's a question of brains so much as drive. I have a lot of white kids from the Carolinas (and the rest of the Confederate 12), and at least two of them are very smart. But from what I know about them, they were encouraged to do only what their daddies did (or go to war) and forget about the world "out there."
>
> Most of my Negro boys don't trust me at all—I'm the white man who gives orders. Far as they're concerned, I might just as well be wearing a bedsheet and carrying a burning cross. Luckily, I have a very good Negro sergeant named Lincoln (there must be a million Negroes named for Abraham Lincoln, and another million named for George Washington and Thomas Jefferson—does that mean Negroes are our best patriots? Only kidding), and he seems to trust me.
>
> The trouble with war is it really screws up what you think is important. The same people you would never share a meal with, or work next to, or introduce to your sister (hah hah), the same people you might cross the street to avoid (see what four years of college does?) are the people who might save your life. Or take it. Bizarre.

Marshall's request to Rachel for advice on a condolence letter—which came about four months into his first tour—was striking in its rejection of sentimentality:

> . . . The dilemma, Roach, is this: On the one hand, I don't want to hurt the feelings of any kin; on the other, I don't want to give

them any overblown ideas about what kind of soldier their son, or husband, was, or that he died in some splendid, noble way. I realize this might sound kind of heartless, but I don't want to give the kin the impression that a death on the battlefield is heroic just because it happens there. It isn't: A lot of guys die—maybe most—because they're stupid or careless or chicken. And I don't want to send the same letter about *those* guys that I do about guys who really were heroic. Maybe I need two form letters—one for soldiers who are getting a posthumous decoration and one for those who aren't. What do you think?

P.S. If relatives write asking for details of a guy's death, what's the best way to finesse that? If I were blown into chopped chuck, how much would you want to know? Do you think that maybe needs *another* form letter?

Nowhere in his letters did Matt Marshall mention Cricket or Eve McGowan, or any other woman—except for this:

. . . No, Roach, it's nothing like the movies, where the wise old CO advises his young troopers on the dangers of falling in love thousands of miles from home. The young troopers don't come to the CO with their romantic troubles—unless they want a transfer because some hard-used local girl has gotten pregnant with their child. The biggest problem for enlisted men is that all American women are off-limits. The nurses are officers and can get in legal trouble for sleeping with enlisted men (not that they do—they confine themselves to colonels or upward). And the Red Cross girls and the USO girls seem to have their own crazy code, and it doesn't extend past warrant officers (chopper pilots, mostly).

This means enlisted men are restricted either to very poor rural women or whores, overt or covert; or, of course, rape. Generally speaking, everybody behaves badly all the time—the girls, their families, their pimps, the soldiers. The less I have to do with it, the happier I am.

Nor did Marshall write explicitly to his brother or sister about the massacre. The only allusions I found were in two letters to Rachel in July 1971.

. . . You keep clinging to this "Six o'Clock News" version of war (it's actually a Hollywood version), and I wish you would just let it go—it has nothing to do with the way we live here. On the ground, there's no such animal as war. There's only maiming and killing, which is not the same thing. War happens in the White House, or Congress, or the Pentagon, or maybe in the cockpit of a B-52, or on the deck of a battleship. But here, on the ground, people shoot at us, and we shoot at them. They blow us up, we blow them up. Very simple. It doesn't sound much different than what I read about World War I, except for the newness of the weapons.

We shoot, they shoot. We usually shoot better, because we have better guns (not to mention bombers and fighters and choppers and napalm), and they die, because they are very good at dying. In the "Six o'Clock News" version, if we kill a lot of them, we win. But on the ground, when we kill a lot of them, we don't win because they keep coming back—they are very good at coming back. And when they come back, they do it very, very stealthily, and then they kill a lot of us very meanly. (They are just as good at killing as they are at dying.) This makes my troopers very, very angry and makes them go kill more of them. Lots more of them. Lots. That is the way we live here—we are not in the war business, we are in the maiming and killing business. Sometimes we enjoy it.

Second:

. . . It's hazardous to form deep attachments, especially to people you have responsibility for. I don't really remember most of the men I've lost, and I'm glad I don't. Right now, there are only a couple of men who matter to me in the way I think you mean. Doc Woolff, who's one of our medics and has managed to stay a human being (don't ask me how); and a corporal named Tim Cleary, who I'm not sure was human to begin with.

Doc is real good at what he does and acts completely unafraid. He tells everyone he's terrified, but to get to a wounded soldier he'll place himself right in the middle of fire. Believe it or not, there are plenty of troopers who can't stand him—plenty of Medevac pilots and nurses and doctors, too—because Doc puts Vietnamese on our choppers. He even does that with POWs and suspected VCs, and *everyone* hates him for that (me included). The one who hates him most is Tim Cleary. I think Cleary might be crazy, I mean medically crazy: He's killed more people than anyone in the company. He loves killing, the more cruel, the more he loves it—but I'm willing to bet he's saved as many lives as Doc. He's a perfect soldier. His only emotion is loyalty to his buddies. And to me.

Matt Marshall's second set of letters—those he wrote in 1974 and 1975, when he went back—told me even less than the combat group. In none of the letters did he mention a woman, or a child, or a search. Nor did he mention Ma or Terry Quinn. The letters read like messages from a dismal summer camp:

. . . The country, as you can imagine, has changed for the worse. Nowadays, Saigon resembles the lowest kind of boom town, filled with hustlers and sharks from everywhere, and there are God knows how many refugees camped on the edge of the city. Everyone believes the government is crooked from top to bottom, the ARVN is impotent, and if there's a crisis, the Americans can be counted on to let the country down.

We (people who work for contractors) are detested by just about the whole world. Easy to understand, really, because most people who come over here for work are misfits of some kind or other, and they act like it. They pick fights, they steal, they rape (present legendary seducer excepted, natch), and they're immune from any punishment.

Matt Marshall's last letter from Vietnam was dated April 16, 1975, two weeks before the fall of Saigon, and at first it appeared as unrevealing as the rest:

. . . I don't know what the press in the U.S. is telling you, but the city is teetering on hysteria. The fall of Da Nang terrified everyone, and people suspect the same thing is going to happen here—panic, panic, panic. Most of the American civilians I know have left, and the last holdouts are making arrangements to get out. All the military people and the USAID people and CIA people are getting their relatives out, and some of them are working like crazy to save their Vietnamese workers. This can be a very lucrative racket, I've learned. Two families came to me yesterday and offered me several bars of gold to find a place for them on a flight out.

Then came this passage:

I've already bought my places, via three different flights. Every day, I visit all my contacts and sweeten the bribes to make certain I won't lose the seats.

Why "places"? Why "seats"?
Matt Marshall was only one passenger. Was it a slip of the pen? Was he confused about his grammar?
What came next didn't clarify matters any:

The way things look now, Roach, the NVA won't surround the city till late May or early June, so I've got a month before I have to get out. See you the Fourth of July!

Emptying my mind, I reread all three passages. Where I wound up was here: The city was teetering on hysteria, the North Vietnamese army was at the gates. And Matt Marshall, who had a loving wife and baby son in North Carolina, was hanging around Saigon and buying places on flights out. Places, plural.

CHAPTER 24

RACHEL HAD IT RIGHT: I knew. I just didn't have any evidence for what I knew.

In April 1974, Matt Marshall went back to Vietnam, and stayed a year, until the fall of Saigon. His ostensible purpose was to work for a contractor, and nothing in his letters to his brother and sister contradicted that. (I found it impossible to believe that his purpose was that simple, but I had no evidence.)

His references to buying places, plural, on flights out could be interpreted as sloppiness. His decision to stay till the last moment could be attributed to his love of risk—he was, after all, a combat veteran who'd won several medals. (I was sure he'd bought more than one seat and equally sure he stayed in Saigon because he hadn't found Cricket and his child, but I had no evidence. Despite the photo of Terry Quinn on his wall, I had no evidence he'd flown out with Quinn.)

Equally significant, at the time Matt Marshall made his last trip to Vietnam—staying a year—he was already married to Beth Marshall, and they had a son.

Beth Marshall had not mentioned this last trip. Perhaps she had forgotten about it, or perhaps her reason for not mentioning it was perfectly guileless. (I could not conceive of Beth Marshall withholding a piece of information like that guilelessly, but I had no evidence.)

Three possible lines of inquiry: contractors (of 1974 to '75); airlines (of 1974 to '75); and Beth Marshall.

The third line was superficially the easiest, but I didn't dial. I wasn't even tempted.

If I asked Beth Marshall why she hadn't mentioned her husband's return to Vietnam, she would lie to me. That I was sure of. It would be a plausible lie, delivered candidly and charmingly in her seductive musical voice, but it would be a lie. More, if I asked her, she would find out that I knew she'd kept the trip secret, and I didn't want her to find that out. Not yet. Not until I had evidence of the trip.

After spending a day entering all my notes in the computer and making diskette copies to take home, I began tracing Vietnam-era airline operators and contractors.

By 1974, when Marshall returned, there were only a handful of civilian airlines flying to and in South Vietnam: Pan Am, Air Vietnam, World, Air America, which the CIA ran, and Global, Terry Quinn's outfit.

Pan Am was gone, and nobody I found who used to work there could tell me whether the line had kept any passenger rosters during the war, let alone if they were stored anywhere. Air Vietnam had been taken over by the North Vietnamese. Somebody thought World had been swallowed up by another charter, but there were no records of it. Air America had split and resplit like an amoeba. Everybody I talked to either at any of its progeny or at the CIA itself refused even to admit it had flown in Vietnam. Some even refused to concede that there was such a place.

Global was also gone, Chapter Seven bankruptcy—which meant liquidation—in 1981. No successor company. If Terry Quinn had started another airline, I couldn't find a record of it, or of him. If Terry Quinn was still alive (I found no death certificate) and in the United States, he'd gone underground. Eve McGowan had said he'd died taking refugees out of Sarajevo, so I called the State Department.

Five people put me on hold, two people hung up on me, three people instructed me to send a letter. Two warned that the letter needed the signature of a relative, one suggested I file a request under the Freedom of Information Act, and one concluded that I'd do better at the United Nations, since Bosnia had been a UN matter.

As I was searching through my reference books for a UN phone directory, Wilson Laird called.

After telling me how very, very glad he was to hear my voice, he asked me if I'd changed my mind about submitting interim reports. No, I said, I hadn't. What a pity, he said; he did so enjoy reading them. Was there anything I wanted him to know, he asked. No, I said, there wasn't. Was I satisfied with my progress, he asked; as much as could be expected. Was there any way he could be of assistance, he asked. I was about to say no, when I had an idea:

"Senator, while you were in public office—" I almost heard him inflate, "—did you have any dealings with people at the UN?"

"All the time," he said magisterially. "The president knew his weaknesses—and my strengths. Why do you ask, Mr. Bruno?"

Beseechingly, I said, "I need your help, Senator."

"Of course, Mr. Bruno, of course. Tell me what I can do for you."

"Well, Senator, without compromising my source, I can inform you that I've learned of the existence of a Red Cross volunteer who was totally knowledgeable about Mr. Marshall's situation in Vietnam. I've also learned that this volunteer saw some service in Saravejo during the nineteen ninety-three airlift. Now, who can I talk to at the UN about Sarajevo so I can find this volunteer for you?"

"Hang on a moment, Mr. Bruno, I want to check my Rolodex," he said, and put me on hold long enough for me to draft a letter to the State Department. When he came back, he said, "Mr. Bruno, I've just gotten off the phone with a Mr. Karel Rasic—you'll be hearing from him momentarily. In case you don't, his number is 555-9970."

"Thank you, Senator."

"Anything for our mutual cause, Mr. Bruno." He paused. "You may need to use your powers of persuasion."

An hour later, when I hadn't heard anything, I dialed the number, and after two rings, a flexible baritone with a mild Yugoslav accent said, "Karel Rasic."

"Mr. Rasic," I said, "my name is Adam Bruno. Wilson Laird said that you might be able to help me with a matter . . ."

After a brief silence, Rasic said, "I'm sorry, Mr. Bruno, but Mr. Laird encouraged you prematurely. I cannot help you."

"Are you sure, Mr. Rasic—maybe he didn't explain the matter clearly? Why don't I—"

"Forgive me for interrupting you, Mr. Bruno, but Mr. Laird explained the matter quite clearly. You are looking for a Red Cross volunteer who served in Sarajevo during the airlift, not so? But that is not the point. The point . . ." he hesitated fractionally to find the proper diplomatic phrase, "the point is that I am not in a position to help you. Which I told Mr. Laird. My deepest regrets." And he hung up.

I gave him enough time to light a cigarette or pour a cup of coffee and called back:

"Karel Rasic."

"Mr. Rasic," I said, "Adam Bruno. Sorry to bother you again, but can you not help me because Mr. Laird asked you to, or can you not help me, period?"

"Whichever satisfies you better, Mr. Bruno," he said facetiously. "Good-bye."

This time, I didn't wait as long, and when he picked up his tone was chillier:

"Karel Rasic."

"Mr. Rasic, if I told you that I don't like or trust Wilson Laird, either, would you consider helping me?"

"No, I would assume that you are saying that merely to manipulate me."

"If I told you I lied to Wilson Laird about what I wanted, would you consider helping me?"

"Are you saying you did?"

I threw the dice. "Yes."

"Why would I want to help a liar?" he said.

"Because I lied to a man we both dislike and distrust. Because we're on the same side."

"Mr. Bruno, you're jumping to conclusions," he said, but he didn't hang up.

"Am I wrong to?"

"One is always wrong to jump to conclusions," he said. "But in this instance, it is understandable."

"Does that mean you'll help me?"

After a long pause, Rasic said, "Well, since you've been so persistent, the least I can do is listen to you."

"Mr. Rasic, I'm not looking for a Red Cross volunteer. I'm looking for a man named Terry Quinn."

Rasic coughed politely to interrupt me: "Why did you lie to Laird about this?"

"Laird is the executor of a large estate and he hired me to find a missing beneficiary. Terry Quinn is a link to the beneficiary, but I don't want Laird to know about Quinn yet because I'm afraid Laird has a conflict of interest."

Rasic chuckled. "Continue."

"During the war in Vietnam, Terry Quinn ran a charter airline, and I was told he rescued children from Sarajevo in nineteen ninety-three. I was also told he was killed while he was doing that."

"The name of the charter?"

"In Vietnam, it was called Global Airways. I don't know what it became."

"Q-U-I-N-N?" he spelled.

"Right. First name, Terry."

"You wish to confirm his death, is that it?"

"I'd rather find him alive."

"I see." He laughed softly. "Mr. Bruno, did you happen to give Mr. Laird a name for your imaginary volunteer?"

"No."

"Well, why don't I call Mr. Laird and tell him I had a change of heart about helping you, and make him a gift of a name? A gift from me, of course, not from you."

"Sure," I said, enjoying Karel Rasic a whole lot.

"What does Mr. Laird know about our volunteer?"

"That he was with the Red Cross in Vietnam and with the airlift in Sarajevo."

"No nationality?"

"Uh uh."

"Good. Excellent. Hmmm. I like Switzerland, don't you? The home of the Red Cross, renowned for its neutrality—but not one of those untrustworthy nonaligned countries, with people who worship strange animals and speak in strange dialects and practice strange medicine. A Swiss is good. Everybody believes in Swiss volunteers. What shall we call our selfless Swiss volunteer? Schiller? Dürrenmatt? Frisch? Klee! But not Paul—some educated person might point that out to Mr. Laird. What do you think of Anton? Anton Klee. Swiss. Of . . . Geneva? No, too obvious. Zurich? No. Bern. Anton Klee, of Bern. Do you approve, Mr. Bruno?"

"I sure do," I said, thinking that if he ever left the diplomatic life, Karel Rasic had a future either as a writer or a con man.

"Good. Anton Klee lives. As soon as I learn more about the fate of Mr. Quinn, I will be in touch."

"Thank you, Mr. Rasic."

"My pleasure, Mr. Bruno."

While Rasic went to work on Terry Quinn, I went to work on contractors. In 1974 to '75, there had been many, many more contractors than airlines in Vietnam, so tracking them (or their successors, or their successors' successors) was like following skeins in a closely knit sweater.

None of the contractors I reached—and over the next four days I reached dozens—recalled Matt Marshall's working for them in 1974 to '75; none of them had easy access to their old employment and payment records. Back then, those records weren't entered in computers. Only three contractors could tell me where I could (maybe) locate their old records (if the paper hadn't been recycled, and if the storage bill had been paid, and if the warehouse hadn't burned down); and only one of those three had any mechanism at all for searching through those old records, and it would take at least six months to put that mechanism into place. And another six—at least—to do the actual search. Was I still interested? Ha ha ha.

At the end of a week, though I was sure there was no point in nagging him, I called Karel Rasic. There *was* no point: He hadn't yet found out anything about Terry Quinn.

Three possible lines of inquiry: contractors, airlines, and Beth Marshall. Two I'd more or less exhausted, and the third I fervently wanted to avoid.

"Fuck you, Marshall!" I said to my computer screen, and just at that instant, Sandy the UPS route man walked in, gave me his usual friendly hello, and saved my ragged ass by handing me an overnight letter from A. Nonni Muss.

CHAPTER 25

I WASTED NO TIME in calling Nicole Maldonado. Her machine said she was in court, and to leave a message. I did. Then, later, another. And two more. She called me back at six-thirty; I told her the news and offered to pay double her usual rate if she came right over. Tomorrow, she said. She was having dinner with her parents, and she was cooking. What time did she expect them, I asked, I could get there in ten minutes. They were due almost immediately, she said; her mother liked to oversee the cooking; or, more accurately, control it. I leaned on her: "Just tell me where do you live—I'm on my way."

"Seventy-first, off Central Park West." Before I could ask the house number, she added politely, "Mr. Bruno, I don't think even you can get up here in ten minutes. Please let me visit your office before court tomorrow. Tell me what time."

"How late do they usually stay?"

"Not late—they have to drive back to New Jersey, but—"

"What if I come by at, say, nine . . . ?"

"They might still be here then, and—"

"Nine-thirty—will they be gone by then?"

"It's hard to say. Mr. Bruno, I don't see them as often as I'd like, and I don't want to rush them out, so—"

"Absolutely not, Ms. Maldonado," I said, leaning harder. "Why don't I come at ten, and if they're still there, you can introduce me—I'd love to meet them. I'll bring dessert—what do you like? What do they like?"

"Introduce you, Mr. Bruno?"

"Ms. Maldonado, I feel as if I know your mother already. You did use

158

her as a consultant on the first letter. Why don't we just make it official?"

"Mr. Bruno, you are ruthless."

"I plead nolo contendere," I said. "What time?"

"Mr. Bruno, I really believe—"

"I'll bring wine as well—what time?"

After a pause, she said, "Ten would be all right, however, I must—"

"Thank you!"

"However," she continued, "I must ask something of you, Mr. Bruno."

"Whatever you want."

"If my parents are still here, may I have your permission to translate the new letter in their presence?"

Caught: "Yes, you may."

Nicole Maldonado lived in one of those West Side brownstones old enough to have a set of stone steps leading up to a set of stately oak-and-glass entrance doors. It was the kind of building in which the interior staircase seemed to have been installed by a drunk: No matter where you placed your foot on the stairs, or rested your hand on the banister, you slipped into a tilt.

At 9:55, after she'd buzzed me in and I'd climbed the drunken staircase to the fourth floor, I knocked on her door. In my right hand, I had a bag containing a pint of raspberries, a pint of blueberries, a lime tart, and two bottles of sauterne. In my left, I had my case.

After the usual New York noises—three locks being unlatched—the door swung open. Maldonado, in tailored wool pants, an Egyptian cotton blue dress shirt, and an NYPD Hostage Negotiator baseball cap, stood in her tiny vestibule with a bag of El Pico coffee in her hand.

"Good evening, Mr. Bruno," she said in her demure way. "Welcome to my home." She stepped backward, allowing me in. As I closed the door behind me, I heard voices from another room. "They're still here," she murmured.

As she led me toward the living room entrance, she called out, "Mr. Bruno has arrived," so by the time we reached the archway, her parents were standing there. "Mr. Adam Bruno," Maldonado said, "may I present my mother and father."

Passing the shopping bag to Maldonado, I offered my hand to her mother, who, like Maldonado, was slender, black-haired, oval-eyed, and riveting to look at. "How do you do, Mrs. Maldonado?"

Nearly inaudibly, and with a mild but unmistakable accent, her mother said, "I am honored to meet you, Mr. Bruno," and briefly enclosed my fingers before lowering her eyes and giving way to her husband.

Maldonado's father stepped up. He was short, lithe, and muscular—he could have been a boxer—but with an almost too handsome face, like a waitress's fantasy of a Latin lover. He also had an accent—New York Puerto Rican Lite—but he was a long way from inaudible. He gripped my hand, smiled eagerly, and boomed, "Luis Maldonado. Hi. Adam, right? Nicci says you've got the sweets and wine."

For the next twenty minutes or so, we ate tart and berries and drank sauterne. Luis Maldonado talked about the difficulty of running a small business (LM Heating & Air Conditioning) in a high-tax state (New Jersey); Nicole Maldonado talked about the unwillingness of Asian and Indian women to testify against their husbands in abuse cases. And after two glasses of wine—Mrs. Maldonado (her name, I learned, was Tuyet) talked about how proud she was that her daughter had accomplished so much in so hard a trade.

"You are satisfied with her efforts, are you not, Mr. Bruno?" she asked.

"I understand she had your help, Mrs. Maldonado."

Like her daughter, Tuyet Maldonado constantly lowered her head and turned it sideways when she spoke, and the effect was almost equally beguiling. "My daughter tries to honor me by telling you this, Mr. Bruno . . ." she touched Maldonado on the cheek, ". . . but the help is all the other way."

"Mama . . ."

"It is like this, Mr. Bruno: Sometimes, when my daughter and I speak on the telephone and she hears a certain tone in my voice, or if we are together and she sees a certain look in my eye, she will say, Mama, I have a Vietnamese passage, it's very subtle and I'm puzzled by it, please help me. Naturally, I cannot refuse this request. But you must understand, Mr. Bruno, this request is my daughter's way of comforting her mother, of making her mother feel valued."

Maldonado listened to this in daughterly silence, nodded to her mother so briefly it bordered on impolite, turned to me and said, "Mr. Bruno, may I have your permission to translate the letter now?"

No expression passed across Tuyet Maldonado's placid face, but from the deliberate way she folded her hands in her lap and directed her eyes from Maldonado to her empty berry dish, I knew mother and daughter— who were sitting only inches away from each other on the couch—were having their own decorous version of a cat fight.

Pretending things were fine, I opened my case, drew out the new letter, and passed it to Maldonado.

Without hesitating, she moved right next to her mother and held the letter between them. Tuyet Maldonado kept her gaze on her berry dish.

Before Nicole Maldonado could say anything—and even she couldn't hide that she was burning to—I produced a second copy of the letter. "Ms. Maldonado," I said, "would you mind if your mother followed along with her own copy? It might make things easier."

"Not at all, Mr. Bruno," she said. I held out the letter, expecting Tuyet Maldonado to take it, but that, apparently, wasn't the protocol, because Maldonado took it and, bowing microscopically, offered it to her mother.

"Thank you, Nicole," her mother said, with a comparable bow. "You honor me."

"Yes, I do," Maldonado said implacably.

While Tuyet Maldonado took her glasses from her purse and put them on, and I placed my recorder on the coffee table, Nicole Maldonado, echoing her actions in my office, moved to the front of the couch, sat up very straight, and translated:

Dear Captain Matthew:

Following your advice, I have written of my situation to the Defense Attaché in Bangkok, the United States Embassy there, and the refugee assistance organizations you describe. I have described my service to the military forces of the United States, and the decorations those forces awarded me. With your gracious permission, I have noted your name.

Please allow me, my dear comrade, to thank you for your efforts on my behalf while I was in Bien Hoa. The knowledge that you were so steadfast in your efforts helped keep my courage alive for those three years, and that was as useful—more useful—than anything practical you might have done. I will wait until we are united to describe my flight from my homeland.

I am desolate to report that the Thais—supposedly our allies—treat us as badly as did the North Vietnamese. To the Thais, we are not refugees but prisoners. There are as many regulations here as at Bien Hoa, and the punishments are equally severe: An infraction means either a murderous beating (with a bamboo stick) followed by a head-shaving and solitary confinement. Infractions include gambling, drinking, or exchanging goods or money with Thai natives (which we must do to survive).

In theory, we are under the protection of the United Nations High Commission for Refugees, but in fact we are at the mercy of the Thai authorities, because all food and supplies go through them. This means either there is very little food left, or we are charged an extortionate premium to obtain it. Since few people here have any funds (they must be sent from the outside, and likewise go through the Thais), we pay our premiums either with our labor (the men, mostly) or with our bodies (the women, if they are young enough— Thais prefer their illicit sexual relations with children).

Release from the camp is purely a matter of influence and politics. There is no set sentence because we are not prisoners, we are refugees. Prisoners are released when their sentence is up. Refugees must wait until someone (some person *and* some country) is willing to give them refuge. As you must know, this is no longer as easy as it was soon after the war ended. For a short time, South Vietnamese were regarded as victims. No longer. For these reasons, very few people leave officially, although some flee. At the moment, the camp contains upwards of 6,000 people.

This brings me to the little I have learned about your friend and her child. According to a refugee family here, your friend and her child were caught trying to escape from Vietnam by boat (cousins of the refugee family here were passengers of the same fleet) and were placed in a reeducation camp near Tay Ninh. From Tay Ninh—they were prisoners for only six months—your friend and her child returned to the place of her birth, but were forced to leave because her mixed-blood child alarmed her neighbors.

Maldonado glanced at her mother, who did not raise her head from her copy of the letter. Maldonado went on:

From her birthplace, your friend and her child (and approximately 20 others) took to the water once more and made their way to Malaysia, where they were put back to sea for lack of bribe money. From Malaysia, your friend and her child sailed to Guam. That is all I know of her movements—I cannot tell you whether they are still on Guam or have gone to the United States or have been put back to sea.

I did, however, learn that during her journey she traveled under the name Nguyen Thi Dinh—

"Say that again," I interjected, scarcely believing my ears and my luck. More slowly, Maldonado said, ". . . She traveled under the name Nguyen Thi Dinh." I signaled her to go on:

I pray that the next missive you receive from me will be sent from a place of true freedom (my uncle is in San Pedro, California, and awaits me). I salute you and wish you all my admiration and affection.

Ghost.

I opened a notebook to a fresh page, tested my pen, and said, "Can we talk about the name—what is it again?"

Simultaneously, mother and daughter said, "Nguyen Thi Dinh," and spelled it for me.

"Is there anything special about it—could it be a code of some sort?"

After mouthing the name silently a few times, Maldonado said, "I don't see anything special about it. If it is a code, that's not obvious." She looked to her mother.

"My daughter is correct," Tuyet Maldonado said. "But . . ." she paused to touch a paragraph. "In my own poor judgment, Mr. Bruno, I do not think this name—Nguyen Thi Dinh—truly belongs to this woman."

"Why is that?" Maldonado said, beating me by a hair to the question.

"Mr. Ghost writes . . ." She found the sentence: " 'I did, however, learn that during her journey she traveled under the name Nguyen Thi Dinh.' This is her *traveling* name, the name she tells other people, the name that will not bring her sorrow if it is known."

Though it was speckless, she brushed her skirt several times before continuing: "In all the years my sisters and I tried to escape, we never used our true names except with each other, and then only if we were alone. Alone with each other. With strangers, no matter who, we used a false name. Many false names—one for each stranger, one for each episode. I do not think this woman is truly Nguyen Thi Dinh."

"Do you think she'd keep that name?" I asked, trying to suppress the hope in my voice.

Tuyet Maldonado thought about it, and, shaking her head doubtfully, said to Maldonado, "Didn't Captain Matthew give her a name—what is it?"

Together, Maldonado and I said, "Cricket."

"Cricket," Tuyet Maldonado said, testing the word a few times. "Perhaps she will name herself Mrs. Cricket."

"He also called her Chau Chau," I said. "It kind of means cricket in Vietnamese, doesn't it?"

With just the barest flavor of accusation, Maldonado said, "I don't recall you mentioning Chau Chau, Mr. Bruno."

"I just found out," I said to her, and then turned to her mother and waited.

"Chau Chau," Tuyet Maldonado said, and tested that for a while. "Mrs. Chau, perhaps."

"Not Mrs. Nguyen Thi Dinh?" I asked.

Tuyet Maldonado shrugged microscopically. "I do not know why she chooses this as her traveling name. If it means something sacred to her, as sacred as Cricket or Chau Chau, yes, perhaps she will keep it."

Scrupulously, I looked from mother to daughter and back. "Is there anything else in the letter that caught your attention?" I said.

While Nicole Maldonado skimmed the letter, Tuyet Maldonado cleared her throat discreetly, glanced at me, lowered her eyes, and said, "Mr. Bruno, forgive me, but I am a foolish old woman, and I am not keen enough to help you when I know so much less, so very much less, than you do . . ."

Like daughter, like mother; I didn't bother with subterfuge. "Mrs. Maldonado," I said, "so I don't have to be long-winded, can you tell me what your daughter has told you?"

Carefully, she answered, "My daughter has told me that she is helping you to find the forgotten child of an American soldier and a Vietnamese woman. That the soldier is recently taken from us and has wished on his forgotten child much of his great fortune."

I took a moment to order the story.

"In 1971, a married American Army officer named Matthew Marshall—the Captain Matthew of the letter—sent two Vietnamese girls who were wounded in a battle to a military hospital. During a visit to the hospital, he formed an attachment to one of these girls. After she was released, he fell in love with her and she bore his child. I'm not sure what happened next, but in 1972, Marshall went home to his wife and son in the United States. Do you have any questions?"

Tuyet Maldonado shook her head.

"In April 1974, Marshall returned to Vietnam to work for a contractor—I don't know which one—and he stayed there until the fall of Saigon in April 1975. During this time—"

Uncharacteristically, Nicole Maldonado interrupted me: "Mr. Bruno, you didn't tell me he'd gone back."

"I just found out," I said. "During this time—a full year—his letters make no mention of a woman and a child. However, I believe he did in fact return to Vietnam to search for them."

"Oh, yes," Tuyet Maldonado said, as though I'd just announced that the sun rose in the east.

"After Marshall came back here in 1975, he continued his search, long distance, using Ghost as his man in the field. To answer your questions in advance, I don't know where Ghost is or whether he's in the United States. I don't know if the woman and child came here, or stayed here. I don't know a whole lot."

Tuyet Maldonado said, "Mr. Bruno, I cannot understand—you do not know where Mr. Ghost is, but you have his letters. Where do the letters come from—will they not lead to Mr. Ghost?"

"No," I said shortly. "What I mean, Mrs. Maldonado, is that the letters . . ." I trailed off, not sure what to say. "The letters . . ." I glanced at Nicole Maldonado, who shrugged at me in perfect innocence, which meant, I was sure, she was enjoying watching her mother put me on the spot. "The letters are not something I found. They *arrived*. Like this: copies, not originals. I can't demonstrate it, but I don't think the letters lead back to Ghost."

"Who do they lead back to?" Tuyet Maldonado said. "Surely that would help us."

At that moment, I realized that any new company would be Maldonado, Bruno & Maldonado, or maybe Maldonado, Maldonado & Bruno, since both of them seemed to be more than capable of doing my job.

"Yes, you're absolutely right," I said, "it would help us, but . . ." Trying to recover: "Can you accept that I don't know anything more about the source of Ghost's letters than you do?" Both women nodded solemnly. "Thank you," I said gratefully. "Is there anything else that caught your attention?"

They scanned the document. Tuyet Maldonado rested her finger on a place in the letter. "He says 'child'—he does not say boy or girl. Which is it?"

I was about to say, "I have no idea," but then dimly remembered a passage in the codicil. Unearthing it from my case, I found it on the first page and read it aloud: " '. . . Cricket became pregnant. Before the birth of this child—which I have no doubt was mine—we were separated by the fortunes of war, and I never saw Cricket again.' Which means he never did meet his child."

As I looked up from the codicil, I was startled to see Luis Maldonado reach out and grip his daughter's hand. Almost instantly, Tuyet Maldonado placed her hand on both of theirs, and the three of them sat clasping each other, locked so deeply into their intimacy as a family that I had to turn my head. Finally, Luis Maldonado gently pulled away, breaking the spell, and looked at me:

"Adam, you said your guy stayed till the fall—when do you mean exactly?"

"I don't know," I said, finding a copy of Marshall's last letter. "This is dated April sixteenth, but he says he's got a month before he has to leave. So, from mid-April on."

"What does he look like?"

From my case I pulled several twenty-year-old pictures of Marshall and passed them to Luis Maldonado. He went through them slowly and shook his head. "I thought maybe I'd have run into him someplace. How'd he get out?"

"My guess," I said, "is that he flew out with an airline run by a guy named Terry Quinn. Global Airways, but—"

"Mia Madre!" Luis Maldonado exclaimed.

"What is it?" I said.

"Terry Quinn!?" he said, in a mix of surprise and delight. "Your guy flew out with Terry Quinn?"

"Marshall had a picture of Quinn on the wall of his cabin," I said, "so I'm guessing he did, but—"

"You got a copy of that picture?"

I pulled out a batch of mystery-wall blowups, found Quinn's photo, and handed it to him.

For a long minute he stared at it, muttering, "Jesu Cristi!" to himself. Then he leaned forward and offered the photo to his daughter.

She held it by its edges and studied it, first matching the face with her twenty-years-back memory of the man, then frowning, as if she were hunting the missing piece of a puzzle. "Where's his gun, Papa?" She held the picture up so he could see it. "He always had a gun." She touched her heart. "Right here."

After looking at the picture, Luis Maldonado said, "Bet it's under the seat. He didn't wear it at the controls." He turned to me. "He carried a silver forty-five pistol in a shoulder holster—on the outside of his shirt, like a bodyguard in a movie. It used to drive the embassy guys crazy, because he wouldn't take it off when he went to see the ambassador." He laughed at the memories, then deduced the obvious and said, "Why didn't you ask Quinn?"

"I've been told he's dead."

Nicole Maldonado's head jerked up, as though somebody had flicked her sharply under the chin.

"Bullshit!" her father shouted, suddenly on his feet. "Bullshit! Bullshit!" He glared at me. "How? Where? Who killed him? I don't believe it. Not for one bullshit minute!"

"I was told he got killed rescuing children from Sarajevo in nineteen ninety-three."

Looming over me, he snarled, "Did you see the body? Did you see a death certificate? What kind of proof you got?"

"Papa . . ." Maldonado said gently, "Mr. Bruno doesn't know. He's only passing on what he heard."

Luis Maldonado wiped the back of his hand across his eyes, sat down on the love seat, and glared at his shoes.

"Luis," Tuyet Maldonado said, and though I heard no admonishment in her tone, he did.

Without lifting his head, he said, "I'm outta line. It's Nicci's house and you're her guest. Sorry."

"Just for the record," I said, "I don't know that he's dead, but I haven't been able to find him in the United States, and I haven't found an airline, either." I added some sweetener: "Of course, I've only just begun looking . . ."

He swiveled a couple of inches so that he could see me with one eye. "Got it." He swiveled a bit farther. "It's not like I think you don't know what you're doing, it's just . . . Terry Quinn is not a guy who should die on people. He's too big a deal in their lives, you know what I'm sayin'?"

"Yes, I do," I said. I had a useful thought. "Luis, can you do me a favor?"

After taking a deep breath, he lifted the empty sauterne bottle to the light. "If my daughter the hostess can find us something to drink . . ."

"I'm glad it depends on me," Maldonado said. She rose, handed him Quinn's photo, and headed for the kitchen.

On the coffee table in front of Luis Maldonado, I placed the other pictures from Marshall's mystery wall—pictures, I now suspected, that belonged to 1974 through '75. "See if there's anybody you recognize."

Luis Maldonado picked up the top photo, studied it, shook his head, and placed it face down. At the third photo, he stopped—it was the same picture that had nudged Eve McGowan, the shot of several suited men drinking in a rooftop restaurant.

"Nicci," he called out, but she was no longer in the kitchen. She was behind him, leaning over his shoulder so that her head was between his and mine, but so close to mine that her hair brushed my temple. I turned very slightly to let it brush my eyelid, and a tantalizing scent radiated from her, a blend of shampoo, wine, cologne, and nighttime flesh; for an instant I wanted to fill my lungs with it and hold my breath until I'd consumed her. I didn't.

"I'm here, Papa," she said.

"You got a magnifier?"

She nodded, handed me a fresh bottle of wine, and went to what I assumed was her bedroom. By the time I'd refilled the glasses, she'd returned with the magnifier and given it to her father. He examined each face in turn and, like McGowan, picked out the man with the rakishly tilted straw hat. "I don't know who he is, but I know him."

"His nickname is B.H.," I said.

"B.H.?" he said in puzzlement. "Uh, uh."

At the sixth photo—of a man speaking into the mike of a portable recorder—he again stopped. "This guy was some kind of reporter."

I looked up my key. "Buzz," I said.

"Buzz?" he repeated. "Uh, uh."

He went right past the photo of Ma and stopped only once more. "Holy shit!" he cried when he did. "Holy shit!"

The picture was of an ascetic-looking man, in a seersucker suit and a fatigue hat, holding a machete over burlap sacks labeled LONG GRAIN RICE PRODUCT OF TEXAS.

"Uncle," he said, in wonderment. "Honey, it's Uncle." He left his seat, knelt in front of his wife, and held the picture up so she could see it. Both her hands leapt to her mouth and then upward, to hide her eyes.

Luis Maldonado passed the picture to his daughter. "Do you recognize him, Nicci?"

She studied the photo, then put a finger on it to cover the fatigue hat. "The man with the servant," she said. "The one we kept going to see every day."

By then, my key had confirmed that the man with the machete was nicknamed Uncle.

"Do you remember his last name?" I said.

"Sure," Maldonado shouted happily. "Spiegel. Sam Spiegel. Uncle Sam! He worked for USAID—United States Agency for International Development." He glanced at the photo of Quinn, then at the photo of Uncle. "Oh, yeah, this makes sense!" he said, rapping each photo with his knuckle for emphasis. "If your guy is trying to get a kid out, Uncle and Terry Quinn, that's where he goes."

"Are you still in touch with Uncle at all?"

Maldonado must have caught the longing in my tone, because he patted me compassionately on the shoulder as he said, "Sorry, Adam, not for years."

By then, Tuyet Maldonado had rejoined us. If she had been weeping, her face didn't show it. "Mr. Bruno . . ." She glanced at my face, then dipped her head to say, "Mr. Bruno, even though we are not related, and we are only meeting for the first time, you are my daughter's guest, so will you allow me to ask something of you—something of sacred value?"

"Mrs. Maldonado, it would be my honor."

After an apologetic glance at her daughter, she said, "Mr. Bruno, may I ask you to present me a copy of these memorable photos?"

"As many as you want, Mrs. Maldonado."

Without looking at me, Tuyet Maldonado reached for her daughter's hands, gripped them, and said, "Mr. Bruno is the kindest of men."

CHAPTER 26

"... THE THING WAS THAT Tuyet and Hiep—Hiep's her cousin, or cousin of a cousin, and she worked for me as a cook—both had kids by Americans, and all I could get that day was two seats. So, one seat for the two kids, one seat for Tuyet's husband—what'd you say his name is? Carlos?"

"Luis. Luis Maldonado."

"That's it—Luis," Sam Spiegel said. "He was a Marine, I think, or maybe Special Forces. Very emotional; he cried more than Tuyet or the child. Of course, she was around ten, and by that age, they didn't cry much anymore."

Spiegel took a bite of his bran muffin and a gulp of his coffee milkshake and stared wistfully at the unopened pack of French cigarettes on his crowded but organized desk. "It's two years; I keep them in front of me for the discipline."

Usually smokers gain weight when they quit, but Spiegel hadn't. He looked more ascetic than ever, partly because his hair had gone all gray, partly because his skin had grown tighter over his bones.

"What was her name?—the kid, I mean? Michelle?"

"Nicole," I said.

"Nicole. I knew it was French." He shut his eyes for a moment, remembering. "Is she still beautiful?"

I hesitated. "Yes."

"When she was ten, she was beautiful like you can't believe. Like you rub your eyes." He laughed and theatrically beat his heart with his fist. "Soft heart. Mush. A sucker for beautiful children, and Vietnam was full of beautiful children. Or maybe they looked beautiful because they were doomed. Or I thought they were doomed. Do I sound like a sentimental asshole? Fine. I am a sentimental asshole."

He picked up the pack of cigarettes, lowered his eyeglasses from their resting place on his head, and read the warning label. "Will one wake up all my dormant cancer cells, do you think?"

He hadn't been hard to find: The Agency for International Development isn't nearly as paranoid as the Pentagon, and they told me he'd left AID in 1978 to work as legislative director of the House Foreign Affairs Committee in Washington. In 1980 he took a job as a counselor for alcoholic and drug-addicted veterans in San Diego. After two years there, he moved to Pittsburgh, where he ran the student-aid office at Carnegie Mellon. From Pittsburgh, he moved to Cambridge, where he was supposed to do the same thing at MIT, but instead opened a bookstore named Sam's Inc.

At first look, it seemed an old-fashioned sort of shop, almost anachronistic—no display racks of best-sellers, no greeting cards, no tote bags, no calendars, no sections for self-help or psychic healing; just lots of literature and history, with a pretty good assortment of politics and anthropology. Not musty exactly, but not up-to-the-minute, either. But Sam's Inc. merited more than a first look.

In one-half of the basement he had a huge collection of computer books and software; in the other half, an even huger collection of business and finance texts, some dating back to the eighteenth century. And just to ensure his profit, upstairs, on the balcony, he had a sensational library of theater, movie, and TV books—and a computer console devoted solely to a CD catalogue.

Behind him in his ramshackle office, which had once been a potting shed and still faintly smelled of earth, stood a wooden rack on which rested half a dozen assorted hats, including the fatigue cap he'd worn in the 1975 photograph. The photograph itself, or one taken around the same time, hung on the only wall in the office that was not covered with shelved books. Hanging beside it were similar shots, the largest of which showed Spiegel squatting in front of a hootch, demonstrating to a group of naked Vietnamese children how to use toilet paper. There were no pictures on the wall of a wife or children, even though he wore a wedding ring.

Spiegel put the unopened cigarettes in his top desk drawer and slammed it shut. "Is it middle-class indulgence to worry about what's going to kill you?" Without any transition, he leapt back to Vietnam:

"It was a time of impossible choices, okay? In April 1975, the only choices were bad or awful. Agony or annihilation. Send your kids away, probably forever, or watch your kids get killed. Say good-bye to everyone you love, or let the NVA round you all up and do whatever the fuck they want.

"Those were the choices—that's what we set up for them, us the allies, the good guys, the white hats, the saviors. We said We're your friends, trust us, and they did, and then we said Fuck you, friends, die. But we meant that part. They could trust us about that part." He saw the baffled look on my face. "Do you know anything about the end?"

"Not really."

"Okay, let me try to give you the short cartoon version. I'll do my best to sound objective.

"In the ten years we were there, we hired thousands—no, scores of thousands—of Vietnamese. Everybody hired them—us, the Army, the Marines, the Red Cross, the USO, the networks, the newspapers, contractors, banks, airlines, the CIA, the embassy, everybody. And everyone we hired had lots of relatives, so when the time came to get out, when the NVA was sweeping across the country, there were scores of thousands— maybe hundreds of thousands—of Vietnamese who *needed* to get out because they were at mortal risk. At mortal risk because they'd worked for us, or were related to people who'd worked for us.

"Now, obviously, getting that many people out was bound to be a monstrous job. And the only way it could ever be done was if you planned for it, planned for it the way you plan for any massive military retreat. And the only way you could plan for it was to acknowledge that Hanoi might win. But that was the one thing we wouldn't do. Our line—our religion—was that Saigon eventually would win. With enough training, and enough arms, and enough supplies, Saigon would prevail, and therefore there was no danger.

"Since there was no danger, there was no reason to plan an evacuation. By the time Saigon and Washington even noticed that maybe possibly conceivably arguably perchance there might be a danger, it was way way too late to plan properly—even if they'd wanted to, and they didn't.

"Well, a bunch of us—people in all the agencies, in the military, even the spooks—couldn't accept that. We began covertly planning evacuations, not only for ourselves but for our Vietnamese and their families. At first, all we could manage was a trickle—the immigration rules were incredibly rigid when it came to Vietnamese. Then, a miracle happened. Da Nang fell, State panicked, and Immigration changed the rules.

"If you were Vietnamese and you had an American relative in Vietnam, *any* American relative, you could get out—and you didn't need to wait for your relative to get out.

"That was enough for us: We concocted a document that said if a Vietnamese could show he or she was a direct relation of an American, he or she was eligible for an exit visa. You can imagine. Suddenly, everybody wanted to get married, everybody wanted her baby adopted, and if they couldn't actually get married or get the baby adopted, shit, the papers would be enough."

He burst into laughter and said, "We went even further. If they couldn't get a marriage certificate or adoption papers, we gave them a chit that said, 'Owing to the horrors of war, the papers have been lost, but So-and-So—fill in an important American official name—vouches that once upon a time the bearer used to have the proper papers and give him every consideration blah blah blah.'

"The whole fucking thing was out of Beavis and Butthead, but we had a pipeline, more than one. Everybody had a pipeline, every agency had at least one person who was trying to do the right thing. Even the fucking CIA had people who were trying to do the right thing, and it was working. We were getting them on planes, we were getting them on ships, we were getting them. out, we were doing it! We were fucking doing it!"

By then, he realized he was shouting and abruptly shut his mouth. Letting his head fall to his chest, he muttered, "Shit. Is it really a generation ago?"

One of his salespeople, a reed-thin Filipino woman of twenty, stuck her head in the office doorway and said, "The guy with the Mayhew just called again to change our appointment to inspect it—that's the fourth time."

Spiegel raised his head to look at her. "When did he change it to?"

"A week from Friday."

"Call him back tonight, late—say eleven—and tell him we found another copy and if we can't inspect his, here, in the store, by four tomorrow, we're going with the other seller." He smiled thinly. "Either he'll show up, or his copy's shit and we'll get rid of him. Order me another shake, okay?" She nodded and left.

"Who's Mayhew?"

"The Studs Terkel of nineteenth-century London. Or maybe Studs Terkel is the Henry Mayhew of twentieth-century Chicago. He went around interviewing poor people and criminals about their life and work. You enjoy books?"

"Reference books mostly," I said.

"Of course," he said, with no sarcasm. "In your profession, that makes sense."

I put a fresh tape in my recorder and said, "Did Matt Marshall come to you for help in getting a Vietnamese woman and a child out of Saigon in April 1975?"

"In a way," he said. "But I met him long before that." Before I could ask him what he meant by "in a way," Spiegel was launched on his tale:

"Marshall first came to see me in the summer of nineteen seventy-four. Very polite, which was unusual for a contractor. Most contractors, and the people who worked for them, were lower than snake shit—these are the guys who used to kneecap Vietnamese for not getting out of their way on the sidewalk. I didn't like contractors, and I wasn't that crazy about southerners. I come from a long line of immigrant Jews, and we were brought up to believe that southerners would lynch a Jew just as fast as they would lynch a black."

Spiegel smiled. "Marshall brought a quart jar of creamed herring. Don't ask where he got it, but there it was, Vita Creamed Herring, with onions. 'Your pal David at Reuters said you eat this stuff,' he said, and put it on my desk. 'Is it some kind of religious thing?' I told him it wasn't, opened the herring right away, and served us a couple of portions. If he didn't enjoy it, he sure put on a great act.

"He'd stopped by, he said, because David at Reuters and Les at USIS and Gene at Chase Manhattan and Carly at Federal Electric and Phillipe at the French Consulate had all told him I had lots of contacts at orphanages, and he needed to talk to somebody with lots of contacts at orphanages, and didn't I think Charles Dickens had said all there ever was to say about orphans and orphanages? . . .

"I don't know why—maybe because he was southern, maybe because he dropped one name too many, maybe because I resented the fact that he could find herring just like that, maybe because I didn't like the way he casually invoked Dickens—but I told him USAID didn't arrange adoptions. I assumed that's what he was there for. Why didn't he try Friends for All Children? I asked, or one of the other big agencies. He said sure, thanked me, and left.

"A few weeks later, he showed up again, to thank me, he said, for sending him to Friends for All Children. He brought me another jar of herring—and a warm loaf of bread he'd gotten at the French Consulate." Spiegel licked his lips in remembrance. "But he saved the best for last: a first edition of *Martin Chuzzlewit*—do you know it? Second-best Dickens, but a favorite of mine. Don't ask me how he found out, or how he got it and had it sent ten thousand miles, but he was a master at that kind of shit. I said something like How can I repay you?—no way was I going to say I can't accept this—and he said, 'Take me to dinner.'

"At dinner, he told me that he was looking for his own child and her mother. He told me how and where they'd met, and how the child was conceived, and when he'd last seen her. He said he understood that lots of Vietnamese women gave up their mixed-race children, and that he wanted to go around to the orphanages and see if anyone recognized the woman he called Cricket—he had a photo. He wondered if maybe once in a while, when I wasn't busy, say on free weekends—he'd cover all the expenses—I'd help him, since my Vietnamese was so strong and his was so weak.

"There were around a hundred sixty to eighty orphanages in Vietnam, and we went to most of them. But it didn't do Marshall any good—not that that was any surprise. You see, when a round-eye shows up and tells the people in charge he's looking for his woman Cricket and their kid, first the people in charge go through their incomplete and totally fucked-up records to see whether anyone named Cricket deposited a kid on their doorstep in whatever it was, seventy-two or seventy-three or seventy-four.

"Then, the people in charge call in all the grownups who were around in those years and show them Marshall's picture of Cricket. When nobody recognizes the picture—and nobody ever does—they call in all the kids who might be the right age, which is, say, three years old, and they show the picture of Cricket to them and ask Is this your mama? . . ." He paused in his flow to say, "Ever visit an orphanage?"

"No."

"Ever feed pigeons in the park?" Before I could get the connection, he said, "That's exactly what it's like—you've got kids all over you like fucking pigeons. Hanging on your arms, hugging your legs, sitting on your feet, grabbing your fingers. I've had five kids holding on to all five fingers of a hand. I mean holding *tight,* death grip. You show an orphan kid a picture of a Vietnamese woman and ask Is this your mama? and standing there is Matt Marshall, big, strong, white, rich—all Americans are rich—who's going to bear me away to the Promised Land, if only he'll notice me, and every kid in the room shouts Yes, that's my mama! because the kid has figured out Shit, man, this is somebody's father, and he might just as well be mine.

"Now, you might ask, what the hell are the people in charge doing showing a photo to three-year-old kids? Kids that age can't identify people from a photograph—assuming they even remember the person and they've ever *seen* a photograph. Well, I guess if I were running a Vietnamese orphanage and a big, rich, white American came in looking for his child, I might do the same. In fact, I *know* I'd do the same."

"But Marshall didn't go for it?" I said.

"Uh uh. He wasn't there to adopt a child. He was there to find *his* child."

"And he kept on looking for how long?"

"Till he left."

"Do you know when that was?"

"Near the end—last week in April, I'd guess."

"You don't know what day? What flight he took out?"

"I don't know what flight *I* took out."

"You don't think he ever found them?"

He raised his eyebrows at my stupidity. "If he had, why would you be here?"

"He found them, he hated her, he hated the child, he decided he'd forget it and go home . . ." I proposed.

"Doesn't fit the pattern," Spiegel said brusquely. "What he did earlier—fuck her and desert her—*that* fits the pattern. The ones who came back—look at Luis Maldonado—came back to find their women and kids and take them home."

I suggested a variation: "He found them, she hated him for deserting them, and she refused to go with him."

"Not credible," Spiegel said. "Not in Saigon in the spring of seventy-five. And even if she wouldn't go, even if she hated him that much, she'd send the child—not a prayer she'd keep the child in country if somebody could take it out."

I returned to where I'd begun. "When I asked you if Marshall came to you for help in getting a Vietnamese woman and a child out of Saigon in April nineteen seventy-five, you said, 'in a way.' What did you mean by that?"

"Well, once he'd learned how things were done, and once it got more and more obvious that the South was going to lose, he said to me—it must have been February seventy-five, maybe early March and we were on our way back to Saigon from yet another orphanage—he said, 'Sam, I'd like to put everything in order: marriage license, birth certificate, adoption papers, exit visas, airline tickets, you name it. I'd like to put it all in place—just in case. Help me out, Sam . . .'

"Well, by that time, I'd gotten a bit tired of chasing around to orphanages, and I more or less told him I wasn't a private service bureau for Matt Marshall, and I didn't need any more herring, or French bread, or even first editions of Dickens, and that in any case I certainly wasn't about to use up my leverage getting documents for an intangible woman and an intangible child. There were plenty of tangible women and tangible children I could help, and come back if you find your own."

"How'd he take that?" I asked, truly curious.

"Politely. As always. About a week later, just as I was closing up the office, he wandered in and said he needed my opinion of something. He trusted my opinion, he said. He knew I would tell him the truth; it wouldn't take but a minute, he said. Okay, I said, if I can deliver my opinion in one minute, it's yours. Starting now . . .

"He took a sheet of paper from his inside suit pocket, passed it to me, and said, 'Sam, can you tell me if you think that's genuine?' It was a confidential CIA report on me—actually not me but a woman I was seeing, kind of living with, really—and the report said she'd been born in the North and was probably a low-level enemy spy. Well, spy is too grand a word. Maybe they said agent, maybe they said sympathizer, maybe they said pawn—but you know what I mean. 'Is it genuine, do you think?' Marshall said.

"Naturally, my first instinct was that he was ready to blackmail me, but before I could figure out how to deal with *that,* he said, 'If it is genuine, and she means anything to you, it might be a good idea to get her out of your life. Or, at any rate, your house. Do you think it is?'

"To this day, I don't know why I trusted him. Hell, this was a guy who'd been using me for months, as an information bank, as a conduit to all of official American Saigon—all of official American Vietnam, really— and who'd just handed me a CIA document, which meant he was in bed with those cocksuckers. But I did. I said, yes, I think it's genuine. And I picked up the phone to warn her.

"Quick as a gunshot, Marshall pointed at the phone with one hand and cupped his ear with the other, to let me know that if the CIA had done all this work on her, maybe they'd tapped my phone, too. 'Thank you, Matt,' I said, 'and what can I do for you?' 'Take me to dinner,' he said.

"First, of course, we scooted over to my house to get my friend out of there. I packed her things, while he kept her calm by making her tell him the Vietnamese word for every item in the bedroom. Then we dropped her off at her cousin's. At dinner, he said, 'Sam, I'd like to put everything in order, can you help me out?' " Spiegel laughed appreciatively.

"So you did it?"

"Is that a serious question?"

"Do you remember what name you used for the woman on the marriage license—her maiden name, I mean?"

He thought, then shook his head.

"Does Nguyen Thi Dinh ring a bell?"

"No. But that doesn't mean it wasn't Nguyen Thi Dinh—it's twenty years."

"What about Chau, or Chau Chau?"

"Same answer."

"Do you remember what name you used for the child?"

Once more, he thought. "Something with M. Maybe just the initial. I think just the initial, because he didn't know whether it was a boy or a girl."

"What about for the exit visas and tickets?"

"Marshall, of course," he said. "Otherwise, they wouldn't have been able to leave—they had to be relatives."

"Did Marshall have a nickname?"

Spiegel thought. "No."

From my case I drew the mystery-wall blowups and put them on his desk. "Do you know any of these people? Marshall had their pictures on his wall."

He put on his glasses and began flipping through the pictures: At Ma, he hesitated. "I think I saw him around." Sheepishly, he added, "Despite my liberal principles, I'm no good with Asian faces, either."

"Does the name Ma, or Ghost, mean anything to you?"

"No," he said. He flipped anew, then paused, "Terry Quinn," he said fondly. "I heard he was dead. Is that true?"

"I haven't confirmed it."

He stopped at the picture of the man speaking into the microphone. "I think this guy was a stringer for a bunch of radio stations in the Midwest. I never really knew him—nobody wanted to talk to USAID people—but I saw him around a lot. He was always stoned. What's his name?"

"Buzz is all I know."

"Didn't he become somebody—I seem to remember that—one of those guys who parlayed Vietnam into a career?"

"Somebody, how?"

"I don't know," he said. "But somebody. The kind of somebody who gets a paragraph in *People* magazine. Or did he get killed?" He thought anew. "Now I'm confused. I think he did get killed."

When he came to the picture of the group seated at the rooftop restaurant, he stiffened, and very slowly his face turned red. At last, he said, "I always have to remind myself that Marshall didn't play any favorites. He made everyone his best friend." He brought his finger close to the photo to touch a face, but changed his mind and picked up a letter opener to use as a pointer.

"Hal Dunbar, *Time* magazine, or maybe *U.S. News,* or *Life*—he's dead now. We used to call him Mister Knees, because that was the position he took vis-à-vis anyone in authority, especially the ambassador.

"Les Fisher—USIS; nice guy, but a eunuch; he was famous for sincere, inaccurate leaks. Last I heard he was with Radio Free Europe, maybe Radio Marti. Any place where he could honestly lie for his country.

"This is D. D. Kenilworthy, Defense Attaché's office. If you wanted to be sure to be double-crossed, this was the guy to see. Guaranteed to fuck you over. I have no idea where he is or if he's alive or dead. Let's hope dead.

"And this . . ." He moved the tip of the letter opener to the image of the man in the rakish straw hat. ". . . is everybody's favorite spook, Barry Randall."

"I have a nickname of B.H.," I said.

Spiegel smiled nastily. "For Bleeding Heart. It was used ironically. Barry Randall's heart didn't bleed."

The undisguised hatred in his tone made me ask, "Did Randall write the report on your friend, do you think?"

"No. Barry Randall was much too important to write reports on the Vietnamese girlfriends of USAID wonks."

"Could Marshall have gotten the report from him?"

"Maybe." Spiegel studied the face under the straw hat. "He's got to be the reason for the picture. He's the only one in this bunch who would have been useful to Marshall. Barry Randall was very useful to lots of people."

"Do you know where he is?"

"Where he is? *If* he is is more like it. I mean, do spooks exist when they're not spooking? Retired is my guess. He was never much of a bureaucratic player, and the CIA is like a Wall Street law firm—it's up or sideways, and sideways is out. They usually wind up in think tanks—think tanks believe spooks bring class into the room."

CHAPTER 27

THE THINK TANK WAS named the Delaware Institute. But when I called and asked for Barry Randall, the receptionist said, "Mr. Randall is not available."

"Does that mean he's tied up, or does it mean he's not on the premises?"

"He's not available," she repeated.

"When will he be available?" I said.

"I can't actually say. Please hold." She answered another call, or maybe three other calls, and returned. "I can't actually say."

"May I leave a message?"

"If you like," she said. "But since I don't know when he'll be available, I don't know when he'll retrieve it."

"I'll take a chance," I said, but by then I was on hold again.

Back she came. "I'm waiting for your message."

"Ask him to call Adam Bruno—B-R-U-N-O," I said and gave her my office number. "I'm an attorney-at-law."

"Subject of message?"

"Tell him the tests came back positive, and my client is prepared to go to court," I said.

In less than two hours, Randall called back, his voice under control, but at a cost: "Mr. Bruno, this is Barry Randall. Before anything else, can you give me your home and office addresses and phone numbers, and your Social Security number? In the light of your message, I need to confirm you are who you say you are."

Since I was sure he'd already confirmed that, I gave him the numbers, which, I could tell, surprised him. "The message was just a ruse," I said amiably. "I figured if I told you I wanted to talk to you about Vietnam, and Matt Marshall, you wouldn't have returned the call."

"You're right," he said, "I wouldn't have."

"When would be a good time to get together?"

"I have nothing to say about Vietnam, and I've never heard of Matt Marshall."

"Mr. Randall," I said, "I'm not after state secrets—it's a boring domestic matter."

"I have nothing to say about Vietnam, and I've never heard of Matt Marshall."

"You were over there, weren't you?"

"I have nothing to say about that."

"I've got a photo of you with Hal Dunbar, Les Fisher, and D. D. Kenilworthy—you're at a rooftop restaurant in Saigon."

"I've never heard of any of those people."

"Mr. Randall," I said, "I don't know what you think I'm up to, but all I'm doing is a simple trace job for Matt Marshall's estate, and I can use your help."

"I couldn't care less what you're up to, Bruno, and I don't want to help you."

Quickly, I played my ace. "By the way, Sam Spiegel sends his regards— you've heard of him, haven't you?"

A quick intake of breath, then calm. "No, I've never heard of Sam Spiegel."

"Are you sure, Mr. Randall? USAID? Skinny guy. Lots of hats. Had a local girlfriend, a live-in, actually—you heard of her, didn't you?"

"I've never heard of Sam Spiegel or his live-in girlfriend or Matt Marshall, or anyone else you've mentioned," he said flatly, and I knew he was about to hang up.

"Are you at the Delaware Institute every day?"

"If you come here uninvited, I'll have you arrested for trespassing," he said, and did hang up.

After entering my notes of the conversation into the computer, I looked for a lever to use on Randall.

A waste of time. Barry Randall—or, at least a version of Barry Randall—existed in various data banks, but all the material was so conspicuously innocent that it had to be sanitized. To the world, Barry Randall was an upright, boring civil servant who'd resigned in good grace from the federal government, had taken a Ph.D. in international studies at Columbia University, and found a cozy nest in the world of think tanks. (The

Delaware Institute was his third.) He had even published some well-received monographs on the future of back-channel diplomacy under the new world order, and—the academic's wet dream—a killingly dull piece on industrial espionage on the Op-Ed page of the *New York Times*.

In two hours, I learned nothing useful about Randall, so I decided to punish myself further by writing an interim report—to me alone—as a way of taking stock:

> Matt Marshall returned to Vietnam in 1974 to find his woman Cricket and their (unnamed, unsexed) child.
>
> In order to do that, he definitely made allies of: Sam Spiegel and (I'm sure) Barry Randall (and of an ARVN officer named Ghost).
>
> He possibly made allies of: Hal Dunbar, Les Fisher, and D. D. Kenilworthy. (And a radio reporter nicknamed Buzz.)
>
> He probably booked tickets with Terry Quinn.
>
> Sam Spiegel says he never saw Cricket and the child, and doubts Marshall found them.
>
> Barry Randall will not talk to me, and I don't have a lever to make him talk.
>
> I don't know who Buzz is, and Sam Spiegel believes he got killed.
>
> I don't know who Ghost is or who can tell me.
>
> Terry Quinn is either dead or so far underground I can't find him.

The phone rang, interrupting me.

"Mr. Bruno, Karel Rasic. Are you well?"

"I hope you're about to make me better," I said, feeling my adrenaline rise like a geyser.

Rasic laughed warmly. "Oh, I do hope so, Mr. Bruno, I do fervently hope so. Are you terribly busy Saturday?"

"I can always find some time."

"Excellent," Rasic said. "Our Swiss friend, Mr. Anton Klee of Bern—do you remember Mr. Anton Klee of Bern?"

"How could I forget?"

"Excellent. Mr. Anton Klee of Bern will be making a stop in the metropolitan area on Saturday, and might be willing to have a cup of coffee with you."

"Do you know where yet, Mr. Rasic?"

"No, I'm sorry, I do not," he said solemnly, "Mr. Anton Klee has not yet made up his mind, but I'm sure if Mr. Klee is willing he will inform you exactly. Or perhaps I should say, expressly—my English is very clumsy sometimes."

"No, you express yourself very precisely," I said. "By the way, have you heard from our mutual acquaintance?"

"Mr. Laird has been in touch. Naturally, I have told him that Mr. Anton Klee of Bern might be willing to speak to you this weekend. He approves."

"Naturally," I said. "Thank you again, Mr. Rasic."

"You're more than welcome, Mr. Bruno."

The Federal Express guy arrived at 3:37. The overnight envelope—sent from K. Rasic at the Yugoslav Mission to the United Nations—contained a Polaroid snapshot of a bearded sixtyish man sitting at the controls of an aircraft. He wore a safari jacket and a White Sox cap; from under the cap flowed a long, bound ponytail. I found the 1975 photo of Terry Quinn and compared it to the Polaroid. It took me a while to be sure, but it was the same man.

On the back of the snapshot was scrawled: MacArthur Airport, 6:30 A.M. Saturday.

CHAPTER 28

HE STROLLED INTO THE terminal at 6:45, wearing exactly what he'd worn in the snapshot. I was unprepared for how big he was—I put him at six-four and 270, easy. If he had a pistol under his safari jacket, I didn't spot it.

I gave him a small wave, and he casually changed direction and wandered over to me. When he reached me, he looked me over and said, "If you're Adam Bruno, who am I?"

"Anton Klee," I said.

He grinned and offered his hand. "The former Terry Quinn." He pointed through the window to a DC-9 parked at a distant hangar. "We can eat there."

Once we settled in the cockpit, Quinn took off his boots and his safari jacket—he did have a pistol in a holster, but it looked like a 9-millimeter, not a .45—and served us his version of a healthy breakfast: bagels with cream cheese, smoked salmon, onion, and tomato; a pecan ring cut in quarters; apple pie; strawberries and bananas; and coffee. As he laid it out, he explained that the meal contained balanced portions of all four main food groups.

While we ate, we chatted about flying, commercial airlines versus charters, jumbos versus corporate jets, tower IFR versus satellite IFR, stabilizers, emergency chutes, that kind of thing. Two or three times he used a cellular phone to call somebody to say, "Well, where are they?" But he didn't sound anxious or impatient, and when I asked if he was waiting for anyone, or if I was keeping him, he said, "They'll get here."

I couldn't tell whether he was sizing me up or if he didn't like to talk about serious matters while he ate; in any case, it wasn't till he'd finished the apple pie, poured us a third cup of coffee, and belched contentedly that he said, "Okay. Let's boogie."

After turning on my recorder, I said, "In nineteen seventy-four, seventy-five, a man named Matt Marshall went to Vietnam to look for a woman and a child—his child—so he could take them out of the country. I don't have any real evidence that he found them or got them out, but I know he tried. A few weeks ago, Marshall died and—"

I stopped because Quinn had gone bleached white, and was about to let his coffee cup fall from his grip. Hastily, I leaned over and took it from him.

"Died of what?" he said accusingly, as though I'd been the cause of death.

"A stroke," I said. "It was in all the papers."

"I don't live here," Quinn said. "I don't see the fucking papers." He opened a First Aid cabinet, found a bottle of Wild Turkey, took his cup back from me, poured a shot into it, poured a shot in my cup, and closed his eyes for a few seconds. When he opened them, he said, "You ever meet him?"

"No."

"Your loss," he said, so matter-of-factly that the hairs rose on the back of my neck. "Okay. Okay. He died of a stroke a few weeks ago. And . . . ?"

"And he left half his estate to the child he had with the Vietnamese. In his will, he said he believed the woman and child made it to the United States. The executors hired me to find the child. Your picture was on his wall, and in one of his letters home he talks about booking airline seats . . ."

Quinn tasted his coffee and added another few drops of Wild Turkey. "Three seats. But I don't think he found the woman and kid—he flew out by himself."

"With you?"

"With me. The last civilian flight out of Saigon. April twenty-seventh, nineteen seventy-five."

"What names did he book the seats in?"

Quinn rapped his forehead with his knuckles. "He had a name for the woman, some kinda creepie-crawlie . . ."

"Cricket."

"Right. Matthew Marshall, wife Cricket Marshall, and minor child . . . minor child . . ." He rapped his forehead again. "Minor child—M. Marshall."

"Did Marshall have a nickname?"

"A nickname? Uh uh. Everyone called him Matt."

For a few minutes, we sipped our laced coffee in silence. Then, Quinn said, "You got any kids?"

"No."

"I got sixteen—five wives, sixteen kids. They're all over; talk about your scattered seed. We stay in good touch. When I fly in, I call, I take 'em up, I take up their kids. We get along good. I get along good with the wives, too—I love every one of 'em. Love every woman I ever fucked. But staying home . . ." He shook his sadly. "Staying home . . . How come you never had any—you got weak juice?"

"Just when my wife and I wanted them, we didn't want them with each other," I said.

"You should've had 'em anyway," Quinn said in amiable disapproval. "Had 'em with anyone; they're much better than goddamn grownups when you get older." His cellular phone rang. "Yeah . . . you gotta be kidding? . . . How long is it going to take to change it? . . . Okay, okay, don't stop to get laid . . ." He hung up. "Stupid goddamn flat tire."

Offhandedly changing topics, he said, "I'll tell you for nothing, that Cricket was a fucking knockout."

"What?!" I shouted explosively.

"Jesus!" Quinn cried, leaping up and spilling his coffee. "He had a picture! A picture. I never saw her." He found a cloth, wiped up the coffee, and refilled his cup. "Man, don't shout, okay. Wave, but don't fucking shout."

"Sorry," I said. "I've been having a hard time."

"A knockout," Quinn said wholeheartedly. "You know the way they get over there when they're right . . ." He ran out of words, and shaped a face with his hands. "I could never decide whether the Vietnamese or the Laotians or the Thais were more beautiful. Then I met a Cambodian. I married her: wife number three. If you're standing at the Gates on the Day of Judgment and the Lord says, you can take one Asian lovely with you for all eternity, you'd go crazy before you could make up your mind." He laughed in elation. "I've moved on—these days I'm married to a Haitian. Pitch black. What a great fucking world!"

More thoughtfully, almost to himself, he said, "Matt's problem was he had to have just that one, his Cricket, nobody else, and that will kill you. He knew that. He *knew* that—but he got hung up, hung up on her, hung up on the kid. He'd never seen the kid, but he was hung up on it, anyway."

He focused on me: "You think you're having a hard time; you're not.

You're looking for a Vietnamese in a country where Vietnamese are *visible*; you're looking in a country where there's no war. You're not having a hard time. This is a hard time: End of March, beginning of April nineteen seventy-five, the American Embassy gets crazy fucking jealous of me because I am running this ferry service for kids, damaged kids mostly, but orphans, all of 'em. I am delivering planeloads of kids every day to churches and foster agencies and Christ-knows-what-else in the United States, and I never lose a kid, and the embassy is pissing a hundred percent pure green bile. They still hate me for Da Nang—shit, I am the guy goes in there with two 727s—this is after the place is crunched—and pulls out three hundred people. I am the guy taking rice and guns into Cambodia when they're telling me if I land the Khmer Rouge is going to barbecue my balls for breakfast. Every time I go near the embassy, the Marine guards are loading special soft-tip rounds just for me.

"Now, I mean *this* jealous: One day, the embassy goes to Friends for All Children, and they say, listen, we need your help, we want to take out the orphans, us, not Terry Quinn, the publicity-hungry, gun-toting millionaire misfit, us the good guys, the guys who really know what we're doing in 'Nam. We'll take a couple of thousand kids off your hands, and we'll call the whole thing Operation Babylift. What do you say?

"Well, what could they say? Yes, is what they say, and the embassy gets right to work. Operation Babylift—the government can't do anything without sticking the word *operation* in front of it—is officially launched. Phase One, two hundred fifty kids are gonna fly to freedom, courtesy of Uncle Sam. Okay, what's coming in, somebody says? A Galaxy C-5A—you remember them? humongous fuckers—is due in. It's loaded with guns and ammo and rockets for our stalwart ARVN allies. They can't believe their fucking luck! Get the reporters, get the photographers, get the TV crews, get every government flack that can walk and talk, we are into movietime! We're going to unload the guns and load the kids! Oh, man!

"The Galaxy circles Tan Son Nhut so everyone can see it, and then it lands. It pulls up nice and slow and stops at a perfect angle in the sunlight. It shines, it gleams—I think they actually waxed the fucker. They open the doors and start unloading guns and ammo; in the meantime, a bunch of buses jammed with kids pull up on the taxiway; the cameras start turning, the flashbulbs start popping. The flacks start loading the kids onto the Galaxy.

"The littlest ones and the blind and the crips upstairs, to the seats on the flight deck, two in a seat. The other kids down below, in the cargo hold, strapped in like baggage. You got no windows on a Galaxy; it's a freighter, you don't need windows. Once they shut the doors—you know those doors at the back? They look like giant clamshells. Once they shut the doors, it's dark except on the flight deck.

"Okay. Doors are shut. Up they go with two hundred fifty kids and one hundred grownups, escorts and crew. No space, no light, but what the hell, the orphans are flying to freedom. Freedom!

"There's one little thing about a Galaxy C5A—every once in a while, when it's airborne, the clamshell doors, they blow. Actually, maybe more often than every once in a while. Nobody's keeping statistics. But it's a freighter, who gives a shit? You lose a few tons of rice, a few tons of guns, the ARVN only sells them to the VC anyway, no big deal.

"That day, it was a big deal.

"Around fifteen minutes out, the pilot sees one of his cute little red lights flashing: rear hatch trouble, clamshell door trouble. Hey, he's used to it, he'll just swing back to Tan Son Nhut, check it out. He tells the tower what he's doing and heads back. He's just about got the field in his sight, and boom! Rock and roll! The monster grows a mind of its own, and nothing he does helps; nothing fucking helps, the monster is going down, man. Down down, down.

"You guessed right: The clamshell doors blew." Quinn smiled ghoulishly. "The lucky kids got killed right then—when they got sucked out of the plane. Whooooosh!

"The pilot's a genius, he brings it down in a rice paddy, and he slides it along for a few hundred yards and finally he stops; water and mud come pouring in to the cargo deck. A fire starts.

"This is on a nice clear day, so everybody sees him go down and everybody sees the smoke. Air America gets its choppers there right away. They are on the case.

"Just about now, Matt and me show up at Tan Son Nhut. We're supposed to go to Nha Trang; I'm gonna ferry some people outta there. The NVA is getting closer; Matt's gonna visit some nuns who have a small orphanage there. We're planning a nice little outing.

"We walk into this fucking nightmare. Air America choppers are coming in waves, whup whup whup whup whup; every goddamn ambulance in Saigon is screaming up, waaaoooooooooo; clerks and typists and press agents are helping doctors and nurses carry these *things* from the choppers to the ambulances. Not one of these things is moving, not one of these things is crying, not one of these things is pissing down its leg.

"Now don't forget this: I'm with a guy who's been looking for his kid in orphanages for maybe nine months, and this is a Galaxy full of orphans. Now maybe he's checked out these kids one time or another, maybe in his head he's sure none of them is his, but . . . but . . ." Quinn stopped to glance at his hand, which was shaking slightly. He put down his cup and methodically cracked all his knuckles while continuing.

"You ever seen a lot of dead kids? I don't give a shit what else you ever see in your whole stupid life, it is a birthday party on the fucking beach compared to seeing a lot of dead kids. And if you believe one of those kids maybe is yours—if you *imagine* one of those kids maybe is yours—you are so deep in the shit, you can't believe you'll ever come up. You are staring at the bleeding end of the fucking world.

"They lost about two hundred kids in Phase One of Operation Babylift, and, surprise, surprise, there was no Phase Two—after that, they left it up to me. I took the last load of kids out on, lemme think, the twentieth or the twenty-first. Church in San Jose wanted them. Those Christian shouters love their crips."

"You said he was going to visit an orphanage in Nha Trang . . . ?"

"Yeah, a bunch of nuns ran it. French nuns. Ex-whores, somebody told me."

"Did you take him around to a lot of orphanages?"

"I didn't take him to any—if there was one where I was going, he hitched a ride."

"Did he talk to you about what he was doing?"

Quinn shrugged. "The usual: He'd gotten a Vietnamese girl in a family way and he'd dumped her, and now he was looking to do the right thing."

"Nothing else?"

"Like what?" Quinn said, sounding genuinely puzzled.

"Like what he planned to do with them if he found them and got them out . . . ?"

"He didn't talk about that."

"Did you ask?"

"Not my business," Quinn said harshly.

"But you knew he was married . . . ?"

"What are you, some kinda fucking priest?!" Quinn shouted. "He did the right thing! He came back, man! You know how many just knocked 'em up and went home? Sent 'em a letter full of lies and a ten-dollar bill, or a twenty-dollar bill, and went home. Wouldn't give 'em a ribbon, or a unit patch, or a goddamn dog tag. No! That was for the little woman back on the homefront, the one blowing the weight lifter down at the Texaco station. That's who they saved their names and souvenirs for. I know who came back, and anybody who came back, I don't give a shit he was married, he did the right fucking thing. Yeah, I knew. So fucking what?"

Placatingly, I said, "What I wanted to find out was whether he'd told you his plans. Was he going to get a divorce? Were he and Cricket and the child going to make a new start somewhere? Was he going to stay with his wife and set up Cricket and the kid in a place close by? Far away? Did he have friends he could count on to take care of Cricket and the child—that's the sort of stuff I'm trying to find out."

More composed, Quinn said, "He didn't talk about it."

"And you never asked . . . ?"

"Sure I asked," Quinn said. "I liked him. You like somebody, you ask 'em things." He shrugged. "He said he didn't know what he was going to do. Maybe he was lying to me. It's twenty years, I can't tell anymore." He looked searchingly at me. "You been on him a while, you think he was lying to me?" His voice shook very slightly. "Is he the kind of guy who lied to people who liked him?"

"No," I said firmly. "That doesn't fit with what I've found." I hesitated, and Quinn tensed slightly in reaction. "Once in a while," I said, "he left things out. But if he told you he didn't know, he didn't know."

Quinn's phone rang again. "Yeah," he said into the mouthpiece. "Okay . . . about one hundred yards east of the United hangar . . . don't worry about it, it's aced." He disconnected and said, "The flat's fixed, and they're rolling."

I opened my case and passed him the later batch of pictures. Efficiently, he began flipping through them. "These guys—the ones in hard hats—they worked for the same contractor Matt did."

"Do you remember their names?"

"Nah."

"What about the name of the contractor?"

"Something Electric. Something Wireless. Something Communications. Something Power." He continued flipping. "Don't know, don't know, don't know; this is that doctor who stitched up kids at one of the native hospitals. He got killed in Ethiopia, or maybe Chad, or maybe Somalia, one of those famine countries." He barely paused at the photo of Ma. "I never had anything to do with ARVN officers; major on up, they're all fucking murderers."

He stopped at the picture of Buzz, the radio reporter. "I remember this guy—he was one of the crazies who stayed after the fall. Who is he?"

"All I have is Buzz."

"Right. Buzz."

"Do you recall his last name?"

"Uh uh. Just Buzz." He laughed. "That's what he always had on. I don't think I ever saw him straight. Booze, hash, grass, smack, acid, no wonder he stayed—he thought he was tripping. Did he get out? I heard not."

"Sam Spiegel thinks either he got out and became a minor celebrity, or he got killed. Do you know?"

Quinn slowly shook his head. "Not for sure. It was after the NVA took the city. But I heard he bought it." He went on to the next photo: "Dunbar, he worked for one of the weekly magazines—he went to Da Nang with us; shit in his pants when we hit the runway. Fisher, he was with the propaganda guys; he was okay, kinda a good-hearted stuffed doll. Kenilworthy, DAO, a sack of pus that resembled a man. This is as fine a pack of pussy-whipped liars and douchebags as you'll ever meet, though the rumor was Dunbar took it up the old Hershey Highway."

He moved his finger to the image of Barry Randall and put his fingertip on the face. "You find this guy yet?"

I pretended I didn't see where his finger rested. "Which guy?"

"Barry Randall."

"Uhuh."

Trying to mask the anxiety in his voice, Quinn said, "Did he tell you him and Matt were friends, or what?"

"He wouldn't talk to me," I said.

"Nah, they weren't friends," Quinn said decisively. "Barry Randall never had a friend in his life—Matt was covering his bases."

"How do you mean?"

"Randall was Exit Central—you wanted to get your Vietnamese out, Barry Randall was the guy to see."

"Not Sam Spiegel?"

"Sam was AID—he had channels, but not like Randall had. Randall was CIA; he was wired into everybody." Quinn stared through the windshield to watch a Gulfstream take off. "He got a lot out. The ones he didn't burn."

"Burn how?"

"To the fucking bone," Quinn said. He licked the tip of his finger and rubbed it in a tiny circle on Randall's face.

"You went to him, and you said, Mr. Randall, sir, I got so-and-so and so-and-so I need to get out—my maid, my secretary, my radio operator, my driver, my clerks, my typist—and Randall said Okay, gimme some honest ID so I can do the right thing; no bullshit ID, honest ID, so you won't have a problem with the Vietnamese Foreign Ministry.

"So everybody gives him honest IDs. Randall vets the IDs, with the Foreign Ministry, with ARVN military intelligence, with our military intelligence, with State, with his own people, and if anyone's dirty—and dirty to Barry Randall is having a tenth cousin north of the thirty-eighth parallel—he calls 'em in and puts 'em to work. He makes minispies of 'em, and the targets are their brothers and sisters and aunts and uncles and cousins and husbands and wives and kids.

"If they don't spy, he tells 'em, he won't help 'em get out. So, they spy. If they come up with shit, he says This is shit, this won't get you out. If they come with good stuff—true good stuff, or fake good stuff, it's all the same to him—he says Okay, this isn't shit, this is good stuff, this gets you out, but these people, your relatives, they gotta stay—they're the enemy, and you just proved it."

"What about the people who were clean?"

Quinn laughed. "Even better. You're clean, Randall says, okay, you're exactly the kind of Vietnamese immigrant we want in the good old U.S. of A. But I'm a bit worried about your boss—your American boss, the one who came to me to help you get out. So you watch him, and you report to me."

Quinn grimaced in disgust and flipped to the next picture, which was of Sam Spiegel standing over the bag of Texas rice. "What's Sam doing these days?"

"Selling books near Harvard."

"He always did read too much," Quinn said. "Whatever happened to that girl he lived with?"

Caught off-guard, I said, "Girl?"

"Yeah, a Vietnamese. Nice. Big tits for a local. I thought they had something really good going."

Neutrally, I said, "We didn't talk about it."

Not neutrally enough. "You wanna give that another try," Quinn said, "but without the bullshit?"

"He heard that she might be in trouble, and he got her out of his house."

"What kinda trouble?"

"She was originally from the North, and somebody told him the CIA was watching her."

Quinn flipped back to the photo that included Randall and shook his head in regret. "I had a chance to kill him; I let it go by. Stupid." He squared the edges of the pictures and passed them back to me.

"Did Randall ever burn you?" I asked.

Quinn snorted. "Nah, Randall never burned me. Wanted to. Was ready to. But I heard about it. One night I took him out for a drink—the place in the picture—and I told him there was a rumor going around he was he was planning to burn me. And before he could smile his ugly

fucking barracuda smile, I told him I'd paid a visit to Cao Lee Hanh."
Quinn mimed pulling the chain of a toilet. "Terry, he says real fast, Terry,
it's only a rumor, don't believe a word of it, Terry, I admire you; you're
a great humanitarian; you're a patriot; I wouldn't hurt you, Terry."

"Cao Lee Hanh was who?" I said.

"Randall was no different than anybody else—he liked a piece of local
ass, and Lee was his. Trouble was, Lee was a couple of other people's, too.
He got wind of it, and told her he expected exclusivity, and she told him
he could have exclusivity so long as he picked up all the tabs, otherwise
anyone who picked up any tabs had a claim. He didn't like that. She didn't
give a shit he didn't like it, and she kept on doing whoever she was doing.

"So he tried to burn everybody she was fucking, two guys, three guys,
I'm not sure, but one of them didn't stay burned—guy from AP or UPI
or Agence France Presse. Big guy, bigger than you. Mean drunk. He goes
looking for Randall and finds him at the Alamo. Walks up to him and
kicks him in the balls; breaks both his thumbs and sticks a swizzle stick in
his left eye. Rams it so deep, he almost kills him.

"Randall crawls into his cave and licks his wounds and plots away. He's
too shrewd—or too chicken—to go after the guy, so he goes after Lee
instead.

"One morning around first light, he takes her up in an Air America
chopper, strips her, fucks her on the deck, throws her out the door at
thirty-five thousand feet, and sends the coordinates of the drop to the guy
from Agence France Presse. He comes to me, I borrow a chopper, and we
go look. The coordinates are on the money; Lee's there. Pieces of her,
anyhow."

Faintly, a horn sounded twice, and Quinn peered through the window.
Coming toward the plane was what once had been a school bus. "You
about done?" Quinn said.

I nodded and put away my tape recorder, notebook, and photos. Once
I packed up, he escorted me to the door and let me precede him to the
ground. At that moment, three school buses—which were crammed with
passengers—pulled up alongside the plane. Quinn signaled the drivers to
wait at their wheels. He turned to shake my hand.

"Thanks for the talk," he said. "It's nice to remember him."

"If I need to reach you," I said, "where are you based these days?"

"Jamaica," he said and found a business card in his shirt pocket and
passed it to me. The raised lettering read: "Lilliput Airlines, Dean J. Swift,
executive director."

"Lilliput Airlines?" I said.

"We're a tiny outfit."

"Are you Dean J. Swift?" I said.

"I have that honor," Quinn said, laughing. "Swift was Irish, just like me." He glanced at the bus drivers, put his arm around my shoulder, and unmistakably pushed me toward the terminal. "As we say in the old country, may the road rise to meet you, may the wind be always at your back."

CHAPTER 29

"MR. RANDALL IS NOT available," the operator said, and put me on hold.

When she returned, I said, "May I leave a message?"

"If you like," she said. "But since I don't know when he'll be available, I don't know when he'll retrieve the message. Please hold."

A leisurely wait, then: "I'm waiting for your message."

"Ask him to call Adam Bruno—B-R-U-N-O," I said. "The number is—"

"Please hold," she said. Another interlude. She came back: "Are you Mr. Bruno?"

"Yes," I said.

"You're certain you're Mr. Bruno?"

"Yes, I'm certain," I said.

"Mr. Randall left explicit instructions to take no messages from Mr. Bruno," she said, and hung up.

"Fuck you and the horse you rode in on," I said to the dead receiver.

To calm down—and to evade any more immediate disappointments in the outside world—I busied myself doing a full-scale organizing job on everything I'd collected on Matt Marshall. After entering my notes of the conversation with Terry Quinn in the computer, I reread all the raw interviews, wrote summaries of them, printed the summaries, and, finally, updated and printed my interim report.

Matt Marshall returned to Vietnam in 1974 to find his woman Cricket and their (unnamed, unsexed) child, but apparently did not find them.

[NOTE 1: Marshall's brother and sister knew he made the trip but not why; who else knew (Beth? Twomey? Laird?) and how much did they know?]

In order to find his child, Marshall definitely made allies of: Sam Spiegel and Barry Randall (and of an ARVN officer named Ma/ Ghost who acted as his eyes and ears in Asia once Marshall returned empty-handed to the United States).

He possibly made allies of: Hal Dunbar, Les Fisher, and D. D. Kenilworthy. (But Kenilworthy may be dead, and the other two don't appear worth following up.)

He probably made an ally of a radio reporter nicknamed Buzz, but Buzz appears to have been killed.

He definitely booked three tickets with Terry Quinn (under the name Marshall) and undoubtedly with other charters.

Sam Spiegel says he never saw Cricket and the child, and doubts Marshall found them.

Terry Quinn says he never saw Cricket and the child, and doubts Marshall found them (and knows Marshall flew out of Saigon by himself).

[NOTE 2: There is no trace of the woman under any combination of Cricket, Chau, Chau Chau, or Nguyen Thi Dinh; and to search under MARSHALL—without more exact information—strikes me as futile.]

I don't know who Ma/Ghost is or who can tell me; I don't know who is sending me his letters; I believe his version of Cricket's escape from Vietnam; there is no evidence Ghost ever saw Cricket or the child.

[NOTE 3: Of the people Marshall served with, only McGowan has corroborated the existence of Cricket (Chau Chau), and she never saw her. McGowan speculates that if anyone among Marshall's troops ever saw Cricket it would have been Woolff or Randall; my interviews don't support this.]

Barry Randall will not talk to me, and though I believe I have a lever (Cao Lee Hanh) to make him talk, right now, I don't know how to use it.

Carefully, as if it truly mattered, I typed and edited the report, copied it on to disks, and printed it. Anything to feel functional. A few minutes after I finished, while I was ineffectually searching for a method to open up Barry Randall, the phone rang and Matt Marshall, Jr., came on: "What time can I expect you?" he said sunnily.

"Expect me?" I said, and then remembered receiving one of his invitations and forgetting to copy the date in my calendar. "Is the opening tonight?"

"Five to seven," he said, "and I expect you no later than five forty-five." Lowering his voice to a stagy conspiratorial whisper, he added, "All the usual suspects . . ."

"What?"

"I told Mollie Wharton you were coming, and I'm sure she told Wilson Laird, and I'm sure Wilson told Mother, and I'm sure Mother told Wendy and Fred. And I'm sure all of them are dying to find out if you're making any progress. Me, too."

Openings of photo shows—or any art shows, for that matter—weren't in my usual line, but I'd been to just enough of them to suspect the guests rarely gathered to look at what was hanging on the walls. I'd never heard of the two photographers on display—Ruth Orkin and James Van Der Zee—but I got the impression most of the people there had never heard of them, either. An impression Matt junior confirmed.

"Of course not. Maybe a dozen people here know who they are. People who know don't come to openings; people who know come when it's quiet and they can look at the pictures, or even consider buying them." While he talked to me, he kept a keen eye on the throng, saluting or nodding or blowing kisses to visitors as they wandered by.

"Ummmm," he said gratifyingly, and for my benefit tipped his head toward the door. I glanced that way to see Wilson Laird leading Beth Marshall into the gallery; a few steps behind them were Wendy and Fred Marshall. All four managed not to see Matt junior or me, and they wasted no time finding pictures to admire at the far end of the gallery.

Matt junior leaned close and said, "Talk to me before they decide to notice you. What have you learned in your travels?"

"My travels?" I said.

"Aunt Rachel said you danced with Abigail." He laughed. "Did you have to keep your arms stretched out straight—to protect her ever-developing unborn?"

"No, she wanted people to feel it."

"Ah, she is her mother's daughter."

"How come you weren't there?"

He made a tsk tsk tsk noise. "I wasn't invited." Mock-confidentially, he added, "Rachel has this ludicrous idea that I want to debauch her son. Did you have a good time?"

"Very good."

"People usually do at her house." He cranked up his most dazzling, debonair smile. "Maybe one day she'll have me back. You can intervene on my behalf." A brisker tone, "So, what did you learn in old San Francisco?"

"About what I expected."

He leaned back, studied me from under a perfectly raised eyebrow, and opened his mouth to speak. Before he could, a familiar raucous voice behind me muzzled him:

"Is this where I have to schlepp to see you? To Soho and the anorexic art crowd?"

Herschel, with Mollie Wharton in tow, shook his head moodily, shouldered past me, and stuck his hand out to Matt junior. "Herschel O'Hara. You're Marshall's number one son, right? You know Mollie Wharton; she says you're the smartest of the kids. I trust her judgment; nice to meet you."

"Herschel!" Wharton said.

"He's smart. Where I live, that's a compliment. Isn't it a compliment among the goyim?"

"No," Matt junior said, laughing. "It isn't." He glanced over Herschel's shoulder toward the door. "Excuse me, I see a critic. Time to tastefully go to my knees."

He drifted off, and Herschel seized two glasses of champagne from a passing waitress. He handed one to Wharton, who sipped and said, "Are you making progress, Mr. Bruno?"

Herschel gazed at the ceiling while I composed my answer. "Yes, Ms. Wharton," I said. "I am."

Herschel burst into laughter, and Wharton looked at him crossly. "Did I miss the joke?"

To me, he said, "What kind of progress?"

"About what I expected."

"Can you be more specific?"

"Not without unintentionally misleading you."

"Misleading us how?"

"Anything I tell you at this point is so ambiguous, it will feed either your optimism or your pessimism, and I'd rather avoid doing that."

By that time, Wilson Laird had moved himself into our knot, and Beth Marshall and Wendy and Fred Marshall were only a couple of feet behind him.

"Ambiguous how, Mr. Bruno?" Laird said. "Excuse me, I'm forgetting my manners. Are you well this evening?"

"Very well, Mr. Laird," I said. "Mrs. Marshall . . . Ms. Marshall, Mr.

Marshall." I avoided Herschel's eyes—I knew he'd try to break me up—and focused on Laird. "Ambiguous in the sense of equivocal."

"Ahhh," Laird said. "Ambiguous in the sense of equivocal. Very much like politics."

"He's mocking you," Wendy Marshall said.

"Mr. Bruno?" Beth Marshall said. "He would never do that, would you, Mr. Bruno?"

"Never, Mrs. Marshall."

"We missed the first part of your conversation, Mr. Bruno," she said, more southern than magnolias. "Did Ms. Wharton happen to ask you if you were making any progress?"

"She did," I said, "and I told her yes. Then, she asked what kind of progress, and I told her, about what I expected. Then she asked if I could be more specific, and I told her, not without intentionally misleading her, and she asked in what way, and that's where you came—on ambiguity."

"Oh, for God's sake!" Wendy Marshall said.

"Is this what we're paying you for?" Fred Marshall said, in a tone that often starts bar brawls.

"Easy, pal," Herschel said, "it's a Soho party, not Friday night at the fights."

Ignoring him, Fred Marshall repeated, "I said, is this what we're paying you for?"

"Mr. Marshall," I said, "you're not paying me at all. You believe you are—because the estate is paying me, and you believe the estate belongs to you. It doesn't. It belongs to whomever a court says it belongs to."

Fred Marshall's face went red, and he could barely keep from bunching his fists.

Herschel rolled his eyes and said to Wharton in a stage whisper, "This is not one of the smart ones, right?"

Fred Marshall whirled on him, and instantly I blocked his way. "Herschel . . ." I said warningly.

"Sorry, Adam," Herschel said laconically. "I didn't mean that to be overheard."

Beth Marshall signaled Fred Marshall to back away, and when he did she moved to my side. "Mr. Bruno, you're absolutely right—we're not paying you, we're not your clients. However . . ." She paused as though searching for words. "We do have an interest. Can you at least tell us how much longer you think your inquiries will last?" She offered her most captivating smile. "The tension is terrible."

"Mrs. Marshall," I said, smiling back at her, "if I knew, I'd tell you. But I don't. I've made a lot of progress, but this is the kind of case in which progress doesn't count. What counts is the result. Everybody needs to know for sure, one way or the other—isn't that right? And until I get there, anything I tell you is just noise."

Beth Marshall nodded courteously, then looked pointedly to Laird, who cleared his throat before saying, "Mr. Bruno, this is an inappropriate time and place to talk business, but I wonder if you and I could get together next week . . ."

"For what, Mr. Laird?"

"Mr. Bruno, we—by we, I mean the executors—are not comfortable paying you without having any confirmation that you're actually working. It's no reflection on your integrity to say that this is not a businesslike way of doing things. Usually, reports are submitted, records are verified; after all, Mr. Bruno, the estate's money is being spent. We—the executors— need something to make us comfortable." He smiled as though he were asking for my vote. "I'm open to suggestions, Mr. Bruno."

I pretended to give it some thought. "Why don't I defer billing you till I get a clear-cut result, one way or the other?" I said. "At that time, I'll submit fully documented invoices; if you object to anything, I'll accept third-party arbitration."

Matt junior had wandered over; Beth Marshall nodded infinitesimally. Wendy looked away, and Fred Marshall said, "This is a private conversation."

"Is it really, Fred?" Matt junior said. "Adam, is it? Is my family having a private conversation with you, my guest, at my party, in my gallery? My, my, my."

I answered him. "Mr. Laird isn't comfortable paying me without proof that I'm working. I've offered to defer my bills until I get a clear-cut result, and then let him challenge anything he objects to."

"What could be fairer?" Matt junior said.

Mimicking him nastily, Wendy Marshall said, "What could be fairer?" Turning to me, she said:

"I believe what you're doing, including this offer to defer your bills, is nothing but a scam to milk my family—excuse me, to milk my father's estate—for as much as you can." By then, she was talking loudly enough so that people in the vicinity were turning their heads to listen. "I believe you already have a clear-cut result and that you have no intention of revealing it until you've ripped us off some more. I believe you're a liar and thief," she ended in a near shout.

Before I could tell her what I thought of her, Herschel leaped in front of her and cried:

"It's all right, Ms. Marshall, it's all right! We'll get you your medication.

Don't panic, there's a drugstore right around the corner. Don't panic! It's okay, everyone!" he called out. "There's no history of violence, she's a very docile patient, there is absolutely no history of violence. But stand back! She becomes incontinent, she can't control her orifices. Stand back! Watch your shoes!"

Everybody near us hopped out of the way, and an anxious babble percolated through the gallery.

Herschel hooked one arm in Wharton's and the other in mine, shook his head sympathetically at Beth Marshall, nodded to Wilson Laird, winked at Matt junior, and guided us backward toward the exit.

Herschel took Wharton and me to dinner at a Tuscan place he'd read about, and neither of them brought up the Marshall case again until dessert.

"You owe me something, pal," he said, waving at the waiter for more coffee. "I got you out of the snake pit."

"What do you mean, something?"

Not even bothering to be coy, he tilted his head in Wharton's direction. "For Mollie. I don't want her knowing less than her boss. It's humiliating."

Trying to think of something to tell her that wouldn't damage me if she repeated it either to Laird or Beth Marshall, I finally said, "I don't know if the mother and child are alive, or if they're here. But I know they did escape from Vietnam and got at least as far as Guam. I also know Marshall devoted a year of his life to looking for them." Before Wharton could ask me any questions, I held up my hand. "I can't give you any more details without compromising my investigation."

Measuredly, she said, "I accept that. Can you say whether you think you'll find them?"

"I have no idea. I mean that."

"But you're getting closer, aren't you?" she said.

"Some days, some days not. Today, not," I said, thinking of Barry Randall's refusal to see me.

"Why not?" Herschel said.

"I've got a source who I think can be very useful, and I even have something on him, but he won't talk to me, he won't return my calls, and he won't take my messages."

Herschel hummed "Anything Goes" for a few bars, then began to laugh, and I felt a shiver of anticipation. When he stopped, he said, "Schmuck, little Denny Eagen and the former Secretary of Defense . . ."

CHAPTER 30

WHEN HERSCHEL AND I were still partners, we used to argue about who should take which impossible case. We had a reputation—earned in blood—of doing well with impossible cases, and we got a lot of referrals from lawyers who didn't have the stomach for the work. Our arguments were loud but not serious, because each of us knew the other's preferences, and we weren't dumb enough to let vanity get in the way of victory for the client.

For instance, as much as I hated multiple-death drunk drivers—and I hated them worse than contract killers—contract killers chose their victims, drunk drivers simply killed what was in their way—I loved defending them because juries, especially suburban juries, wanted to be convinced that drunk driving was not a crime but a sort of exuberant extension of, say, double-parking, and I never had much trouble convincing them (not even with a judge's son who spotted what he thought was a deer by the side of the road, steered that way, accelerated, and tore into it. The deer happened to be a sixteen-year-old kid changing a flat tire. My client's car cut him in half and kept going, slashing the fuel line of the sixteen-year-old's car. It caught fire, and the kid's brother, two sisters, and mother and father were incinerated. My client lost his license for a year and did 180 days of community service).

Herschel, on the other hand, hated sexual predators, but he loved to defend them—the more notorious the better—because he knew exactly which emotional buttons to push to confuse jurors into either an acquittal or a deadlock. The only sexual predators Herschel hated to defend were politicians. Herschel believed all politicians were guilty until proven innocent and should be either spit-roasted or injected with nitric acid.

One day, we got a referral from a very eminent law firm that specialized in bond work for the state. The firm wanted us to handle the criminal case of one of its erstwhile senior partners, a former Secretary of Defense who'd moved on to a California think tank called the Crisis Endowment.

The former Secretary of Defense was about to be indicted for felonious statutory rape and sodomy, and since he was a man of integrity and probity and had children and grandchildren, he was refusing to cop a plea and insisting on mounting what lawyers call a vigorous defense.

The moment we hung up, Herschel shouted, "This cocksucker's all yours."

Just as quickly, I replied, "Your meat, Herschel, no pun intended."

We went back and forth for a while, but even though Herschel was dead serious, he knew I detested pols almost as much as he did—especially Republican pols—and that he truly was far better at this kind of case.

At the first conference—Herschel asked me to sit in and tape every word—the former Secretary of Defense, the man of probity and integrity, told this story:

When he'd been in New York six months earlier, he'd stayed at the Pierre, where he always stayed, and one night there was a knock on the door. He opened it to find a boy named Dennis Eagen standing in the hallway in a T-shirt and Jockey shorts. Denny Eagen had locked himself out, he said; could he stay in the former secretary's room till his sister came home from the theater . . . ? Gallant fellow that he was, the former secretary ushered Denny Eagen into his suite and ordered a tray of cookies and a couple of bottles of Lafite Rothschild to wile away the hours until Denny's sister returned. (She was seeing *Beauty and the Beast*.)

Somehow, during those hours, Denny Eagen caught the former secretary off-guard and seduced him—he was ashamed to admit it since he was a happily married grandfather—after which the former secretary fell asleep. When he awoke the next morning, Denny Eagen was gone, but on the pillow was an envelope with a note in it, demanding $7,500 and asking that it be slid under the door of a room down the hall. The former Secretary of Defense was outraged—after all, he'd thought Denny Eagen had seduced him out of love, or admiration, or something. He tore up the note and the envelope.

A few weeks later, he received a phone call from a woman claiming to be Denny Eagen's mother, telling him that Denny Eagen was only fourteen years old and demanding $7,500. He refused. A few weeks later, an envelope arrived at his office: In it was a Xerox of Denny Eagen's birth certificate (he was, in fact, fourteen years old) and a bill for $7,500. He threw it out. A repeat of that envelope arrived a month later, again at his office. He threw it out. A month after that, the Eagens, mother and son, went to the district attorney of New York County and filed a complaint of statutory rape and sodomy.

"That's your story, pal?" Herschel said, with an inflection that would have made an innocent man punch him out.

"Yes, that is my story; and I prefer to be addressed as Mr. Secretary," the client said.

"According to the guy who sent you here, you want to litigate this, is that right, pal?" Herschel said.

"Absolutely," the former secretary said. "I am not your pal."

"Can't help you, pal. Not with that story."

"That story is the truth."

"Sure, pal. Whom do we bill for the consult?"

It was hard for me to tell whether Herschel was bluffing, to smoke out the former Secretary of Defense, or if he was actually ready to let him walk. Herschel didn't ordinarily toss away the kind of money we'd be charging the former secretary—if we litigated, the fee was bound to be six figures. But he *did* detest pols.

"Herschel," I said, "why don't we ask the secretary a couple of questions . . . ?"

"I got one question," Herschel said.

"Yes?" the former secretary said.

"Why the fuck are you lying to us?" Before the former secretary could answer, Herschel gunned on:

"Try this story, pal: You made a deal with Denny Eagen's mother. It's a deal you've made before—not with her, maybe, but with other mothers for other sons. Your tastes are not exactly a state fucking secret. I don't know what the price was—my guess is twenty-five hundred, three thousand—that's about the going rate these days for an all-nighter with a clean kid.

"Okay. What next? Did you ask him to do something and he refused? What'd you ask him to do? Or maybe you didn't ask him. According to the complaint, he's four-eleven, maybe ninety-five pounds. What'd you do to him that he didn't like? Why'd he up the price to seventy-five hundred dollars? And we know he upped it. No way you make a deal for seventy-five hundred for a one-nighter with a fourteen-year-old."

Coldly, the former secretary said, "I made no deal with Dennis Eagen. I never met his mother, and the boy—man—told me he was twenty-one years old. That is my story. If you can't defend me with it, I'll go elsewhere."

"Please, pal, the door. That way; right there. But before you go," Herschel snarled, "listen to my partner. Adam, tell him how it works in New York County; give him the standard sex crimes speech. And call him Mister Secretary, otherwise he'll cry."

"Mr. Secretary," I said, "in New York County, we have a very zealous woman in charge of the sex crimes unit. Her name is Graciela Lopez, and if she could put away a Republican former Secretary of Defense for rape two—that's what statutory rape is in New York State—her career would be made. She'd ascend to the bench in a year."

"Appellate division," Herschel brayed.

"Your defense is that you had consensual sex with a male you honestly believed was of age. The jury will want to hear that from you—they always do when the defense is consent. Which means you will have to take the stand. Now, in addition to being insanely ambitious, Graciela Lopez is capable. She's as good a cross-examiner as you'll ever meet. So when you are on the stand, she will work you over pretty good. Now let's say that's not a problem for you—you've been on the grill before, you can take it, and you come out of cross unmarked—"

Herschel let loose a boisterous, disbelieving laugh.

"It could happen, Herschel," I said. "It could happen. But, Mr. Secretary, Graciela Lopez doesn't need to destroy you during cross, not if she's got willing witnesses. And she has: the boy and his mother. And she will prep them, I promise you. She will prep these willing witnesses to Academy Award level.

"And if by chance Denny Eagen's mother testifies that when she negotiated with you, you explicitly asked how old her son was—and she'll tell the jury that, for sure; and if by chance Denny Eagen testifies that you begged him to call you 'Daddy'—and he'll tell the jury that, for sure; the jury will not see a former Secretary of Defense, the jury will see a dirty old man who likes to buy little boys; and then you will be staring at a D felony. You see, Mr. Secretary, let's say Mrs. Eagen pimped her son to you—"

"Yes?" the former secretary said avidly.

"That's a separate case. If Graciela Lopez wants to bring it. But it is not a mitigating factor in your case. Not under the law, and not with a New York County jury."

After a silence, the former secretary said, "I sincerely believed he was twenty-one."

Herschel jumped in: "How old are your grandchildren?"

"One is eleven, another is—"

"And you're telling these jurors that you believed this child—poor little Denny Eagen—ninety-five-pound, angel-faced Denny Eagen—God, you can hardly see him in the witness stand—you believed this baby was twenty-one years old? Is that your story?" Herschel turned to me. "Send this butt-fucker to Rabinowitz."

After a longer silence, the former secretary said, "Do you always use these tactics?"

"You got it, pal," Herschel said. "We don't defend people who bullshit us, and in my experience, rudeness saves time. Tell us the truth, stop patronizing us, and I'll see what we can do."

The former secretary slumped in his chair, and Herschel poured him a glass of water. After sipping, he said, "I made a deal with his mother for twenty-two hundred dollars. That was supposed to include anything I wanted except . . ." he hesitated.

"Fist-fucking?" Herschel said.

"Yes," the former secretary said. "And it was supposed to be . . ." again he hesitated.

"No condom?" Herschel said.

"Yes. Instead—"

"Did you say that explicitly—for twenty-two hundred dollars I'm not going to use a condom . . . ?"

"I said, 'I don't like using condoms.' "

"What did his mother say?"

"She said that was okay with her."

"Nothing more—that's okay with me . . . ?"

The former secretary snapped, "We were negotiating an illegal sexual act—I didn't take notes."

"What'd you give her in advance?"

"Half. Eleven hundred dollars."

"So, after you've made the deal, paid eleven hundred up front, and little Denny has arrived at your suite, and you munch your cookies and you drink your Lafite, you pull out your joint. What did the kid say?"

"He said, 'Do you have a rubber?' I said no. He—"

"Did you tell him explicitly his mother said that no rubber was okay?"

"No."

"Then what?" Herschel said.

"Dennis grinned and pulled a pack of condoms from his shorts and offered me one. Actually, he volunteered to put it on for me. It was quite sweet."

"And you refused?"

"Well, yes."

"At that moment, did you say, 'Your mother told me no rubber is okay'?"

"No."

"And then?" Herschel said.

"Then, he left."

"Right then?"

"Well, not *right* then." The former secretary looked away; we waited. "I tried to explain that I was sixty-three and medically safe and sound, and he had nothing to fear, but he was stubborn. Very stubborn."

We waited some more; finally: "I asked him again—I even offered him an extra hundred dollars for himself, just between us, he didn't have to share it with his mother, but he refused. Then, I told him I'd made a deal, and I expected him to keep his end of it. I ordered him to do what I told him. He refused." The former secretary licked his lips. "He offered to masturbate me. Not knowing what else to do, I let him. Then, he asked me if he could watch television—the room had the sports channel and he didn't have that at home—and we turned it on.

"While we were watching, I reached for him, and this time he wasn't so stubborn—perhaps it was the wine, perhaps the wine relaxed him. But when I tried to . . . when I tried to get him to fellate me—"

"Without a condom?" Herschel asked.

"Yes. Without one. He pushed me away, quite hard, and I struck out—it was a reflex really, a slap. Nothing serious. A slap. At most, two slaps. Barely slaps. Pushes actually. The way you'd push away a child. Discipline a child—if you have children, you know what I mean. And he got frightened and ran into the bathroom and locked the door. It was so silly. I would never hurt him—he's a beautiful boy. I must have fallen asleep, because when I woke up he was gone."

"Did he actually leave a note on the pillow?"

"No. But his mother did ask for seventy-five hundred dollars, both on the telephone and in writing."

"Did she say why?" The former Secretary of Defense cleared his throat, and Herschel leaned very close to him. "No bullshit, pal . . ."

"She enclosed some doctor's bills. Not for that much, but for nearly thirty-one hundred dollars. Orthopedist's bills."

Herschel leaned back and shook his head in amazement. "Why didn't you just fucking pay?"

"He cheated me!" the former secretary said adamantly. "We made a deal; he reneged."

"Yeah, I can see why you'd believe that," Herschel said. "Let me tell you where you stand. If we go to trial, you will get killed. I mean, fucking killed. By the time Graciela Lopez is through with you, you will be known as a child molester who was ready to give a little boy AIDS—"

"I don't have AIDS!"

"Have you ever been tested?"

"Of course not!"

"So you might have it. And you took a chance of infecting a *child*. Of cutting off seventy years of Denny Eagen's young, untouched life." Herschel smiled ferally at me. "For the first time in my career, I wish I was prosecuting."

The former Secretary of Defense looked at me and repeated, "He cheated me. They both cheated me."

Herschel rolled his eyes before saying:

"This is what we can do, pal: I can go see Graciela. If the Eagens don't have any real evidence of injury—let's pray their goddamn orthopedist didn't take Polaroids—and if we can find other customers of theirs, Graciela might listen to reason. With luck, and a heartfelt remorseful speech at sentencing, I can get you off with a fine and community service. It wouldn't be a bad idea to tell the court you'd like to pay for any therapy little Denny might need, and you'd like to set up a college trust fund for him, Yale maybe, or Columbia, someplace where he'll feel at home."

"A college trust fund at Yale?" the former secretary said incredulously.

"It's a lot cheaper—and quieter—than defending yourself in a twenty-million-dollar civil suit, and I promise you Graciela Lopez will advise the Eagens to bring one."

After a moment's thought, the former secretary said, "What would I have to plead to?"

"Sexual abuse three. Unlawful sexual contact with a person under seventeen."

"Sexual abuse?" he said in a hushed voice. "Isn't there a way to leave out the sex part? Can't I plead to assault? I don't mind pleading to assault."

Shaking his head, Herschel said, "Even if I could get Graciela to go for it, the Eagens'll never buy it."

"Why not?" the former secretary said.

Herschel made the kind of face he makes when he can't believe a defendant's stupidity. "Because they gave you a chance to buy your way out, but you were too cheap to take it. Now, they're pissed off, and they want to hurt you."

"Can't you persuade them not to?"

"I can't talk to them. I can only talk to Graciela, and I don't have anything to persuade her with. Sorry, pal, in Graciela Lopez's eyes you are no kind of candidate for special treatment. Except maybe gelding. Sexual abuse three."

"Will I have to plead in public court?"

"That's the drill," Herschel said.

"I don't think I can do it."

"Sure you can, pal," Herschel said, in the robust tone of a bungee instructor encouraging a first-time jumper to leap off the edge of a cliff.

"You stand up, you clear your throat, you glance shyly at your faithful wife, you nod contritely to the Eagens, you look at the judge, and you admit that you touched Denny Eagen's round, downy cheeks and you brushed your fingertips across his precious, hairless privates.

"Then, you tell the court how terribly sorry you are, and how if you hadn't been under stress and recovering from prostate cancer and taking Halcion, or Prozac, or Twinkies, or Frosted Flakes, you'd never never never have done it; and you swear you'll stay in therapy for as long as it requires; and you beg the forgiveness of your faithful wife and your kids and your grandkids—and most of all the forgiveness of poor little angel-faced Denny Eagen and his sainted mother; and you go home.

"Otherwise, pal, you go to trial, and poor fragile little Denny Eagen—pathetic tears streaming down his Irish altar boy's puss—testifies to twelve horrified respectable Democrats that you tried to stick your naked sixty-three-year-old dick in his tender, vulnerable fourteen-year-old mouth."

Unsurprisingly, the former Secretary of Defense grasped Herschel's logic and copped to sexual abuse 3.

Herschel got him exactly what he'd promised: a fine and community service—and he even persuaded Graciela Lopez to let the former secretary do the service in California, so he could go back to his floor-sized win-dowed office at the Crisis Endowment. The trouble came when we submitted our bill. For months, we saw nothing. Then, a check arrived—for one-quarter of what he owed us.

Herschel called, and the former Secretary of Defense didn't take his call and didn't return it. I called, and got the same treatment. We sent a bill for the remaining three-quarters of our fee. Nothing. Herschel called the former secretary's old law firm to explain our problem. Nothing. We sent a letter to the former Secretary of Defense, copy to the executive director of Crisis Endowment, warning him that we were prepared to go to a collection agency. In return, we got a letter from the executive director of Crisis Endowment, copy to the former Secretary of Defense, copy to the law firm of the Crisis Endowment, warning us that economic harass-ment was a violation of the California Penal Code.

We schemed and schemed, and finally Herschel, in one of his more radiant maneuvers, sent another letter to the former Secretary of Defense. It read:

Dear Mr. Secretary:

As per your instructions, in the next 72 hours, we will be faxing a verbatim transcript of your New York County sentencing hearing to the following recipients . . .

Then, we listed every foundation, university, and think tank in the country.

A day later, Federal Express delivered the former secretary's certified check.

I got the fax number of the Delaware Institute and sent Barry Randall a message:

Dear Mr. Randall:

Thank you for agreeing to see me. My assistant inadvertently purged the time of our appointment from my datebook file, but I seem to recall Friday after lunch—please call with the exact hour.

My publisher and I look forward to hearing your anecdotes about the fall of Saigon, particularly the role played by your associate, Cao Lee Hanh. How would you feel about somebody like Joan Chen for the movie version?

CHAPTER 31

"I WOULDN'T HAVE USED her full name," Barry Randall said, taking my fax from his inside pocket. "Lee would have been enough. More coffee, or would you like a glass of wine? The Delaware Institute is proud of its cellar."

That was no surprise: The Delaware Institute, which was nowhere near Delaware—not the state, not the river, not the county, and not the gap—was housed in a neo-Gothic mansion on about eighty acres of awesomely expensive land right outside Greenwich, Connecticut. At the west end of the ground floor of the mansion was an oak-paneled dining room, which the Delaware fellows donnishly called the cafeteria, and where Randall and I were having coffee and warm pecan cookies.

Delaware had a board of thirty-five eminent citizens and a rotating band of sixty fellows. It was unclear whether the board got paid, but the fellows did, and, according to Delaware's annual report, very nicely, too. As with most think tanks, the source of Delaware's tax-exempt money was a bit vague, but from what I could deduce, much of it came from a midwestern brewer who'd been advised by his press agent that donations to the Cuban American Foundation and the Aryan Nation had lost some of the cachet they'd had under the Republicans.

Delaware specialized in supplying conservatives with position papers on international strategy (who to bomb and when) and domestic economics (how to eliminate taxes on the rich and which illegal immigrants made the best workers). And though most of its fellows were second-rate academics who spent a lot of time kneeling before third-rate politicians, it did dress up its letterhead with a couple of Nobel laureates. It also gave shelter to a couple of dozen retired generals and diplomats, and among those retired diplomats there had to be at least a handful of retired spies.

I hadn't had much experience with spies, so I couldn't tell whether Randall fit the mold or not. He looked more like a tenured teacher at a small liberal arts college than a character out of Ian Fleming, or even a character out of John Le Carré or Graham Greene. He was a bit taller than average, maybe five-eleven, and trim for his age, which I put at around fifty-five. He moved neatly, but not gracefully, the moves of a man who played ball every day but never got good enough to play well. He had a trimmed, graying beard, which seemed out of place, till I realized he must have worn it to obscure his thin, bloodless lips.

Randall ran his palm up and down the fax, trying to flatten the ever-curling thermal paper. "You didn't mention Lee on the phone . . ."

"I hadn't heard about her," I said.

"May I ask who told you?" he said.

"You may ask," I said, "but I won't tell you."

"Did you plan to use any information you have?"

"If necessary," I said.

"What would make it necessary?"

"Mr. Randall, I won't waste your time. Sometime in early nineteen seventy-five, a man named Matthew Marshall approached a man named Sam Spiegel to ask his help in getting a Vietnamese woman and her child out of Saigon."

From my case, I took the envelope with the 1974 to '75 blowups, drew out Spiegel's photo, and put it next to Randall's plate. He glanced at it with no expression.

"I believe Marshall also approached you," I said, and put Randall's photo on top of Speigel's; again Randall glanced down with no expression.

I went on: "Marshall booked three tickets on all the airlines still operating, but when he left Saigon, he left by himself. No woman, no child. Marshall died a few weeks ago, and his estate has asked me to find that child.

"I want you to help me, Mr. Randall, by telling me everything about your dealings with Matt Marshall and everything he told you—or everything you learned on your own—about the woman and the child."

Randall didn't respond at all, so I leaned closer to him and said, "If you don't, or if you lie, I will publicize what I know about you and Cao Lee Hanh."

"Which is what?" he said indifferently, folding the fax and returning it to his pocket.

"Which is enough to make you wish you'd never taken an early-morning flight in an Air America helicopter."

Randall picked up a pecan cookie, inspected it for flaws, found flaws, put it back on the plate, picked up a fresh one, inspected that, and took a tiny bite. After chewing deliberately and rinsing his mouth with coffee, he said, "Do you want to ask questions, or shall I tell you what I know first?"

"Tell me what you know."

"The first time Marshall and I talked at length was around September of nineteen seventy-four. I'd heard about him, of course, because he'd been so busy making friends with everyone. We'd even run into one another a few times—maybe at one of Dunbar's dinners, or at a USIS cocktail party. Marshall was a popular man. Unlike most contractors, he was pleasant, soft-spoken, and gracious with women. By the standards of Saigon in those days, he was a desirable social catch.

"As likable as he was, I didn't trust him, not at all. It was no secret that he was chasing all over the country with Sam Spiegel, and Sam Spiegel is—" He broke off, then said, "You mentioned Spiegel when you called me. Have you talked to him?"

"Uhuh."

"At length?"

"At length."

"What did he say about me?"

"Nothing, really."

Randall signaled the waiter for fresh coffee. "I don't believe you, Bruno," he said. "Sam Spiegel hates me, and if you talked to him at length, he must have said something."

"He said you were very useful to a lot of people—he meant in getting Vietnamese out of Saigon—and that your nickname was . . ." I made a show of searching my notebook. ". . . was Bleeding Heart—is that right, Bleeding Heart?"

"Yes."

"Why did they call you that?"

"Because I was anything but," he said, with more than a trace of pride. "Sam Spiegel and his ilk were the bleeding hearts. They were the ones who wanted to give away the country. They were the fifth column, they were the hidden enemy—not hidden from me, but hidden from everyone else. They lost Vietnam for us, not our soldiers or ARVN. Sam Spiegel, and all the others who thought Vietnam was a country when all it was was a prize. A *prize*. That's all it was."

Rapidly, he moved cookies around on the plate.

"Over here, China and the Communists; over here, us. In the middle, Vietnam. And Cambodia and Laos and Thailand and Burma and Malaysia. Prizes. Not prizes for oil or uranium or gold or bauxite or copper or even cheap labor. Prizes in the ultimate game—do they control the world, or do we control the world? Whoever wins the most prizes controls the world, because if you win enough prizes, the other side quits. If we hadn't made a deal at Potsdam, all those countries—Poland, Hungary, Yugoslavia, Romania, Czechoslovakia—would have been ours instead of theirs. If we'd hung tough, there would have been no Cold War. If we'd hung tough in Korea, China never would have expanded through Asia. China would be an imprisoned nation of illiterate, impoverished peasants.

"That's what the Sam Spiegels of this world can never understand. Vietnam for the Vietnamese! As though Vietnam is a real country. As though those people have any idea of what they want or how to run their lives."

He picked up the cookie that represented the West and said, "We are a great power. We are the equivalent of Rome before Christ, or England in the nineteenth century. We have obligations; we have responsibilities. Without our help, freedom dies. Freedom dies. Every country in the world turns into North Korea or the country of your choice in black Africa.

"Sam Spiegel—or Paul Vann, or Neil Sheehan, or Mohr, or Halberstam, or Safer, or Page, or Schanberg, any of them—is a traitor. They put their insignificant, piss-ant personal morality above the honorable interests of the United States, and by doing that, they betrayed their country. They cost us fifty-eight thousand men and the respect of the world.

"Once upon a time, we were *it*. Now, we're just like the rest. Or they're just like us. Muslims are as good as Christians, Hindus are as good as Jews, and Buddhists are as good as everybody. There's no difference between their ideas and our ideas; there's no difference between freedom and captivity. We all want the same things, we all want to live well—let's make a deal. We make deals with people we should be at war with. If Germany invaded Poland tomorrow and rebuilt Auschwitz, we wouldn't go to war, because going to war would stop BMW from building a factory in Tennessee, and that would cost four thousand jobs. War is not a crime. Weakness is a crime."

"You must have really enjoyed Vietnam," I said.

"I did," he said forcefully. "I enjoyed the whole thing—the intrigue, the danger, the power. And, most of all, I enjoyed mattering. We mattered. Even a traitorous sonofabitch like Sam Spiegel mattered." He glanced around the plush dining room and scowled. "Things were at stake," he continued. "Big things, not just whether blackened snapper is on the menu, or the location of your parking space; or how many frequent-flier miles you need for a week in Maui; or which coaching service will help your kids do well on the SAT; or whether an Op-Ed piece in the *Times* will be more effective than a donation to the chairman of the Senate Foreign Relations Committee. The real stuff.

"Do you have any idea what it's like to matter and then not matter? Can you even begin to get your mind around that? Can you?"

"No," I said, and tried to rein him in: "Matt Marshall . . ."

He shut his eyes an instant, shook his head, like a dog shaking off water, and said, "The first time we talked at length was around September of nineteen seventy-four. He told me he'd gotten a woman pregnant a couple of years earlier, and he wanted to find her and her child and take them home. I asked him why he thought I could help him, and he said that he'd heard that I was tight with every CIA station chief in country, and he knew that every station chief employed lots of natives, and he wondered whether there was a way to persuade the station chiefs to ask their native employees to keep an eye out for the woman and her child."

"Wow," I said, impressed.

"Wow is right," Randall echoed. "Not many people would have the nerve—or the brains—to request the help of the complete CIA network in Vietnam to look for a little mongrel bastard. But Matt Marshall did."

Curious, I asked, "Did he bring you a present?"

Randall nodded. "Oh, yes. He gave me the names of the Western reporters who'd discovered our phone taps. Very shrewd, when you think about it. It didn't hurt them, and it didn't really help us, except we stopped bothering to transcribe the tapes. A clever present."

"Did you agree to help him?"

"Not a chance—not for chicken-feed like that. Which I told him. He thanked me and left. Over the next several weeks, he made a point of running into me and casually giving me some tidbit. For a while, I thought he wasn't too quick—I'd made it plain I wasn't about to put the CIA at his disposal for the junk he was bringing me. Then—he must have been doing some very serious and discreet homework—one day he showed up at the Continental with an ARVN officer and invited me to his table for a drink."

As if the word *drink* reminded him, Randall summoned the waiter for more coffee before continuing.

"The officer, Marshall explained, worked at the heart of the Saigon government, in a security position. What position he wouldn't say. What he would say is that he was sure the officer would prove helpful. Now, it

so happened, we'd just lost somebody in the heart of the Saigon government, so if this man was legitimate, he was pure gold."

"Was he?"

"Twenty-four carat," Randall said. "Better than the one we'd lost. Far
better."

"So after that, you helped Marshall?"

"Absolutely. In fact, to this day, I have no doubt we got the best of the
deal. What the hell, all we had to do was keep an eye out for a woman
and a child."

"Did you have any luck?"

"No. And we didn't dog it—we looked for them," Randall said emphatically.

"For how long?"

"Till March perhaps. Till things got terrible."

"Did you ever get the impression he found them?"

"Not at all."

"If he had, do you think he would have told you about it—I mean,
were you friends?"

"No, we weren't—but he would have told me. He'd told just about
everyone what he was doing; I can't imagine he would have hidden it if
he'd been successful."

"Then why did he come to you for help with exit papers? He did,
didn't he?"

"Anybody who was smart did. By then, the pressure to get out was very
high. The smart ones got everything in order so in case the NVA arrived
ahead of schedule—which they did—nothing needed to be done in a
panic at the last minute."

"Do you remember when he came to you for papers?"

"March, I imagine."

"Do you remember what names he used for the documents—the
woman's maiden name, or the child's name?"

"No. I'm sure they were false—he was married, after all," Randall said.

"Does Nguyen Thi Dinh ring a bell?"

"No."

"What about Chau, or Chau Chau?"

"No."

"Cricket?"

"No."

"Do you remember what name he used for the child?"

"Good God, no."

"Did he have a nickname, do you remember?"

"I called him Matt."

"Do you know when he left?"

"I have no idea."

"When was the last time you saw him?"

"I don't remember," Randall said testily. "By April, we were inundated, we were buried. We had tons of classified files to burn; we had millions in U.S. currency to either ship out or destroy; we had South Vietnamese bullion to get to Switzerland. We had stations all over the country screaming for help, and we had nobody to call on for extra planes: The military was busy evacuating Cambodia, and Langley refused to release any of theirs. We had emergency rosters of locals to prepare—and we had to run evacuations all across Vietnam, for Americans first, and then for Vietnamese: C-141s during the day, C-130s at night; we even ran a secret evacuation for anyone too hot to transport openly.

"We had to deal with the defeat of Cambodia, we had to deal with the collapse of the Saigon government, we had to deal with nation after nation refusing to accept Vietnamese refugees. We had a Secretary of State who wasn't talking to the Secretary of Defense; a Saigon station chief who was heading at warp speed toward clinical psychosis; and an ambassador who'd *passed* clinical psychosis. The NVA was surrounding the city, and South Vietnamese troops were killing women and children to beat them to the boats and airplanes. I didn't devote a lot of time to thinking about Matt Marshall and his baggage."

From the envelope, I drew out the photo of Ma and passed it to Randall, who hesitated too long to lie.

"That's him," Randall said. "What's he up to?"

Casually, I said, "I heard he wound up in San Pedro."

"Wouldn't surprise me," Randall said. "Plenty of ARVN people wind up in Los Angeles."

Even more casually, I said, "Do you remember his name—I have different versions . . ."

"I just knew him as Ma," Randall said offhandedly. "It means 'mother,' but it means a lot of other things, too."

"Ghost?"

"Possibly. I've forgotten most of my Vietnamese."

"His real name would really help me."

"No doubt."

"I'll be discreet—I won't expose him."

"I can't help you."

"You never heard a real name?"

"Wouldn't have wanted to," Randall said. "If I know his name, no matter how careful I am, I might let it slip—and that puts him in jeopardy."

It sounded reasonable enough to be true, but not coming from Barry Randall. Matching his moderate tone, I said, "It's hard to believe you would have used a source placed that centrally and not tried to find out who he was . . ."

"I can't help what you believe."

"Is he in San Pedro?"

"I can't tell you."

"When was the last time you were in touch?"

"Years and years."

"You're sure you don't know his name?"

"I don't know his name," Randall said, in a way that made it obvious he was lying and didn't give a shit whether I knew it or not. Before I could mention Cao Lee Hanh, he patted the pocket that held the fax and said, "If you carry out your threat, the worst that can happen is the end of my career. If I tell you Ma's name—assuming he hasn't changed it and assuming he's still alive—and you're careless with that name, he could get killed, assuming he hasn't been killed already. I can't allow that. If I have to lose my career to prevent that, fine."

"I didn't realize he meant that much to you," I said.

"He did; he does. He was loyal to me—he never betrayed me, or the agency, or the United States. That's enough for me not to put him in danger of being killed."

"I see," I said, furious at his resistance and unable to subdue the fury. "Loyal agents you protect. Unfaithful girlfriends you waste. That's a value system any patriot can admire. Does your wife know? Do your kids? How did you tell them? Was it over dinner? Or during an outing to Disneyland—Lee was doing these other guys, so I tossed her out of a chopper—did it go like that?"

Without realizing it, I'd moved my face close to his, and he moved his chair back to get some room. As he did, he turned away and stared through the window for a few minutes. At last, without turning back, he said, "I thought she was just a fuck. I didn't know I loved her." He glanced at me obliquely. "Has that ever happened to you?"

Still angry, I snapped, "Has what ever happened to me? Thinking someone is just a fuck? Not telling my wife I threw a fuck out of a chopper? What?"

"Confusing your feelings. Not understanding them at the time. Finding out too late. Goddammit!" he said. "Do you know when you love someone?"

"Yes," I said, mostly to trump him.

"I don't believe you," he snapped. "You're a petty little shyster. You don't know anything."

Idly, I picked up my fork and read the institute logo on the shaft. "My father used to say, Adam, fifty percent of the people you meet you'll dislike on sight; fifty percent of the remaining fifty percent, you'll learn to dislike. And fifty percent of that last fifty percent, you'll learn to hate. That's your category, Mr. Randall."

"Is there a point to this, or are we finished?"

"Mr. Randall, let me tell you a story. A couple—"

"A story?" he said contemptuously. "Must you?"

"It's not very long, Mr. Randall. Humor me." I took a breath. "A couple of years ago, some old Jews in Boca Raton got in touch with me. They believed that one of their neighbors had been a guard at Treblinka, and they wanted me to find out whether that was true. If I could supply evidence that it was true, they would take that evidence to the Justice Department to get this man deported.

"The leader of these old Jews was named Leah, Leah Stein, and she was dying. She had one kidney, bone cancer, and emphysema. With tears in her eyes, she told me that before she died she wanted to see this man— Stefan Waldheim—sent back to Germany. That's all. She didn't want to hurt Waldheim; she didn't even want to see him put on trial. She simply wanted him sent home so that she and her fellow Treblinka survivors could die in Boca in peace.

"I took the job. A few weeks later, I found enough evidence for Leah and her friends to take to the Justice Department, and I gave it to them. They gave me a check, discounted appropriately for their age and station.

"A month after I came back to New York, I noticed a one-paragraph story in the *News:* An elderly couple had died in a fire in their Boca Raton home. The police suspected arson, which, of course, was why the fire rated a paragraph in the paper. The victims were Stefan and Mathilde Waldheim."

"You're threatening me."

"No, Mr. Randall, I am telling you an anecdote about my professional life. Here's another. My next case is going to be a search for the documentary wartime history of a former CIA operative. When I find all the documents—the letters, the tapes, the photos—I'm going to put together a beautiful, leather-bound scrapbook, dedicated to the memory of Cao Lee Hanh. Then, I'm going to send the scrapbook to the CIA operative's family. I want his family to know how he spent his war." I stood, tossed the fork on the table, and walked out.

On the way to the parking lot, I felt exhilarated. But by the time I pulled onto the highway, the feeling was evaporating. I still didn't know Ma's real name, or have a clue to any name he might have taken, or how or where to look for him. Ma had been my strongest connection to Cricket. In fact, he had been my last connection to Cricket. By the time I drove across the Tappan Zee Bridge, I felt like shit.

CHAPTER 32

AT THE OFFICE, I found eleven messages on the answering machine. Seven were unimportant. Two were from Herschel. The first said: "Hey, pal, did it work? The Secretary of Defense folded like a new pair of pants—what about the prick you went to see? Did he give it up?"

And the second: "Call me before four—I've got tickets to the Knicks and Pistons. After four, I invite somebody worthwhile."

And three were about the Marshall case:

"Mr. Bruno, Matt Marshall here—notice, I don't say junior. Wendy and Fred have only awful things to say about you, and Mother is not far behind. Just to let you know they're about to gang up on you. By the way, I can offer you a real good price on the McCullum picture."

"Mr. Bruno, Mollie Wharton. It's an official call. The family is taking the position that the estate is frittering away money by using you, and is prepared to formally request that you either be replaced or joined by another detective. The firm's position is that you're doing fine. Call me so we can straighten this out."

"Mr. Bruno, this is Nicole Maldonado. We have not spoken for a while and I wondered whether you were making any progress in your quest."

It was after four so there was no point in calling Herschel, not if I wanted to see the game, and I was in no mood to talk to Matt junior or to Wharton. I called Maldonado.

"I'm making no progress," I said, once we exchanged greetings. "I'm stuck."

"In what way?"

"I can't find Ma; I seem to have run out of people to talk to; and I don't know what to do except go over the same old ground again; and I don't feel like going over the same old ground again." I heard my tone and caught myself. "Sorry. I'm quacking."

"Quacking?"

"My ex-wife's word—bitching, whining. Like a duck." I made duck noises, and she laughed.

"Is there anything I can do to help? Would you like my mother and me to examine his letters again?" she said.

"Do you think it would do any good?"

After a pause, she said, "No." Quickly, she added, "Sometimes, if you must go over old ground, it helps to do it with another person—to get a fresh perspective . . ."

". . . About ten years ago, Marshall wanted to buy a small electronics company—it specialized in virus-detectors for communications software—so he invited the president of the company to a premiere at the New York City Ballet. Mind you, the company was in a suburb of Minneapolis, and the president had no plans to come to New York.

"Two weeks before the premiere, Marshall sent the president four aisle tickets to the ballet. He sent four because the president had a wife and two daughters, and Marshall had found out that both girls were studying dance, and the wife had once studied dance. A week before the premiere, he sent the president's daughters a receipt—in their own names—for a thousand-dollar donation to the New York City Ballet Scholarship Fund. And three days before the premiere, Marshall sent his corporate jet to Minneapolis to fly the president and his family to New York. He put the family up at the Pierre. He had a limo at their disposal twenty-four hours a day, and after the premiere, he escorted them to the party, where they got to shake hands with Balanchine and Baryshnikov."

"And of course the president sold him the company," Maldonado said.

"Of course," I said. The waiter had momentarily disappeared, so I filled our glasses. "Matt Marshall did everything right. He had a knack for doing everything right. If he needed charm, he used charm. If he needed cunning, he used cunning. Ruthlessness, likewise. He had all the moves all the time. He never dropped a stitch. So why don't his wife and children seem to care that he's dead? Is there something I don't know about the way rich Protestants mourn? Am I mistaking discipline for indifference? The point is this: A lot of people loved Matt Marshall, but I haven't found one who believes he loved them. I've found people who *hope* he loved them, but no more. What's missing?"

I said the last more sharply than I intended—the couple at the next table stopped eating and looked my way—and I covered myself by taking a sip of wine. Maldonado and I had spent the first ninety minutes of dinner going over old ground—not accomplishing a thing—before I returned, as I inevitably did, to the elusive character of Matt Marshall.

"Have you never come across anybody like him? I can't believe that," she said.

"Oh, sure. There are plenty of people in the world who cast their nets, and catch you in them, and take what they want from you, and discard you, and move on. Maybe everybody does that sometimes. Marshall's not unique. He's just the one I'm obsessed with right now."

The waiter appeared, handed us dessert cards, and retreated. Maldonado ignored the card. "Why?"

"Temperament. I get tenacious—obsessive, if you like—when I take a case."

"And angry," she said mildly.

"Angry?"

"Cecile Boulanger believes anger is your driving emotion." Delicately, she added, "Do you agree with her?"

"No, I don't." Then I remembered something and laughed in concession. "Of course, it is true that when Herschel and I were partners, everybody at the courthouse used to call us the last of the raging injustice collectors. For a while, we considered using that as the name of the firm—Bruno & O'Hara, Raging Injustice Collectors."

She glanced at the dessert card. "Will you share a zabaglione with me?" I nodded, summoned the waiter, and ordered the dessert and two espressos.

After he went out of earshot, Maldonado said lightly, "How did you become a raging injustice collector?"

"My father."

"Is he very political?"

"Not a bit," I said. "He was a small-time bookmaker, and he used to get arrested regularly as part of his deal with his boss. It was all very civilized. Until one day, two detectives new to the vice squad—in those days, gambling was a vice—didn't like his accent, and made him repeat a sentence over and over again. Every time he stumbled, they hit him. The sentence was, 'I am a foreign piece of shit, and I am ruining this country for real Americans.' After they got tired of hearing him say that, and tired of hitting him, they took him to central booking and then to night court. I went there with the lawyer to meet him. When they brought him in from the holding pen, he had blood on his face.

"We finally got the story from him—he whispered it to us because the detectives were standing just a few feet away—and I asked the lawyer what we could do to them. Nothing, he said. Why, I asked. Because they're cops, he said. Cops do what they want.

"That's when it began. It wasn't conscious. I didn't make any vows—I was only a kid. But that night is as fresh in my mind as if it were yesterday. Today. The dried blood around his mouth and nose, the bruises on his neck and temples, the pain and fear in his eyes. On the way home, we stopped at a bar. He said he needed a brandy. Before he ordered it, he went into the men's room to wash the blood off. But the mirror was broken, so he called me in there to wipe his face. When I touched him, he flinched. My father had never flinched at my touch. I've hated those two detectives since that night. I'll always hate them. Does that answer your question?"

"Yes," she said. She thought for a few seconds. "Is there an injustice here?"

"It hasn't happened yet," I said. "But it will." She waited for me to explain. "The law belongs to those who can buy it. Rich, powerful people don't go to the electric chair, or serve hard time in overcrowded prisons—or lose their fortunes to poor, powerless people. Rich, powerful people win. Unless the Marshall family makes a colossal mistake, or unless a miracle happens, they will win, and Cricket and her child will lose."

The waiter arrived with the zabaglione, two spoons, and coffee. After tasting the dessert, Maldonado said, "So you have to believe in miracles, correct?"

"Correct."

"Which you do not?"

"Correct."

After taking Maldonado to her door, I came home to find a message on my answering machine:

"Adam Bruno, it's Sam Spiegel in Cambridge. I was wrong about Buzz. He wasn't killed in Saigon. He's a shock jock in California, and his last name is Oliver. Buzz Oliver. You got it? Buzz Oliver."

CHAPTER 33

"... ALL RIGHT! ARE YOU ready for two minutes of the outside world—weather, traffic, and lies. Or news, if you like euphemisms. We'll be back with our guests Carolyn Blum and Adam Bruno to talk about sex, violence, power, love, marriage, the fall of Saigon, and my good buddy, the late and, believe me, lamented Matt Marshall."

Buzz Oliver finished just as the second hand of the large studio clock touched the numeral 12. He pulled his earphones from his head, lowered the volume of the studio speakers so he wouldn't have to listen to the news, checked his log, and said into his mike, "Can we get some fresh coffee in here? And I mean fresh, not reheated in the goddamn microwave."

"You got it," his producer said from the control room, and nudged a gorgeous production assistant to get moving.

When I'd tracked down Buzz Oliver to KHWD in Los Angeles and called to talk to him, his assistant informed me—in a tone that implied I should know it—that Buzz did morning drive time for KHWD and he was Number 2 in his time period, and gaining on Number 1 and was *very* busy. She suggested that I show up at KHWD at six A.M. Wednesday, since he had only one guest booked and maybe he could fit me in. I tried to explain that I wasn't a guest, that I merely wanted to talk to him, and that after the show would be fine with me, but in Buzz Oliver's very busy world, even people who weren't guests had to show up at dawn simply to make an appointment to see him.

I'd flown out Tuesday and arrived at the station at 5:30 A.M. Wednesday, expecting to make the appointment. Instead, his assistant quizzed me on why I wanted to see Oliver. I summarized what I was up to, she scribbled notes on a clipboard, nodded, smiled, vanished for ninety seconds, and then reappeared with the producer.

The producer, whose name was Victor Vance and who looked like a fullback gone to seed, confirmed what I'd told the assistant, had me pronounce my name several times, and mimicked me perfectly. Then, *he* vanished for ninety seconds.

When he returned, he was nodding happily. "Cool, very cool," he said. "Buzz wants you for the whole show; what do you like for breakfast?" Before I could demur, the other guest arrived, and Vance introduced me to her—Carolyn Blum, who taught psychology at UCLA Medical School and had, I found out later, a thriving therapy practice. Blum seemed unnaturally cheerful for 5:40 in the morning, but it turned out that Oliver used her for that very quality; the policy was one grouch per program, and that was Oliver himself.

"Here's the script," Vance said to Blum, who scribbled shorthand notes as he rattled on. "Back in the dark ages, Buzz was in Vietnam, and Adam here's got news of a friend of Buzz's, so you're gonna talk about the war, and the girls they left behind, and the girls they found over there, and kids. Shit like that. Buzz and Adam'll talk about the friend. And whatever else comes up. This cool with you?"

Blum thought for a moment and said, "Is there a choice? Get me some basic stuff on war brides. Immigration numbers—how many Vietnamese are here, where are they, how they do—that kind of thing. Just so I have something to fall back on when I run out of ways to compliment the host."

"By airtime," Vance said, and went.

Blum looked at me, smiled, and said, "It's radio—you can spill your coffee or pick your nose and nobody'll know it. And Buzz is very good— he makes everyone sound brilliant."

"Even after three hours?" I said.

"Oh, yes," she said. "In the third hour, he really rolls, and all you have to do is roll with him."

"*Exactement!*" said a voice behind me. I twisted my head, and there stood Buzz Oliver, a cup of steaming coffee in one hand, a marked-up *Los Angeles Times* in the other. He resembled his 1975 photo in a distant, almost postcorporeal way. He reminded me of people who'd served time in maximum-security prisons—they'd been purged down to their essence. He wore lightly tinted glasses, and they made his eyes look like those of a rare nocturnal predator.

"You're Adam Bruno," he said in a gravelly radio voice. "I'm Buzz Oliver. You met Lady Carolyn? Great. Smartest shrink in California. Is that saying anything? No. But she's got brains anyway. Don't let the blond hair fool you—it's frosted. Victor tell you how it works? What does Victor know?

"Here's how it works: It's my show. But I want you to look good. *When* I want you to look good. Sometimes, to make a point, I need you to look shitty. It's not personal—it's purely for the show. Let me tell you the best way to ride. Don't depend on winging it; don't get hung up on one question or one answer. Have your story, and use your story as your base. Your story is your search for Matt Marshall's woman and kid. You can do a million variations on that, and you can bring Carolyn in whenever you want. She knows all about men and women and affairs and marriage and families and kids. Bring me in.

"Buzz, you say, with as plaintive a tone as you can fake, you've got a huge audience, how can we enlist your audience in my search . . . ? Like that. But whatever it is, wherever I go—and I go all over the goddamn place—don't lose the thread of your story. Cool?"

"Actually, Mr. Oliver," I began, "all I want to do is ask you a few questions about Matt. I didn't really plan on—"

"Adam, I get it," he said brusquely. "You want my help? It's yours. On the air. It's a great story, it's going to make a great show. Cool?" I hesitated and glanced at the wall clock. "Adam, I'm a busy guy; I can't help you—except on the air. Are we cool?"

"Yes."

"Great!" he said, and he smiled wolfishly at Blum. "Are you cool, buns of steel?"

"No, I'm not—unless I know more." Blum referred to her notes. "All I have is: You were in Vietnam, and Adam has news of a friend of yours, and you want to talk about the war, and women and children."

"Okay," Buzz said. "The friend served over there, got a girl pregnant, went back after his tour to look for her and the baby, couldn't find them, went home to his wife. A few weeks back, he died. In his will, he left a huge chunk to the missing kid. The estate hired Adam to find the missing kid. Adam's been looking up everybody the guy knew—including me. Now: What are you going to do?"

"Thank you, King Buzz," Blum said. "What about the male love of the mysterious and the forbidden? Starting with the Old South and the master's unquenchable lust for slaves."

"See why I'm hot for her?" Oliver said to me. "She knows how to please a guy. We all cool? Great."

The first hour I felt stiff and awkward, but it didn't hinder me, because instead of beginning with me and Matt Marshall, Buzz Oliver—before he even introduced Blum and me—stuck a lozenge in his mouth and began with himself:

". . . Victor, find us some Doors, find us some Who, some Stones, some Hendrix, we're going back, Victor. We're taking a trip on the Time Machine. Hear me now." Moving his mouth closer to the microphone so his breath formed a wave on which his words could ride, Oliver continued:

"1965: Lyndon Johnson sits on his throne; Richard Nixon sulks in Pat's lap; JFK is dead and RFK is taking aim at 1968. I'm in St. Louis doing City Hall reporting for the local Dumont affiliate. With luck, my future is to read the news on the half-hour. Except. Except ten thousand miles from home is a war—a cute, easy, TV-screen-sized war. I grab my Uher tape recorder, I stiff my landlord for the rent money, I hock my watch, I hock my Harley, I forge a letter telling the Pentagon that the station has assigned me to 'Nam, and I find the cheapest way to get my ambitious ass over to Saigon."

Under Oliver's voice, the engineer faded in Jimi Hendrix's "All Along the Watchtower," and Oliver sang a couple of bars with the song.

"All right," he said impatiently. "Let's move on. We're not going to do a whole show about the war. We're not going to weep crocodile tears for the Vietnamese, or for democracy, or even for the fifty-eight thousand names on the wall in Washington. This isn't then, this is now.

"My guests today are Carolyn Blum—if you listen to me, you know Carolyn: smart, no bull, right-into-your-bad-place Carolyn—and Adam Bruno. Adam's new to us; he's out here from New York. But you'll dig him, he won't disappoint you. Adam's out here on a quest, and I don't mean one of those wussy New Age quests where you look for God in the artichoke heart, I mean a quest even a grownup can dig. Story time:

"When I was in 'Nam, I met a guy named Matt Marshall. I didn't meet him when he was soldiering over there, I met him later, in 1974, after our troops had gone. Dig it, vets, while Matt Marshall was soldiering, while Captain Marshall was winning medals, he fell in love. And he did what soldiers do when they fall in love. He figured he'd die, so he stopped thinking about home and he followed his heart. His girl—he called her Cricket—got pregnant. But Matt Marshall didn't die; he lived; and he went home. End of story, right? Finito. So long, Suzy Wong.

"Not! Matt Marshall came back. He wanted to find his Cricket and her baby—*their* baby. Victor is waving at me—what is it, Victor? . . . Okay, we got money to earn here . . .''

Oliver pointed a finger at the control room, slid his earphones down around his neck, and wiped his damp face with a handkerchief. As the first of a batch of commercials played, he checked it off on his log, popped another lozenge in his mouth, and glanced at me. ''You cool with this?''

''Sure,'' I said.

''Carolyn, I'm about to throw you a cue—jump in hard, okay? I don't want to stay in this mood too long.''

A minute later, Oliver did as promised, wasting no time getting to his point: ''. . . Adam, lemme tell you the dirty little secret about 'Nam, and I mean *dirty*.''

Blum interjected: ''Everybody. Buzz is leering. He is leering like a teenager at a topless beach.''

''No, a degenerate old man at a topless beach. Hear me now, Adam. We were in 'Nam more than ten years. We've never been anyplace ten years. Not Beirut, not Panama, not Kuwait, not Cuba, not Mexico, not the Dominican Republic, not even Nazi Germany. If the women in 'Nam looked like the women in Kuwait, or Panama, or Beirut, or anywhere else we've been, we'd have gotten out of 'Nam in ten minutes. But the women in 'Nam were drop-dead, double-cross-your-best-buddy beautiful. And docile. We like our women docile, Adam.''

''Speak for yourself, Buzz,'' Blum said.

''I speak for millions,'' Oliver brayed. ''Anytime I hear a man say, 'I like my women independent and outspoken,' I know I'm hearing a fraud or a hairdresser. Shut up and lie down—that's my motto. Or shut up and iron. I could never figure out why we didn't bring home more Vietnamese. They do anything you ask them to in bed, and they never get in your face.

''In Vietnamese, the word for beautiful is my, spelled M-Y, pronounced me. They always used it about America. Two minutes of the outside world. Hang in.''

By the time we got into the second hour, I had joined Blum in feeling entirely at ease. Oliver assumed that anyone he invited as a guest could be entertaining, particularly with a little help from him, and he helped all the time. He also knew exactly how to make an audience wait.

It wasn't till the beginning of the third hour, after we'd argued about the scholarship records of Oriental children at American colleges, and the abandonment of bastards in wartime, and Asian-American marriages, and the future of worldwide miscegenation, that Oliver finally cued me, and I told a drastically edited version of what he had taken to calling "Adam's quest." While I talked, I spread the 1975 Vietnam photos on the table before him, and closed by saying, "Buzz, you knew him better than anybody back then—help me out here . . ."

"Matt Marshall is my perfect legman," Oliver said. "He's handsome, he's brave, he's smart—all those adjectives you and me never once hear about us. Which means he can talk to people I can't even get near—not unless I catch them naked in a whorehouse or near comatose in a saloon. I don't get invited to embassy teas; Matt Marshall does. I don't get to hear lonesome Foreign Service wives repeat their pillow talk; Matt Marshall does.

"But I know the dark side—the black marketers and the drug dealers and the buyable cops and the two-hundred-dollar hitmen and—most important of the lot—the whoremongers and the barkeepers. Because the whoremongers and the barkeepers are the ones who hire good-looking young girls. And Matt Marshall is hunting for a good-looking young girl—named Cricket." He took a beat and, in a gentler voice, said, "Why do I keep saying 'is'? I mean 'was.' Matt Marshall is a was."

He glanced down at the pictures and said, "On my desk, I've got a bunch of photos, courtesy of Adam Bruno, lawyer, quester, and all-round early-morning man. These are photos of the friends of Matt Marshall—it's like a reunion of the spirits. These are the people Adam has been talking to. Where are they now? I'm here, but what about the others. Fill us in, Adam. I'm holding up a picture of Sam Spiegel—where is he now?"

"He runs a bookshop in Cambridge," I said.

"No more rice, huh?" Oliver said, picking up another photo. "Terry Quinn. Is it true he got killed in Sarajevo?"

"That's what I heard. Nobody's ever confirmed it."

"Let's hope they never do. What do we have here? Oh, boy: Dunbar, Kenilworthy, Fisher, Randall. Not a great group in this picture, Adam. I don't even want to know where they are." He picked up another photo:

"I'm holding a shot of an ARVN officer who used to call himself Ma, which means Ghost. Ghost was the man to see if you needed a pipeline into the South Vietnamese government. Or into the CIA. Or the French intelligence service. Or the English. Or the Polish. He lived a charmed life until the Communists rolled in. Then, prison, torture, the works. Sorry bastard. Where is he now, Adam?"

"I haven't found him yet," I said. "The last I know of him he was in a refugee camp in Thailand, but he talked about coming to San Pedro."

"Then, he's here," Oliver said. "With his background he's not safe anyplace but southern California. We got a lot of ARVN vets down here. Safety in numbers. They hang together like rabid bats."

"Do you remember any other name he used?" I said.

"Ghost is all," Oliver said, spinning his finger in a rapid circle, indicating, come on, come on. Finally, I got it:

"Buzz," I said, forcing a catch in my throat, "Ghost is just about my last hope. Is there a way to call on your vast audience to help me find him?"

"Everybody, Adam wants our help. Can we say no? Not on his life. Victor, give me some search music. Everybody—Adam, we're talking to eleven states—are you paying attention? Especially in Los Angeles, Orange, and Santa Clara counties.

"If you served in the army of the Republic of South Vietnam and you were a friend of Matt Marshall's and your name is Ghost—Ma—call us. The number is 1-800-555-KHWD. That's 1-800-555-5493. If you can convince Adam that you're Ghost—and he is a hard, hard man to convince—Adam will pay you . . ." Oliver drew a question mark in the air, and in return I drew a five. "Five hundred dollars. From there, you negotiate with him."

Oliver got a cue, glanced at the clock, and said, "Time to hear some lies and pay some bills. When we come back, Saigon in the spring of nineteen seventy-five. Evil. And the last time I saw Matt Marshall. Hang in."

He slipped off his earphones, signaled for fresh coffee, and said to me, "We need a secret fact the girls at the switchboard can use as a test. You got something, Adam? Victor, pay attention to this."

"All ears," Vance said from the control room.

After skimming copies of Ghost's letters, I said, "The real Ghost will know the name that Cricket traveled under when she escaped from Vietnam."

Oliver brooded on that for a few seconds. "That's too on the nose. It's cool for you, but it's not cool for the show. I want more than one finalist for you to talk to. Have you got something a lucky guess might hit?"

I checked the letters again. "Ask whoever calls where the Communists first put him in prison."

"You get that, Victor?"

"Where the Commies first put him in prison," Vance said, picking up a phone. "And that is where, Adam?"

"Bien Hoa. B-I-E-N H-O-A."

"Bien Hoa," Vance repeated, first for me, then into the phone.

"Victor," Oliver said, "when you get six finalists, let me know so Adam can talk to them." He bared his teeth at me. "How do you like radio?"

"It gets better every minute," I said.

231

"Yeah, it's like oral sex that way," Oliver said.

"Giving it or getting it?" Blum said dryly.

"Both, sweet lips," Oliver answered instantly. "Let's do a show on that at Lent." Oliver glanced at the clock. "Victor, start with 'Paint It Black,' then get some soul ready. No lightweight girl groups, okay?"

"No lightweight girls," Vance echoed.

"Welcome back, everybody," Oliver said, waited for "Paint It Black" to fade in, and slowly turned to stare at Blum. "Carolyn, do you believe in evil?"

"How do you mean, Buzz?"

"Evil. You wake up in the middle of the night, and there's a dark presence in your bedroom. It's so potent a presence that you turn on the light in sheer terror. You look around, but you don't see anything. You don't smell anything. You don't feel a breeze. But the presence is still there. Maybe a little weaker—maybe the light frightens it—but it's hanging around. You listen to some music, you read a book, you watch some TV. You turn out the light. Still there. So you leave the light on until the sun comes up. By then, it's gone. That kind of evil."

"Did you swallow anything, or smoke anything before this presence dropped in to your bedroom?" Blum said.

"She doesn't believe."

"I didn't say that, Buzz."

"Sure you did. Cool. Don't believe. I know what's real. The fall of Saigon was that kind of evil. No matter how much you did right by people, and there was a *lot* of that, the evil was always present.

"Victor! Serious soul." Vance faded out the Rolling Stones and faded in Aretha Franklin's "Gotta Find Me an Angel" as Oliver continued:

"The last time I saw Matt Marshall . . .

"At cocktail hour on April twenty-sixth, nineteen seventy-five, Matt Marshall and I meet for a drink. After a year of looking for Cricket and their kid, Matt Marshall's string has run out. If he stays in country, he dies—at least, that's what everyone official is telling him. He's scheduled to leave the next day.

"We drink all night; we smoke all night; we talk all night. Just before sunup, a few hours before he has to head for the airport, Matt looks into my eyes and says, 'Buzz, if you were me, what would you do?'

"What would I do? In front of me is a tortured man. At home in North Carolina, he's got a wife and child. Somewhere in Vietnam, he's got a lover and child. He thinks. He believes. He hopes. What I'd do, I tell him, is . . . Carolyn, what would you tell him to do?"

"He's your friend, Buzz."

"Adam . . . ?" Oliver said.

"I don't know," I said, and I didn't.

"I tell him . . ." Oliver took a beautifully timed pause—even I held my breath. ". . . I tell him, I'd get on the plane and go home. I'd go back to my wife and child. That's what I'd do, Matt. 'Why Buzz?' he said. Because, I said, even if I believe Cricket and your kid are out there someplace—and I don't—even if I believe they're out there, it's over. The romance is over. 'Nam is over. Time to pack up and get back to the real world."

In the control room, Vance held up six fingers and waited till Oliver saw the gesture and gave a thumbs-up sign. Oliver took a breath and said, "Get back to where you once belonged, I told him. Matt stared at me with that thousand-mile stare. You don't think they're out there, do you, Buzz? No, Matt, I don't: They're dead, believe me. Go home."

Another magnificent pause. "Well, everyone, Matt Marshall went home—but he didn't believe me. Before he drove to the airport, he found Ghost and he begged him to keep an eye out for his Cricket and their child.

"Victor!" he cried, and pointed dramatically at me, "put a caller through to Adam!"

A light on the phone console in front of me began to blink. "Push the button, Adam," Oliver said, "you'll hear him through your earphones."

I pushed the button. "Hello," I said, and heard only breathing.

"You're on with Adam," Oliver said peevishly. "Say something or get off."

"Mr. Adam," an accented male voice started uncertainly, "I am the Mr. Ghost. When they take me in prison, they take me in Bien Hoa."

"Mr. Ghost, what name did Cricket travel under when she escaped from Vietnam?"

After some muffled whispering, "What name?"

"Yes, Mr. Ghost. What name?"

More whispering. "It is very far long time. I hardly may remember."

Oliver drew his finger across his throat, but I shook him off and said, "Mr. Ghost, how did you stay in touch with Matthew Marshall after he went home?"

More whispering. "Letter, I think."

"And how did you address Matthew Marshall in your letter?"

"Address? Where he live."

"What did you call him at the top of the letter?"

"Oh, oh, oh. Address. Mr. Marshall."

"Thank you," I said and signaled to Vance. A different light on the console blinked.

"Number two," Oliver said. "Number one was a fake."

"Hello," I said.

A slightly lighter accent. "Mr. Adam, I address Mr. Marshall in my letter as Dear Matthew. We are total close."

"And Cricket's traveling name?"

"Madame Marshall."

"Thank you." Vance anticipated me, and a third light went on. "Hello."

"Bien Hoa," the caller said. "Two years Bien Hoa. Marshall love me. I love Marshall. Many letter. Bien Hoa."

"What did you call him in your many letters?"

"My dear friend."

"Thank you." The fourth light blinked. "Hello."

"Woman Cricket travel with many names," the caller said, more calmly than the others. "One is Chau Chau."

Tensing, I said, "How did you address Matthew Marshall in your letter to him?"

"Major Matthew," he said confidently.

"Major Matthew?" I repeated.

"With dear in front. Dear Major Matthew."

"Mr. Ghost," I said, scanning the letters, "where did you go from Bien Hoa?"

A pause. "From Bien Hoa? What is from?"

"Where did you go next—your next stop?"

"Oh, where next. New country. Safe place."

"Where was that?"

Another pause. "Hong Kong."

"Thank you." The fifth light. "Hello."

To my surprise—and dismay—I heard a woman's voice. Barely comprehensible, she said, "Mr. Adam?"

"This is Mr. Adam."

"I am widow of Mr. Ghost. I go very slow. Yes?"

"Fine," I said. Oliver shook his head in irritation.

Syllable by painful syllable, the woman said, "My husband letter send to Dear Captain Matthew."

"Thank you, Mrs. Ghost. Where did your husband go from Bien Hoa—his next stopping place after Bien Hoa?"

"Refugee camp."

"Where, Mrs. Ghost?"

"Thailand."

My excitement must have pervaded the studio, because both Oliver and Blum were leaning forward intently, and in the control room Victor stood dead still.

"Mrs. Ghost," I said, powerless to control the quaver in my voice, "what name did Cricket travel under when she escaped from Vietnam?"

"Nguyen Thi Dinh," I heard her say.

"Please repeat that, Mrs. Ghost. Slowly and loudly."

"Nguyen Thi Dinh."

Oliver rescued me deftly: "I can tell from Adam's face that we have a winner! Is that right, Adam—do we have a winner? Adam is shaking his head like a man with advanced palsy. Mrs. Ghost, stay on the line. Victor, Mrs. Ghost stays on the line or you look for a job. The rest of you, thanks for calling. Weather, news, traffic, sports, stock market. Ugly life. Hang in."

He slipped off his earphones and popped his usual lozenge. "This is a long break, Adam, why don't you go make a date with her?"

Ghost's widow, who called herself Mrs. Cuong, was not free to see me until the weekend. That was fine with me, because it gave me time to book a room, buy an open plane ticket, track down Nicole Maldonado, and tell her I needed her in Los Angeles for the weekend.

CHAPTER 34

GHOST'S WIDOW REFUSED TO let us come to her home; she wouldn't even tell me where it was. She suggested—insisted, really—that we meet outdoors. Since she seemed so anxious, I let her pick the time—noon, Sunday—and the place—on the promenade overlooking the Pacific Ocean at the foot of Arizona Avenue in Santa Monica. She told me she'd be bringing along her second husband because he spoke better English than she.

Maldonado and I arrived at a quarter to twelve, but before we could stroll to the lip of the bluffs and take a few minutes to enjoy the spectacular view, a middle-aged Vietnamese couple appeared from behind a large palm. Each was casually dressed in cotton slacks and a print shirt, and each wore a floppy straw hat and dark sunglasses. The man carried a striped canvas folding chair. Tentatively, they approached us.

"Mr. Adam Bruno?" the woman asked. I offered each a small bow. "I am Mrs. Kim Cuong, the widow of Mr. Ghost," she continued. "Here is my husband, Mr. Philip Cuong."

After I introduced them to Maldonado, who murmured a greeting in Vietnamese as well as English, Cuong guided us to a bench, wiped it with a handkerchief, and, while we sat, opened the folding chair and placed it opposite us for himself.

Ghost's widow looked at me expectantly.

From my case, I took a twenty-year-old picture of Matt Marshall. "Mrs. Cuong," I said, "if we could—"

I stopped because Ghost's widow, after a hurried glance at the photograph, frowned and leaned forward to whisper urgently and audibly to her husband.

Maldonado brought her mouth close to my ear and murmured, "Mr. Bruno, did you promise her a reward?"

"Thanks," I muttered, found the envelope in my jacket pocket, and drew it out. "Mrs. Cuong," I said, "allow me to give you this before we resume."

With a tiny bow, she accepted the envelope and passed it to her husband, who opened the flap, expertly counted the $500 in twenties with his thumb and nodded to his wife.

Ghost's widow smiled at me.

"Mrs. Cuong," I said, offering her the photo, "this is Matt Marshall—Captain Matthew."

While they studied the photo, I told them what I knew of Marshall's connection to Ghost, what he had asked Ghost to do, and what I was after. As I spoke, Cuong delivered a rapid, mumbling translation to his wife. When he finished, I said, "Mrs. Cuong, may I ask you some questions now?"

For the first time, Cuong spoke directly to me, "Mr. Bruno, I know my wife will be more happier with business arrangement in the place . . ."

"Mr. Cuong," I said, "I can't do that until I know the quality of your wife's information."

They put their heads together for a moment. Then, he said, "How is quality decided?"

"Mr. Cuong, I'm looking for Captain Matthew's child. If what your wife tells me leads me to the child, I will pay well. Otherwise, I will pay nothing."

"How are we know you will pay?" he said.

"Mr. Cuong," I said, indicating the envelope in his hands, "I pay."

Once more, they put their heads together. "One-third in advance," Cuong said. "Please state offer."

"One-third in advance?"

"Yes, one-third," he said briskly. "Now, please state how much you pay?" He squeezed his wife's hand. "Finding child worth very much dollars, I am sure."

"Mr. Cuong," I said, "before we get into a negotiation over very much dollars, I have to find out a little bit more about your wife and her first husband."

"What more?" he said.

"I need to feel comfortable that her first husband told her enough about this business so she can help me."

"He told."

"Good," I said, "then she'll have no trouble answering a few easy questions."

He shook his head. "No questions to wife. Please state offer."

With a slight bow, I took the picture of Marshall from his hand and opened my case to put it away. "Mr. Cuong, if I can't ask your wife some preliminary questions, then I'm not going to make any offer."

"Questions worth money," he said.

"Not these questions," I said. Ghost's widow tugged at his sleeve, and I took the opportunity to add, "Mr. Cuong, anytime you believe a question is worth money, stop me, and I'll go on to another one." I paused. "If you stop me too often, I'll assume your wife can't help me . . ."

Cuong put his mouth against his wife's ear and explained, and she finally turned to me and nodded.

"Mrs. Cuong, where did you meet your first husband?"

"When we are came here from the camp in Thailand in nineteen eighty-three; we are met on the ship."

"After you came here, did your husband get in touch with Captain Matthew?"

She waited for Cuong to translate, then said, "Yes."

"By phone or letter?"

She hesitated, and I mimed writing and dialing a phone. Instead of answering immediately, she glanced at Cuong, who looked at his feet.

"Phone," she said.

"Do you remember when?"

"Soon, very soon. Nineteen eighty-three."

"Did he talk about Nguyen Thi Dinh?"

Without bothering to consult his wife, Cuong rubbed his fingers together in the universal sign for money.

"I'm not asking *what* he said, but *if* he talked about Nguyen Thi Dinh?"

Cuong put his lips against her ear and translated. When he stopped, she said, "Yes, he talk."

"Did your first husband call again?"

She glanced at Cuong, and he said, "Many time."

"Your first husband called Captain Matthew many times?" They nodded. "Once a month—twelve times a year—that many times?"

They conferred. "Not so much," Cuong said.

"Once every two months—six times a year?"

"Not so much," Ghost's widow said.

"Once every six months? Once a year?"

A conference. "Yes," she said.

"When was the last time your first husband called Captain Matthew?"

Cuong translated, and she gazed out to sea for half a minute before saying, "Nineteen eighty-seven."

"Why was that the last time?" I said, expecting Cuong to stop her from answering. He didn't.

Ghost's widow reached into her purse, drew out a copy of a newspaper clipping, and handed it to me. It was in Vietnamese, so I passed it to Maldonado.

She skimmed it, then offered key snatches: "We mourn the death of our companion, Colonel Chu Trung, known to his intimates as Colonel Ma; murdered by his enemies 4th July 1987 while sleeping aboard his boat. . . . The explosion also took the lives of Major Ngoc Hai and two other as yet unidentified former soldiers. . . . A Requiem Mass was said at Our Lady of Perpetual Help. . . . Among the pallbearers were many who bore arms with Colonel Ma in his native land. . . ." Maldonado raised her head to indicate she'd given me the essentials.

"So the last time your first husband and Captain Matthew were in touch was the year of his death, nineteen eighty-seven . . . ?"

"Easter," she said emptily.

"Did they talk about Nguyen Thi Dinh?"

Cuong didn't bother translating for her; he merely rubbed his fingers together in the money gesture.

"Not *what* they talked about Nguyen Thi Dinh, but *if* they talked about her . . . ?"

Cuong smiled minimally at me and shook his head.

Smiling back, I nonchalantly said, "And since the death of your first husband, what about you, Mrs. Cuong, have you been in touch with Captain Matthew?"

But I barely got to the end of the question before Cuong was impatiently rubbing his fingers together, leaving me maddeningly unsure of where I stood.

Part of me believed that Ghost's widow had answered my questions well enough so I could safely make a deal with her and get on with the real job. Another part of me didn't. While I looked over my notes, Maldonado casually leafed through the 1975 blowups and chatted in Vietnamese with Ghost's widow.

A thought occurred to Maldonado, and she broke off her conversation to turn to me. "Mr. Bruno, may I have your permission to show Captain Matthew's photograph of Colonel Ghost to Mrs. Cuong?"

I assented and went on with my interior struggle.

Maldonado pulled Ghost's picture from the stack and passed it to his widow. While Mrs. Cuong looked at it expressionlessly, and Cuong resolutely stared out to sea, Maldonado reread Ghost's obituary.

"Mrs. Cuong," she said in puzzlement, "I don't see Captain Matthew's name here—couldn't he serve as a pallbearer for his comrade-in-arms?" Ghost's widow looked confused, so Maldonado translated what she'd said into Vietnamese.

After a glance at her husband, Ghost's widow made a muted reply, and Maldonado said, "Mr. Bruno, Mrs. Cuong says Captain Matthew did not attend the funeral of his murdered comrade-in-arms."

"No tell Captain Matthew," Ghost's widow said.

"Why not?" I said.

Cuong took a very long time translating those two words, and when he was done, Ghost's widow said, "No want to give pain to Captain Matthew."

"Did you ever tell him?" I said.

Very slowly and mournfully, Ghost's widow shook her head, and passed the photo back to Maldonado.

Maldonado reached out and took her hand, saying, "Was Captain Marshall a distant man to you, Mrs. Cuong? Sometimes, the comrades of our husbands do not honor us properly, do they?" Once more, Ghost's widow looked confused, and once more Maldonado translated for her.

Ghost's widow conferred with her husband. When she finished, she spoke in Vietnamese to Maldonado, who explained: "Mrs. Cuong is humiliated to admit that Captain Marshall met only with Colonel Ghost; like many soldierly men, he rejected the company of wives."

Maldonado pulled the twenty-year-old picture of Marshall from the stack and put it side by side on her lap with the picture of Ghost. "Yes," she said reflectively, "soldiers, comrades-in-arms." She held both pictures in front of me. "You see, Mr. Bruno?"

Before I could tell her no, I didn't, Cuong snapped a command to Ghost's widow, and she jumped to her feet. He did the same, folding his canvas chair the instant he was upright and using it to angrily prod his wife toward the street.

By then, I was up, taking my first steps after them as they raced across the avenue, dodging traffic.

Maldonado stopped me by seizing my arm and forcing me to turn to her: "He can't help you!" she said with frightening conviction. "He will tell you whatever you wish to hear to get what he wants. This is what he does, Mr. Bruno. This is what he did with Captain Matthew."

By then, Cuong and his wife had climbed into a black Sable and were starting to pull into the traffic.

"With Captain Matthew?" I said.

"Of course," Maldonado said, and held up the photo. "Mr. Cuong is Colonel Ghost."

I kept a lid on it the rest of the day and night, and most of Sunday. But about three hours into the flight to New York, after we'd eaten and were having drinks, and I was tired and frustrated and past sober, I brought it up.

"Ms. Maldonado, I wish you'd tell me in advance when you're going to play detective. That way, I can try to stop the prey from running off."

Before she spoke, she put down her drink and folded her hands in her lap. "Mr. Bruno," she said even more formally than usual, "I apologize for not alerting you to my little improvisation—at the time, I didn't know how—but even if you had stopped them from leaving, it would not have helped you. You must know that."

From the dish on the tiny table, she took a mint, unwrapped it, and slipped it into her mouth.

"No, I don't know that," I said. "What I know is I never got a chance to get at the truth."

"From that man?" Maldonado said, her voice soft but her tone fierce. "His letters are false, his name is false—even his death is false. Why do you think he would ever tell you the truth?"

"Even false people do, when it's in their interest," I snapped.

"Only if they know it!" she said. "He did not, so he would have lied. No matter how much money you gave him, he would have lied."

"I wanted to determine that for myself," I said, "not have the decision taken out of my hands."

"That is outrageous!" she said, still without raising her voice. "I found him out, and I revealed him to *you;* I did not confront *him.* I did not force the issue. He ran away on his own—which should make plain the kind of man he is. A false man; a liar!"

She bit her lip and lowered her head; when she raised it, she'd reverted to her obliging facade. "Mr. Bruno, may I please order a Sambuca?"

While I signaled the flight attendant that we wanted more drinks, Maldonado unwrapped another mint. Instead of putting the whole thing in her mouth, she balanced it on her forefinger, brought it close to her lips, and delicately licked the chocolate coating with the tip of her tongue.

"Mr. Bruno," she said between flicks, "do you truly believe my behavior today sabotaged your inquiry?"

"Sabotage implies intent," I said. "I know you didn't intend to do any harm."

She dipped her head politely. "Do you believe if I had not exposed Colonel Ghost he would have helped you?"

I was saved from answering immediately by the arrival of the flight attendant; once she left, I said, "I don't know. I do know that no matter how unreliable you think he is, I have to talk to him again."

"That would be a complete waste of time," she said so confidently I wanted to pour her Sambuca on her head.

"I don't have to waste yours, Ms. Maldonado!" I said.

Instead of responding either to my words or my inflection—and it was vicious—she glanced away, swallowed hard, then leaned close enough that I could feel her minty breath on my face, and said, "Mr. Bruno, do you believe Colonel Ghost truly loved Captain Marshall and truly wanted to help him?" She brought her hand near my eyes and mimicked Ghost's finger-rubbing gesture. "Do you believe that about the man you met yesterday?"

"I'd have to think about that," I said flatly, but I didn't. Ghost was a dead end, and I knew it. The trouble was I couldn't accept it because I had no clue where to turn next.

"What will you do now?" she said, in another of her exasperating flashes of telepathy.

"I don't know," I said. "At the moment, I'm feeling a bit lost."

"You're not lost, Mr. Bruno," she said. "You're thirty-seven thousand feet in the sky, with your faithful interpreter."

CHAPTER 35

THERE WERE FIVE OFFICE suites on my floor, and they had done all of them. They'd also done two of the three suites on the floor below. Only one of the seven suites had a remote alarm system—the building was meant to be secure—and the alarm sounded at a private company, not at a precinct. The private company logged it but didn't respond to it. So nobody discovered anything until the start of the business day on Monday.

When I arrived at 8:45, I found the assistant manager standing in front of my open door. Talking to him was a thirtyish heavyset guy who, unsurprisingly—given his suit, his shoes, and his suspicious eyes—turned out to be a cop.

"Detective Marty Jacoby," he said to me when I reached them, blocking me from entering. He didn't offer his hand—they rarely do, and then only to deceive. "You Adam Bruno?" he asked, indicating my name on the door. Instead of answering, I showed him my driver's license. While he glanced at the license photo, I glanced at the door lock. It had been jimmied, masterfully. Jacoby handed me back my license and said, "Can you show me your place?"

Nodding and pushing the door wide, I stepped across the threshold and looked around.

They had taken just about everything electronic—the computer, the printer, the typewriter, the fax, the answering machine, a portable recorder, and a postage meter. The only item they'd left was a copying machine, which because it was a rental had been bolted to the floor.

They had opened all the drawers in my desk, including the two locked ones, and left them open, both to save time and make no noise. They had done the same with the locked file cabinets and the locked diskette cabinet and the locked supply closet. "Okay if I check the desk?" I said to Jacoby.

"Sure," he said. He fished in his pocket and found a couple of stolen-property forms. "I'll leave these, okay, and you can fill 'em out when you like." He fished in another pocket for his notebook. "I'll just write the special shit. You keep a licensed weapon here, long gun or pistol?"

"No," I said.

"Unlicensed?"

"No."

"Don't bullshit me about that," he said. "We don't want some perp running around with your piece."

"I don't keep a gun here."

"What about large amounts of cash?"

By then I'd discovered that they'd taken from my desk a shoebox-sized steel box in which I kept petty cash. "Maybe six hundred dollars," I said. "They got that."

"Six hundred dollars?" he said, letting me hear his disbelief. "That's all?"

"I never keep more than a thousand here."

"Sure," he said, in the same skeptical way. "Bearer bonds in large amounts?"

"No."

"Large amounts of securities that maybe somebody could sell at a discount?"

"No."

"Jewelry or valuable timepieces?"

"No."

"Paintings, sculptures, antique documents—either yours, or something you're holding for somebody?"

"No."

"Anything at all of special value, either yours or somebody else's?"

"No."

"Any controlled medication? Codeine? Sleeping pills? Tranqs? Diet pills—that kind of stuff?"

"No."

"You got a safe?"

"No."

"How come?"

"I've never needed one."

"So you got nothing in here anybody wants?" Once more, his tone was skeptical bordering on rude.

"Like what?" I said, echoing the nastiness.

"I dunno," he said insinuatingly. "Maybe evidence in something you're working on."

"I don't follow you, Detective," I said. "Why don't you tell me what you're talking about?"

"You're a lawyer, right? Criminal lawyer? You defend criminals. That kinda evidence." He smiled fixedly. "I dunno, maybe a coupla keys."

I smiled back at him. "Detective—it's Jacoby, isn't it? Marty Jacoby. Detective, keeping contraband here would be a crime." Ostentatiously, I raised my voice so it could be heard easily in the hallway, if not in the street. "Are you accusing me of a crime, Detective? Is that what you're doing to the victim of a burglary?" I stepped toward the door. "What's your partner's name, Detective?—I'd like to call him in here to witness this. If I'm going to be accused of a crime, I'd like a witness present."

"Nobody's accusing you of shit!" he said, enraged.

"Good," I said, lowering my voice. "Is it okay if I fix the lock now?"

"When they've dusted!" he barked, and marched out.

After calling the locksmith to come in the early afternoon, I inspected the office the way a team of narcs would, inch by inch.

Beginning with the printed files—open case, closed case, interim reports, interview transcripts, interview summaries, open informer, coded informer, local police sources, county sources, federal sources—I went on to the diskette shelves. I examined each floppy diskette to make sure the label had my handwriting and that no blanks had been substituted. Next, the supply cabinet, and, last, the desk: I emptied and replaced each item in each drawer, making an inventory as I went.

Though they had searched everywhere—looking for cash, presumably, since people kept cash in all kinds of places—and had ransacked all the paper files, they seemed to have taken nothing. They had taken no floppy diskettes. That meant I had lost no data, nothing, not even what had been on the computer's hard disk, because every night I copied everything on the hard disk onto floppies.

Taking as much time as each would give me, I called on the other six victims. Their offices had been plundered exactly as mine had—cash and equipment, no damage. No water coolers smashed, no Crazy Glue on the coffee machine, no shit on the carpet. The burglars had jimmied the door, taken what was saleable, and scrammed.

In total, they got maybe $10,000 in cash and equipment worth around $125,000 new; if they had a place to store it and could sell it piecemeal, they could get, say, $25,000. If they sold it in one batch, $15,000. If there were three of them, that was $8,000 to $11,500 each. Not a lot, but not a lot of work either, especially if they did more than one job a night, which was easy enough.

All the signs pointed to a simple burglary—except that I was working a case that involved $105 million, so for the time being I assumed that all the signs were a cover.

If I had wanted to disguise my purpose in a burglary, I would have done exactly what this burglar had done. I would have hit as many places as possible, and I would have taken the same sort of booty from all of them.

I went through the place again, this time trying to think like that burglar. If I were he, and Adam Bruno were the target, I'd be looking for information: paper files, or diskettes, or a hard disk. Perhaps he took the computer just to get the hard disk. Right.

Wrong: There was no useful information on the hard disk.

Could he have gambled that all the information he wanted was on the hard disk? Insane: You don't loot seven offices to get a hard disk that might not contain what you want when floppies that might are sitting on a shelf. You take both, and you do the same thing in the other offices to hide your intentions. Your victim might be suspicious, but at least you'd have the goods. This way your victim was suspicious anyway, and you had nothing.

Maybe all the signs were right: a simple burglary.

While I waited for the locksmith, I ordered a replacement computer and called the insurance company to explain that I'd had a break-in and would be submitting a claim. The insurance company told me my premiums would go up.

Just before lunch, a crime-scene team came in and dusted for prints. They were in a very good mood, and why not? Commercial burglaries were a holiday for them—no self-important paramedics or peevish homicide cops; no hysterical relatives; no screaming, orphaned infants; no rabid pets; no curious neighbors; no uniforms stepping all over the evidence and taking it out of the room on the soles of their shoes; and, most important, no rank bodies, no maggots, and no blood, which meant no trying to get prints from things you'd rather not see, never mind touch. In an office, most of the surfaces are smooth and retain prints easily. Assuming the thieves leave them. "You have any luck anyplace?" I said.

The head of the crime-scene team looked up from his work. "You're shittin' me, man? This be professional work." He thought of something and softened his tone: "What's the matter, you don't have no insurance?"

"No, I'm okay," I said.

"That's cool," he said, returning to his task. "I be thinkin' maybe you be askin' 'cause you be expectin' to be gettin' your shit back."

"How'd they get in the building?" I said.

"Fire door in the back alley," he said.

"There's an alarm on that door," I said.

"Sure be," he said, "and the door be reinforced steel, and it have two deadbolts and a Fox." He smiled lewdly. "The night porter, he leave it unlocked weekends so his lady, she be able to stop by."

"Did she stop by last night?"

"Two-thirty, two-forty-five," he said. "Stay till his shift be done at seven. Them two be way too busy to hear no thief." He burst into admiring laughter. "He have a queen-size sofabed down there, man. Sheets. Pillows with pillowcases. Shee-it!"

Right after the crime-scene team left, the locksmith showed up and fixed my door. Forty minutes after that, the computer dealer arrived, and we spent the next two hours setting up my replacement system and testing it.

Once he'd gone, I rounded out a bleak, wasted day by drafting a report for the insurance company. That took longer than it should have, since I was still brooding over the burglary, but I finally finished it, printed it—with the inventory, it ran four pages—and took it to the Xerox machine, to make copies for the insurer and the police.

I put the pages in the feeder, set the dial for two copies, pushed the START button, and waited for the first page to go through. Sometimes the first page jammed; the machine was temperamental that way. Sure enough, the first page jammed, and I opened the machine to release it. As I was working the page free of the rollers, I checked the paper tray to make certain there was enough fresh paper. The tray was full—which made me stop and think.

Whenever the paper tray dropped to the quarter-full level, I reloaded it, but only up to the three-quarter mark; anything higher jammed the machine, something I had never been able to get across to the rental serviceman. Whenever he reloaded the tray—which he did when he came to check the counter—he always reloaded it to the top. Full. Had he loaded it last? Had I loaded it last?

I found the machine counter, copied the total—it was 7,989—and called the copier rental house. The woman who answered wasn't happy to talk to me—normally, if customers called for their previous readout totals, they were calling to protest a bill—but I persuaded her that wasn't my aim, and asked her for my last recorded total and whatever averages her computer had available.

"Je-sus," she said. "What's your problem?"

"My secretary's secretly writing a screenplay, and I suspect she's making copies of it."

"What's it about?" the woman said, punching keys.

"Sex and violence," I said. "You got the numbers?"

"Gimme a minute," she said. "What kinda sex?"

"She won't let me read it, but I think it involves a Saint Bernard in some way," I said, expecting that to quiet her.

"Yeah, my sister-in-law's into that," she said. "Here we go . . . Last six months: monthly . . . low 1,190, high 1,360, average 1,275; weekly . . . low 274, high 368, average 335; daily, all I got is average, which is 64. Your last recorded total—that's six business days ago—is 7,155. You say your present readout is 7,989, so you did 834 copies since then, which is 139 pages a day. Yeah, unless you had a lot of extra work lately, I'd say somebody's ripping you off."

"Thanks," I said and rang off. With some effort, I made myself sit dead still and think.

My office had been penetrated. Nothing could be done about what had been copied—and I had no doubt that only the Marshall material had been copied—so there was no point in removing it. In fact, removing it would be stupid: If the burglars returned for another taste, they would immediately grasp that I knew what they had come for. The smart thing to do was leave everything where it was and simply not add to it, or add to it in a way that it would make no difference if it were stolen.

That was easy enough. The harder part was figuring out what to do with any new material once I'd gathered it. Actually that didn't seem so hard either: I picked up the phone and started dialing Herschel's number.

But as I punched the fifth digit, my stomach tightened and I hung up. Herschel O'Hara was sleeping with Mollie Wharton. Mollie Wharton worked for Wilson Laird. Did that mean I couldn't trust Herschel? I didn't know, but I knew I wasn't brave enough to gamble.

Feeling treacherous and hating it, I opened my phone book and began looking for somebody who had absolutely no connection to the Marshall case, somebody I could count on to safeguard any documents I left with him and not repeat anything I told him; somebody I could trust.

I only had to get as far as the B's. She wasn't in, so I left a message:

"Ms. Boulanger, it's Adam Bruno—I need to talk to you. I'd like to renew my retainer."

CHAPTER 36

"... As I UNDERSTAND IT, you want to retain me to hold the material you give me today and any material you might send me, either on paper or on disk, or both—correct?" Cecile Boulanger said, and preceded me through the revolving door into the federal courthouse.

"Yes," I said, once I got inside and caught up with her as she strode toward the elevator bank.

"And as I understand it," she continued, "none of this material is—so far as you know—stolen, or is evidence in a crime—correct?"

"Yes."

An elevator came and we got into it, along with a crushing throng of lawyers, clients, and clerks. She waited till we reached her floor and were headed along the hallway to her courtroom before picking up: "And as I understand it, you want me to consider any conversations we have about the Marshall matter privileged?"

"Yes."

"In the event I accept you as a client, do you have any objection if I peruse the material you give me today—" she indicated the crammed tote bag I was holding, "or any material you send me?"

I'd anticipated the question, but it still wasn't easy for me to say, "I have no objection."

Ceremoniously, she nodded, and I passed her the bag, which held four 10 by 13 envelopes stuffed with files and diskettes. She hefted it, cleared her throat, and said, "May I ask you something? ..." I nodded. "Why did you come to me—why not Herschel O'Hara?" I hesitated, and she said, "Is he somehow involved with the Marshall case?"

"Not exactly."

"Translate that, please."

"He's involved with one of the executors," I said, and as I did, my back began to sweat. "That's privileged," I added uncomfortably.

"Of course," she said, not troubling to hide her smile. "May I summarize this for myself, please?"

A couple of lawyers greeted her, and she waited till they'd passed before saying, "A one-hundred-five-million-dollar estate is at stake; you've been keeping progress reports from the executor; the executor and the surviving Marshalls believe you already have a result; and you are convinced the burglary of your office was to purloin your material on the case . . . ?" I nodded. "You don't have a result, do you—you haven't found the child?"

"No, I haven't found the child," I said, with more vehemence than I intended.

We'd reached the courtroom doors. She glanced at her watch and said, "Well, what is it that you have found, Mr. Bruno, that you want me to protect?"

"I don't know," I said. "All I know is that it's in the Marshalls' interest to demonstrate to the court that the child does not exist. Or that its existence can't be proved."

"Does your material offer proof of its existence?"

"No; no proof. Hearsay. Weak hearsay, in fact."

A court officer stuck his head through the doors and said, "He's on his way in, Ms. Boulanger."

Boulanger nodded her thanks; to me, she said, "How would your material help the Marshalls—or anyone else?"

"I don't know," I said with some heat. "I went over it last night, and I couldn't find anything that would be seriously useful. I have to go over it again."

"Good luck," she said.

"Thanks," I said and opened the door for her.

"Any time," she said, with a hint of conquest, and slipped into the courtroom.

Two nights later, at 5:35 in the morning, I found it, and it hurt so deeply I wanted to believe that whoever had burglarized my place had missed it; had not found it, had somehow, while he was reading all my material, glided right past it the way I'd glided past it.

But I couldn't believe that, not even for a minute.

Six and half hours earlier, at 11:04, while I was deciding whether to return to Los Angeles to give Ghost another shot, the narration from the

TV set penetrated my consciousness and I looked at the screen:

". . . Although authorities said this was the twenty-ninth bombing of an abortion clinic this year, it was the first explosion set off during office hours."

On the TV, a reporter stood next to a fire truck in front of a shattered one-story building. Tendrils of smoke rose from the wreckage behind him. In the corner of the screen, a uniformed cop followed a leashed Labrador as it sniffed the debris.

At the bottom of the screen, white lettering read, LAKELAND, FLORIDA.

"So far, there are three known dead," the reporter continued. "Beverly Dornan, a local right-to-life activist who police believe planted the bomb in the bathroom of the clinic; a seventeen-year-old girl who was in the midst of an abortion at the time of the explosion; and Michael Woolff, the doctor who ran the clinic. . . ."

Footage of Woolff appeared and was followed at once by footage of the man with the cross I'd run into outside Woolff's house. The reporter said:

"The Reverend Arthur Bartley, with whom Ms. Dornan often demonstrated, declined to condemn the bombing:

"I mourn for Beverly Dornan and the babies she will no longer be able to save," Bartley said. "I cannot mourn for Michael Woolff, Hitler of the unborn."

The TV picture changed to one of Miriam Woolff, her tear-soaked face resting on a filled black body bag as it was borne on a gurney to an ambulance.

"Dr. Woolff leaves his wife and two children," the reporter said, as the picture changed to a still of the kids.

A commercial appeared, and I pulled my eyes away from the TV set. My face was clammy and damp.

What devastated me most at 5:35 was how easy I had made it for them. They hadn't needed to go through reams of material; all they'd had to do was read my interim report to myself—it was in the third bracketed note:

[NOTE 3: Of the people Marshall served with, only McGowan has corroborated the existence of Cricket (Chau Chau), and she never saw her. McGowan speculates that if anyone among Marshall's troops ever saw Cricket it would have been Woolff or Randall; my interviews don't support this.]

CHAPTER 37

MIRIAM WOOLFF IGNORED THE Lakeland detective's resentful looks and maintained a deliberate pace while she emptied the drawers of her husband's desk into two large accordion envelopes. She also ignored the stench—an ugly, pungent combination of scorched paint, charred wood, melted plastic, singed cloths, piss, shit—the bomb had been placed in the bathroom—and, piercing through it all, burnt flesh.

Her hands were steady as she worked, and if she was about to fall apart, it didn't show. It was an impressive performance, but I guessed that living with the threat of violence every day had conditioned her. When she finished, she said to the detective, "I'd like to look in Room B."

The detective, whose name was Orville Hatch, wriggled in discomfort. "You're supposed to be collecting his personal stuff, Mrs. Woolff. You're not going to find anything in there. We gave you everything."

She touched her throat. "He wore a chain, with a little gold heart. You didn't give me that."

"Maybe he didn't wear it that day."

"He wore it," she said. "It never came off!"

"Okay, okay," Hatch said. "Let me have a couple of days, and I'll get a team to do a good search."

"I want to look myself," she said unyieldingly.

He shrugged at me and led us down the debris-filled hallway to the demolished doorway to Room B. There, he stepped out of the way to let her go in.

His reluctance made sense: Every surface in the room was spattered with blood. Chunks of flesh clung to the walls, and entrails dangled from the twisted furniture. Bits and pieces of machinery—the aspirator—were embedded in the wallboard. Parts of a teddy bear were strewn near the window; its glass eye lay wedged between the slats of the blind.

"May I move this?" Miriam Woolff said, pointing to the mangled aspirator.

"Sure," Hatch said from the doorway.

She bent down and shoved the aspirator a few inches to the side. From her purse, she took a large comb and began to sift through the rubble and dust on the mock-tile floor. She paid no attention to either of us.

"I'll show you the rest of the place," Hatch said, pushing me down the hallway to the reception room. Once there, he rolled his eyes and gratefully lit a cigarette.

"I hope that chain is worth it," he said. "Crawling around in that shit." He sucked deeply on his cigarette. "I hate fires and I hate explosions," he said. "I came down here from Detroit to get away from fires and explosions.

"People break up weird—I mean, it's not like TV, where the parts fall off on the seams. The girl on the gurney, the one getting vacced—chili; you could have served her with rice and beans. The doc, he was between her legs—not between her legs, but you know, between her legs like a doc—he caught a piece of faucet through the eye and a section of drain-pipe through the belly. Oh—and a shard of glass through the neck. Bet that's why they didn't find the goddamn chain."

"What about Beverly Dornan—where was she?"

"In the bathroom with her goddamn bomb," he said in wonder. "Can you believe it?" He laughed mordantly. "If you think the doc and the girl got ripped, you should have seen Bev. You need all of your parts to get to Heaven, no fucking way Bev gets there." He made a face. "I hate explosions."

"No doubt it was her, is there?"

"We got matching prints and dental work. It's Bev."

"You think she did it on purpose—stayed with the bomb, I mean?"

"No way," he said with some force. "These people talk a very big game—every one of them is ready to die for their beliefs, but somehow it's never more than a hundred-dollar fine and seventy-two hours in the lockup. When was the last time you heard of a right-to-lifer getting killed? Bev fucked up; no way that bomb was meant to go off just that second."

"Did she ever try anything like this before?"

"Couple of rinky-dink fires," he said. "They like to set night fires—usually a clinic, sometimes a car. A doc's car, a nurse's, a counselor's. We got Bev on three of those: misdemeanor arson, sentence suspended." He shrugged. "The judges down here are serious Christians."

"What about her mentor, the Reverend Bartley—he ever do anything like this?"

"Not him himself. One of his people shot a doc a couple years ago down in Pensacola. Another stabbed one this March up in Jacksonville. They didn't connect Bartley up to either of them."

"Have your guys?"

"The official position," he said, pinching his nose to show his opinion of the official position, "is Bev did it all on her own, and there's no evidence of anyone else's involvement, 'specially not the Reverend Bartley, and no cause to waste manpower and money looking for anyone."

"Is that your position?"

"I don't have a position."

"You're saying, as far as your bosses are concerned, the case is cleared?"

"Sure," he said. "Bev hates the doc, Bev builds a bomb, Bev sneaks it in the clinic, Bev takes it in the bathroom, Bev puts it next to the plumbing—and boom!"

"Do you believe it?"

"I believe she hates the doc, I believe she sneaks the bomb in the clinic, I believe she takes it in the bathroom, I believe she puts it next to the plumbing, I believe the boom." He gestured. "I got to believe the boom. But I have a hard time believing she builds it."

"Why?"

"I busted Bev a lot of times. She can't drive a stick shift." He shrugged. "Hey, everybody's happy, they got a slam-dunk." He laughed meanly. "Except the prosecutor—he's shitting walnuts. He was having wet dreams about Court TV."

"You know, something just occurred to me," I said, as if it had. "Do you think—since the case is cleared—do you think your boss would let me look at some of your reports . . . ?"

"Our reports?" he said warily.

"For the lawsuit," I said, gesturing toward Miriam Woolff in Room B, "and for . . . whatever."

"What's . . . whatever?"

"I'm getting calls," I said. "There's other media possibilities apart from Court TV."

Hatch lit another cigarette. "I'm not sure it's a great idea to ask my boss," he said with excessive thoughtfulness. "Any media shit comes along, he hears about it, he expects to get right in the middle of it."

"Oh, you mean like a technical advisor?" I said.

"You got it—and it's not like he did the work."

"Well, if you can't ask him, you can't ask him," I said. "Is there another way to get at those reports?"

"It's official stuff," he said. "It's not like it can walk out of the building on its own."

"Is there a way to copy them?"

While he thought about it, Miriam Woolff emerged from the door of Room B. Her dark suit was smudged with dirt.

"Sure there's a way," Hatch said. "But we don't have print shops on every corner in Lakeland. It's a lot of money to copy official stuff down here."

"What are we talking about?"

"Oh, we're talking about, say, a dollar a—we're talking about two dollars a page."

Miriam Woolff walked slowly along the hallway toward us. When she came close, she held up two fingers; hanging from them was a thin gold chain with a tiny heart attached. "I guess you missed it," she said to Hatch.

"I guess we did," he answered.

"Thanks for bringing me," Miriam Woolff said once we'd pulled away from the curb in front of the clinic.

"Sure," I said. "I'm glad you found the chain."

"Yes," she said, holding it up so the sunlight glinted off it. "I gave it to him the night I first decided to sleep with him. I wanted him to know I was giving my heart, too. Left at the light."

After I made the turn and we rode a few blocks, she said, "Why did you come here?"

When I'd called her from the airport, I told her I'd come to pay my respects because I'd upset Woolff so much when I'd been there last. At the time, she made no comment—simply asked me to take her to the clinic so she could collect some of his things—and I was wondering whether it was worth a second pass when she said, "And please don't tell me it was to pay your respects to Mick. I don't believe it."

I didn't want to lie, but I wasn't ready to tell her my speculations about Woolff's murder: "I came because I still hope to find something that will lead me to Matt Marshall's girlfriend."

"What a waste of your time," she said.

"Maybe," I said, "but when I was here last, your husband held things back. I think he believed I was here for a different reason than I told him, and he didn't trust me."

"That's right, he didn't," she said.

"I understand that," I said, "but I really did visit him about Matt Marshall."

"I don't know anything about Matt Marshall," she said, "and I don't care."

"Did your husband keep any mementos—diaries, cassettes, photos?"

"No. I don't know. No!" Bitterly, she said, "He wanted to forget the war. You prevented that, and it left him messed up for days."

"I'm sorry," I said.

"Goddamn right!" she shouted, and pressed her face against her door window.

I waited till she sat back in her seat. "In the last couple of weeks, did your husband mention Marshall at all?"

"No."

"You're sure?"

"I'm sure."

"Did he get any unsolicited calls or visits?"

"You mean at the house?" I nodded. "We don't get much traffic there—you know, the Reverend Bartley . . ."

"What about at the clinic?"

"He's a doctor. Somebody's always trying to sell doctors something."

"Anyone he made a point of telling you about?"

"He doesn't do that, not unless it's really unusual. Didn't do that, I mean."

"It wouldn't have been a salesman—more likely someone doing a survey about Vietnam and veterans, or someone doing an article about the war. Anything like that?"

She shook her head, then looked at me closely. "Why are you asking?"

I couldn't tell her; I lied: "The Marshall family is worried that someone's trying to do an unauthorized biography."

She made a rude noise and pointed through the windshield at the intersection. "Right at the four-way."

I left her in peace for a few minutes before saying, "If you're not sure about the mementos, I could stop by and help you look—I'm going to be here a while anyway."

"No!" We rode in silence for a few miles before she said, "Over there," indicating the ranch house. Without the pickets marching in front of it, I didn't recognize it.

When I pulled up, she turned down her visor to inspect her face in the vanity mirror. "Are my eyes red?" she asked, and turned toward me.

I looked carefully. "No."

"The kids get crazed; they don't want me crying away from the house. If I cry, they want to comfort me." She made a sharp, angry gesture. "What am I talking about—they're with my parents. Goddamn, I'm losing it!"

She opened the door. She still had Woolff's chain clutched in her hand. "If you're going to be here anyway, why don't you call me," she said, and got out of the car.

Chapter 38

Orville Hatch wanted to earn his two dollars a page, so he copied nearly 300 pages of reports. In addition to interviews with patients, counselors, janitors, and a dozen of Bartley's pickets, he included material from the coroner's office, the forensic team, the bomb squad, the fire department, the health department, the buildings department, and the consumer affairs department. By 2:30 the following morning, I'd been through everything twice, and I was pretty sure I'd wasted $568. Whether because they thought it was a slam-dunk or because they were incompetent, they'd done a terrible job.

Once they ID'd Beverly Dornan—which was right away since they found her wallet on their first sweep after the explosion—they went to autopilot. They had a method, they had a motive, they had a perp. Why bother with nuances?

Typical of their efforts was this by the bomb squad:

Our preliminary investigation shows that the device (see hypothetical sketch) was, by modern standards, quite rudimentary: easily obtainable hardware-store dynamite (not plastic) surrounded by several poly bags filled with kerosene to multiply any incendiary effect. The detonator can be obtained on the surplus market, or copied from an Army manual (or several radical handbooks). The timer is homemade and assembled from any one of a number of cheap watches. (We have recovered portions of all parts of the device.) It is extremely unlikely the device was designed to be exploded by remote control. The device reminds us of the devices formerly used by the KKK and other such supremacist groups when they attempted to destroy black churches. There is nothing unusual about it, although it is not seen very often these days.

Based on the forensic evidence in the clinic bathroom and on the body of Beverly Dornan, the device was contained in a cardboard Nike shoebox, which was hidden under some women's clothing in a plain supermarket shopping bag.

Then, they gave themselves a reason to stop work:

It is not unusual for homemade devices like this one to explode when they are not expected to. This can be the fault of the detonator or the timer. We believe this is what happened in the case of the device at the clinic.

Also, since the components of a device like this are so easy to obtain or build, we think it is inadvisable at this time to devote man-hours to tracing the source of them.

The interviews were no better.

Nobody in the clinic that day—staff or patients—noticed Beverly Dornan come into the clinic, which meant nobody noticed whether she came in alone; which meant nobody noticed whether she went to the bathroom, or whether she went alone or somebody went with her. Nobody noticed who went to the bathroom right before her. Nobody recognized Beverly Dornan—and it was hard to imagine that not one of the women there for an abortion had never seen Beverly Dornan on the news or on a picket line—which meant she disguised herself in some way; but since nobody noticed her, or recognized her, nobody could describe her disguise. And, of course, nobody noticed what she might have been carrying.

All of the pickets who were there the day of the bombing—including the Reverend Bartley—were asked whether Beverly Dornan had said anything about her intentions, and all of them said no. (No other pickets associated with Bartley were even interviewed.) All the pickets who were there that day were asked whether Beverly Dornan picketed, and all of them said no. All of them were asked whether they saw Beverly Dornan go into the clinic, and all of them said no. None of them were asked any follow-up questions.

The police didn't bother with anybody who wasn't a patient or working at the clinic the day of the bombing, so no repairmen, or deliverymen, or anybody who stopped by were interviewed. Nor was anybody on staff interviewed for a possible connection to Beverly Dornan.

Her son was interviewed; he said he knew nothing. Her father was interviewed; ditto. Her estranged husband was not interviewed, since he was considered a hopeless drunk.

The only worthwhile piece of information to come out of the interviews was from one Teresa Torres, the receptionist at the clinic. She told the police that Beverly Dornan did not use her own name to register.

"I already speak to the police. I speak to the ones in the car; I speak to the one in the stupid hat, Hatch; I speak to his partner, I don't know his name, the one with mean eyes; I speak to the one who does the bombs; I speak to the one in the gray suit, the FBI one—why I got to speak to you?"

Teresa Torres stood in the doorway of her small, spotless house and held her right arm just under my chin. Since the arm was encased in plaster, I took it seriously. Torres reminded me of a movie version of a Latin American—black hair, ruby lipstick, flashing eyes—except that she was tall, and movie Latins are short, and, it turned out, she had good reason to resent authority.

"I'm not the police, Miss Torres," I said. "I work for Mrs. Woolff—I'm trying to collect some information on what happened so she can file a claim." I found a business card, handed it to her, and took a step back to give her some room.

"May I come in?" I said.

"Ten minutes," Torres said. "Not a minute over."

Torres led me to the living room and pointed sternly to the couch. As I began to lower myself, three small children appeared; they were trailed by a younger, plumper version of Torres, who came over to me and mimed that she wanted to hang up my raincoat.

"He's only going to be here five minutes, Maria; he can keep his coat on," Torres said.

Maria smiled nervously at me and turned to snap in Spanish at Torres. I didn't follow much of it, but the gist was that since Maria shared the house with Teresa, I was her guest, too, and *her* guests were not obliged to sit in their raincoats. She turned back to me. Avoiding Torres's glare, I slipped out of the coat and passed it to Maria. She nodded and carried it to the hall closet, smoothing it as she went.

"She still thinks she's home," Torres said contemptuously. "Don't kiss everybody's ass, I tell her, this isn't Oaxaca, but what does she know? She knows about cleaning bathrooms and having kids. Take an English course, I tell her; I'm scared, Teresa, I'm scared; they'll make fun of me. Hah!"

Maria returned with a tray on which were three cups of coffee. "For Jesus's sake, Maria! He's a lawyer, not the goddamn president of Mexico!"

At the word *goddamn*, Maria glanced at an icon on the wall and quickly crossed herself.

"You see what I'm saying? Hopeless."

"*Muchas gracias*," I said to Maria, who blushed and lowered her head.

"What are you doing?" Torres cried. "She'll think you want to marry her. He doesn't want to marry you, Maria. He's a lawyer. Everybody knows they're all *maricones*."

"*Este caballero no es maricon*," Maria said.

Half an hour later, after Maria had put the children to bed and poured us more coffee, things were less amusing.

"I tell you over and over what I tell the others over and over," Torres spat. "I sit there the whole goddamn day and I work. Busy! You know what busy is? You think they give me the job because I'm a Latina and I work cheap? I make more than the last two girls they have, and they were both Anglo. They give me more because I work. And what about my unemployment? What's going to happen to that? Tell me. You work for Mrs. Woolff, answer me that. We have a lot of mouths here—do you know what these four eat? What about my unemployment? Is Mrs. Woolff going to help me with that?

"I work like a burro—damn phone every minute, dumb girls who don't how to put the words in the right place on the form. It says right on the wall—no personal checks. They don't care. Please, please, I didn't know, I don't have that much cash, I don't have a Visa or a MasterCard. Of course you don't—you're only fifteen stupid years old, who's going to give you a MasterCard? Will you help me with this part—I don't understand this part. An idiot can understand it, Maria's kids can understand it, but not those girls. Miss Dumb Latina has to help the girls do the form." She took a breath.

"First: Everybody who comes for an abortion goes to the bathroom all the time. There's pressure down there." Maria crossed herself. "They're scared. They go. Sometimes, they go every twenty minutes. A man wouldn't understand. The people who come with them also go, because they're nervous. It's traffic all the time. This woman—this horrible Dornan woman—I'm sure she goes. I didn't see her go. When I first started, I used to worry about people passing out in there, but it can't happen—there's too much traffic.

"I don't pay attention if more than one person goes, because that happens all the time. It's not like a bakery, where you take a number. Sometimes, whoever's with the girl takes her in the bathroom—maybe the girl feels faint, maybe she wants company; even boyfriends go. They take them to the door and they wait just outside. It's nice. It shows heart.

"Next: Everybody who comes here carries a big bag, a tote, even an overnight; the poorer ones have a plastic shopping bag. Double bag. They need it. They always bring a change of underwear, sometimes a pair of slippers, their own towel, maxipads, lots of makeup, aspirin, heating pads. Nobody comes for an abortion with a little beaded evening bag."

She picked up a newspaper with a photo of Beverly Dornan on the front page.

"Next: She doesn't look like this. I'm not saying she don't come in—they found her in the bathroom, she must have come in. But she doesn't look like this. When they come in, they don't want to look like who they are. They tie their hair up—sometimes they even cut it; they wear a shawl or a hat. They wear sunglasses, and they sit in them the whole time. I don't know if I can recognize one out of ten who come in there if I see her someplace else.

"Next: Most people come in with *somebody,* but usually whoever they come in with just sits down—doesn't come over to me—and I don't notice unless there's something very special about them. Kids I notice. We ask them not to bring kids, but they do anyway. Very old people. Very dirty people. People without shoes. People with dogs or cats—we don't let the animals in. Drunk people. Drug people. People in uniform—once in a while, we see that. Different color couples. Very loud people. If there's nothing really special, why should I notice? I've got lots of work. Busy."

I shuffled through the papers on my lap, found a list of patients, and said, "Miss Torres, you told the police that Beverly Dornan didn't use her real name to regis—"

"Wait a minute!" she said, jumped to her feet, marched into another room, and returned with two sheets of paper. Brusquely, she signaled me to move over, sat next to me, and held out her hand. "Let me see."

I passed my list to her; she rapidly compared it to hers. "The same," she said, nudging me hard.

I peered at her list. Next to each name was a series of marks. "What do all these mean?" I said.

"The cross means they've filled out the form and paid—C is cash, CC is certified check, K is credit card. Double cross means they've seen the counselor. Star means they've had the procedure."

In the upper left-hand corner of her list was a penciled heading, NS, and under it were three names. In the upper right-hand corner was the heading, CO, and under that were two names and a question mark.

"What are these?" I said.

"NS is no-show—they call up to make an appointment, and they never show up." I copied the three names. "CO is chicken out—they show up, but they don't have the *cojones* to go through with it."

"Why the question mark?" I said.

"No name. Most always, the COs fill out the form and bring it to me, and then chicken out. This one never filled out the form. I give it to her and I give her a pen, but she never brings it back to me."

"Do you remember how long before the explosion she came to your desk to get the form?"

Torres tilted her head up, then looked at her watch. "Fifteen minutes, maybe. More."

"What did she do then?"

"I don't know—goes back to her chair, I guess. Somebody else come up to the desk. It's Saturday, we're very busy Saturday. They like to do it on the weekend, so they don't lose a day's pay."

"You didn't see which chair?"

"It's Saturday!"

"And you didn't see her leave?"

"No! All I know is she never brings the form back to me—sometimes, they do that. They hold the form for a long time. They get this idea if they fill out the form, they're promising to go through with it. It scares them. A man doesn't understand."

"Would you have seen her leave?"

"Not if she didn't have the procedure—they can just sneak out."

I reached for the newspaper with Beverly Dornan's picture. "The woman who came over to your desk to get the form and never returned it, did she look anything like this?"

Torres scrutinized the grainy photo. "I don't know," she said. "I didn't look close at the CO, but she didn't look like this. That I know."

"What do you remember about her?"

"I tell you, it's Saturday. I don't remember."

"Sure you do," I said. "You're observant. Here, I'll start you and you pick up. She's white . . ."

"Si."

"She's big . . ."

"Ummmm, no," Torres said.

"Small . . ."

Torres scrunched her eyes shut and kept them shut while she remembered: "She's not very big, she's not very small—she's a little bit fat . . . kind of loose coat, raincoat maybe, but loose, to hide herself . . . floppy hat . . . scarf around her hair . . . I don't see earrings . . . sunglasses . . . no lipstick . . . jeans—no, not jeans, what do they call them, chinos . . . running shoes . . ."

By then, I was comparing Torres's description to the forensic report on Beverly Dornan. Everything matched, including the running shoes, which meant that Beverly Dornan did indeed take a bomb packed in a Nike box into the bathroom of the clinic and get blown up when it went off.

Torres opened her eyes. "Was it her?"

"I can't really tell," I said, crossing my fingers behind my back. "Did she have a bag?"

Torres started to nod, then paused. "She must have, but . . ." she hesitated. "Maybe she left it at her chair. I don't remember seeing it."

"Did you see her come in?"

Torres shook her head. "Unless it's very slow, or unless somebody is making a fuss or is very special-looking, I don't see them come in."

"So you don't know if she came in with somebody?"

"No."

"What do they do when they come in?"

"They come to me, but on a Saturday they have to wait." She gestured widely. "We have chairs all around, on all the walls, and three rows in the middle, and they wait in the chairs, and they always know who's ahead of them and who's behind them. They pay pretty good attention. So when it's their turn, they come over. There's a chair at my desk—Dr. Woolff doesn't like them to stand."

"Before she came over to you, do you remember where she was sitting?"

"How am I supposed to remember that—I tell you, I didn't see her come in."

"Don't try to remember *her*. Remember the others."

Once more, Torres shut her eyes. For a while she kept silent. Then, pointing tentatively to different parts of the room, she said:

"Over here is the little black girl, she's with her mother . . . over here is the older lady, she's with a man but he's a *maricon* . . . over here is the Jewish girl with her boyfriend . . . over here is—no, that was Friday. Over here is the college girl—Catholic!—with her two friends. They make a lot of noise . . . over here is . . ." She paused, her finger wavering. "Here. She's here." She opened her eyes. "The last seat by the hallway."

"Who was next to her?"

"Some man."

"Did they talk to each other?"

"I don't know."

"What do you recall about him?"

She shrugged. "Nothing special." She laughed. "Not even good enough for Maria."

"Teresa!" her sister said.

"Young?" I said. "Old?"

"Middle," she said. "Middle everything; not skinny, not fat . . ."

"Nicely dressed? Jacket? Tie? Shorts?"

She shrugged. "I don't remember."

"Brown hair? Blond hair? Gray hair?"

She thought. "Bald. I think."

"Why do you think that?"

She patted the top of her head. "Hat." Something teased her recollection. "Sunglasses," she said, touching her eyes. "Sunglasses."

"Yes . . ." I said.

"Very expensive. Like from a magazine. With a name. He didn't look like a man who wears sunglasses like that. They're hundreds of dollars, those sunglasses."

She rubbed her eyes. "I'm getting all mixed up," she said. "I'm mixed up now if it was him in the hat and the sunglasses, or if it was the Jewish girl's boyfriend in the hat. Maybe it was the boyfriend of the girl who die. I'm mixed up."

"We can take a break," I said.

"No, no more," she said, touching her temples with her fingertips. "It hurts me to remember."

"I can come back tomorrow."

"No more!" she cried. "It hurts!" A tear formed in each eye. "She was seventeen; from Ecuador. She ask me to hold her hand during it, but I can't on Saturday; it's too busy." She crossed herself, and Maria did likewise. "I can't remember her name this minute. Poor *poquita*. Poor Dr. Woolff."

CHAPTER 39

"THAT'S LAST JUNE," MIRIAM WOOLFF said, "on Bonnie's tenth birthday. Mick let her take the helm."

We were in the middle of the living room carpet, surrounded by scrapbooks and videotapes. The TV showed a tape of the Woolff family aboard a sailboat; his daughter, in a shocking pink sunsuit, stood earnestly at the wheel. Woolff lounged on a seat a few feet away, pretending, without any success at all, to ignore her.

Night had fallen. We'd eaten pizza and cherry-vanilla ice cream, and Miriam Woolff had taken me, pictorially, through just about the entire history of her life with her husband. At first, I thought she was doing it out of malice—forcing me to look at every photo and videotape of their years together before she would show me anything from his time in Vietnam.

But after a half hour, I realized that malice was the farthest thing from her mind—and so was Vietnam. Miriam Woolff wanted to show me her scrapbooks and her tapes because she needed to share her husband with me. His work had isolated them, had made them pariahs, so she didn't have many people she could share him with. I might have been a stranger, but, by her standards, I wasn't a hostile one.

The tape stopped and the TV screen went sky blue. Miriam Woolff rested the back of her head on the ottoman of the knockoff Eames chair—the chair her husband had liked—and stared at the ceiling.

"It's not easy explaining death to a ten-year-old," she said, "or an eleven-year-old, for that matter. See, they understand their daddy's not coming back, but they want to know if he'll get French fries in Heaven, and whether there are sailboats up there. Is it cold, they want to know? Will someone bring him coffee in bed in the morning?" She pantomimed carrying a tray. "They brought him coffee—he woke up earlier than me—and they liked to be standing at the bed with his coffee when he opened his eyes. Especially Bonnie."

"Are they okay?" I said.

"I can't tell," she said, sitting up and stretching for the bottle of wine behind her. She filled our glasses and took a swallow. "They're taunted every day about their father the baby-killer, so they hide pain very well. I don't know whether they're okay. Did you meet them last time?"

"Sure," I said. "They had dinner with us."

"Right," she said, touching her forehead with her knuckles, "Right. Did you like them? They liked you."

The question surprised me, and I had to think back. "They were pretty quiet—very good manners."

She smiled. "They show them off for adult company. You'd like them. They're cool."

Abruptly, she climbed to her feet, saying, "Be right back," and left the room. First, I heard her in the hallway; then I heard her go into the kitchen and open the door to the garage. Finally, I heard her above me, in the bedroom.

Twenty minutes later, she returned carrying a crate marked Indian River grapefruit. She lowered it to the rug and wiped the dust from it with a paper napkin. It was sealed with duct tape. "I've never seen what's in it," she said.

I drew my knife from my pocket. "May I?" I asked. She nodded: I cut along the seams and pulled the flaps back, releasing a haze of dust, which made us both sneeze.

Mickey Woolff hadn't saved much: A dozen aid kits, two dozen ampules of morphine, dog tags, a waterproof flashlight, a unit patch, a fatigue cap, three knives, including a K-bar, some yellowed newspaper clips, several crumpled blank applications for colleges and nursing schools, a .45 pistol and eight loaded magazines, an ancient Merck diagnostic manual, a reference book on drugs, a primer on field surgery, a copy of *Survival, Evasion & Escape,* and underneath the books and tied neatly with twenty-year-old suturing thread, a modest bundle of photographs.

While Miriam Woolff painstakingly examined all the items in the crate, I went through the photos. Many of them were of the same people Matt Marshall had on his combat-era wall, and told me nothing.

There were two exceptions.

In the first, Matt Marshall and Tim Cleary squatted on either side of a

Vietnamese girl who sat on the ground with her feet stretched out and her head bowed so her face was in shadow. A surgical dressing was visible on her abdomen.

In the second, Mickey Woolff was changing the girl's dressing; again, her head was bowed and her face—though more visible than in the first shot—was indistinct.

I turned the pictures over to see whether Woolff had captioned them. He hadn't.

"May I copy these?" I asked.

She leaned closer to see them. "What are they?"

"This is Matt Marshall—he was your husband's commanding officer. This is Tim Cleary—he served with him. And this—I'm pretty sure—is Matt Marshall's lover."

She nodded in recollection. "Aaah, that's what you asked Mick about when you were here." She frowned in puzzlement. "Why wouldn't he tell you?"

Lamely, I said, "I think maybe he thought I wanted to know about, uh, another, uh, aspect of the whole thing."

"What are you talking about?"

"It's not important now."

"Tell me."

"It's not important now."

"Tell me!" she insisted. "What did he think you wanted to know that made him hold out on you?"

After a silence, I said, "I think he believed I wanted to know about a massacre. This girl lived in a village that Marshall's troops annihilated. I didn't know about it when I was here before, but I'm sure my questions misled your husband."

She lost all her color. "Did Mick—?" She stopped, helpless to take her next breath.

"No," I said. "All he did was bind people up and put them on a Medevac. Including this girl and a friend of hers."

"You're sure?"

"Yes."

She seized my hand. "You're absolutely sure?"

"I'm absolutely sure," I said. "Wait . . ." I searched my case for one of Marshall's letters and read to her:

> Doc is real good at what he does and acts completely unafraid—he tells everyone he's terrified, but to get to a wounded soldier he'll place himself right in the middle of fire. Believe it or not, there are

plenty of troopers who can't stand him—plenty of Medevac pilots and nurses and doctors, too—because Doc puts Vietnamese on our choppers.

Before she could ask, I said, "I'll have a copy made and send it to you."

"Thank you." She looked at the Vietnam pictures. "Who did you say this is?"

"His name is Tim Cleary."

"Was he a friend of Mick's?" she said. "Maybe he'd like to know he was killed . . ."

"I'll be sure to tell him."

"Have you talked to him about this girl?"

"Not yet," I said. "I'm going there from here."

CHAPTER 40

WHEN I TURNED INTO Tim Cleary's driveway, I did exactly as I'd done the time before: I pumped my horn, braked to a stop, shut off the engine, and sat waiting with my hands visible on the steering wheel.

As before, I tried not to let the rustlings of the leaves alarm me. I tried not to fidget, and I kept my eyes focused on the mirrors.

Five long minutes went by, then ten. By fifteen, I decided to risk leaving the car. I took a breath, wiped my hands dry on a paper towel, climbed out, slammed the door as loudly as I could, and headed for the house.

As I came closer to the porch, I heard a low buzzing. Squinting and shading my eyes from the bright morning sun, I traced the source of the sound: a swarm of flies hovering over a trail of small, dark spots—blood—on the clean, wooden steps. The spots led all the way to the front door—which only then did I notice stood slightly open.

Slowly, forty-five degrees at a time, I turned in a circle, scrutinizing each quadrant; no movement, no sound. Next, I did the same in reverse; no movement, no sound. Next, I studied the house the same way, piece by piece. Finally, I shut my eyes and listened. No sound.

Stamping hard on the steps, whistling shrilly, I walked up to the door, put my hand on the knob, shouted, "Cleary!" and waited. "Cleary! it's Adam Bruno. Cleary!" I shouted for a third time, and pushed gingerly.

The door swung open noiselessly, and I stood still for a moment, barely breathing, not sure whether Cleary would prod me in the back with his shotgun, or the sill under my feet would explode. Neither. Resuming my whistling, I let go of the doorknob and stepped warily into the room.

The functional unpainted chairs stood in the same place; so did the huge round coffee table and the cast-iron pot-bellied stove. The walls still had no pictures, the floors no rugs. The three gun cases were still locked and filled with weapons. The thick dark curtains still covered the windows, and the expensive stereo and hundreds of cassettes still occupied a full wall. If it hadn't been for the heavy silence, I wouldn't have been surprised to see Cleary emerge from his kitchen, bearing cheese, apples, and beer.

Except Cleary had already done that: the cheddar and Granny Smith apples were on the coffee table, only a few inches from the hat and the sunglasses.

Teresa Torres had remembered right: The sunglasses were Porsche, and the hat was a handsome, gray Borsalino. There was no blood on the hat, but there were a couple of specks on the left lens of the sunglasses, not very much really; nor was there very much on the plate of cheese and apples. It was impossible to tell whether the blood on the apples and the glasses came from Cleary or his visitor. The floor was more helpful: There were spots of blood on either side of the coffee table, and on the side where the visitor had sat were two .45-caliber casings.

If Cleary had behaved the way he'd behaved with me, he would have ambushed the visitor in the driveway, brought him inside, put away his rifle, invited the visitor to remove his hat and sunglasses and take a seat, fetched apples, cheese, and beer, sat down opposite the visitor, and placed his K-bar on the coffee table.

Did the visitor talk? Did he ask about Cricket? Did he mention Mickey Woolff? Did he mention me? Or did he just wait for the right moment, and shoot? The guest shoots, the host stabs, both are wounded, the guest gets out and . . . what?

Did Cleary follow him? Did he go to a hospital? Was Cleary on his way back? Or was his visitor outside somewhere, waiting for a chance to return and finish the job?

I made myself stop imagining. My choices were simple—leave, or look for what I came for: images of Cricket.

The house was small—only the ground floor, an attached workshed, and a cellar—so it didn't take long to discover that, unlike Matt Marshall, Tim Cleary kept no shrine to Vietnam. Whatever past he had, he carried in his head; it wasn't on display in his home. Nowhere in the house—the living room, the bedroom, the kitchen, the sunroom, the workshed—did I come across a diary, a journal, a letter, a birthday card, a holiday greeting, a pressed flower, a whimsical knickknack—anything to indicate that Cleary ever had a memory that he wanted to preserve.

On top of that, the present didn't seem to matter to him, either. He had no Rolodex, no daybook, no address book, no contact sheet; the door of his refrigerator held no urgent list of people to call—not that it would have done any good, since he had no phone.

He had not saved old driver's licenses or registrations or tax returns or sales receipts or guarantee cards or appliance instruction booklets. He had no voter-enrollment card and no library card. He did not belong to a church, or a club, or a civic group; he did not lead Scouts or coach Little League, or work as a volunteer fireman.

His correspondence consisted of mail-order catalogs from hunting-supply houses and a few bills—water, oil, electricity, taxes. He paid the bills with post office money orders; he had no checking account and no savings account. He had no stocks, bonds, or mutual funds; no insurance polices (except for those legally required for the truck and the house); and no subscriptions to magazines.

He had a few dozen books—a King James Bible, the Bhagavad-Gita, the Koran, the I Ching, several dictionaries, a text on poisons, three firearms reference works, a plumbing manual, an electrician's manual, a fine-woodworking manual, and, to my surprise, most of Joseph Conrad. All the books were well thumbed, including the sacred ones. And, of course, he had his wall of music, which though it concentrated on the late 1960s and early 1970s, went all the way forward to the Pretenders and the Eurythmics and Nirvana. Cleary loved his rock and roll.

I went through all the books and tapes and found no photographs of Cricket, or anyone else.

The entrance to the cellar was outside: a slanted, ground-level wooden hatchway built into the foundation. It was fastened with a simple latch. I fetched a flashlight from my car, unlatched the splintery doors, tugged them open, shined the beam ahead of me, and cautiously went sideways down the concrete steps.

The cellar was as orderly as the rest of the house. On one wall was an oil tank; on another, the oil burner; on another, a water pump and water heater. There was no debris, no dust, no leaks. In the center of the room was a large, immaculate table on which lay tools for repairing guns and loading and testing ammunition.

Neatly stacked against the fourth wall were dozens of green military ammunition boxes.

At random, I pulled a box from a stack and opened it: 7.62-millimeter NATO rounds; I pulled another box from another stack: 30-caliber carbine; another: 30-06.

As I reached for a fourth box, a sharp thump sounded on the hatchway, and I froze. Very quietly and slowly, I picked up the flashlight and brought it above my head. Without breathing, I turned first my eyes, then my head in the direction of the hatchway. I saw nothing but a patch of daylight. Another thump, making me gasp and tighten my sphincter, hard.

"Cleary?" I called out. "Is that you? It's Adam Bruno. Can you come down here and give me a hand? I can use some help." I counted to ten. "Cleary? Tim . . . ?"

There was a third thump, and then a screech, and the nesting owl I'd disturbed flew from its hiding place near the hatchway out into the sunlight.

"Fuck you!" I shouted at the owl, and let my heart rate retreat to near normal. Then, I reached for the next box: .22 long rifle; .357 magnum; 12-gauge, double-O buckshot.

The forty-eighth box, which was the third from the bottom in the next-to-the-last stack, contained 9-millimeter hollow points. It also contained, in waterproof wrappings:

Eighteen 3.5-inch computer diskettes; a copy of the supposed obituary of Ghost; three letters in Vietnamese, presumably the originals of the pair I'd received, plus one more; and several photographs.

The first photograph was a twin of the shot that showed Mickey Woolff changing the girl's dressing; the second was a twin of the shot that showed Marshall and Cleary squatting on either side of the girl; the fourth was a cousin of that shot.

A cousin and not a twin, because the girl's face—Cricket's face, I didn't doubt for a minute—was pointed straight at the camera.

After I'd packed the pictures and diskettes in my briefcase, I got in my car and sat behind the wheel for a few minutes, sorting out what to do next.

As much as I wanted to drive straight back to the city and get hold of Nicole Maldonado to translate the three letters, I couldn't. I wasn't sure what I owed Tim Cleary, but I owed him something, at the very least a word to the only people who seemed to care whether he lived or died.

CHAPTER 41

HOLLOWAY AND SKLAR SAT on either side of me in Holloway's private office. Not touching-close, but close enough so that it wouldn't have been a stretch for either of them to reach me. Not that they ever made a move to, or even leaned my way. But between them, they weighed at least 450 pounds, and their sheer bulk was more than enough to keep me sitting very still. Each had a container of coffee before him, though only Sklar touched his. They'd offered me coffee, but I'd refused. They'd offered me a doughnut, and I'd refused that, too.

When I walked in and told them I'd been to Cleary's house, found the door open and bloodstains on the floor, and no sign of Cleary, Holloway nodded a few times and casually invited me into his office. On the way, he ordered Sklar to ride over to Cleary's and check things out.

He offered me a chair and a magazine, and left the room. There I waited, first leafing through the October bulletin of the Association of Chiefs of Police, then reading it, then reading the September bulletin, until he and Sklar returned ninety minutes later. Sklar bore a cardboard boxtop that held three containers of coffee and a pack of doughnuts.

"Is it as I described?" I said to Sklar.

"Let's talk a bit first," Holloway said, pulling up a chair beside me. Sklar did the same. Holloway picked up a doughnut, stared at the powdered sugar on it, and lowered it back into the box. Turning to me, he said, "Tell us again the part about going in. You drove up, you sat in your car, you waited for Tim to jump you, he didn't, you got out of your car, you walked to the house, you called his name—I'm kind of clear up to then. It's the next part—tell me about the next part."

"I pushed the door open," I said, "and—"

"The door wasn't locked?" Sklar said.

"Unlocked, and slightly open."

"You're sure of that?" Holloway said. "You didn't turn the knob?"

"No. It was open. Maybe three inches."

"Then what?"

"I called his name again and went inside."

"By then, you saw the blood?" Holloway said.

"The first time I saw the blood was outside, on the steps and on the porch."

"Okay. You're in. What do you see? Go slow, now," Holloway said, and signaled Sklar, who pulled a notebook from his pocket and flipped it open.

Deliberately, I told them what I'd seen. As I talked, Sklar followed along in his notes.

When I finished, Holloway said, "Did you touch the bullet casings?"

"No."

"Did you touch the sunglasses?"

"No."

"What about the hat?"

"No. Or the apples and cheese."

"Did you step in the blood?"

"I don't think so," I said and twisted each foot in turn to see whether there was blood on my shoes. "I can't see anything."

"Then what?"

"I looked though the house for Cleary."

"All through the house?" Holloway said.

"Ground floor, workshed, and cellar."

"No sign of Tim?"

"No sign of anybody."

"Any bloodstains anywhere else in the house?"

"No."

"Any bullet casings?"

"No."

"Any knife, or icepick, scissors—like that?"

"No."

"Did you notice anything else that didn't look like Tim's?"

"How do you mean?"

Holloway said, "Car keys, maybe. Cigarettes. A lighter. A pen. A notepad. A nail-clipper—anything the guy might have taken out of his pocket?"

I shut my eyes for a second. "Not that I can think of. Of course, unless it was obviously not Cleary's—like the sunglasses and hat—I don't know how I could tell."

"Did you take anything?" Holloway said.

My stomach tightened. "No."

"You sure?"

"I'm sure."

"Did you search the place?"

"I told you, I looked for him in the house, the workshed, and the cellar."

"Yeah, we know you looked for him. Did you look for anything else?"

Again, my stomach tightened. "I looked for more bullet casings. I looked for a weapon. I looked for anything that might tell me who the visitor was."

"Like what?"

"A business card. Slip of paper with a name, or a phone number. Like that."

"You find anything?"

"No."

"Did you move anything?"

"I'm sure I did, but not the plate on the table, or the hat, or the sunglasses, or the casings."

"And you didn't see anything unusual at all?"

"Not that I could tell. It all looked exactly the way it looked the last time I was inside."

After a pause, Holloway said, "When was that?"

"You want the exact date?" He nodded. I pulled my notebook from my briefcase, found the date, and told it to him. He carefully printed it on a pad.

"How'd you get in that time?"

"I waited in my car in the driveway till Cleary ambushed me with an M-16."

Holloway laughed. "Yeah, that's how he'd do it." He stretched out his hand, and Sklar passed his notebook. Holloway skimmed a few pages before saying, "You didn't see any cars?"

"No. Not near the house."

"You ever see those sunglasses or hat before?" Holloway asked.

"No," I said truthfully, since I hadn't.

"You got any idea who the guy might be?"

"No," I said. "You'd know Cleary's acquaintances better than me."

"He doesn't have any acquaintances," Sklar said.

"Not since Marshall died," Holloway added.

"He didn't hang out with *anybody*?" I said.

"Hanging out wasn't Tim's thing," Sklar said. "Not unless he was waiting for a kill."

For a moment, we were all quiet.

Sklar said, "Could have been a stranger."

Holloway twirled his finger for Sklar to continue.

"Insurance salesman, somebody like that. He stops in the driveway, Cleary bushwhacks him, hauls his ass inside. They get in a beef, the salesman pulls a piece, Cleary sticks him with the goddamn K-bar . . . ?"

Holloway said, "Yeah, and?"

"And what?" Sklar said.

"And where are they?" Holloway asked. "Tim's pickup isn't there; the other guy's car isn't there. Nobody's turned himself in to a hospital. If the guy's just a salesman and Tim sticks him, why doesn't the guy go to a hospital? Why doesn't he call us and say, I went to see Tim about a car policy and he stuck me, and I had to shoot him? Why doesn't he do that, Eph? Or why doesn't Tim come in and tell us he had to stick a guy? Tim's not afraid of us." He gestured toward me. "He didn't stick Bruno. He brought him to us. Where are they? Why isn't either of 'em still at the house?" He shook his head. "Uh uh, Eph. Wasn't a stranger."

"Maybe somebody from the war," Sklar offered. He chuckled. "Some guy buggy as him."

Holloway glanced my way.

"Maybe," I said. "It makes as much sense as anything else. Couple of guys from the war, having a beer, reliving some weird memory in some weird way. You know Cleary better than I do. It's not impossible." Holloway wasn't objecting, so I pushed the logic further. "After all, there's not much blood, and both cars are gone—which means both of them were strong enough to drive. Maybe patched each other up, had another beer, and went somewhere to shoot something living. That's not impossible, either."

"Yeah," Sklar said, laughing. "Let's hope the fucker's got four legs."

"Okay," Holloway said pleasantly, "I can't think of anything smarter right now. Okay." He tilted his chair back. "Why'd you go see Tim today?"

I'd been preparing for the question since I'd left Cleary's house.

"During the war, Matt Marshall fathered a child with a Vietnamese. I'm looking for the child, and I'm hoping Cleary can help me identify its mother."

"Is that why you were up here before?" Holloway said.

"Uhuh."

"How come you didn't tell us?"

"The estate wanted everything kept quiet. Marshall was a prominent guy—they didn't want the world to know he fathered a bastard in Vietnam."

"Is there any money involved?" Sklar said.

"They don't tell me," I said. "All they tell me is, find the kid."

"I bet there's a shitload of money involved," Sklar said, his voice dense with envy.

"Maybe," I said. "Can I ask you something, Sheriff?" Holloway nodded. "When Cleary goes off by himself, hunting or whatever, does he have a special place he likes?"

"I don't know," Holloway said.

"He was superprivate," Sklar added.

"You never went hunting with him, either of you?"

"He went by himself, or with Marshall," Sklar said.

"He never said anything when he came back, dropped the name of a village, or a lake, or a mountain?"

Sklar shook his head.

"You don't know if he built a shack someplace that he used as a kip?"

This time, Holloway shook his head.

I got to my feet and shook the stiffness from my arms and shoulders. "You need me for anything else?"

Holloway thought it over. "You don't carry a piece, do you, Bruno?"

"No."

"So you wouldn't mind a toss . . . ?"

"Not at all," I said, raising my arms.

Holloway nodded. Sklar quickly and efficiently searched me. "No," he said to Holloway.

Knowing the risk I was taking, I pointed to my briefcase. "Do you want me to empty that for you?"

Holloway nodded.

Item by item, I laid everything out in rows on his desk. Most items were in envelopes of different sizes. Sklar reached for the thickest envelope, which contained the diskettes. I picked it up, slid the diskettes out, let them see that's all that was in there, and repacked them. I did the same with all the other envelopes, making sure they never saw the front of any photographs and explaining, "These are all confidential, Sheriff, so you'll forgive me if I don't let you peek." I smiled innocently. "After all, you're looking for a gun, right?"

A minute later, they walked me outside. While I gave my card to

Holloway and asked him to call me when Cleary showed up, Sklar searched my car. When he was finished, he and Holloway strolled back inside.

As I left Knickerbocker County, I thought about Cleary and the bombmaker and what it might mean that neither was badly hurt and both of them had gone underground.

Did it mean that Cleary was looking for me to ask what I knew about the bombmaker? Did it mean that the bombmaker was looking for me to ask what I knew about Cricket? Did it mean that Cleary and the bombmaker both were looking for me? Did it mean that I was a target? Or did it mean I was merely a conduit to a target?

An hour from the city, my head aching from brooding about Cleary and the bombmaker, I called Nicole Maldonado and invited her to stop at my home that night. I said nothing about blood, or the sheriff of Knickerbocker County. I told her I wanted her to translate three letters. I didn't mention the pictures. I wanted to save those for her presence.

CHAPTER 42

"BEFORE YOU BEGIN TRANSLATING, would you mind looking at something?" I said to Maldonado, and casually drew the photographs from my pocket.

Maldonado put her cup on the coffee table, wiped her fingers on a napkin, accepted the photos—I'd arranged them so that the shot showing the girl full-faced was on the bottom—and studied the top picture: It was of Marshall and Cleary on either side of the girl.

"This is Mr. Marshall, I know," she said. "Who is this?"

"His name is Tim Cleary; he served under Marshall."

"Tim Cleary," she murmured. "And this?" she said, pointing to the girl. "Is this Chau Chau?"

"Keep going."

Maldonado put the picture on the coffee table and went to the next shot—of Woolff changing the girl's dressing. "And this?"

"His name is Mickey Woolff. He also served under Marshall. As a medic—that's why he's taking care of her."

"Mickey Woolff," she said. "Taking care of Chau Chau, correct?"

"Keep going."

She made a disapproving noise, put the second photo on the coffee table, and picked up the third. As it came into focus, she drew in a short, sharp breath and touched herself protectively under the breast. For a long moment, she stared at the girl's face. "Why did he call her Chau Chau? Insects are not beautiful—she's beautiful."

She put the photo next to the other two on the coffee table, bent close, and scrutinized all three. "I don't believe she's pregnant here," she said.

"Probably, it's too soon after her wounding." She glanced at me. "It is Chau Chau, isn't it? Cricket?"

"Yes," I said, "I think so."

"It must be," she said. "Who else could it be?" The obvious occurred to her. "Can't you ask either of these men?"

"No, I can't."

Her gaze returned to the shot that included Woolff, and she frowned. "Mickey Woolff . . . Mickey Woolff," she said to herself. "Dr. Woolff! The abortionist in Florida—the one who was killed," she said. "His name is Dr. Woolff—I heard that on television. Dr. Woolff. Medic. Doctor. Yes?"

"It's the same man," I said, cursing myself for underestimating her yet again.

"Ah," she said, "that's why you couldn't ask him."

"Right," I said.

Maldonado looked up from the photographs and, for the first time since I'd met her, kept her eyes locked on my face. She held them there so long it made me fidget, compelling me to ask, "Is something bothering you?"

"I must admit, Mr. Bruno, it seems a bit odd that you would show me a picture of a man who has just been blown up and not mention that. That bothers me."

Feeling trapped and hoping it didn't show, I said, "I didn't want to clutter things up."

"Of course," she said, in the same uninflected voice she'd used when I'd lied to her at our first meeting. "Shall we do the letters now?"

"Can we clear this up first?" I said. "Whatever it is that's bothering you."

"I've already told you."

"No, you haven't. You said it seems a bit odd. What exactly does that mean—a bit odd?"

"It means, I wish you'd stop . . . shading the truth. Do you imagine I don't watch TV or read the papers? Do you imagine any woman in America hasn't heard about this bombing?"

Once more, her eyes were locked on my face, and I knew I'd have terrible difficulty lying to her. "What do you know about it?"

"A religious woman took a bomb into a clinic, and it went off while she was still present. She died, and so did a teenage girl, and so did Dr. Woolff."

"I believe that somebody used that religious woman as an in-strument—a willing, enthusiastic instrument but, still, only an instru-ment—to kill Mickey Woolff. I don't believe that woman—her name was

Beverly Dornan—planned the bombing or built the bomb. I believe somebody else gave her the bomb to carry. I also believe that person set the timer so that Beverly Dornan would die in the explosion."

She ingested that and said, "I don't understand. A man makes a bomb to kill an abortionist, he gives the bomb to somebody who also wishes to kill the abortionist, but he sets the bomb so she will die as well. Who is this man?"

"I don't know."

"Where is he?"

"I don't know that, either."

"Have you told the authorities about him?"

"The authorities have a perfect case against Beverly Dornan, and nobody wants to ruin perfection. Telling them about the bombmaker . . ." I hesitated, unwilling to describe what I suspected, and feared. Finally, I said, "I don't really have anything to tell the authorities about the bombmaker."

"Why would he set the bomb to kill the woman?"

"Ms. Maldonado," I said, "I don't really want to say anything more."

"Why not?"

"I can't."

She picked up her cup, found it empty, lowered it, and turned her head just far enough so she could look past me.

"Ms. Maldonado, you're going to have to trust me on this," I said.

Without looking at me, she said, "No, I'm not."

"Goddammit!" I said. "All right. All right. I believe that the killing of Mickey Woolff is connected to this business—the Marshall business. Okay?"

"Aaahhh," she said, dragging out the sound mournfully as she exhaled. "In what way connected?" As I began to frame an equivocal reply, she held up a finger in warning and said, "Please, no shading . . ."

"Mickey Woolff was killed because he was one of two people who could identify Cricket. This man, Tim Cleary"—I picked up a photo of Cleary—"is the other. The killer went to Cleary's home. That I know. But when I got there, nobody was around. That's all I can tell you."

"Aaahhh," she said again, and peered into her cup. "May I have some more tea?" I nodded, took the cup, and went to the kitchen to refill the kettle.

A moment later, while I was unwrapping a fresh tea bag, she appeared in the doorway. Surprised to see her there, I awkwardly said, "It's not from Vietnam, it's from China—I hope it's all right."

"Excellent," she said. "You are a most considerate host." She cleared her throat in a preparatory way. "Mr. Bruno, may I ask you something?"

"Of course."

"Is there anyone else who can identify Cricket?"

"Not that I know of."

"So nobody else is in danger?"

"On the face of it, no."

The kettle whistled; I picked it up and poured boiling water into her cup. Maldonado wrapped a napkin around the cup to protect her fingers, turned toward the living room, and then stopped in midpivot.

"But Mr. Bruno, what about Cricket—when you find her, won't she be in danger—she and the child?"

"No," I said, terrified that I was as transparent to everyone as I was to Maldonado. "No, not at all. Once they're exposed, they're safe. Perfectly safe. But, if it would make you feel better, when we find them, I'll take precautions."

"It would make me feel better."

Once in her seat, Maldonado picked up the first letter in her free hand, scanned it, and read: "Dear Captain Matthew: I hope this reaches you. I have given it to somebody I cannot really trust, but I know he has the means to escape, and it is the only way I am able to send a message . . ." She trailed off but continued reading to herself.

A second later, she said, "This appears to be the original of the first letter I translated for you. Shall I go on to the next?" I nodded, and she picked up a second letter: "Dear Captain Matthew: Following your advice, I have written of my situation to the Defense Attaché in Bangkok, the United States Embassy there, and the refugee assistance organizations you describe . . . " Once again, she trailed off and read to herself.

"That's the second letter, isn't it?" I said.

She nodded, put it on the coffee table, picked up the third letter, and started to scan it.

"Oh my God!" she said with real urgency, and placed her cup on the table. "Oh, my dear God."

"What?" I said.

She made as if to explain, shook her head, put her forefinger on the first line of the letter, and translated:

"Dear Dinh—"

"Dinh?" I said. "Who's Dinh?"

"Please, Mr. Bruno!" she said. "Listen!

Dear Dinh:

I write to you to beg you not to search for me.

I do not know if you search now, but I do know you searched in past days. I must beg you never to search again. Many years ago, you and I lived a short short life. Now, I live a new life in your country, but you must not appear in my new life. You must not. I beg you, for the sake of our child, please leave me my life as I left you your life.

My dreams will always belong to you.

Cricket

For a moment, Maldonado sat motionless, her head bent, her forefinger pressed to the last line of the letter. At last, she raised her head. "There is no address," she said. "Is there an envelope?"

"Not that I found," I said. "Is it dated?"

She looked. "August twentieth, nineteen eighty-one."

"Is there anything special about it?" She stared at me as if I'd lost my mind. Speedily, I said, "I mean on top of the special fact that it's from Cricket?"

She studied the letter, shook her head, and then turned it over. She peered at what was there, left her chair, sat next to me, and held the letter between us.

Written on the back, in light pencil, was a list of names, each followed by a question mark and an X.

"I believe Mr. Marshall disobeyed her," Maldonado said. "These are the names he must have guessed she might use."

One by one, she touched them: "Nguyen Thi Dinh. Chau. Cricket. Marshall. Thong Che—"

"What's Thong Che?" I asked.

"It is Vietnamese for marshal," she said. She shrugged. "I assume from this"—she pointed to the X after each name—"she did not use any of these names."

"May I?" I said, and she handed me the letter. I looked at it minutely, not expecting to find anything Maldonado had missed, but unable not to devour it, the only evidence from Cricket herself of her existence in Matt Marshall's life.

I could tell nothing from the paper—it was the kind of paper available in any chain store—and certainly nothing from the handwriting. I held it near my nose, hoping to catch a scent, perfume maybe, or even a hint of Cricket's breath or body—I'd come across women who kissed their notepaper after they wrote a love letter or touched themselves with it. I smelled nothing except ink and paper and perhaps—I wasn't sure—the faintest trace of soap or talc.

I noticed Maldonado watching me. "Sometimes people leave an odor," I said, and lowered the letter.

She nodded in understanding, and said, "Mr. Bruno, may I ask how you came by it?"

"Tim Cleary," I said, gesturing toward the photos.

"Ahhhh," she said, picking up a picture and inspecting it. "Is he a good friend to Mr. Marshall?"

"Better than I guessed," I said.

"Could he not tell you anything?" she said.

"Cleary didn't give me the letter. I found it at his home. He was safekeeping it for Marshall."

"Was he safekeeping anything else?"

"A few pictures—the clear shot of her. Ghost's obituary. Some computer diskettes."

Her eyes brightened. "Is there anything on them that can help us? Surely there must be," she said intensely. "If Mr. Marshall left them along with her photo, there must be something helpful on them."

"I don't know," I said, and I could hear the tightness in my voice. "They're encrypted, and I don't have any passwords. I don't have any passwords for his computer, either. I can't get in anywhere. I'm shut out. He's shut me out; he shuts everybody out. It's what he does."

Maldonado looked at the penciled list on the back of the letter. "Have you tried all the names he tried?"

By rote, I said, "I tried variations of his name, his wife's name, his children's names, his parents' names, his brother's name, his sister's name, his sister's nickname, all his nieces' and nephews' names. I tried all his phone numbers, his birthday, his social security number, his zip codes, his license plate numbers, his addresses—all of them, a number I found in his night table. I tried all the names of the people in the photos on his wall, first, last, and nicknames, forward and backward. I tried Tay Ninh—the camp Ghost said Cricket was held in.

"I tried Cricket, I tried Chau and Chau Chau. I tried Nguyen Thi Dinh, and I tried Nguyen and Thi and Dinh separately. I haven't tried Thong Che because I didn't know it till just now. Shall I try it? Why don't I try it? It would complete the cycle if I tried it. It would make me happy. It would make you happy. It would make the whole stupid universe happy!"

While I was talking—shouting, by the end—I was hauling Marshall's laptop onto my desk. I opened it, gestured brusquely to Maldonado to join me, and turned it on.

It hummed, and the usual message appeared: TO INVOKE PROGRAM, ENTER PASSWORD.

"You do it," I said. "Maybe it doesn't like my touch. Maybe it likes a gentler touch. Go on, sit down. Please." Not happy with my coercion, she sat anyway.

"Okay, type THONG CHE and hit ENTER." She did; on the screen appeared INVALID PASSWORD. "Try CHE THONG, and ENTER." She got the same result. "You see?"

"Does Mr. Marshall have a nickname?" she said. "A secret name only the two of them would know?"

I couldn't help smiling. "If I only knew that," I said, "I wouldn't be behaving like such a fool."

"He called her Cricket—what did she call him?"

I showed her the salutation: "Dear Dinh. She calls him Dinh. I tried Dinh."

Stubbornly, she typed DINH. INVALID PASSWORD. Without looking at me, she said, "Forgive me. I had to."

I looked at the salutation, and I stopped feeling sorry for myself. "Ms. Maldonado, read this, please . . ."

"Dear Dinh . . ."

"If it said—in Vietnamese—dear Chau Chau, and you were translating for me, what would you say?"

"Dear Cricket."

"Okay. Do it with this."

She took the letter from me and scrutinized the salutation.

"Dear . . . Nail . . ."

"Nail?"

"Yes, nail. Not a fingernail—a nail you hammer."

"Try it," I said.

She typed NAIL and hit ENTER. INVALID PASSWORD.

"Try NAILS," I said, "with the S." She did, and the same message appeared. "You sure it means nail?"

"Written like this, yes, nail."

I carried over another chair, turned on my computer, and began scanning the summaries of my interviews. I knew no one had given me a nickname for Marshall, but I wanted to make doubly sure I'd asked everyone. I hadn't. I'd skipped Buzz Oliver, perhaps because he constantly called Marshall Matt; and I'd skipped Rachel and Paul Marshall, perhaps because I was too comfortable in their presence.

Since it was nearly eleven, which meant nearly two in the morning in California, I called Paul Marshall in North Carolina first. I got a machine and left a message.

"Fuck it all," I muttered and dialed Oliver's home number; I got a machine there, too. "Buzz," I said, "it's Adam Bruno in New York. I need to know if Matt Marshall had a nickname. Call me anytime and leave a—"

"If he had a nickname, don't you think I'd have used it on the air, you putrid maxipad!" Oliver shouted at me. "Jesus, I thought you had brains. Why did I think that? You're a lawyer. Everybody I went to high school with who became a lawyer or a doctor was dumber than kitty-litter."

"Just checking," I said. "Did I wake you?"

"No, but you woke *her*. Honey, go back to sleep. Turn over. I don't want to look at your face unless I'm kissing it." To me he said, "How's it going?"

"Slow."

"You'll get there. Call me when you're out here."

He hung up, and I dialed Rachel in San Francisco. "Hello," she answered cheerfully. "If you don't talk and merely breathe heavily, I'll send my lover after you, and she's on parole for manslaughter with a chain saw."

"Hi, Rachel, Adam Bruno."

"Adam!" she cried gaily. "Are you here? Can you stop by for a drink? I have the most stunning granddaughter ever born in the history of the race. The human race. We have the movie—wait till you see her pop out!"

"I'm in New York," I said, "and I need your help."

"Oh, okay," she said mock petulantly. "Don't come over, don't celebrate with us. What do you want?"

"Did Matt have a nickname?"

"A nickname?" she said. "No."

"Nothing? He called you Roach—didn't you have a name for him?"

"Are you talking about when we were kids?" she said.

My stomach flip-flopped. "Anytime."

"When we were little, little kids, I called him Candy. For M and M's. He—"

"Hang on, Rachel." To Maldonado, I said, "Try Candy. C-A-N-D-Y." She did and got INVALID PASSWORD. "Try M-M; then, M-N-M, then M-and-M."

She did and got the same result every time.

"I beg your pardon, Rachel, I interrupted you. What were you saying?"

"I was saying, he made me stop calling him Candy because he thought it was a girl's name, thank you very much for rejoining me, Adam, it's really nice to know there's at least one gentleman left in the world."

"Sorry," I said.

"You should be," she said. "In any case, he made me stop that, and for the next few years, I called him Spike. Actually, we both did because he carried a hunting knife and—"

"Spike?" I shouted.

"Shit, Adam, don't yell in my ear. Yes, Spike."

"Spelled S-P-I-K-E?" I said.

"I guess," she said.

"S-P-I-K-E," I said to Maldonado, and she typed along with me as I voiced each letter. She hit the enter key: INVALID PASSWORD.

"Are you there, Adam?" Rachel said.

"Did he have any other nicknames? Even if only for a short time—one like Candy, one you used that he asked you to stop using. A mocking one? A mean one?"

"Spike was it till eighth grade, no seventh. From then on, he was plain old Matt."

"You sure it was Spike?"

"I'm his sister."

"Spelled S-P-I-K-E?"

"Who knows?" she said crankily. "We were kids—kids don't write their nicknames down. Until I got to high school, I thought Roach was spelled R-O-C-H-E."

"Hang on, Rachel," I said. "Nicci, try S-P-Y-K-E."

Maldonado typed the letters. For five seconds the screen went blank. Then—sending my spirits soaring as high as they'd been since I took the case—this appeared:

INVOKING SYSTEM PROGRAM.

Click, hum, whirr, click, hum, whirr. Message:

TO VIEW MENU, ENTER PASSWORD.

Maldonado again typed SPYKE and got INVALID PASSWORD.

"Adam, for crissake, are you there?"

"Sorry, Rachel, sorry," I said. "Listen, you've been wonderful. Let me get off and test this, okay? I'll call you tomorrow. I promise. Thanks."

"Come and see the baby!" she cried, and hung up.

"What do you think?" I said, as I sat next to Maldonado. "His nickname, her nickname? Try Cricket."

She typed CRICKET. It didn't work.

"May I?" she said, but didn't wait for me to say yes before typing CHAU CHAU. That didn't work; neither did CHAU.

"Try Dinh," I said. She did, and DINH worked.

A menu appeared, offering several different application programs, including a word-processor. Maldonado moved the cursor to it and hit ENTER.

INSERT DATA DISK AND ENTER PASSWORD.

Rushing, I inserted one of the diskettes I'd found in the ammunition box, and Maldonado typed each password in turn. CHAU CHAU brought a menu of directories to the screen, but the titles weren't descriptive: there were MMNYC, MMNC—I assumed that meant North Carolina; MMASS, which could have meant assets, or mistresses; MMDRK, MMTEL, MMART, MMSW, and dozens of others. I pointed to MMDRK, and Maldonado moved the cursor to it and hit ENTER.

ENTER PASSWORD.

Maldonado went through the list, and CRICKET opened MMDRK, revealing a list of files whose names were even less evocative than the names of the directories.

"You pick it this time," I said. Maldonado moved the cursor to MMDRK-3, and tried each password in turn. When she typed THONG CHE and hit ENTER, a message read:

PLEASE WAIT. RETRIEVING FILE.

After a few milliseconds, the screen filled with words. MMDRK-3—all of it—read:

Every time I think of selling this house, all I have to do is take the dogs for a walk at night. Even overcast nights are extraordinary up here. The clouds form new shapes every two minutes, changing the look and feel of the world over and over in a half-hour walk. I have never felt safer than I do up here—and the dogs sense it. They love me in town, but up here they adore me. I can feel it in the way they stick their noses into my hand and the way they can't stop bringing me presents. Not to throw for them to fetch, simply presents. Do they know I owe them my life? Is there a way to let them know that? I doubt it. I can't even let TC know I owe him my life, how can I let Bitch One and Bitch Two know?

In its entirety, MMDRK-8 read:

Beth asked again this week if she could come up here; I refused. She accused me of using it as a hideout for love affairs; I told her I had somewhere else for that. Cruel, I guess. But why does she want to come here? She has places. This is *mine*. Mine and the dogs. We don't want to share it, do we, Bitches? No, we do not."

My eyes itched and I leaned back, rubbed my neck, and checked the time. It was nearly 1:30. We had read two files in a single directory. There were nine directories on that one diskette and probably a dozen files in each directory. There were eighteen diskettes in the ammunition box I'd found in Tim Cleary's cellar.

"Maybe we should call it a night," I said.

"Now?" Maldonado said, incredulously. "We've only just begun! How can you stop now?"

I tapped my watch. "It's one-thirty."

"Are you tired?" she said. "Do you have to get up early? It's Sunday tomorrow—do you have to go to church?"

"I was thinking about you," not entirely truthfully.

"I don't have to go to church, I'm not tired."

"No, my point really was that you don't need to do this—it's really my respon—"

"Excuse me, Mr. Bruno!" she said. "Are you dismissing me? Now?"

"No, I'm not dismissing you, Ms. Maldonado. I just think it's a good idea to take a break. A break. You can come back tomorrow."

"I don't see why we can't go on."

"Because at this rate, it's going to take all night, and we're tired—excuse me, *I'm* tired—and the longer we stay on it, the greater the chance of screwing up."

"You're not dismissing me?"

"I'm not dismissing you."

"You're sure?"

"I'm sure. Never."

"Oh, never." A smile crept to her face. "Then, I apologize for my outburst. What time shall we start tomorrow? Is nine too early?"

"I was thinking more like ten-thirty," I said.

She looked at her watch and raised her eyes. "I will start at nine. You can start later."

I felt my brow crease in puzzlement. But before I could tell her she was mixed up, she shocked me by bringing her hands to my forehead and gently smoothing the furrows. Then, shocking me even more, she let her fingertips float slowly downward, brushing my eyelids shut, gliding over my cheeks and lingering to stroke the corners of my mouth until I was afraid to breathe for fear she would stop.

The rush was so powerful and so fast-moving I couldn't tell whether it was spreading from my eyelids, my lips, or my throat. For a disconcerting instant, I was back in high school, overwhelmed with heat and longing, and the giddy disbelief that a touch could cause so much havoc.

When I opened my eyes, I pulled her chair nearer to mine, let my hands fall on her back, and pressed just hard enough to feel her flesh through her linen blouse. She put her arms around my neck, tilted her head upward slightly, and softly and slowly blew her warm, scented breath onto my left eyelid, then shifted and did the same to my right. Again, and again, and again, and again.

I brought my hands around so they were at her waist and slid them upward along her trunk, into her armpits, where I let them rest until I could feel moisture. Then, I slipped them up along her shoulders, her neck, her cheeks, till I came to her temples. There, I caressed the veins before moving my fingers to her ears to play with the lobes and then explore the inner hollows until I knew them by heart.

I bent to kiss her throat, and she arched her neck and licked her lips, like an animal who had just tasted its kill. She opened her mouth, and the wetness gleamed on her dark pink tongue as it darted along her sharp white teeth. When I finished kissing her throat and my eyes came level with hers, she brought her lips within a hair of mine and parted them still further so that she could draw air from my mouth.

We stayed that way, inhaling and exhaling each other's breath, regulating one another's heartbeats until, it seemed—I'll never know—we could no longer tell them apart. Then, simultaneously, we let our lips gently fasten together, and we tasted each other for the first time.

CHAPTER 43

WE DID GO TO work at nine. We chose a diskette at random, loaded it, and began unlayering Matt Marshall's life.

From a file dated 23 September 1981, and titled MMCR-1:

> . . . I can't find her in any Vietnamese communities in the country under Chau, Chau Chau, Thong Che, or Nguyen Thi Dinh, or different combinations of those. I can't find any combinations of Marshall with a Vietnamese name, or any Marshalls with an address in a Vietnamese community. The trouble is I don't have a clue as to how she would choose a name or a place, because I don't have a clue how her mind works.
>
> So I don't know whether she's telling the truth in her letter—I must beg you never to search again. You must not appear in my new life. *What* new life? Are you married? To a Vietnamese? To an American? Which? For the sake of our child, please leave me my life as I left you your life. I don't want to leave you your life, especially not for the sake of our child. What is our child? Does it piss standing up or sitting down? Does it have my blue eyes or your brown ones? What does it look like? Does it speak English? Vietnamese? French? All of them? Is it miraculous? Its conception was miraculous, it must be miraculous. *How* is it miraculous? I want to know! Where in my country? Where, goddamn you?

From a file dated 2 December 1983 and titled MMCR-2:

. . . Ghost called, announcing he's in Los Angeles and looking for work. Promised as soon as he found a job he'd go back to the search, if I wanted. His usual routine; payment first, services later, if ever. But I said no. No. I told him I'd help him get a job but I wasn't looking for her anymore. She'd made a new life. Twomey's in mine.

From a file dated 25 July 1987 and titled MMCR-3:

. . . Getting Ghost's obituary in the mail ruined my day; I could do nothing but think about her, and I've managed to mostly keep her out of my thoughts for years. Her presence invaded my head and lodged there. There was a moment after I got up here when I actually saw her walking through the trees toward me and I called out her name. I stood there, between the car and the front door, calling out her name, sniffing the air for her. I actually dropped to my knees and and buried my nose in the grass, smelling like a dog for a piece of her. It's really over now; he was the last link.

From a file dated 19 June 1986 and titled MMEM-1:

. . . The moment I came back from Washington I got a list of detective agencies, ready to start the hunt all over again. Going to the wall was a mistake. Taking the kids was a terrible idea. I didn't prepare them, and I couldn't deal with them while we were there. For the time we were there, I don't know who my life belonged to. The past, the present, the future. What future? Whose future? Every other minute, I thought I saw somebody from back then—Lincoln, Eve McGowan, Doc Woolff, Angel—and every time I thought I saw somebody I looked for her. Why wasn't she nearby? Why wasn't she with us? Where had she gone? So when I came back to New York, I was ready to search for her again. But I stopped myself. I drove up here and got hold of Tim Cleary and we went killing. Rabbits, since it was out of season.

From a file dated 1 June 1995 and titled MMEM-6:

. . . At the wall last week, Matt junior asked me whether I was crying for all of them or for anyone in particular. It's like him to ask something like that. For a split second, I thought of saying, no, my dear queer son, I've cried for my men, now I'm crying for a wounded girl I sent away when she told me she felt our child begin to form in her belly; I'm crying for somebody I was ready to leave you and your mother for 20 years ago; I'm crying because in 1975 I fled from Saigon instead of staying and finding them; I'm crying for the one time in my life when I felt another person enter my soul and allowed me to enter hers. I don't believe in that, I've never believed in that, I will die not believing in that. My dreams will always belong to you.

Without a word, Maldonado left her chair, picked up our cups, and went to the kitchen.

After a few seconds, I followed her and found her filling first the kettle, then the coffee machine. She turned on a burner and put the kettle on it. Then, she put a filter in the machine, took the coffee beans from the refrigerator, ground them, and emptied them into the receptacle. She sprinkled a tiny bit of salt on the coffee, pushed the receptacle in place, and turned the machine on. She worked methodically and fastidiously, the way people did when they concentrated fiercely on a physical task so their feelings wouldn't smother them.

"Why do you do that?" I said. "The salt, I mean?"

"It brings out the flavor. You can only use a little. If you use too much, you taste it." She paused. "My father taught me."

For the first time since she'd left the computer, she looked at me. "Do you like my father?"

"Very much."

"Do you like my mother?"

"Even more."

"She's stronger than she seems."

"I noticed."

"Did you? Most people don't."

"You're similar that way."

The kettle began to whistle, and she lowered the flame, rinsed both our cups, wiped them, unwrapped a tea bag, and dropped it in hers.

"They have that," she said. "My mother and father. They have what he's talking about. Soul to soul. Sometimes, they look at each other and it's like seeing them naked. Not erotic naked. Naked like babies. No cover." She glanced at me. "Do your mother and father have that?"

"No."

"What about earlier, at the beginning?"

"I don't think they ever expected it," I said, realizing I'd never talked about my parents this way. "They were very European. He was born in Trieste and came here when he was about five; she was born here, but her parents had only arrived from Austria a year or two earlier."

"Was it an arranged marriage?"

"No, not really. But . . ." I tried to think how to describe the marriage of Isaac and Clara Bruno without making it sound like a caricature. "Their expectations were different. Both of them were Middle European, both children of the Depression; my guess is they saw marriage as something people did so they could survive better together than apart."

"Are they still together?"

"Yes. It's more than forty years."

"So they must have *something*."

For a moment, I reflected on all the ways in which my parents managed to avoid each other while occupying the same house. I remembered my mother's throttled tears over the vanished rent money, bet on sure things at Belmont and Jamaica; over the three A.M. phone calls from my father's card partners, demanding payment of his debts. I remembered her bitter acceptance in our lives of Marty the big-time bookie and his courtier, the lawyer Carillo. I remembered the evening after the first day that she found out that I was running for my father and regularly went to night court to watch his arraignments. She threatened to leave him that day, screaming at him that he was a fraud, that he'd always been a fraud, that she could have married a real provider instead of a criminal, that she would spend the rest of her life thanking God that she'd had all those miscarriages and couldn't bear more children. And I remember being shocked that my father, instead of slapping her hard across the mouth—which he did when she raised her voice to him in front of me—simply said, "You don't like it, get out. Earn your own way for a change."

"Yes," I finally said. "They have something, but I can't tell you what it is. Mutual fear, maybe. Huddling together like small animals in the dark."

"What about you?" Maldonado said. "You were married once, weren't you?"

I tried to make a joke of it. "Heat," I said. "Unstoppable lust. Need. If you don't actually dislike one another, lust and need can fool you for a long time."

"Fool you . . . ?"

"Into believing it's love. Fool you into believing what Marshall described—soul to soul."

She glanced away. "Does that mean that now you're like Mr. Marshall—you don't believe anymore?"

As lightly as I could, I said, "My dreams will always belong to you, Nicci."

"Yes, Adam, they will," she said equally lightly, as the machine sputtered and the last drops of coffee dripped into the carafe. She filled my cup with coffee and hers with water, and we lifted them at the same time.

After we each took a sip, we edged closer to one another until her right thigh pressed gently against my left hand. The heat rising between us made me dizzy.

"Are you dizzy?" I said.

"Yes."

"Maybe we should lie down."

"If you think it will help."

"I do."

From a file dated 11 June 1995 and titled MMDIE-1:

. . . I tried to talk to Beth, but the moment I said I needed to discuss our future, she cut me off. Our future is fine, she said—our past is fine, our present is fine, our future is fine. She obviously believed I was about to ask for a divorce or a separation, and no matter how often I said it was way too late for that, she wouldn't believe me. It is too late for that. It is too late for everything. I tried to tell her that, and she told me she really wasn't in the mood for my fashionable midlife crisis. Fair enough. The next step is to talk to Hewitt.

From a file dated 6 July 1995 and titled MMDIE-2:

. . . It's done. I went in yesterday and Mollie Wharton drew up a codicil. They expect me to stop in after Labor Day to consult with them, and then they incorporate the changes in the will. I threw away the prescription but kept copies of the number in the night table up here and in the car. The number is 651594. Hewitt says I'll have no trouble with the druggists.

From a file dated 26 August 1995 and titled MMDIE-3:

. . . Everybody is on vacation, which is good, otherwise somebody would say, where are you? where have you retreated to? what's going on—stuff like that. Maybe not. Maybe I overestimate their interest. Or maybe by now they regard my withdrawals as normal, and wouldn't notice at all. Either way. I can't claim any rightness or smartness in this. I can't claim anything at all. I like my life but I want to love it, and I don't know how. I did once, and whether it was because it was the time, or because she was in it, I can't tell. All I can

tell is I don't love it now, and I haven't for years, and I don't believe
I ever will again. Will anybody notice that I'm not taking the dogs
with me? My dreams will always belong to you.

By five o'clock Monday morning, we had read all the files on Matt
Marshall's diskettes. We found out a lot about Marshall, especially about
how and maybe even why he had ended his life, but we found nothing
that told us Cricket's name, or the child's name, or their whereabouts.

While I entered notes in my computer, and made copies for Boulanger,
Maldonado did one last search, skimming through the more likely files on
Marshall's laptop.

"Merde," she muttered.

"Right. *Merde.*"

For want of something to do, I picked up the original letters and studied
them. All they told me was that Cricket and Ghost had drastically different
handwritings.

Maldonado watched me for a moment. "How did you get those?" she
asked. "Not the ones in your hand, I mean the copies you received?"

Trying to smile, I said, "A. Nonni Muss sent them."

"Who could A. Nonni Muss be?"

"Almost anyone," I said. "The first letter is sent to Marshall in the late
seventies. Who has access to him then? The next letter is sent in the
eighties. Who has access to him then? Did he keep the letters with him?
Did he put them away? Did he give them to Cleary for safekeeping? After
each arrived? How long after? Separately? Together?

"In nineteen eighty-six, he says he's ready to go on the hunt all over
again. Did he recover the letters from their hiding place? From Cleary?
From his wallet? Who had access to him in nineteen eighty-six? See what
I mean—over the years, almost anyone."

Musing aloud, she said, "Many years ago, or not so many years ago,
somebody with access to Mr. Marshall finds a letter, two letters, in Vietnamese. This person, instead of returning the letters to Mr. Marshall,
copies them and has them translated and . . . then what?"

"Sends them to me. Which means this person figured out their value
to me."

"Who could have found the letters?" I said, and began to type a list.
"Who would have copied them and translated them? Who would have
saved them?" I said, and added to my list. "Who would have sent them
to me?"

CHAPTER 44

"I DIDN'T EXACTLY FIND them," Trish Twomey said. "Matt brought them with him to East Forty-eighth Street, sometime in the summer of eighty-six, and one morning I woke up before daylight because I heard the sound of weeping, and he was sitting on the toilet reading them. At the moment, I had no idea what they were." She shook her head. "I'd never seen him weep.

"I asked him what was wrong, and he said, nothing, he'd gone to the Vietnam Memorial and had a bad flashback, and would I get the fuck out of the bathroom while he was trying to take a shit. Sure, I said, but what's that in your hand, and he shouted, none of your fucking business and kicked the door shut. We weren't at our best in those days—it was only a couple months before we stopped being lovers—and I got pissed off and made a vow to myself to get hold of whatever it was he was reading that made him weep and be mean to me.

"At the office that day, without telling me why, he had me get references on several detective agencies, and that night he brought the material with him to East Forty-eighth Street. We had a couple of drinks, did a quickie, and . . ." She frowned at the recollection. ". . . he went to meet Beth at Carnegie Hall for a concert. He said he'd be back by midnight. While he was out, I found the letters, took them down to the twenty-four-hour print shop on the corner, and copied them.

"When he came back, we had a couple of more drinks and I asked him what was going on. Going on how, he said. Going on with you looking for a detective agency after spending half the night sitting on the toilet in tears, that's how."

Twomey pulled her robe tight around her and drained her coffee cup. I'd rung her bell just after 6:30, giving her no time to shower or dress or put on makeup. She had managed to run a comb through her hair, but she looked tired and edgy, which is exactly the way I wanted her, since tired, edgy people don't lie very well.

"Did he tell you what was going on?" I said.

"Later. Four o'clock. Five. This time, I found him in the living room. He wasn't weeping, but he was drunk, and he looked horrible. What is it? I said. He said he needed to go upstate, he had to get away from temptation. For a minute, I levitated—I thought he meant me. He meant the temptation of looking for her."

Twomey left her chair, opened the refrigerator, found a bag of coffee beans, and began to brew a fresh pot in the fancy machine she'd lent to the apartment at East Forty-eighth Street. Keeping her back to me, she said:

"He met somebody in Vietnam, he said. He fell in love with her, she got pregnant, he lost her, he went to the memorial with his kids and it made him want to look for her. That's why he'd asked me to vet detective agencies. But looking for her was out of the question."

"Did he say why?"

"He said, 'It's over.' "

"Did he tell you what the letters were?"

Twomey turned around. "He said they were from some South Vietnamese officer he'd hired to look for her."

"Did you believe him?"

"No, I thought they were from her."

"Did you ever tell him you took them?"

"No."

"When did you have them translated?"

She hesitated. "A week or two later."

"So when I interviewed you, you knew all about the girl and the child."

"Yes," she said. "I lied to you. Sorry."

"Did you and he ever talk about it again?"

"No. Only that night."

She poured herself coffee, saw the expression on my face, and reluctantly filled a cup for me.

"Thanks."

"You're welcome," she said, and sat down again.

"Why did you save the letters?"

She closed her eyes briefly. "They were so important to him; I guess I had some idea of using them to hang on to him. Using them as a lever."

"Did you?"

She shook her head. "I couldn't."

"Couldn't because you didn't figure out how, or couldn't because of scruples?"

"Fuck you," she said conversationally.

"Why did you send me the letters?"

As though she were reciting her social security number, she said, "I hate Beth Marshall, and her shitty kids."

"No other reasons."

She looked away, and for a long time, she neither spoke nor stirred. At last, she turned to me:

"When he told me he'd met somebody in Vietnam and fallen in love with her, I felt it—here." She touched her heart. "But I didn't really feel it here." She touched her belly and slid her hand down to her crotch. "Until he said he got her pregnant. With child—isn't that the expression in the South? With child?" She pressed her abdomen hard. "Pregnant. Beth. Her. But not me.

"I need to see her. I need to see the child. I need to see who it is who did this to him."

"Do you hate her the way you hate Beth?"

The question appeared to surprise her. "No," she said, after weighing it. "No."

"How come?"

She considered before explaining.

"That night, dawn really, before he drove upstate, I asked him if he believed she loved him—I was being cruel. I wanted to convince him she was nothing but a little Vietnamese slut who was fucking the big Yankee conqueror so her miserable family could eat.

"He said . . ." Almost imperceptibly, she gagged. "Yes. He said, 'Yes, I believe she loved me. I believe she did because she wouldn't tell me she loved me in English—because she knew Beth told me in English. She would only tell me she loved me in Vietnamese, or in French.' "

With hindsight, of course, I should have picked up on it a lot sooner, and Maldonado even sooner than I.

As it was, it only took me another two hours. I was at the office, entering my interview with Twomey into the computer, and on the screen was the last of it:

". . . she wouldn't tell me she loved me in English—because she knew

Beth told me in English. She would only tell me she loved me in Vietnamese, or in French."

Quickly, I turned on Marshall's computer, inserted the proper disk, and brought up the first Cricket file, MMCR-1:

". . . What is our child? Does it piss standing up or sitting down? Does it have my blue eyes or your brown ones? What does it look like? Does it speak English? Vietnamese? French? . . ."

I left the screens as they were, locked the office, ran to the library at Pace University and asked for all the French-English and English-French dictionaries they had.

The French word for cricket is *grillon* or *sauterelle* or *caroubier;* for spike, *cheville,* or *clou.*

The number of combinations of GRILLON, SAUTERELLE, CAROUBIER, CHEVILLE, and CLOU is limited, even throwing in CHAU, DINH, and THONG CHE.

By 4:30 that afternoon, starting with counties known to have a large Vietnamese population, I'd done a nationwide computer search on all the name combinations, concentrating especially on marriage and divorce records; citizenship and green card applications; formal name changes; adoptions and school registrations; and narrowed it to twenty-six possibilities. By 7:45, after calling the twenty-six, I'd narrowed it to three, one in Denver, one in Corpus Christi, and one in San Jose. By nine, after calling those three, I'd isolated it to one.

By noon the next day, Maldonado and I were airborne, bound, via San Francisco, for San Jose.

CHAPTER 45

"WHEN I SAY HIM, Dinh, I am going to have your baby, he say me, all you girls say that, and I say, who is all you girls, and he say, all you girls, you Vietnamese girls, that's what you say when you want money, or big hooch, or job in place with lots of rice, you say, I am going to have your baby. I am not born yesterday. I say, what is born yesterday, I no understand, and he say, it means I know old trick when I see one, and I say, no trick. Feel down here. No trick. I put his hand here, and he say, I no feel anything, and I say, feel harder, and he say, I no feel anything, and if I feel anything anyway, how I know it's mine, and I say, your. Your mine. Mine your. But he no believe. He say he no believe."

Before Cricket could continue, the doorbell sounded, and she went to answer it.

She lived in a neat house on a quiet residential street in a town called Gilroy, which is a bedroom community south of San Jose; she called herself Chloe Grillon.

When she landed in the United States, she called herself Clou Grillon (which translated as Spike Cricket); a harried INS agent transcribed the name as Chloe Grillon. She called her daughter—Marshall's daughter—Michelle.

For five years—from 1981 to 1986, during her marriage—she'd been Chloe Quang Bui. Since the husband never legally adopted her daughter, the girl remained Michelle Grillon. The moment the husband divorced her—for somebody with a thriving small business and no children—Chloe reverted to Grillon. Since then, she'd been on her own, first as a seamstress, then as a cook, then a computer-component assembler, then an inspector. For the last two years, she'd worked as a real estate broker, selling commercial properties to other Vietnamese.

When she'd opened the door to us, shortly before twilight, neither Maldonado nor I had any trouble recognizing her. She was smaller than I expected, less than five feet, but as slender as in the nearly twenty-five-year-old photo and looking not much older than when it was taken. Except for the tiniest of crows' feet, her face was unlined, and her features were so perfectly proportioned, they seemed nearly unreal. Her hands were smaller than a child's, and when she offered me the right one, I hardly knew how to grip it. Like both Maldonado women, she had the Vietnamese habit of glancing away when she spoke.

After Maldonado and I introduced ourselves, in English and then Vietnamese, Cricket bowed slightly, backed up to let us in, and pivoted gracefully to lead us into the living room. Once there, she seated me in a huge armchair and Maldonado and herself on the couch. On an oval coffee table between us, she'd laid out tea and several kinds of cakes.

While she poured and chatted in Vietnamese with Maldonado, I let my eyes wander. On the walls were framed diplomas and awards, testifying to Michelle Grillon's achievements—high school valedictorian; summa cum laude, California State; first-year award, medical school. But the room was dominated by a baby-grand piano, and the piano was dominated by the photos on it. They were of the girl, and she'd inherited her mother's cheekbones and eyes, and Matt Marshall's nose and mouth.

"This is my daughter," Cricket said, as she returned to the living room with Michelle Grillon. "Mr. Adam Bruno and Miss Nicole Maldonado."

"How do you do?" Michelle Grillon said, first to Maldonado, then to me. In the flesh, she was even more arresting than in her pictures, no small feat. She wore baggy jeans, high-tops, and a Cal State sweatshirt. Under her arm, she clutched a stuffed worn leather briefcase. She dumped it in a corner, poured herself a cup of tea, waited till Cricket returned to the couch, and sat on a hassock next to her.

For a moment, the only sound was of the four of us sipping green tea.

"So," Michelle said in a strained, jokey tone, "I hear I'm an heiress."

Cricket murmured something to Maldonado, and Maldonado murmured something comforting in return.

"What was that?" Michelle said to Maldonado. "I don't really speak the language."

"Your mother says she wishes sometimes . . . you were more traditional."

Michelle laughed. "You're as indirect as she is."

"Not indirect," Maldonado said evenly. "Tactful."

"Okay," Michelle said. "Am I an heiress? Have I become a Vietnamese-American princess? Do I finally and officially and publicly have a dad?"

"What has your mother told you?" I said.

"That I have a rich dad—a rich dad who just died and mentioned me in his will. Is that right?"

"More or less," I said, glancing at Cricket, who murmured again to Maldonado.

"Mrs. Grillon has told Michelle very little about her father except that he was an American soldier."

"That's all?" I said.

Too cheerfully, Michelle said, "He was an officer, not an enlisted man, and it wasn't rape."

"Did she tell you his name?" I said to Michelle.

"No," she said too airily.

"Do you know what he looks like?"

"No," she said. "Till today, he's Mama's secret."

Reaching for my case, I said to Cricket, "Mrs. Grillon, would it be all right if I showed your daughter a photograph of her father?"

Cricket hesitated, and so did I.

Maldonado leaned close to her and whispered, and, after listening closely, Cricket nodded yes.

"This," I said, passing Michelle a Vietnam picture of Marshall alone, "is not long before you were conceived."

Michelle Grillon took the photo from my hand, theatrically held it at arm's length, tilted her head, and widened her eyes, making a jest of the whole thing. Then, after a nervous glance at her mother, she straightened her head and brought the picture closer, till it was only inches from her face. She swallowed several times, reversed the photo, held it adjacent to her face, and said brightly, "What do you think? Am I my father's daughter?"

Her mother leaned forward, gently took the shot from Michelle's hand, and, without looking at it, handed it back to me. Next, I passed Michelle the picture of Cleary and Marshall with a face-front Cricket between them.

"Here they are together," I said.

"Who's the other guy?" Michelle said.

"His name is Tim Cleary; he served under your father. He's a friend."

Michelle Grillon studied the photo for a long time, then looked over the top of it at her mother. "Why didn't you tell me, Mama?"

"Tell what?" Cricket said.

"That you loved him. That he loved you."

"Not true."

"Oh, come on, Mama. Look at this. Look!" she said angrily, and shoved the picture at Cricket. Her mother resolutely turned her head to one side.

"Not true," she repeated. "No love."

Michelle Grillon bit her lip; then, with an effort, she shrugged, turned to me, and said, "Okay if I keep this?"

After a glance at the immobile Cricket, I said, "I don't see why not."

"Cool. What else you got? What's that?" she said, pointing to the picture of Mickey Woolff changing Cricket's dressing. I passed it to her. "Who's this, and what's he doing to Mama?"

"His name's Mickey Woolff," I said. "And he served with your father too. He was a medic."

Assertively, she held the photo in front of Cricket.

"What's wrong with you here, Mama?"

This time, Cricket accepted the picture and looked at it. "Doc," she said at last. "Kind gentleman."

"Were you wounded?" Michelle said. "Who did it? Did he do it? Did my father hurt you?" She struck a tough pose. "If he did, I'll follow him to Hell and geld him."

Rapidly shaking her head, her mother said, "No. No!"

In the silence, I found a recent picture of Marshall and passed it to Michelle.

"This is about a year ago."

She looked it at. "I've seen this. Is he from around here?"

"No," I said, "but he was in electronics. His name is Matthew Marshall."

"Tel-Mat?" Michelle said. *"That* Marshall?"

"Yes."

"Wow," she said. "I *am* an heiress, Mama." She looked at the photo again. "Very distinguished. Look," she said, and offered the picture to her mother, but less aggressively than she had the others.

Without taking the photo, Cricket bent forward and scrutinized a version of her lover that she'd never seen.

At long last, she lifted her eyes from the image and spoke to Maldonado in Vietnamese.

Maldonado said, "Mrs. Grillon asks who was with him when he died."

"Nobody," I said. "He died alone."

Again Cricket spoke in Vietnamese.

"Mrs. Grillon asks where he was when he died that he died alone," Maldonado translated.

"In his country house. He always went there by himself—it was his private place."

I couldn't stop myself.

"It was his place of memories. Where he went to recollect the past." I touched the photos on the table. "All these pictures were there."

As Maldonado murmured a translation, Cricket leaned over the table and gazed down at the photos.

After a moment, I heard a sound I couldn't recognize, and then I realized—and Maldonado and Michelle realized—that the sound was of Cricket's tears as they dripped onto the Vietnam photos of herself and Matt Marshall.

CHAPTER 46

At FOUR THE NEXT morning, while Maldonado lay asleep on my chest, and I wrestled with my conflicting allegiances, Michelle Grillon called.

"Can I ask you something, Adam?"

"Now?"

"You're not asleep—I can hear it in your voice. It's important."

Maldonado sleepily kissed my chest and shifted to her side of the bed.

"What is it?" I said.

"Are we going to be okay?"

"How do you mean, okay?"

"I mean, is his family going to sit still for this?"

"They haven't told me."

"They're not, are they? I'm the Amerasian bastard, and they're going to fight us all the way."

"They might; there's a lot at stake."

"Mama's scared. Terrified, really. She's not great at dealing with the past." I waited, sensing, and fearing, what was coming next.

"Can you help us?"

"I can recommend a good lawyer, if you want."

"Can't you help us yourself? Mama thinks you're our friend!"

"I work for the executor. I can't take sides."

"Got it." After a silence, she said, "Can I ask you something else?"

"Sure."

"Did you know my dad?"

"Uh uh. I was hired after he died."

"So you don't know what he was like?"

307

"I know a little bit."

"Like what?"

"He was very smart. Good-looking. A charmer."

"What's that—a charmer?"

"Lots of people liked him."

"Lots of women?"

"Men and women."

"He fucked around, didn't he?"

"Why do you say that?"

"Guys that good-looking—they always do." She hesitated again, then said with the same false cheer as at the house, "Well, at least it proves it wasn't rape. I'd hate to think I'm a potential heiress because of rape."

"You're not," I said. "You saw the photos."

"Do you know what kind of dad he was—to his other kids, I mean?"

"I don't know."

"Did he do stuff with the girl—dad stuff, I mean?"

"I don't know, Michelle."

"Got it. Do you have any kids?"

"No."

"When you were a kid, did you do a lot of stuff with your dad—you know, guy stuff—ball games, shit like that?"

"Not much. He worked very long hours. Sometimes, I hung out with him after school."

"Doing what?"

"Running bets."

"What does that mean?"

"He was a bookie; people made bets with him, and he gave me the bets and I ran them over to his bank. Bank, as in Marty his boss, not bank as in Security Pacific."

"You're a criminal!"

"Ex-criminal."

"Did he make you do that?"

"No, I wanted to. It was the only time I could really spend with him."

"Were you scared?"

"Excited—I thought I was going to grow up to be Sky Masterson."

"Who's that?"

"A character in Damon Runyon. Did you ever see *Guys and Dolls*?"

"No." She paused. "Do you have any sisters?"

"No."

"So you don't know what dads do with girls?"

"No."

She laughed. "Me, neither. Except from TV and movies." Again, she was silent. Then: "When I was a kid, I used to sneak into the bookstore and go through all the Vietnam photo books. Maybe he's the one, or maybe him, or maybe him. The mongrel's missing American half. For a while, I pretended he was a pilot, but not a bomber pilot or a fighter pilot, a recon pilot who got shot down and who Mama saved from the angry neighbors. Then, I wanted him to be an advisor—a noble soldier who taught us English and democracy and helped us to be a real country. Then, I wanted him to be a doctor—Mama got wounded, and a decent Yankee surgeon extracted the bullets from her bleeding body and made her whole again."

"That's not so far off," I said.

"He wasn't a shit, was he?"

"No."

"You're sure?—I mean, he *was* rich, *and* he dumped Mama."

"I'm sure."

"Do you think he was ashamed of me—because I'm a mongrel, I mean? Mama is sometimes."

"No."

"I don't want him to be a shit."

"He wasn't one."

"Do you think I would have liked him?"

"I don't know how to answer that, Michelle—I hardly know you."

"Would *you* have liked him?"

"Yes."

"Then I would, too." She faltered. "Do you think he would have liked me?"

"No question."

By then, Maldonado was awake and propped on her elbow, listening curiously. Michelle, I mouthed to her, and she nodded as though, of course, who else?

"Isn't there some way you can help us, Adam?" Michelle said.

"Let me recommend a lawyer."

"Mama won't trust some lawyer, Adam. She trusts you. She thinks you're our friend."

"Michelle, I work for the executor."

"Can't you help us anyway?"

"It would be tricky," I said, when I should have simply said no.

"But not impossible?"

"No, not impossible."

CHAPTER 47

THREE HOURS LATER, AT seven San Francisco time, I sent a fax to Mollie Wharton in New York:

Mollie Wharton, Esquire
Dunlop, Tyler & Laird
This is to inform you that, in accordance with the terms of my contract, I have located a person I believe to be the child referred to in the Saigon codicil; that is to say, the abandoned child of Matthew Marshall.

As per my employment contract, before I reveal the whereabouts of the child, or serve the child with a notice of probate, there is a $50,000 bonus due me. Please let me know how you would like to proceed.

At 9:15, while Maldonado was showering and I was putting the finishing touches on my strategy, the phone rang.

"Mr. Bruno!" Wilson Laird said with his usual fraudulent warmth. "How are you? San Francisco is so lovely this time of year, isn't it?" He chuckled. "When the hotel operator answered, I said to myself, what I most admire about Mr. Adam Bruno is that he always travels first class. Do you mind if I put you on the speakerphone? I have Mollie Wharton and Tom Schuyler with me . . ."

After a click, he returned, sounding, as people do on a speakerphone, as though he were at the bottom of a well.

"Mr. Bruno, you say in your fax—where is it? You say—I quote—'a person I believe to be the child referred to in the Saigon codicil; that is to say, the abandoned child of Matthew Marshall . . .' Exactly what do you mean by that?"

"I believe the person I've located is the child, but I don't know—"

Schuyler, who I'm sure had been restraining himself with a strenuous effort, burst in: "What is the basis for that belief?"

"What I was saying, Mr. Laird," I continued, "is I believe the person I've located is the child of Matthew Marshall, but I don't know what you and the surrogate court require to establish that. Maybe if you tell me the requirements, we can get someplace."

"Hold on a moment, Mr. Bruno," Laird said, and turned off the speakerphone and covered his mouthpiece so I couldn't hear them.

When he returned, he said, "Mr. Bruno, I've asked Mollie to give you a summary of what's required. For the record, there may be additional conditions we've overlooked."

"Understood," I said.

"Adam . . . are you ready?" Wharton said.

I checked my cassette. "Ready."

"As you know, Mr. Marshall has already acknowledged paternity, so that's moot. In that acknowledgment, he's given parameters of the time and place of conception and birth. The estate—and the surrogate—would expect supporting evidence of that. The more supporting evidence the better.

"Best would be a birth certificate, listing Matthew Marshall as father. In the absence of that, testimony from the doctor or nurse or midwife who delivered the child. In the absence of that—and we're cognizant that this child was supposedly conceived and born in a wartime setting—any witnesses who could testify that Matthew Marshall did, in fact, impregnate a woman who subsequently bore this child."

"Not many people are around for a conception," I said, as blithely as I could.

"We understand that," Wharton said. "But we would expect some credible testimony from intimates of Matthew Marshall that he was sexually involved with the purported mother. Naturally, we would want to interrogate any of these intimates. Do you know of any?"

"Oh, sure," I said. "Anything else?"

"You know of intimates?" Schuyler said.

"Know of them; talked to them. What else?"

"A paper trail of some sort," Wharton said. "Correspondence between

Marshall and the child—birthday cards, graduation cards, gifts; the kinds of things that would announce or imply parenthood. Obviously, if there's a letter that says, 'To my dear son—' "

"Daughter," I said.

"—'To my dear daughter,' so much the better."

"What about correspondence to Marshall from the mother of the child?"

"Fine, especially if anything in it directly refers to the child. However," she added warningly, "it would have to be more than a request for support or money. Those are always open to challenge."

Laird again interjected: "Is there correspondence between them, Mr. Bruno?"

"Oh, sure."

"In what language?" Schuyler said.

"Vietnamese," I said. "What else, Ms. Wharton?"

"Nothing springs to mind," Wharton said.

"Okay. Official documents, paper trail, testimony from medical people, testimony from intimates."

"Exactly."

"Ms. Wharton, what about the mother—would her testimony have any value?"

After an electric pause, Laird breezily said, "The mother is alive, then?"

"Very much so," I said.

"Have you met her?"

"Oh, sure," I said.

"What's your impression?" Laird said.

"Very beautiful," I said. "But heavily accented English. How valuable would her testimony be?"

After a whispered conference, Wharton said, "We would depose her, of course, but any testimony she could offer would be so patently self-serving, it probably would have little probative effect."

"Little or none," Schuyler said contemptuously.

"I'll keep it in mind," I said.

Laird said, "Now, given what Mollie has said, Mr. Bruno, where do we stand?"

"I'm not sure I follow you, Mr. Laird. Stand, in what way?"

"What's your impression—in the light of what Mollie has said—do you believe these people can mount a case?"

"Frankly, Mr. Laird, this isn't my area at all, and I think it would be irresponsible to guess."

"Do you think they're frauds?"

"I doubt that, Mr. Laird."

"Why?"

"It's not as if you ran an ad and they came out of the woodwork. I hunted them down. On top of that, I questioned Cricket pretty rigorously. If she's not who she says she is, she's a sensational con artist."

"Mr. Bruno, you believe that the person you found is indeed the child of Matt Marshall?"

"Yes."

"May I ask, how strong is your belief?"

"Strong."

"All right. Based on your conversations with mother and child, and your independent inquiries, how much actual ammunition do you believe they have? Would it be safe to dismiss them out of hand—to say, the executors do not credit your claim of identity? Would that be safe?"

"No."

"Why not?"

"They have enough to sue."

"Do they have enough to prevail?"

"I can't determine that, Mr. Laird. Only a court could determine that."

"What's your impression?" he said insistently.

"Mr. Laird, if I said to you, the second I saw the child—I mean, the split second—I recognized the Marshall genes, what would your reaction be?"

"The court is not concerned with physical resemblances," Schuyler interjected.

"Mr. Laird," I said. "What would your reaction be?"

"The split second?"

"The split second."

Laird took a long breath and said, "You know what I think would be best? I think, for the moment, we should banish our occupational mistrust and assume that everyone is acting in good faith. That would be best. Mr. Bruno has done yeoman work, and we should accept that he believes he has found Matt's child. We should also accept that the woman who claims to be the child's mother—Cricket, Matt called her—correct?"

"Cricket," I said.

"That Cricket is likewise well intentioned and not trying to cheat the estate. Why don't we make that our starting place? What do you say to that, Mr. Bruno?"

"Fine," I said, forming a circle of my thumb and forefinger and showing it to Maldonado.

"Let me propose this, Mr. Bruno: Before we formally serve the child a notice of probate and file the will, why don't we—the executors—meet

Matt's child and her mother? Not for formal interrogatories. Not for an adversarial encounter. Not at all. A get-together. We all want the same thing, for Matt's wishes to be honored. I like that idea. Don't you, Tom? Don't you, Mollie?"

If they did, they didn't say so aloud.

"What do you think of that idea, Mr. Bruno?"

"I'm not in a position to judge."

"Oh, don't underestimate yourself, Mr. Bruno—I value your judgment. After all, we haven't met the parties. You have. Do you think mother and child would like this idea?"

"I can't tell without asking them."

"Would you ask them?" Laird said.

"Wilson!" Schuyler blurted. "I really am not comfortable using Bruno as our go-between."

"Ah, but Tom, I am," Laird said. "Mr. Bruno, I want you to invite Matt's child and her mother to join us in New York for a conversation. Can you do that? Convince them to come to New York?"

"At your expense?"

"Of course, of course," Laird said. "All expenses paid, first class. Do they have any special desires—opera, ballet, theater, rock concerts? Are there any restaurants they'd like to try? Museums? We can arrange for private tours. Baby-sitters? Tutors? We have lots of resources at our disposal. What would make their stay more delightful?"

"Well, this is all new to me, Mr. Laird, but offhand I'd say that for your conversation, Cricket would want a—"

"You're not going to say a lawyer, are you, Mr. Bruno?" Laird inserted smoothly.

"No. I was going to say a translator of her choosing. Cricket's not a young woman, and she's embarrassed about her English. Is that okay?"

Cautiously, Laird said, "At the present instant, I don't see why not."

"And my guess is she'll want me there. I've managed to make myself a familiar presence, and I know she'll need that. Let's be honest, Mr. Laird, you and Mr. Schuyler and Ms. Wharton can be pretty intimidating."

"Oh, you flatter us, Mr. Bruno," he said. "But, if it makes Madame Cricket comfortable to have you in the room, so be it. As long as you understand the limits of your role. Is there anything else?"

"When we arrive, you'll have a certified check for fifty thousand dollars—my bonus."

"Ah, yes, your bonus. It will be waiting for you, Mr. Bruno. When shall I have our travel agent call you?"

"We'll make our own arrangements," I said.

"That's absurd," Laird said. "We have the wherewithal. We'll do it."

"I'd prefer to do it myself," I said.

"What on earth for, Mr. Bruno?"

Because I need to keep our movements secret, I thought, but did not say. Because I cannot get out of my mind the blood and shell casings on Tim Cleary's floor. Because until I get Cricket and Michelle into your office, I'm afraid they're targets of a man in sunglasses and a gray Borsalino.

"Because it would make a neat coda to my quest," I said. "Put it down to my fondness for ritual."

Laird chuckled. "How can a lawyer reject ritual? When should we expect you?"

"Thursday at noon."

CHAPTER 48

"THEY'RE NEARLY FORTY MINUTES late," Thomas Schuyler said in his typical querulous fashion.

"Midday tunnel traffic, I bet," I said, knowing that Luis Maldonado had left the house at eleven, and that it was a thirty-five-minute drive, at the outside.

"If *we* had booked the hotel and the car instead of you," he said, "we could have done everything properly."

"They'll be here," I said laconically.

Once more, I was sitting in the middle of one side of the oval table in the conference room at Dunlop, Tyler & Laird; to my left was Schuyler; opposite me was Wharton; as usual, Wilson Laird occupied pride of place at the head of the table.

"It's all right, Tom," Laird said congenially. "Nobody's in any hurry today. Have something to eat."

He gestured to the folding table behind him, on which rested platters of cold smoked duck, poached bass, shrimp and lobster dumplings, quail eggs, vegetable tempura, sushi and sashimi, hot and cold spiced noodles, bean curd and sprouts, and anything else that the caterer believed spoke of East Asia.

"You think they'd at least call," Schuyler said, and helped himself to some cold noodles. "You think they'd at least observe the elementary courtesies."

"Traffic," I said, praying.

I'd booked the plane tickets under my mother's maiden name, and Mal-donado had arranged to have her father pick us up at Newark airport and take us to her parents' house. It had been easy to persuade Cricket—she liked the idea of being in a place with Vietnamese speakers—but somewhere over the Great Lakes, Michelle wanted to know why she had to stay in New Jersey rather than at a luxury hotel in the city. She didn't need to be with Vietnamese speakers, she said.

"I don't think it's a good idea for Wilson Laird to talk to you till the last possible minute," I said, truthfully.

All the way from the airport to the Maldonados' house, I kept discreetly checking the rearview mirrors, but I wasn't as discreet as I thought, because later, when everyone had gone to bed except Luis and myself, and we were sitting in the kitchen drinking tequila shots, he said, "Was somebody following us from the airport?"

"Why do you ask that?"

Maldonado formed a half-fist and made the universal gesture for jerking-off. "Adam, don't bullshit me, okay?"

"No, I didn't see anyone following us."

"But you were afraid somebody was?" I nodded. "What's going on?"

I had a hundred fall-back positions, but I knew that Luis Maldonado would be driving Cricket, Michelle, and Nicci to the meeting Thursday, and I owed him some facts. My throat was dry, and I swallowed some tequila first.

"When you bring everybody in to the city Thursday, keep a good eye. I can't tell you what kind of car to look for or describe the driver. He might be wearing designer sunglasses and a hat, a Borsalino. He might not. He might not be here. He might be in a hospital. He might be dead. I don't know. But keep a good eye. Take a cellular phone with you. I'll have mine. You'll enter my number in the speed dial."

Seeing his face change, I hastily added, "Luis, this is strictly my paranoia. I think if this guy's around, the only thing he might do—and I doubt he'll even do that—is try to follow me so I can lead him to Michelle and Cricket. That's why I'm not riding with you—just on the off chance he's watching my house. I don't believe there's any danger."

"Okay," Luis said. "I keep a good eye for a guy in designer glasses and a hat. I put your number in the speed dial—but the only risk is the guy might follow you."

"Right."

"Why can he do that and not follow me?"

"He doesn't know about you—nobody knows when and how we came into town. But my office address is in the phone book; my home, too. So if he wants to follow anybody, I would be the one."

"And there's no danger?"

"Right."

He repeated the jerking-off gesture. "Adam . . ."

"There isn't."

"I can smell your sweat from here."

After a breath, I said, "There was a killing."

"And this guy did it?"

"I think so," and before he could ask the obvious, I added, "Nicci knows about the killing and knows the killer might be on the loose."

"Is she at risk?" he said, and the Special Forces warrior in him surfaced to join the father.

"No," I said. "No. No. The person who was killed was somebody who could identify Cricket. Nicci's not at risk. Nobody's at risk anymore."

"Cricket's at risk; Michelle's at risk," he said.

"No."

"Don't bullshit me."

"Only until noon Thursday."

At 12:51, my cellular phone rang and I flung open my case to get it. "Yes," I said tensely.

"Yes is right," Herschel O'Hara said. "I hear you did it. You got your man. Woman. Women."

"This isn't a great time," I said.

He laughed ebulliently. "That's why I called. Mollie says you—"

"Not now. I want to keep this line open."

"Whoever she is, she won't call."

As I rang off, furious with him for calling me and furious with myself for entrusting everything to Luis Maldonado, a man whose abilities I knew nothing about, there was a polite knock on the conference room door. Before anyone else could stir, I jumped up and marched toward it. As I reached for the knob, the door swung open.

Laird's assistant, Gretchen, stepped into the room and announced, "Mr. Laird, Mrs. Grillon, Ms. Grillon, and Ms. Maldonado are here."

By then, Gretchen had moved aside to let Cricket and Michelle walk in. They were followed by Nicole Maldonado, and I couldn't stop myself from touching each of them lightly on the sleeve as they entered. Maldonado leaned close to me and muttered, "Overheated school bus in the Holland Tunnel."

"No other problems?" I whispered.

"None," she said.

Laird and Schuyler were standing, and Laird marched over, both hands stretched out before him.

"Mrs. Grillon. Ms. Grillon. It is an honor to meet you at last. And you must be Ms. Maldonado. I am Wilson Laird; this is Tom Schuyler and Mollie Wharton. Mrs. Grillon, sit here, by me. Ms. Grillon, why don't you sit next to Mollie. And Ms. Maldonado, here, close to Mrs. Grillon, so she'll feel secure. What can we offer you? We asked our caterer to prepare some Oriental dishes, and I must beg your forgiveness in advance if he fell short. He's merely French. Tom, describe those noodles you ate to Ms. Grillon. Mollie, see whether those dumplings are still warm—I never trust paraffin heaters. Would anyone like a glass of wine? Champagne? Mineral water?" Laird said, sounding more and more like a maître d' aboard a cruise ship.

Strangely enough, the babble worked. A few minutes more of it, and we all had plates and glasses in front of us and were chatting pleasantly about Silicon Valley, the growth of San Jose, the vineyards of California, the end of the embargo on Vietnam, and Michelle Grillon's future in medicine. Even Schuyler managed to behave humanly, which stupefied me until I caught the craving on his face when he surreptitiously looked at Michelle.

Forty-five minutes later, after the waiter had served crème brûlée and coffee and tea; after he had cleared the dirty dishes and refilled our cups; after Gretchen had brought in several copies of the codicil and my $50,000 check; and after Laird had ostentatiously instructed her to turn off the sophisticated phone unit at his elbow, he got down to it.

"Mrs. Grillon," he said, "as you know, Matthew Marshall—a close friend of mine for many, many years—made a provision in his will for his child . . ." He waved vaguely in Michelle's direction, as though he couldn't yet quite concede that she was the child. "Without going into all the questions and complications this provision has raised, let me say that as the executors of the estate, we want—if at all possible—to honor Matthew Marshall's wishes to include his child in his bequests. This is our desire."

He waited politely while Maldonado translated into Cricket's ear. Cricket smiled placidly and nodded.

"Did Mr. Bruno happen to describe to you some of the standards that the court might use to determine these matters?"

Cricket listened to Maldonado's translation and then nodded to Michelle, who said:

"Official documents—like a birth certificate; testimony from doctors or nurses who were around when I was born; testimony from intimates—I guess those would the soldiers who were around while Mom and Dad were . . ." Michelle made a mock-modest noise. ". . . conceiving me. A paper trail—letters between me and my dad or Mom and my dad . . ." At the use of the word *dad,* Schuyler and Wharton both jumped slightly, as though they'd touched metal after sliding across a carpet. "And some other stuff I can't remember right now."

"I see Mr. Bruno was his usual precise, unexpurgated self," Laird said, glancing at me kindly. "Mrs. Grillon, can you give us an idea of what you can supply in those areas?"

After conferring with Cricket, Maldonado said, "The birth certificate doesn't include Mr. Marshall's name, and Mrs. Grillon doesn't know the names of the doctors or nurses in attendance. They were Vietnamese, not American. As for testimony from soldiers who served with Mr. Marshall . . ." She paused gracefully and glanced at me. "Mrs. Grillon says Mr. Bruno would know more about that."

Schuyler and Wharton turned to me, and Wharton said, "Are there such people?"

"Definitely."

"And can they be deposed?" Schuyler said.

"They'd love it," I said, joyfully imagining Tim Cleary on the witness stand while Schuyler interrogated him.

"What about the paper trail?" Wharton said. "Did Mr. Marshall write to either of you?"

Both Michelle and Cricket shook their heads; Schuyler stroked his chin to hide the smile stealing across his face.

"That's a bit of an obstacle," Laird said indulgently. "Letters would really help."

"Yes," Wharton echoed. "Testimony from soldiers isn't nearly as strong as documents."

I scratched my nose, and Michelle ingenuously said, "Dad didn't write to us, but Mr. Bruno says he found some other letters—didn't you, Mr. Bruno?"

Laird, Schuyler, and Wharton turned to me simultaneously, as though they were separate wheels connected to a single axle.

From my case, I drew copies of Ghost's letters and passed them to Laird. "Those are not originals," I said, "but the originals exist and can be submitted to the court."

"I take it this language is Vietnamese . . . ?"

"Yes. Why don't you keep those and have them translated by your own people," I said. "In the meantime, do you want Ms. Maldonado to do a version for you?"

"Have the Grillons examined these?" he said easily.

"No, I thought we could all do it together."

"Perhaps we should study them in house first."

"It's up to you, Mr. Laird," I said unassumingly. "But I would think that you'd want the Grillons to know of anything that might be useful to them—wouldn't that be the best way of carrying out Mr. Marshall's intentions?"

After a fitting pause for thought, Laird nodded.

"Good point, Mr. Bruno. We're all on the same side." Taking a pen from his pocket and uncapping it, he said, "Why don't you set the context for us?"

"The letters are from a Vietnamese Army colonel who Marshall knew as Ghost. After Mr.—"

"Does Ghost have a name?" Schuyler said.

"A name, a face, a voice, and an address," I said. "After Mr. Marshall returned to the United States, he asked Ghost to do a favor for him. Shall we have Ms. Maldonado translate the relevant passages?"

Laird nodded commandingly, and Maldonado began:

"This letter was written from Bien Hoa jail sometime after the Communist takeover in nineteen seventy-five:

'Dear Captain Matthew:

I have been very much on the lookout for your dear friend, but . . . I cannot look for somebody with only the nickname you affectionately imposed on her. I must have her own name, at the least the name of her village. Do you know if she has the child with her? . . . If a woman has given herself freely to a member of the invading forces and borne his child, she can . . . be considered a political prisoner . . .' "

Maldonado picked up the second letter:

" 'Dear Captain Matthew:

. . . According to a refugee family here, your friend and her child were caught trying to escape from Vietnam by boat . . . and were placed in a reeducation camp near Tay Ninh. From Tay Ninh . . . your friend and her child returned to the place of her birth, but were forced to leave because her mixed-blood child alarmed her neighbors.

From her birthplace, your friend and her child took to the water once more and made their way to Malaysia, where they were put back to sea for lack of bribe money. From Malaysia, your friend and her child sailed to Guam. That is all I know of her movements—I cannot tell you whether they are still on Guam or have gone to the United States or have been put back to sea . . .

I did however learn that during her journey she traveled under the name Nguyen Thi Dinh . . .' "

"Could you repeat the name, please?" Wharton said to Maldonado. Cricket quietly said, "Nguyen Thi Dinh."

Schuyler, after waiting fruitlessly for Laird to comment, said, "Frankly, Wilson, I'm not impressed. Are you, Mollie?"

"I'd have to study them further," she said.

"What about you, Mr. Laird," I said. "Are you impressed?"

Laird pursed his lips. "Not convincingly, no."

From my case, I drew Cricket's letter to Marshall, and passed it to Laird. "This might help a little."

Laird compared it to Ghost's letters. "I can't be sure, but it looks like a different hand."

"It is. That's a letter from Mrs. Grillon to Marshall."

"To Marshall?" Laird said. "How did you come across it, Mr. Bruno?"

"Serendipity, Mr. Laird. Do you want Ms. Maldonado to translate it for you?"

"Please," Laird said, passing the letter to her.

With a modest bow to Cricket, Maldonado read, " 'Dear Dinh' "— Dinh is Vietnamese for Spike," Maldonado explained, "which was Mrs. Grillon's private nickname for Mr. Marshall."

"Spike?" Laird said. "I never heard of Spike."

"From his boyhood," I tossed in.

"Can that be corroborated?" Wharton said.

"Rachel and Paul," I said.

Maldonado waited through all this, then:

" 'Dear Dinh:

I do not know if you search now, but I do know you searched in past days. I must beg you never to search again. Many years ago, you and I lived a short short life. Now, I live a new life in your country, but you must not appear in my new life. You must not. I beg you, for the sake of our child, please leave me my life as I left you your life.' "

As she finished, Maldonado reached under the table and took Cricket's hand.

"When did you write that, Mama?" Michelle said in a strained voice.

"When I marry Mr. Quang Bui," Cricket said.

"The 'our child' is ambiguous," Schuyler said coolly. "It could refer to the child of Mrs. Grillon and whomever she was presently with, Quang whatever-his-name-is. It's not definitive that 'our child' refers to a child of Mrs. Grillon by Matthew Marshall."

Maldonado translated for Cricket, who very politely pointed to Michelle and said, "Our child." She made a gesture of sculpturing a face and added, "Make good look. Our."

Laird nodded. "Yes, I think anyone who ever knew Matt would be inclined to agree with you, Mrs. Grillon. Of course," he smiled benevolently, "the surrogate didn't meet Matt, and resemblances don't count much in court. Nonetheless . . ." He rubbed his hands contemplatively. "I myself find the letter quite impressive—it would be ambiguous only to someone challenging it. What do you think, Mollie—how does all this appear so far?"

"There's not a whole lot," Wharton said, watching Laird's face for cues. "As you said, resemblances don't count much with the court. Mrs. Grillon has no official documents, the letters from Ghost lack any real specificity, and unless Ghost could be much more detailed in a deposition, I don't see much help there. And Mr. Bruno hasn't told us yet about the reliability and number of his military witnesses.

"This one letter," Wharton said, touching it, "seems to be the strongest evidence, and, yes, it's quite impressive, but it *is* open to challenge. There *is* ambiguity."

Into the silence, Laird offered this:

"Well, Mrs. Grillon, not ironclad on the face of things. But, we're just beginning; you mustn't lose heart. Don't you agree, Mollie? Soldier on, et cetera."

Wharton considered. "Yes, I think so."

"I don't," Schuyler said.

"What is it you're saying, Tom?" Laird asked, almost sounding genuinely taken aback.

"Given what we've heard so far," Schuyler said momentously, "I think that Mrs. Marshall and the named children can mount a strong challenge—a well-financed challenge—to the claim of Marshall paternity posed by Ms. Grillon."

Schuyler looked at Michelle, found her face unnerving, and hastily turned to Cricket:

"Defending that challenge could take years—and millions of dollars. Which unless you have, you would need to borrow since lawyers are reluctant to work on contingency in probate cases. As executor of the estate, I believe—we all believe—it's in everyone's interest to avoid pro-tracted litigation and arrive at an equitable settlement."

"By equitable," Laird said, patting Cricket's hand paternally and not noticing her flinch, "Tom means generous."

"If you believe the Grillons can be successfully challenged," I said, "why do think the other Marshalls would agree to a generous settlement?"

"Mr. Bruno," he said, "I can assure you that Beth Marshall—and the children—will follow the advice of the executor and do the right thing. I will tell them that nobody here challenges the Grillons' moral claim. Do you, Tom? Do you, Mollie? I don't."

Fluently, he continued:

"On the contrary. I believe this lovely young woman is, in fact, the child of Matt Marshall. Unfortunately, the courts demand much more than my belief. They demand incontrovertible evidence, and—it grieves me horribly to say this—we don't see that evidence. So the best we can do as executors—bound by law, not merely belief—is to forcefully urge Beth to live up to the spirit of Matt's intentions."

After listening closely to this, Michelle said to me, "What is he saying?"

"He's saying they don't want to go to court, either."

"You mean, they're making an offer . . . ?"

"They can't make an offer. All they can do is go back to the Marshalls and say that you're willing to entertain the idea of one. Any offer has to come from the Marshalls. Doesn't it, Mr. Laird?"

"Indeed it does."

"Why don't we invite them in?" I said. "It'll save so much time and abstract chatter—don't you think?"

Before Laird could decide what he thought, I leaned over the sophis-ticated phone unit next to him:

"Mrs. Marshall, why don't you join us?"

CHAPTER 49

BETH MARSHALL KNEW ABOUT entrances. Instead of leading a procession into the room, she allowed Wendy and Fred to precede her. Once they'd gotten ten feet in, she followed. She wore a midnight blue Armani suit, and wouldn't have looked out of place on a *Vogue* cover. Pausing graciously to nod to Laird, Schuyler, and Wharton, she strode right up to me and offered her hand. "Mr. Bruno, I'm delighted to see you again. Please," she said, sounding utterly sincere, "introduce me . . ."

"Mrs. Beth Marshall," I said, "Mrs. Chloe Grillon and her daughter, Ms. Michelle Grillon."

"How do you do?" Beth Marshall said, taking Cricket's hand. "Grillon—what a lovely name."

"It means Cricket," Michelle said.

"Of course," Beth Marshall said, and turned to the girl. For a disconcertingly long time she studied Michelle's face. "Yes," she said at last. "Oh, yes."

She beckoned the others closer. "May I introduce . . ." She paused and smiled wittily. ". . . my children, Fred and—"

She halted abruptly because—in one of those moments that usually occur only on stage—the door opened and Matt junior, brilliant smile solidly in place, strolled in.

"Hello, everyone. Sorry I'm late. I would have been on time, but I wasn't invited. How are you, Wilson? Mollie? Mr. Bruno. Fred. Wendy. Mother. Did I interrupt something?"

Without dropping a stitch, Beth Marshall said, "Mrs. Grillon, Ms. Grillon, may I introduce my children, Fred and Wendy and Matthew junior."

When the greetings were done, Wendy and Fred sat beside each other near Schuyler; Matt junior sat at the far end of the table by himself; Beth sat next to me. After removing her gloves and lining them up neatly on the table, she nodded politely to Laird and faced Cricket.

"In the light of what we overheard, Mrs. Grillon, we are prepared to give you two hundred and fifty thousand dollars. We are prepared to pay for Michelle's medical school, help her invest in a private practice or clinic, and give her five hundred thousand dollars. Naturally, we would assume any tax liabilities. In exchange, we would want you to forgo any claims against the Marshall estate."

"That's seven hundred and fifty thousand dollars, plus education, plus a medical practice, tax-free," Fred Marshall said.

Cricket nodded courteously to both Beth and Fred and looked at Michelle, who picked up her copy of the codicil, found a paragraph, and said, "Can I ask about something?"

Fred Marshall flushed. "Don't you have any manners? Respond to my mother's offer first."

It was Michelle's turn to flush. She took several breaths before flatly saying, "According to Mr. Bruno, Matt Marshall's worth more than one hundred million dollars." She tapped the codicil. "And I'm due half. I don't see why I should take five hundred thousand."

After an unreadable glance at me, Laird said, "Yes, my dear, that is correct. The estate is worth about one hundred eight million dollars, and—in theory, at any rate—you are due half. The reason you should take five hundred thousand—for yourself—and two hundred fifty thousand for your mother is because we—the executors—are fearful that the court might dismiss you with nothing at all."

"More than fearful," Schuyler said predictably.

"You see," Wharton said, making it a three-on-one, "from the court's standpoint, you don't have a whole lot."

With no warning, I opened my case and began pulling microcassettes from it and stacking them before me.

"During the past several weeks, I've interviewed a lot of people. Soldiers who served with Marshall, like . . ." I dropped a photo on the table. "Eve McGowan." Another photo. "Mickey Woolff." Another photo. "Tim Cleary. These three have talked to me about the conception of Michelle Grillon, and can testify to it. That's first.

"Second," I continued without giving anyone a chance to stop me, "in the spring of nineteen seventy-four, Matt Marshall went back to Vietnam. Do you remember that, Mrs. Marshall?"

After tipping her head sideways to demonstrate earnest thought, Beth

Marshall said, "He took a job there—work here was hard to find. The work was in his field and paid very well."

"Do you remember how long he stayed?"

She shrugged. "A while."

"Does a year sound about right, Mrs. Marshall?"

"Perhaps; it's a long time ago."

"Do you have a point?" Schuyler said.

Pulling more tapes from my case, I said, "These are interviews with . . ." I laid out another batch of photos. "Sam Spiegel, Terry Quinn, Barry Randall, Buzz Oliver, and Ghost—they're the people who helped Matt Marshall search for Cricket and Michelle in the year he stayed in Vietnam. They can testify to that."

After glancing at the pictures, Laird said, "But can they testify that Mrs. Grillon is the woman they were searching for and that Ms. Grillon is the child?"

"We'll find out."

"Yes, we will," Laird said. "If they can't . . ." He lifted his palms in a gesture of futility. ". . . then, all they can tell us is that Matt was looking for—forgive me, everyone—his lover and their child. There's no linkage, you see? Mrs. Grillon, I don't mean their testimony wouldn't help. I just don't believe it would be determinative. Do you, Mollie?"

"No," she said firmly.

Laird waited till Wharton's confident "no" sank in before saying, "Mr. Bruno, let me say both formally and as a colleague that your work on this case has been truly remarkable. Remarkable. But in the end . . ." He turned to Cricket and gestured to all the material on the table.

"Mrs. Grillon, Ms. Grillon, this is all so very vulnerable. The letters from Ghost are ambiguous; your letter is ambiguous. And everything else depends on the testimony of long-ago, secondhand witnesses, and—to be painfully candid—I have no doubt the court will label that testimony as hearsay. Mollie, what can we do? What can we suggest to the Grillons that would be definitive?"

"I really don't know, Mr. Laird."

"There must be something," he mused. "But what?"

I let the silence build for a while. Then: "Ms. Wharton, what about a DNA match? I know the criminal courts give great weight to genetic evidence. Would the surrogate's court find a DNA match definitive?"

"Not definitive, no," she said flatly.

"What about a DNA match combined with all this?" I said. "Would the court find that definitive?"

"Not definitive, no," she repeated, with a twitchy glance at Laird.

"Okay. Then, how strong? What would Michelle's chances be if she presented all this, plus a DNA match?"

Laird smilingly rescued Wharton.

"Mr. Bruno, there's no answer to that in advance—you know that. Shame on you for trying to force poor Mollie to speculate on the intentions of the Manhattan surrogate."

As he smiled benevolently at Wharton, I said, "Why don't we do the tests?"

Laird started to reply, but Wharton must have found her equilibrium because she waved him off.

"As executor, we would support that, Mr. Bruno. But you do realize that the most reliable DNA matches—the kind the court demands—are parent-child." She cleared her throat daintily. "Which would mean the estate would have to ask for the exhumation of Mr. Marshall's body. The executor has no objection." She looked at Beth. "Do you, Mrs. Marshall?"

"Yes, I'm afraid I do," Beth said, with just the right tinge of widow's regret.

She leaned back in her chair, and so did her children; and so did Laird, Schuyler, and Wharton. As small as their movements were, they reeked of swagger.

"I can understand that, Mrs. Marshall," I said, opening my case. From it I took a copy of Marshall's obituary, skimmed it, and found the passage I wanted.

"This is from the *Times:* '. . . He also built and endowed the burn unit at New Amsterdam Hospital and a blood bank to go with it, along with blood banks at existing burn units at hospitals around the country.' "

I raised my head and said, "Do you think he donated blood himself to the New Amsterdam Bank?" I said. "Or to any of them?"

"It's possible," Laird said easily.

"Do you know, Mrs. Marshall?" I said.

"I imagine he did, but I'm sure some lucky soul has it coursing through his veins by now, don't you?"

"I can't say, Mrs. Marshall. But why guess? Why don't you ask the blood bank at New Amsterdam? And the blood banks at the other burn units? If you ask, they'll tell you." I smiled at Schuyler. "They told me."

"Ahhhh," Laird said.

Michelle waited a few seconds, then said, "Mr. Bruno, if we get a DNA match, what are our chances?"

"Near enough one hundred percent."

"You have no right to say that!" Schuyler shouted, slamming his fist on the table. "You are not an authority. You do not speak for the executors. It is criminal of you to mislead these people. Wilson, I insist we call security and have this man put out."

For a moment, nobody said anything. Then, Matt junior spoke: "Mollie, is he right? Just between us?"

Wharton looked to Laird, who resurrected his previous line: "There's no answer to that in advance."

"Thank you, Wilson," Matt junior said. "Mollie, is he right—are their chances near enough one hundred percent?"

Schuyler was about to shout at her, but Laird held up a resigned hand and said, "We might as well have your opinion, Mollie."

After an apologetic glance at Beth Marshall, Wharton faced Matt junior: "Near enough."

"Thank you," Matt junior said quietly.

"My, my, my," Beth Marshall said blithely, while Fred and Wendy turned to each other for solace. "Near enough one hundred percent." She picked up a glove and examined it as if she sought secrets in the calfskin fingers. At last, she put it back on the table and turned to Michelle.

"I don't want to draw this out, Ms. Grillon, so let me outline a proposal. Under—"

"Beth, please . . ." Laird said. "Don't be hasty in—"

"Thank you, Wilson. Ms. Grillon, under the original will, Wendy, Fred, and Matt junior divided forty percent of the estate—13.333 percent each. Would you agree to an equal share? Ten percent? The same for each of Matt's children? How much would that be, Mollie?"

"Nearly eleven million dollars each."

"Would you agree to nearly eleven million dollars, Ms. Grillon?"

"We haven't agreed to that," Wendy said. "Why don't you give away your money, not ours?"

"Because you will eventually get my money," Beth said icily. "Now, please be quiet, all of you. Would you agree to an equal share to Matt's other children—eleven million dollars?"

Cricket's face showed no reaction, but she slid her fingers around the arm of the chair and gripped it.

Michelle again touched her copy of the codicil. "Can I ask about something?"

"Please answer me, Ms. Grillon," Beth Marshall said, as though she were talking to a servant.

"Fine," Michelle said spikily. "I'm supposed to get fifty percent; why should I take ten?"

"Because the ten percent is guaranteed," Matt junior said pleasantly.

"And if we go to court, we'll tie you up in litigation for so long that even if you get your fifty percent, it will be cripplingly reduced, and you'll be too old to enjoy it. But don't believe me. Or any one of us. Ask Adam."

"Is it true?" she said.

"Not as true as he makes out," I said. "But, yes, they could tie it up for years, and reduce it very seriously. But, keep in mind," I added pointedly, "you don't have to decide right now."

Out of the corner of my eye, I caught a glimpse of Beth's face hardening. "Mrs. Marshall, if you're about to say anything like . . . we make the deal now or not at all . . . don't. No court would enforce a deal made under these conditions—you surrounded by three lawyers and the Grillons with nobody."

"He has a point, Beth," Laird said.

"Fine," Beth Marshall said. "However, that is my offer. Ten percent of the estate; the same as his other children. You can accept it, or we can litigate until you're old and broke and ugly."

Her tone was so laden with hatred that Michelle's lips went white, and she stared at the codicil to cover her distress. At last, she raised her head.

"What about this?" she said, touching a passage. Before anyone could ask her what the passage was, she read:

" 'My child by Cricket shall also have the absolute right to use the name Marshall if he or she wishes.' "

Beth Marshall sucked her breath all the way in and blinked her eyes hard. "No," she said. "No."

"Goddamn right, no!" Fred Marshall shouted.

Michelle took her mother's hand and said, "Mama, I hope you don't mind, but I guess we're going to be in court for a while."

"Is it truly necessary?" Cricket said, gently pulling free of her daughter's grip.

"I think so, yes," Michelle said.

To my shock, Cricket looked at me. "Mr. Bruno, is it truly necessary?"

"I don't know how to answer that," I said.

"If you are uncle, or brother," Cricket said, with a flicker of appeal in her voice, "will you tell her do this? Will you tell her demand this?"

"No," I said finally.

Sounding cornered, Michelle said, "Nicole, if you were my sister, would you tell me to do this?"

"Yes," Maldonado said unhesitatingly.

Urgently, Cricket said, "He is father, they admit, he is father. You no need his name."

"I know I don't need it!" Michelle said hotly. "But I might want it. I might want to call myself Michelle Grillon Marshall. Or Michelle Marshall Grillon. I might want to say, 'Matt Marshall is my dad.' " She turned abruptly to face the Marshall children. "My dad!"

"It not necessary," Cricket repeated.

"Yes, it is, Mama! If I can't use his name, it's as if it never happened. It's as if nobody was my father." She reached for her mother's hand again. "It's as if you never loved him and he never loved you. It *is* necessary!"

CHAPTER 50

IT WAS THE CLOSE OF LUNCH HOUR by the time we rode the elevator down and walked outside. The morning clouds had lifted, and the midday sun had drawn throngs of people to the streets. The air was balmy, the way it sometimes gets in Indian summer in New York, and people moved languorously, as though they feared that any sudden motion would destroy the benign mood. For a moment, the Grillons, Maldonado, and I stood before the building, basking in the lulling atmosphere, letting the warmth of the day and the sweetness of the crowd deliver us of the ugly feelings we'd absorbed upstairs.

For a moment, I stopped thinking about Matt Marshall and his secret life and its bloody effect on everyone who mattered to him. I didn't think about the massacre in 1971, or the annihilation of Mickey Woolff, or the shell casings and stains on Tim Cleary's floor. Whatever happened next in the battle over the Marshall fortune, the mortal danger to the Grillons had passed. They were visible now, public, safe. For a moment, I let my head empty, and simply enjoyed occupying the same piece of New York sidewalk as Cricket and Michelle Grillon and Nicole Maldonado.

So of course, I didn't sense him behind me—not that I ever had before—or recognize his athletic back when he pushed past me. I should have, of course. I should have known that he'd have gone to ground till he mended and then stalked me, because I would lead him to his prey. I should have known that the story belonged to him as much as anyone, and that he more than anyone would bend it his own way.

As he went by, he jostled me just hard enough to break my reverie, and I remember being surprised to notice that the Marshalls had beaten us to

332

the street. I remember thinking maybe that was because Cricket and Michelle had spent so much time in the ladies' room. Even so, I wondered why the Marshalls hadn't stuck around to talk to Wilson Laird, and why Matt junior was nowhere in sight while Wendy and Fred were loitering near the entrance. I wondered why Beth Marshall was thirty feet down the block talking intimately to the man leaning against the illegally parked car. And I wondered what it was about the man leaning against the car that rang a bell—was it his mouth, his nose, his suit, or was it his new Borsalino and his new sunglasses?

But by then, of course, it was too late to wonder. Tim Cleary had pushed past me and was upon them. And in a move as elegant as a dancer's, he brought his gleaming K-bar in a clean, perfect arc out of his boot and right into the man's groin. Once he'd driven it home, Cleary gripped the K-bar with both hands and wrenched the blade upward. Which artery he hit first, I didn't know, but blood sprayed from the man's trunk and showered Beth Marshall. Finally, she screamed.

Everybody moved then. Michelle pulled her mother into the shelter of the doorway; I did the same with Maldonado. Wendy Marshall fell to her knees and cowered in terror, and Fred Marshall knocked people over in his frantic dash to get to his mother's side.

He grabbed Cleary's shoulder, and it was as if he'd shouted Please kill me now. Cleary whirled and kicked Fred Marshall's instep to knock him off balance, and as he fought to stay upright, Cleary seized his hair, yanked his head back so his throat was exposed, and punched him four brutal times in the Adam's apple.

As the last blow struck home, Beth Marshall leaped on Cleary, raking his face with her nails and ripping both his cheeks wide open. Shrieking ferally, she brought her hands high to scratch again, but Cleary—in five moves so swift and sinuous they became one—pulled the K-bar from his first victim's chest, pivoted, drove the blade between Beth Marshall's eyes, twisted it ninety degrees, and withdrew it before her nails could break his skin a second time.

Cleary took a single step back, and Beth Marshall, covered in her hired killer's blood, and with her brains leaking from her forehead, fell dead on the crumpled body of her son. Cleary leaned over her, sliced off her left ear, stuck the ear in his pocket, casually ran across the street, and disappeared into a subway entrance.

I never saw him again, but I never looked for him, and I never sent anyone else looking for him, either.

CHAPTER 51

THE MAN IN THE sunglasses and the Borsalino, the primary victim, the *Daily News* reported, was a former New York City cop named Toby Novak.

Novak, the *News* said, quit the force in 1986 to open up shop as a private detective. During his time on the force, he'd worked armed robbery, the bomb squad, and narcotics, and he'd sent dozens of violent felons to Attica and Green Haven—the *News,* in fact, assumed that one of those violent felons had stalked Novak and killed him. Beth and Fred Marshall, the *News* concluded, just got in the way.

What the *News* omitted was that Toby Novak quit the force in 1986 because he'd been accused of moonlighting as a homicidal enforcer for a cocaine wholesaler. The case never went to trial. Toby Novak had a very smart lawyer.

I found him just after 9:15 in an empty courtroom at 100 Centre Street. He was standing at the defense table, arched over it like a giant bird while he scanned four newspapers simultaneously. When I walked in, he glanced up and grinned sardonically. "What a way to go, huh? You get my messages? I left three at the office."

"I haven't called in," I said, joining him at the table. I doubted he'd left any messages.

Herschel O'Hara tapped the ten-year-old photo of Toby Novak in the *Post.* "I always knew he'd come to a bad end, but to get gutted like a trout on Liberty Street—that's ridiculous." He reached out and squeezed my shoulder. "I'm sorry, pal. I got caught up in love, and I did something real stupid."

When I said nothing, he continued: "She said to me, we can't get any information out of him, he's being a monstrous pain in the ass, we want somebody to monitor him, do you know anybody, is there another detective who could help us?" He touched my chin with his knuckle. "It's not like you weren't being a pain in the ass."

"And you sent her Toby Novak to monitor me?"

"Actually, I sent her Carl Rosenstone, Davey Wender, and Les Bennett as well, but she liked Toby."

"She told you that?"

"No," he said with his usual sarcasm, "she didn't tell me that, but she chose him, so she must have. Adam, I'm sorry, I did something dumb for love. For lust. For whatever. No harm done, pal. Not to you or yours."

From my case, I drew a clip describing the bombing of Mickey Woolff's clinic, passed it to Herschel, and said, "That's Novak's work." As Herschel skimmed the article, I added, "The doctor—Mickey Woolff—he was one of two people, at that time anyway, who could ID Cricket."

"Oh, for chrissake, Adam, where the fuck does that come from?" He shook the clip. "What are you smoking? Mollie Wharton does not hire people to blow other people up."

By then, I realized that he knew nothing at all. "She gave Novak's name to Beth Marshall."

"Oh, bullshit," Herschel said dismissively. "Just because she's a WASP doesn't guarantee she's unethical."

"Yes, she did, Herschel, and Beth Marshall hired Novak to do Mickey Woolff and to do another guy named Tim Cleary. He fucked that one up; and yesterday Beth Marshall was busy hiring Novak to do Cricket, or Michelle, or both of them."

By then, I was close to losing it.

"When you gave her Toby Novak's name, did you tell her what kind of shit he was? Did you tell her he'd been bounced from the force? Did you tell her he'd killed six drug dealers, including one fourteen years old? Or did you just say, precious, Toby Novak's exactly what you need, he's a tough ex-cop, he'll do you fine . . . ?"

A single bead of sweat formed on his forehead. "I said, he's not as good as Rosenstone or Wender or Bennett, but he's an ex-cop, and he'll do you fine."

"Did you ever follow up—did you ever ask her if they were satisfied with Toby Novak's work? Did you ever ask your bitch how the monitoring of your ex-partner was going?"

For the first time since I arrived, he lowered his head. When he finally raised it, though his eyes were rimmed in red, he'd recovered his spirits.

"Hey, pal, Toby Novak's dead, Beth Marshall's dead, you're okay. Life is short—give me a fucking break."

CHAPTER 52

Not long past dawn, Luis Maldonado loaded their bags into the trunk of my car, and Tuyet Maldonado handed each of them a small, beautifully wrapped package. Vietnamese food for the flight, she explained. After Luis Maldonado hugged them, Tuyet embraced Cricket Grillon, then Michelle, then Cricket once more, enfolding her in her arms as though her touch would keep Cricket safe for life.

The moment we all were in the car—Cricket and Nicole Maldonado in the back, Michelle beside me—Tuyet Maldonado took her husband's hand and led him back to the house. Later, I found out she couldn't stand to wave good-bye—bad, bad luck.

". . . This is final call for boarding of flight twenty-four to San Francisco; all passengers kindly proceed through the gate to the aircraft. Final call for boarding."

Michelle Grillon helped her mother up from the waiting room chair while I took the tickets from my inside jacket pocket and held them out to the attendant.

"You're sure we're going to be okay?" Michelle Grillon said, not for the first time.

"Laird is filing the will for probate Monday morning. You're going to be okay."

"What if Wendy and Junior challenge us?"

"They won't."

"I don't want those little shits ripping Mama's life to shreds in a courtroom."

"They won't."

"What if they do, Adam?"

"If they do," I said patiently, "Herschel O'Hara and I go to Cecile Boulanger. Since Beth Marshall hired Toby Novak in New York, the conspiracy to bomb the clinic began here and is prosecutable here, in federal court. You can't prosecute a dead person, but you can take any evidence to the surrogate and explain that a challenge to the Saigon codicil has to be regarded in the light of that conspiracy."

Before she could ask me again if I were sure, Maldonado touched her arm. "It will be okay."

Michelle Grillon nodded, and hugged Maldonado, then stepped aside to let her mother do likewise.

After Cricket released Maldonado, she turned to me and stepped forward; Michelle moved at the same time, and an instant later I found myself wrapped snugly within four arms and felt the press of two faces flush against mine.

We stood that way until the insistent voice of the flight attendant broke in: "Mrs. Grillon, Ms. Grillon, you have to board now. We need to close the aircraft."

Mother and daughter kissed me hurriedly, released me from their grip, and walked into the passageway that led to the plane. Ten seconds later, without waving farewell, they rounded a bend and disappeared.

On the stroll to the parking lot, Maldonado took my arm. A plane roared past overhead, and she tilted her head and shaded her eyes to follow it. "Is that them?"

"If it were a movie, it would be."

She smiled and pulled my arm tight against her left breast. After we'd walked a bit, she said, "Do you feel my heart?"

"Very much," I said, and I did.